MW01681257

over her face and hair in the firelight. The air between them began to thicken, to dance and hum in high-strung, pulsing energy. They both knew in one instant that it was going to happen.

"So what do you think?" he said, eyes teasing, intimate, gently challenging her participation in the game. "Shall we?"

The decision was made; it was only a matter of how long from now. Marielle wanted it to be a long time—as long as she could stand. She would have to remember it always . . .

Also by Jeane Renick

Trust Me

Available from
HarperPaperbacks

Harper Monogram

ALWAYS...

JEANE RENICK

HarperPaperbacks
A Division of HarperCollins*Publishers*

HarperPaperbacks *A Division of* HarperCollins*Publishers*
10 East 53rd Street, New York, N.Y. 10022

Cover illustration by Jim Griffin

First printing: June 1993

Printed in the United States of America

HarperPaperbacks, HarperMonogram, and colophon are trademarks of HarperCollins*Publishers*

❖ 10 9 8 7 6 5 4 3 2 1

For Denise (and Tom), for Rosabel Brown, and for the women who change their lives for children . . .

Prologue

West Africa, February 4, 1874

Daybreak. Miserable, hunkered next to Billy McCafferty on the bank of the Oda River, forty feet wide and waist deep, twenty-year-old Jameson Woods stared at thin wisps of mist lifting into cool morning air from the surface of the dirt brown water. Humping his shoulders, he adjusted the heavy pack of detonating equipment and lifted his gaze to a hole in the leafy canopy some sixty feet in the air. He and Billy were sappers, explosives detail, and edgy from a sleepless night.

He scowled at a sunless sky. "Up yer ass with the 'Gold' Coast, Billy."

McCafferty, spare and blond, fair skin wealed and bloody from insect bites, swiped mosquitos away from his face and said nothing. There was a nervous crackle of gunfire a hundred yards upriver. They heaved themselves to their feet along with the others, rifles at the ready, and stood watch as the team of engineers labored in the treacherous water to finish a makeshift bridge.

Jameson shifted his pack again and spat in the muddied grass. Reality had a bitter taste. Mired in poverty as thick and unyielding as the muck at his feet, he was angry that he'd permitted his hopes to swell with dreams of a better life. Billy's uncle, an agent with the British West Africa Company, had filled their heads with stories of massive gold necklaces, rings and breastplates, even a huge gold palanquin on which "King Coffee" was carried about; of village chiefs with arms so laden with gold trinkets and bracelets that they had to rest their hands on the heads of small boys for support; gold and more gold.

This was the seventh day they'd slogged inland toward the king's stronghold; seven days in a humid furnace of unceasing rain in wet, tangled, trackless jungle by day, and so cold at night you could see your breath. Morning's half-lit silence would be broken harshly by a sudden squawking of birds or the barking of monkeys, and was home to ugly moss-coated animals called sloths, which had proven unfit for eating.

Snakes and slugs and slimy creatures of all description slithered in the decaying rot that sucked at his feet while leeches oozed under his wet clothing and into sodden boots to feed on his living body. A week of hard fighting, and Her Majesty's finest had managed the poor show of capturing a handful of stinking mud villages. Gold in the streets, indeed.

Stalled at the river with barely four days' supplies, Jameson calculated they were at least a hundred miles from the anchored mother ships on the coast. He longed to rest his eyes on the cool blue line of a far horizon. He saw instead the sweating shoulders of the man ahead of him and the walls of solid green that pressed in from either side; he hated the river, the underwater gloom of the West African jungle, the incessant rain and every man jack in his regiment.

He wondered if he would die here.

Finally, the engineers pronounced it ready and he and Billy took their place in the column, inching their way across the wooden snake of a bridge.

"Up yer ass," he snarled again. The sagging bridge swayed dangerously in the water. Billy, sullen, ignored him.

The advance guard reached Kumasi, capital city of

the Asante ruler, King Kofi Karikari, at midday. By then "King Coffee" had fled the town along with most of its citizenry. The troops took possession of the royal palace, a singular stone fortress amid a sea of thatched roofs and mud huts, and set up tents and supplies on the palace grounds without incident.

In the midst of yet another violent rainstorm the next afternoon word arrived that the Oda had risen rapidly and the engineers' bridge was now under more than two hands of water. Jameson's young general promptly declared a victory and issued orders to return to the coast. The city was to be searched for articles of value to compensate Her Royal Majesty for the costs of campaign; thereafter, Kumasi was to be burned and abandoned. Jameson's job was to burn it, and burn the bloody place he would!

That night he and Billy labored in the mud and pouring rain to ring the king's palace with explosives. Billy tugged at his arm. "Look, there."

A short distance away, two officers struggled with a bulky trunklike box of rough construction. It clearly had considerable weight and they carried it along a rain-slick path from a side door of the palace to an outlying hut.

"Sure 'nough quiet about it," observed Billy, in a hoarse whisper.

The sappers watched in silence as the officers returned to the palace, then emerged with a second box, then a third. Candlelight winked and flickered through chinks in the wooden door of the hut.

"Weren't nothin' light, that's sure," mumbled Billy after a few minutes. "They was sweatin' it."

Jameson trailed his spade through the slime ten paces down the palace wall. He proceeded to dig another hole, his thoughts as nagging and insistent as the rainwater drizzling down his neck. Billy was right. And true enough, there was only one reason officers would undertake to move anything that heavy, particularly in a downpour. They'd be hiding something of value. Something secret.

The next morning, he and Billy volunteered to stay behind to detonate the explosives. Their orders were to be certain the last of the column was a sufficiently safe distance, then fire the village and rejoin the ranks. A Royal Fusilier, John Dawes, remained to stand watch.

The last of the troops was barely out of sight when the two men broke for the outlying building. The confused Dawes brought up the rear in time to help kick down the door.

Inside the hut the wooden boxes had been smashed and plundered, their contents scattered about the room. Heaped onto muddied silk robes of every hue was a confusion of abandoned riches. Pouches of gold dust and bags of nuggets lay amid wondrous objects of every kind and description: scimitars with bulbous gold handles; coral necklaces and carved ornaments; intricate headbands; mysterious masks of pure gold with savage faces—wolves' and rams' heads; gold knives and silver canes. Bracelets, breastplates, rings, objects of incredible artistry and perfection were trampled into the mud of the floor and lay gleaming in the thin morning light.

"Mother o' God," whispered Dawes, who crossed himself while McCafferty jigged in glee.

Jameson approached the golden objects in wonder. "Best hurry," he said, breaking the spell.

Abruptly, they grabbed and clawed at the remains of the royal treasure, every man for himself. Golden idols were snatched from the mud and jammed into emptied packs; knives, bracelets, nuggets, were chosen, discarded, then chosen again from the glittering booty.

Moments later, perched amid objects too large to carry, the three made a pact as the incessant rain pounded the thickly matted roof of the hut.

"No one's t'know." Billy's voice was ominously quiet, "or we'll not live t'spend it. Agreed?"

The three stared at each other in wary consent. "Agreed."

Struggling furiously through the knee-deep muck churned by the departing soldiers, Jameson felt the muscles in the calves of his legs burn in complaint. Heat from the stricken city and light from the fires soon disappeared but, buoyed by his change in fortune and some four stone of gold heavy upon his back, he kept pace with Dawes and McCafferty as they caught up to the column.

Hours later, at the Oda River, the listing bridge had all but disappeared under three feet of turgid water. Bowed into a straining half-moon curve by the relentless current, it sagged deeper into the water under the weight of each crossing soldier. Dawes staggered forward in his turn and Jameson watched horrified as halfway across, the exhausted man lost his footing. The fusilier's heavy pack pitched wildly and he toppled over the guide rope; his scream burbled into stillness in the muddy water.

Four men remained. Two abandoned their packs and made it safely across. Torn with indecision, Jameson turned to Billy, who was next in line with his heavy burden firmly in place.

"I come too far, mate." Billy shrugged defiantly. "I'll not give up this close—not in this life, I won't. See y'cross safe now." True to his word Billy turned and, ignoring the water streaming over his shoulders, struggled to the other end of the bridge.

Jameson, heartened, last to cross, began the longest journey of his life. Over the hungry, liquid sound of the water the wet hemp *skreeked* and groaned in complaint, threatened to give him to the Oda while the water pulled and sucked at his belly and added its weight to his pack. He fought his way deeper and deeper into the current. Water licked at his chin, spilled into his ear, determined to have him; he slid both hands along the upstream rope, groping his way and willing his feet not to slip on the slick, canted wood.

It took three men, plus Billy, to haul him out of the shallows and onto the bank.

At the coast, quivering with fatigue, he staggered on board his ship and cached his heavy pack next to Billy's in the munitions hold. They guarded their cargo in turns until Billy, ill with fever, died two days from England's shore.

Thirteen months later, Jameson Woods, service to Her Majesty Queen Victoria fulfilled, bought a small interest in a shipping business and, based on his assured income, was permitted to marry Elizabeth Ann Claymore. The following spring Margaret Mary Woods was born, and two years hence, a son and heir, Boyce Edward. Had anyone inquired, Jameson Woods would have expressed his belief that he would be happy, always. . . .

1

Beverly Hills, California, April 2, 1989

Omens.

Nervous and running late for her appointment with Dr. Lanier, Marielle Tèa Lilia Jonas McCleary managed to puncture two consecutive pairs of pantyhose with her freshly polished nails, ruining manicure, stockings, and temper, in that order. "Always," she grumbled. "Every damn time." She grabbed a handful of cotton balls and began swiping at her nails with polish remover.

Presentable at last in a shift of soft pumpkin silk, the gold cameo locket that had been her mother's favorite necklace, and her nails coated with a quick layer of clear polish, Marielle discovered Digby III, her bubble-eye goldfish, belly-up in his bowl. Unable to endure the knowledge of his inert body floating aimlessly the rest of the day, she carefully fished him out with a plastic spoon and buried him in the window box of geraniums next to Digbys I and II.

Outside the door of the Beverly Hills apartment she'd waited two and a half years to acquire, she watched the elevator stop without its usual warning bell. Compounding its obstinance, the doors closed before she could get to the Stop button. Now very late, she bolted for the stairs.

Omens. Definitely omens.

Proceeding with minimum caution through morning traffic on little Santa Monica, she braked to a stop three cars back from a red light at Elm. A civil servant piloted a rowdy lawnmower along the greenbelt center divider. Marielle sighed and took the moment to relax, breathe deeply, and enjoy the early April morning with its cornflower sky and the green smell of fresh-cut grass.

"It's not brain surgery. It's your basic commonsense visit with your gynecologist."

Somehow, saying it out loud gave the purpose of her mission authority over her apprehension; it was time for a Pap smear and a yearly examination for all the logical, intelligent reasons post-thirty women had to consider.

Computer driven, the watering system on her side of the greenbelt jumped into service. A misaligned sprinkler head three feet away stalled in place and sent an arc of glistening city water through her open window; it trickled down her earlobe to drip off an earring onto her dress, creating an ugly brown splotch on the silk before she had the presence of mind to roll up the window. Definitely omens.

Dr. Lanier's cheery nurse offered her coffee. "He's on his way from the hospital," she chirped. "Mrs. Bartunik chose this morning to deliver. She wasn't scheduled until Thursday."

A pregnant patient arrived with her two-year-old daughter, reminding Marielle of her niece, now almost seven. Heather had been the joy of her life until her brother-in-law moved his family to Detroit the same year she'd divorced Jeff.

Shy at first, the little girl stared at Marielle with huge china blue eyes rimmed with spiky lashes that brushed her cheeks when she blinked. Marielle sat quietly and within minutes the child was next to her on the couch holding out a well-thumbed copy of *The Cat in the Hat* to be read.

"Is it all right?" she asked the mother.

"Be my guest." The woman sighed. "I can recite it in my sleep."

For the next half hour Marielle and the little girl entered the magical, mystical world of cats in hats and talking fish and rainy days with Thing One and Thing Two. Hannah, trusting and fragile, with the smell of little-girl fresh-washed hair, sat next to her and heaved contented sighs when Marielle got all the words right.

Each time she finished the huge blue eyes would seek her face. "Read me." Enchanted, Marielle hugged the little girl gently and with great longing. To have a child . . . Hannah scooched closer and Marielle began again.

Two hours later, she sat stonily in front of her mountain cabin, throat dry and tight from controlling tears. Dr. Lanier had been all concern and kindliness, had held her hand and clucked in sympathy. But all the symptoms she'd ignored, written off as hypochondria, tension, exhaustion, and so on, the missed periods and hot, liquid body flushes, panicky night sweats, had finally added themselves together to a sum total she wanted desperately to deny.

She got out of the car and let herself into the small pine A-frame, haven and sole asset surviving from her failed marriage to Jeff. Inside she placed a call to Dr. Whitlaw in San Francisco and began a strained conversation with her faded former doctor.

"'Course I remember you, Marielle," said the faint voice through the receiver. "What can I do for you?"

"My doctor told me this morning he thinks I'm entering an early menopause. . . ." She stumbled over the barren word.

Dr. Whitlaw interrupted her. "Weelll." He drew out the word, disclosing his Indiana heritage. "Can't say I'm surprised. Nearly always runs in families. Your mother was twenty-nine, as I recall . . . and let's see, your grandmother . . . Caddie Oldham reached menopause at thirty-one. So I'm 'fraid, my dear, the women in your family just aren't long-term breeders. What symptoms you havin'?"

Marielle hovered on the edge of tears as she told him. The old man's voice came back at her in undeniable agreement, his fifty-odd years of practice aligning precisely with the leading-edge, scientific tests Dr. Lanier had relied on. With her family history, at thirty-four years of age, he confirmed her symptoms were entirely too similar for coincidence. The tears spilled over and she huddled in misery, clinging to the old man's voice on the telephone.

"Now you listen here, miss. Don't you go getting all upset. You still got time to get yourself at least one, assuming you've got someone in mind to get the job done. Your grandmother managed it and your mother managed it and I have a pretty good idea you can, too, if you set your mind to it."

She barely remembered to thank him before severing the connection. She was the last member of both the Oldham and Jonas families and the thought of never having a child was devastating. She damned Jefferson McCleary one more time for being such a jerk and insisting that they wait, castigating herself as well for having gone along with his adamant declaration—no children until they were financially secure.

Financial security had been a slippery, elusive term, and its definition hadn't materialized by the time she discovered that Jeff, too, had been slippery and elusive about other women in his life—followed by raging fights and Jeff's rationale. Something about not being absolutely certain she was the "perfect woman" for him and he'd only been continuing to "make sure." She'd used the old-fashioned term. "Cheating."

They'd survived the first episode, but she'd called it quits the second time around. Now, two years after the divorce, her clock was moving into overtime.

One of the better decisions she'd made had been keeping the cabin. Thirty-five minutes northwest of Beverly Hills, tucked in the Malibu Mountains, she'd wondered for a while how many of Jeff's candidates had auditioned here, but had given it up as a dumb reason not to keep the rustic hideaway with its clear spring lake and peaceful canyon view.

But the cabin couldn't work its magic today and, after walking the familiar path around the small lake, she came to the conclusion that Dr. Whitlaw had put his finger on the salient fact. Whether or not she wanted to get pregnant, the plain truth was that she didn't have "someone to get the job done."

Stung by the failure of her marriage, she'd built a wall of protection and succeeded very well at not being hurt again. No one of substance had penetrated the barricade and time had slipped past all too quickly.

Tears spent, she closed up the cabin and maneuvered her car down the canyon road to meet Rose and Shirley for dinner.

2

London, England, April 2, 1989

Father Derning's fingers tapped an untidy rhythm on the bulky envelope in his lap as he waited uncomfortably in the antechamber; under the inquiring gaze of formidable Miss Gibbs, he sighed and broke his rhythm long enough to sip his tea and study the strong signature across the seal. Margaret Mary Woods had been bitter and malicious toward her family until the day she died and he did not like his duty this morning.

At 9:00 A.M. the tall office clock began its round of chimes. Seventy-year-old Rettig Burnside bustled in on the seventh note. He ushered the somber priest into his office and briskly settled himself behind a massive desk. "Sorry to keep you, Father," he offered, with the barest hint of reproach.

"Ah, yes, I suspect I'm early," conceded the cleric, embarrassed at his ill-concealed impatience. "Anxious to dispose of this bit of business, I suppose." He placed the aging envelope on the heavy teak desk and watched the older man read the hand-written instruction: DELIVER 25 YEARS AFTER MY DEATH TO RETTIG BURNSIDE, BOND STREET, LONDON.

"It's the last condition in her estate."

Burnside regarded the large manila envelope with a baleful mixture of curiosity and dread. Margaret Woods had been the spinster daughter of a now-deceased client, an old sapper by the name of Jameson Woods whose shipping business had been destroyed in the First World War and who'd died all but destitute in 1945. He hadn't seen her in some forty-odd years. What had the poisonous old woman cooked up after all?

His mission completed, Father Derning took his leave. Burnside saw him out and after a fortifying cup of Miss Gibbs's tea, called in his partner Avram Halkin to act as witness, whereupon he carefully cut through the signature to find an obscure volume of Spanish poetry and a small envelope addressed to him in Margaret's unmistakable hand.

He examined the poorly bound book. Other than age, it had no apparent value. Puzzled, he leafed through the title pages. Having a spare acquaintance with the language, he was able to decipher only a word here and there. The stiff pages stopped unexpectedly to reveal a hollowed body. Secreted inside were several items, including a richly yellowed wedding invitation addressed to Mr. and Mrs. Jameson Woods with a return address he suspected that he and a New York law firm had been searching for these past twenty-five years.

Reading, England, November 6, 1932

When the post dropped softly through the door into the mailbox, Margaret Woods retrieved it as she had done all her life. Once pretty, the severity of her lost vanity was written in her scrubbed jawline, unrelieved by color, devoid of softening powder. Spare, tautly restrained, she moved firmly about in a worn linen dress, her shoulders covered by a thick woolen shawl, trailing a vague fragrance of dull black dye in her wake.

She started toward the study where her father sat stone quiet, hollow-eyed, then faltered as she identified among the many notes of condolence a fat parchment envelope addressed to her parents bearing a San Francisco postmark. Altering course, she took it instead up the stairs to her bedroom of half a century.

Boyce. It had to be.

At this thought, veins in her forehead seized in harsh constriction, resisting every surge of blood her heart forced through her body; the resulting pain streaked toward a blinding headache and she sank onto her bed.

Boyce had run away to America at seventeen. He'd come to blows with their father over a woman—his father's whore. It had been a night of horror with the two men screaming obscene accusations, striking each other repeatedly until her brother, bloodied and raging, had staggered out never to return. Her mother had shrieked and torn at her hair and taken to her bed with alternate bouts of hysteria and laudanum-induced stupor.

Incredibly, her father had continued to see the woman who'd destroyed his family. He'd denied it, of course, despite her mother's frenzy of accusations and frantic tears. Margaret, nineteen, had pressed pillows around her head to shut out the endless threats and pleadings that seeped through walls in every room of the house, echoed up the stairwell and under the locked door to her bedroom. Eventually, her mother had retreated into an ice-locked silence.

Margaret passed the next twelve years on a tiptoe of quiet until the day she would remember to her coffin: in this house she'd grown to despise, her father ill and taken to bed with fever, Lilia Foxworthy dared enter to talk with her mother. In their house!

Crouched in the stairwell, Margaret had witnessed the confrontation. She'd been shocked at the woman's frowsy appearance—she wasn't young at all—and at the depth of her mother's scalding outrage.

"Whore!" her mother had screamed. "Whore!" She'd gone at the woman with her fists. "You cost me my son! He was my life!"

Lilia defended her swollen stomach. "I swear it's his."

"Never," her mother's voice had shrilled. "I'll shout it in the church! I'll shout it from here to London! I'd starve in the streets before I'll legitimize your bastard! Never!"

"Please, Elizabeth." The woman actually had tears in her eyes. "I beg you. His child . . . "

Her mother regained control and lowered her voice. Margaret had had to listen very closely to hear what happened next in the foyer. Her mother had circled Lilia with a fierce, piercing hatred as she paced her rage.

"What will it take to be rid of it?" Her mother's voice was a seething, whispered fury. "Bastards are costly, my dear, and my husband has nothing. His business is gone, as I'm certain you know. What you see in this house is pledged to the banks, we've naught to sell. Surely, he's told you."

"If you'd see to the babe when it's born."

"Never!" The word was spat in the woman's face. "I'll give you money to get rid of it. You'd best take it. I swear on my life I'll not free him and I'll not see his bastard raised in this house. Not while I live!"

Margaret stole down the stairs to stand with her mother, accomplice to the pact, helpless witness as the woman accepted a letter of credit against her mother's account. An account untouched through her father's business disaster, held aside despite her family's humbling financial difficulties.

The money had been promised to Margaret as long as she could remember, first as a dowry despite the blow to her father's pride in his failure to provide, and when she'd decided not to marry, her mother's inheritance had been an assurance of a comfortable spinster's life. Margaret's secure future was the price being paid to her father's whore to buy peace in her mother's life.

Six months later they'd learned of Boyce's marriage

to Lilia, who'd used the money to go to him in America. She would remember always her mother's crumpled face, her father's disappearance for a full week. Her brother's name had not been spoken in this house from that day. Twenty-five years. On this day of his mother's funeral, he'd be forty-two, Margaret calculated idly.

Lips compressed, she opened the envelope.

Boyce and Lilia Woods invite the favor of
your witness to the celebration of marriage
between their daughter Caddie Lilia and
Charles William Oldham

Her mind exploded at the insult, then fell in on itself; watery blue pupils constricted to pinpoints as a well of black, unseeing rage swept reason aside. Effrontery! An invitation to the wedding of her father's bastard? Claimed as her brother's own! Half sister to him . . . herself as well! Rocked to her soul, she nearly ripped the thing to shreds.

After twenty-five years of silence, this! Twenty-five years. The number burned in her brain. When was enough to be enough? Hadn't Boyce and the whore humiliated her beloved mother beyond grief, cost her everything?

All things, she vowed silently. All things in due time.

A subsequent letter from Caddie Oldham announcing her pregnancy was intercepted, read with contempt, and consigned to the cookstove. Six months later, a birth announcement for Tèa Lilia Oldham was intercepted and burned as well.

Margaret watched the post carefully thereafter but no further correspondence arrived from America. World War II began in earnest, further depleting their lives, and she was forced to husband her father's meager resources; life became frugal survival.

The years passed slowly and she watched him grow old, firm in her duty that he should not enjoy life without her mother. One day she returned from the market to find him sitting in his library, eyes filled with tears. He did not speak to her from that hour until the moment of his death some four days later, nor could he be badgered to explain.

A week after his funeral in a stunned conversation with Rettig Burnside, Margaret learned to her horror that during those four days her father had revised his will to reinstate Boyce.

She flew to the library to consult the hollowed book in its usual place and sure enough, its contents had been disturbed. Her mother's diary was gone, probably destroyed; in its place was a small sealed packet with instructions from her father designed to force her into contact with Boyce. Steeped in the misery of her failure, totally unprepared for the burst of grief for the end of the years of pain between them, Margaret could not bring herself to fling it into the fire.

After a while, she carefully replaced the contents and returned the book to its customary shelf. In the hall she paused to stare stonily at her image in a gray, fading mirror.

"You haven't won, Father. Not yet, you haven't."

Rettig Burnside sighed again and looked out his window to the budding lilacs, wishing for green. Margaret Woods's face, swathed in a dense black veil, rose in his mind. A week after her father's funeral, he'd approached her regarding Boyce, explained about the codicil.

Furiously bitter, she'd stared at him at first in open astonishment, then, with an almost joyous malevolence. "My time has come," she'd hissed at him, tight with satisfaction. "My time has finally come. I'll not help you locate my brother and I pray you never find him."

She'd stalked from his office without another word.

Thereafter, she'd refused to discuss the matter of her brother and declined to her death to answer even the most innocent of correspondence.

In accordance with his wishes, Jameson's house in Reading was quietly transferred to his daughter's name. Checks mailed monthly for her benefit and welfare had been cashed with ruthless regularity until her death twenty-five years ago.

The old man had indicated that his son had moved to America and that Margaret could supply an address; with this information at hand, Rettig had had the foresight to place Boyce's small inheritance in trust with an American investment firm and, with prudent financial judgments and the passage of four decades, he could point with justifiable pride to the fact that the once-modest amount was now a sizable estate.

At last, Burnside opened the envelope addressed to him. Inside was a fragile, faded packet printed in the old man's wavering hand: "To be opened by the last living heir of Jameson Woods."

Predictably, there was no message from the old woman.

"Bad business." He held the sealed packet to the light from his office window. The outline of a heavy key was vaguely visible. "Bad business, indeed." He handed the wedding invitation to Avram Halkin for his inspection. "According to this, Boyce had a daughter named Caddie. Married Charles Wilson Oldham in San Francisco in 1933. Here's an address. We'd best start a search for heirs."

"I'll see to it," agreed Halkin, and discreetly withdrew.

Rettig Burnside sighed heavily. Surveying the items arrayed on his desk this fine false-spring morning, he wondered at Margaret Woods's eccentric, punitive actions against her family. Apparently, the caustic old woman felt she'd succeeded in some sort of revenge as she was finally willing to pass her brother's legacy forward.

He wondered, idly, if she had guessed what her father had kept for his son—now his son's heirs. He did not think so.

3

April 2, 1989

The weekly girls' night out at Tonio's was amiably referred to among the three of them as the Meeting of the Minds.

"Shirley said to start without her." Rose's greeting from the dim twilight of the Mexican restaurant held no preliminaries. Friends some seven years, Marielle adored Rose's ability to bypass subtlety, cut through to the point, and proceed from there. Rose was true to form. "You look terrible. What'd he say?"

Marielle ordered a double margarita for fortification. The Minds had known about today's appointment and while she didn't intend to avoid the subject, she hadn't quite figured out how to discuss it. Rose Brown, two years her junior, openly wanted to have a baby as badly as she did; a hysterectomy had sealed that door forever and Rose's criterion for dating was a divorced man with custody.

Marielle sipped at the salty foam and filled her in on the parameters of both doctors' diagnoses. "They can't tell me how long before it happens, but they both tell me to get pregnant as quickly as possible."

"So, what do you want to do?"

"I want to have a baby."

Rose traced a finger around a water ring on the table from one of the glasses. "God, what a screwed-up world. Too many people and not enough babies to go around. If I hadn't had the operation, I'd have children by now—with or without a husband." She stabbed at the center of the circle as Shirley Canfield lowered her svelte body into the remaining chair at the table.

Josef appeared with a glass of iced tea.

Shirley's was an ironclad rule. No alcohol. Fifty-five, high-spirited, she was an energetic public relations agent for Mason & Pearson; everyone who knew her well was aware she hadn't had a drink since the Sunday in July four years ago when a hangover had kept her from a fatal outing to Catalina. Somehow the boat had capsized and Bill Canfield and their son, Jody, fifteen, had both drowned in the forward cabin.

Marielle filled Shirley in and they ordered dinner. "If I could afford it, I'd have a baby while I still can. Then, if someone came into my life and we fell in love, everything would be perfect."

"I'm going to be the buyer in Swim and Sportswear in three weeks with a huge raise in salary," Rose announced. After a royal toast of congratulations from her friends, she continued. "You have a baby and I'll pay the bills."

Marielle stared at her. "If I had a baby and we both worked . . ."

After a moment Shirley said quietly. "What about a third partner? I've got a house with a tenants' lease that's up soon. I can't live in it and I don't need the income."

Marielle and Rose turned to her in unison, mental wheels in operation.

"With a house, you could do it on one salary," Shirley added.

"Okay." Rose got down to basics. "Housing and economics are covered. So who's going to 'do the job'?"

During dinner, Rose and Shirley laughingly constructed

a list of Marielle's possible paternity candidates and in the considered opinions of the Minds none of them merited fatherhood, let alone "till death do us part." And, they agreed, in light of Drs. Whitlaw and Lanier's professional opinions, time was short.

"First priority?" demanded Rose.

"Intelligence," came the triple response.

"Sexy," said Marielle, with a wide grin.

"Kevin Costner," came Rose's leering opinion.

"Sean Connery," contributed Shirley.

"Respects women. Absolutely adores them," insisted Marielle, well into her third margarita. "And single. Definitely single. Married men need not apply."

"Perfect," decreed Rose.

"The only perfect, eligible, sexy human being is Thomas Saxon," declared Shirley, creating a pause during which Thomas Stephen Saxon, tall, gorgeous actor, unmarried, and totally unattainable, was considered, compared, and categorized in the Perfect department, and found wanting in none of the specifics.

"Mason & Pearson signed him today. That's why I'm late. We're going to work on a campaign for his next movie."

Rose abandoned Marielle midcandidate in her passionate curiosity about the actor. "What's the scoop?"

"Amazingly down to earth for someone in this business," Shirley stated without reservation. "I liked him a lot."

"Well, he is perfect," Marielle tossed in dryly. "However, in view of his major celebrity status and my totally anonymous existence, don't you think we might encounter a few obstacles in this romance?" she teased her friends. "Not to mention his girlfriend?"

"We signed her, also."

"Oh, wonderful. I suppose she's perfect, too."

"Not quite. Pretty, with a bad case of ambition and a thin line of talent."

Thereafter, discussion reverted to serious examination of the conventional possibilities of single motherhood via artificial insemination, as well as adoption procedures, spiced with stories of the emotional battering endured by various friends of friends who'd tried adoption only to have the birth mother decide at the eleventh hour to keep the child.

Josef discreetly slid the bill to the center of the table. Marielle licked traces of salt from the rim of her glass and drained the last of her margarita. "I hereby declare that I, Marielle Tèa Lilia Jonas McCleary have a child in my future," she stated, "and the three of us will raise him or her, assuming we can find a father."

The deal was struck and the bill was paid.

The next evening, Marielle bought a calico goldfish from the pet store on Pico and named him Abernathy. He swam frantically round and round the sturdy plastic bag on her kitchen counter while she washed and rinsed his new home.

"Good luck," she admonished the vigorous little fish, and dumped him unceremoniously into the bowl. "I think you're going to need it, living with me."

Two weeks later she received a slender letter from Haygood, Haygood & Buchanan, one of the most conservative law firms in San Francisco. Oblivious to Abernathy's greedy attack on the fish food floating on his water, Marielle read the painfully brief letter from Milford Haygood:

Dear Ms. McCleary:

We have been advised that you may be a descendent of one Jameson Woods, late of Reading, Great Britain. If so, kindly contact this office in order to discuss documentation of such fact at your earliest convenience.

4

June 16, 1989

My dear Ms. McCleary:

This office has been charged with a trust for the heirs of Boyce Woods, deceased, last known to reside in San Francisco.

We are advised by Milford Haygood that you have satisfactorily documented yourself to be the only grandchild of his daughter, Caddie Lilia, deceased, thus establishing yourself as sole heir to said trust, a portion of which legacy flows to your biological children, if any.

Once necessary inheritance levies have been satisfied, and proper documents executed and filed in Great Britain, we are pleased to inform you that you may expect to receive three hundred fifty-three thousand dollars. Kindly contact Mr. Haygood to indicate the manner in which the proceeds of the trust are to be transmitted.

There is also the matter of an envelope which appears to contain a small physical item, possibly a key. This, of course, will require your personal attention.

Faithfully,
Rettig Burnside

Rose passed the letter to Shirley. "I love the British. 'Appears to contain a small physical item.' If I had an envelope, I'd know whether or not there was something in it."

"It's probably a keepsake of some kind," said Marielle. "According to Mr. Haygood, the family was very poor and any money they may have had disappeared before the Second World War. The trust was set up with something like a hundred and fifty dollars at the time of Jameson Woods's death."

"And now it's three hundred and fifty thousand? Are you sure it's ironclad? Can they change their mind?" Rose could scarcely believe it.

"According to my lawyer, it's absolute." Marielle's eyes sparkled. "I'm rich. It's incredible, but it's true."

"This is too much." Rose, rapt, ignored her dinner.

"I'm going to have a baby," Marielle added softly. "It's what I've always wanted."

Her announcement created a well of expectant silence around the table.

"Are you serious?"

She studied her friends. "I decided the minute he said the money was real."

A slow grin of approval spread across Shirley's face. "If you're sure about this, you can have the house for as long as you want. The price is godmother."

"Wait a minute, I want to be a godmother, too," Rose chimed in.

"I'll do better than that. You'll both be mothers. We'll all be Mothers instead of Minds." Marielle grinned excitedly. "All we need is a father, and enough time to 'get the job done.'"

Two weeks later, Marielle stood in the archway of the Palisade Room at the Hilton Hotel. The occasion was a fund-raiser for a health clinic that enjoyed support from the entertainment community. Stars and producers of varying importance, studio executives, and heads of talent agencies were everywhere; young men of various corporate status were heavily in attendance, socializing in a hierarchy of power positioning understood only by the participants.

Shirley had arranged an invitation and Rose had beamed in approval. "Lots of very smart, very ambitious, and very good-looking young men," she'd pointed out. "Excellent genetic traits for a child."

Marielle had laughed and agreed it would be a good place to practice and sent her one and only basic black cocktail dress to the cleaners.

Fun at first and flattering when her solo appearance garnered a good deal of attention, Marielle was soon uncomfortable. The chasm between theoretical discussion and the enormity of actually choosing a real live human being to father a child was turning out to be overwhelming in its implications.

She spent the evening fending off the attentions of a pair of aggressive men openly wearing wedding bands. Gradually, she became aware of the scrutiny of an attractive young man, just under the wire for tall, with intensely blue eyes. He promptly made an opening bid.

"You haven't been working the room," he scolded with slightly sardonic charm.

"I'm about to leave the room. My feet insist."

"Well, they're lovely feet. I'm Michael Winston." He waited expectantly and when she made no connection, "Liaison with the Committee to Elect Bob Malloy the next governor of California."

At that moment, Shirley paused at her side with a beautiful young television starlet in tow. "I'll be right back," she whispered to Marielle.

"You know Shirley Canfield?" Michael Winston was openly impressed.

"She invited me. She's one of my best friends." Marielle watched him consider this information.

"Are you quite sure you have to leave? I'd love to buy you a drink."

Suddenly her feet didn't hurt half as much and she allowed herself to be persuaded to have one last glass of wine, and when Shirley returned, introduced him. After a moment, Shirley was away again.

"Bob's having a small cocktail party for a few of his contributors this Friday, and I don't have a date."

Marielle paused only a fraction of a moment before pushing herself into the brink. "Actually, I'm free Friday."

May as well start here.

"He's thirty-two, single, and I think he's interested," she reported to the Minds. "He's asked me to dinner again tomorrow night."

"According to a friend on Malloy's staff, he's very ambitious, works hard, and Malloy likes him." Shirley nodded conditional approval with a warning in her voice. "Also says he's been known to climb socially."

"I got the same impression," said Marielle. "The cocktail party was mostly following him around and getting a byplay of who was providing how much money and what kind of leverage Malloy was going to have after the election." She sipped her iced tea, morose.

"So, about our potential father . . . " Rose, the realist, nudged impatiently for information.

Marielle sighed. "To and from the party was mostly about his decision not to marry until he's forty." She dawdled with a tortilla chip. "I feel so guilty. I'm checking him out for fatherhood and he thinks he's making a commitment to an affair." Marielle was annoyed with herself. "He kissed me good night and I felt like a spy. Why can't it be simple—we fall in love and get married?" she lamented.

"Do you want a baby or not?"

Marielle refocused her determination. "Yes, I want a baby. And it's too late for June. I can't get pregnant in July, so I have to wait until . . . "

"Wait a minute. What's wrong with July?" Rose was all business.

"I don't ovulate in July. November, March, and July. I've been keeping track for months. I have to wait till August. The fourteenth."

"So do it August fourteenth." Rose gave her a wickedly benign smile.

Until any possibility of error in the inheritance had been removed, Marielle reminded herself daily that Michael Winston lacked anything remotely resembling commitment. That in mind, she avoided dinner complications by meeting him solely for lunches, lied that she was in Tahoe skiing for two weeks, and between his schedule and hers, managed to avoid his bedroom as she maneuvered herself closer and closer to the August goal.

At first, her resistance only added to his interest and on those occasions when he pressured her for a sexual commitment, she told him the truth, that there hadn't been anyone in her life since her husband and she was determined not to make another mistake. Late in July, however, he tired of the game and insisted on making a firm date for dinner.

Early that afternoon, Milford Haygood phoned to let her know the final paperwork had been filed in London and that a bank draft to her order was waiting in his office. A few more signatures would complete the matter.

"I have a meeting in Los Angeles this evening," said the attorney, "and then I'm catching the red-eye to New York. Suppose I bring the papers and we can finish this."

They agreed to meet at seven o'clock. Happy to have a legitimate excuse for a change, Marielle called Michael and attempted to break the date. "I know it's late notice . . . " She explained the problem.

Michael's reaction was immediate and ominous.

"There's a great deal of money involved," she continued, "and he's leaving town."

"I totally understand and I'll change our reservations. Pick me up at the bar at Morton's."

Winston's shift in interest at her mention of money as well as his determination not to lose control of the evening, set her teeth on edge. Then she rallied. If the moon was right, she was going to make a baby in about two weeks and after that she wouldn't have to see him or lie to him again.

"I'll try not to be too late," she conceded. Better to lose the battle and save the war.

When she got to the restaurant, Michael greeted her with a predatory smile, his interest transparent. "What are we celebrating?"

She decided to tell him. "I've inherited some money."

"No kidding, are we rich?"

"What do you consider rich?" She managed to keep her tone light and teasing. Her ex-husband's idea of financial security had been vague, but always ran in the direction of millions.

"Two, three million ought to do it. How rich are we?"

"If we were that rich, I wouldn't be here," she responded airily.

"Listen," he said suddenly. "Malloy invited me to his fund-raiser in Palm Desert. I wasn't sure I'd make the invitation list, but he says he wants me to come. This could make my career. Major, major, ultrahot guest list. Even Sinatra's supposed to be there." He paused to set up the moment.

Suddenly, she could feel it coming, an avalanche on a downhill run. The hard place was about to come into solid contact with a rock and the question under the question was on the table at last: Is it going to be now or never? Michael Winston was through waiting.

"You want to go? Weekend of the fourteenth."

His voice was coming at her, uncomfortably close.

"Two weeks from now."

She couldn't escape his eyes.

"I'd love to," she said quickly before her brain allowed something negative to come out of her mouth. An immediate sinking sensation swallowed the center of her stomach. "It sounds terrific." The thinnest of lies but the deal was done and committed to. He knew it and she knew it.

He swiveled on his bar stool in order to bring his leg into close contact with her thigh and questioned her with his eyes as he paused, a broad grin charming his face. "Great. We'll be there for the weekend, of course. Black tie and all that. Bring some tennis stuff, the sexier the better, I'll buy you some if you want. Bob likes to hang out on the courts. You play?"

The maître d' signaled and Michael finished his drink to shepherd her to their table. "By the way, I've got a great investment guy if you need one."

"The money's already committed," she said firmly.

"What'd you invest in?" He was quite curious.

Diapers, she thought, resigned to the evening and wondering what kind of look he'd get on his face if she told him the truth. She smiled into his curiosity. "Futures."

Michael Winston was very impressed and ordered a moderately expensive bottle of wine.

5

Palm Desert, California, August 14, 1989

"Here's your copy of the guest list."

Marielle abandoned her view of development rooftops sliding southward beneath the light commuter plane, to take the sheet of paper.

It had taken monumental efforts to sidestep Michael's intentions since accepting the invitation. PMS had worked for a week followed by a mythical business junket. Rose and Shirley were invaluable in conjugating a series of crises relative to the trip: fittings and manicure appointments gone awry, late work at the office, a disaster at the hairdressers.

But this day had finally arrived and she was en route to Palm Desert sans birth control, and somewhere in the belly of the plane a glamorous Neiman's gown that had cost a small fortune was carefully packed next to her basic black cocktail dress in luggage borrowed from Rose.

"Major contributors, essential to know," Michael continued. "I'll need your help working the wives. Sometimes they're more important."

Marielle scanned the names to see who she was expected to "work" and stopped in the *B*'s to read:

"Bellemy, Alissa—Actress, guest of Thomas Saxon." She skipped instantly to *S*. His name was there with two ballpoint stars. According to Shirley who was in New York on business, Thomas Saxon hadn't been able to clear his shooting schedule and wouldn't be attending.

She read the brief biography for the internationally famous actor: "40, divorced, born in Detroit, college basketball star, knee injury destroyed pro career. Two major motion pictures, *Restless, Shotgun Summer;* television series, 'Murder 101.' Guest: Alissa Bellemy, 26, single, former Miss Willow Grove, Texas."

"What's this?" She pointed to the inked-in stars next to Saxon's name.

"No-show," mumbled Michael. "Girlfriend's coming, though. She's real sharp. Got him hooked and reeling him in, I hear."

Marielle pretended to study the list for the balance of the flight, preoccupied with her own agenda. At the hotel, they were speedily settled into a luxurious room with a grand view of the San Jacinto mountains and a huge king-sized bed.

Michael was quickly in and out of the shower and dressed in a conservative tuxedo. "I have a couple of details to take care of," he told her. "Shouldn't take more than an hour. How long will you need to get beautiful?"

"It's going to take a while," she countered, uncomfortable. "Why don't I meet you downstairs?"

"First business, then pleasure." He moved across the room to take her in his arms. "We've been waiting a long time for this."

She didn't resist as he kissed her and opened her mouth to his. Trying very hard to bring forth special feelings—for this man and for this night—she willed with all her might to call forth a surge of passion to celebrate the circumstance, to create an interest in him sexually, curiosity even, anything to convince herself to go forward.

There was nothing except the insistence of his mouth and his probing tongue. When he held the embrace too long, a thin line of rebellion clawed its way to the surface; she managed to smile as she extricated herself and walked him to the door. Michael grinned back at her and paused a moment in the doorway to deliberately slide his hand in ownership from her waist down her body to her thigh. "Mmmmmm," he murmured appreciatively. "I do have plans for us."

Marielle locked the door.

You're still being unrealistic. She punctured her search for a fantasy evening with the reality of the situation. *You're looking for a way to convince yourself this is about love and caring. The truth is it's about calendar dates and belt notches.*

She castigated herself into action and began unpacking. Both gowns had traveled without so much as a wrinkle. "This is your doing, not his," she admitted to herself. "Stop trying to make him the bad guy and concentrate on getting through this evening."

She stripped to her skin in the artificial cool of the hotel room and stepped into the bathroom to start the shower. Studying her flat stomach in the vanity mirror, she tried one last time to imagine her future—see her belly taut with a child inside.

"You've been through all the reasons to do this," she lectured her fading self. "You made his list because you haven't been to bed with anyone since your divorce. And you know why he made yours, so what's the decision? Yes or no?"

The silent face in the mirror steamed over and she stepped into the shower.

Later, slipping into the creamy Luxuria knit, she caught her image in the bedroom mirror. In the soft evening light, the gown became the color of her skin. "Endowed" had been her mother's subtle term for her generous bustline. Well, she was endowed, all right, and there was nothing subtle about it in this dress; at first glance it was impossible to tell where the low cut of the gown ended and her skin began. Her seductive reflection added flutters to her stomach and a blush of nervous color to her cheeks.

She turned away from the sexy hourglass image to step into cream satin pumps with three-inch heels; with her hair twisted high into a sophisticated chignon, she was fully six feet tall as she turned back to the mirror. When she clipped on long, airy clusters of seed pearl earrings, suddenly her long swan's neck came into balance with the rest of her body. She entered a curious calm; as clear as her reflection came the knowledge that her life was her own and the decision that might change her future could be made and unmade a hundred times before the night was ended. It would be what it would be. In the meantime, the woman in the mirror was going down to join the beautiful people at the party.

Michael's jaw dropped satisfactorily when she joined him at the hors d'oeuvres table and if the looks she'd received crossing the room were any indication, all she had to do was say the word and the Minds were going to wind up Mothers this weekend.

Despite her confidence, the parade of celebrities was boggling. As the evening continued, she occasionally scanned the room, but Shirley's information proved accurate; Thomas Saxon was not to be found.

Michael kept her at his side as he worked the room and introduced her to name after name from the guest list, including a courtly, charming Frank Sinatra. She found she was having a grand time listening to familiar voices roll out of the famous faces. The men were interesting and attentive; some of the women, up to here in diamonds and down to there in pearls, were less receptive, but others were wonderfully refreshing in their candor and wit.

Eventually, Michael's possessive manner and his insistence on towing her in his wake became oppressive. She decided to take a few moments to enjoy the evening on her own terms. It was late. The sixty-four dollar question for this circled-in-red night was approaching at light-speed and she needed some distance.

As she passed the dessert table, a particularly luscious, red-ripe strawberry beckoned in long-stemmed, fruity perfection; it simply could not be refused. Dipping it in a small bowl of crème fraîche, then adding a sinfully rich coating of brown sugar, Marielle lifted the treat to her mouth and stopped, berry suspended, as she recognized teasing, dark-as-molasses brown eyes openly studying her from across the room.

Surprised by his presence, distracted by his obvious interest, her pause allowed a portion of the heavy crème to slide off the berry and drop wetly onto her bare breast.

Flashing his famous wicked smile, Thomas Saxon, incredibly handsome in a white tuxedo jacket, persistently held her gaze while the crème, warmed and melting, began a slow downward slide toward the hollow of her breasts. She realized he was waiting for her to decide how to retrieve the crème.

Breaking away from his gaze, she scooped the dollop of crème onto her little finger. Saxon appeared an instant later, all six foot six of him, directly in front of her and entirely too close. He gently took her wrist and delicately brought his mouth down over her finger. Her body became sweetly hot at the intimate touch of his tongue and she began to drown in rich brown molasses.

He sucked her finger with exquisite care, then pulled it slowly from his mouth. Merry eyes locked with hers—masculine, compelling, possessive—he opened his mouth to receive the berry. Somehow she managed to feed it to him with nerveless fingers.

Over the next few seconds, somewhere in the

remote-control section of her brain, she watched him take a black silk handkerchief from his breast pocket and offer it for her use. Unfolded, the beautiful silk was heavy with the smell of subtle, expensive cologne.

Eyes crinkling slightly at the edges, Thomas Saxon dropped his insistent gaze to study her neckline with gentlemanly discretion. "I believe you've missed some."

The sound of his voice sent light waves cascading through her stomach as she used the pliant silk to touch up the errant crème. He observed her efforts with a total, undivided attention that was overwhelming and completely disconcerting.

"For a moment . . ." His deep voice paused, a man carefully candid with the influence of much champagne. "I was tempted to do something I'd probably regret." He allowed a final lingering glance at her chest and sighed. "Might have been worth it."

Frozen in time, hopelessly lost in the maze of copper-gold filaments in the riveting brown eyes, aware of the perfect dimple on the left side of his gorgeous face, she tried to believe he was flirting with her.

Before she could martial her thoughts and force her mouth to create speech, she heard a woman's petulant voice in sugary complaint. "Tommy, I am positively exhausted. Can we possibly say our goodnights?"

Thomas Saxon turned from Marielle in slow motion and tilted down to the former Miss Willow Grove who'd arrived in a grand flourish of radiant auburn hair and an expensive splash of red sequins on black satin.

"Oh, hello." A blank, patent-leather smile floated for a split instant in Marielle's general direction. "Frank's been gone for ages, Tommy. Nobody who's anybody is still here. Good night." This last was directed to Marielle in specific eye-to-eye contact and dripped with undisguised dismissal as Alissa Bellemy took possession of Thomas Stephen Saxon.

Marielle returned to life. Before she could speak,

Michael Winston materialized at her elbow, urbane and charming. "Tom, Alissa, Bob was so glad you could make it. Listen, we were about to call it a night. How about joining us for a nightcap?"

Marielle held her breath. The wet sensation of the actor's mouth flashed a sweet echo in her brain and his eyes heated hers for a brief moment before Saxon responded. "I'm sorry but Alissa's exhausted. We were just leaving."

"I'm here till Sunday, offer's open."

Marielle felt the firm tug of Michael's hand on her elbow as he propelled her forward in his determination to accompany Thomas Saxon from the room.

"Thanks. Another time." Saxon's tone was firm but polite and he walked with Alissa toward the elevator in an unhurried easy gait.

Marielle was heavily aware of the ripples of attention brought about by their exit; there was a palpable shift of tension as eyes in the room followed their progress. Different from the interest she had enjoyed earlier, this was speculative attention, taut with examination and envy. Thomas Saxon was leaving; his departure would create a shift in the balance of power for the remaining people in the room. He's like royalty, she thought. His presence changes things whether he intends it or not. Life in a fishbowl.

Her voice sounded scratched and damaged in her ears, a worn recording, but she managed to say good night to the beautiful couple. They stepped into the hotel elevator, and she watched the faces of passengers change to pleasure as they realized they were privileged to share their space with Thomas Saxon. Facing front, eyes unreadable, the famous actor smiled slightly and held her glance until the doors closed.

While Michael spoke animatedly with another guest, Marielle's heart churned a steady trip-hammer beat. She stood silent and dared to wonder how would it feel, just once, to make love with someone like Thomas Saxon.

Reliving every second of her encounter, smoothing the precious square of black silk through her fingers, Marielle resolutely tuned out Michael's essay of who was or wasn't who for the evening until he took her aside to put his arms around her waist, pull her body into close contact with his, and whisper, "How about that nightcap?" The sexual suggestion in his voice and the lack of subtlety in his body language left no doubt of his choice for the next question. "Or do you want to just go to our room?"

His actions jolted her to attention. Michael. What on earth to do about Michael? The thought of sharing his bed was suddenly repellant. No way she could open her body to this man, child or no child. Not with Thomas Saxon's attention warm and liquid in her mind. Not tonight. Probably not ever, but absolutely, positively, not tonight.

Predictably, Michael was furious and vented righteous indignation without pause. "This is ridiculous! There were a hundred girls who'd sell their grandmothers to be here," he raged at her. "You've been playing me coy for weeks. If you didn't expect to sleep with me, why'd you come?"

It was a fair question and for a brief moment Marielle considered telling him the truth but sanity prevailed and she rejected the idea. Michael didn't wait for an answer, simply thrashed on, furious. Finally he brandished the room key at her.

"Find somewhere else to sleep and don't be here when I get back." He slammed out, key in hand.

All first-class hotels hold emergency rooms for VIP guests who create situations to be dealt with. Thus, it took Marielle about five minutes to make a deal with the desk clerk and for an outrageous sum of money she was given a tiny single with a view of the hotel parking lot. From the musty smell, she suspected it hadn't been used in months but for twenty dollars the bellhop managed to have her moved in less than fifteen minutes.

Cheap at any price was her new motto. She pulled aside the curtains and threw open the windows to clean, night desert air. Michael Winston disposed of, all she wanted to think about was the sensation of Thomas Saxon's mouth. The warm-slick feel of his tongue gliding along her little finger wouldn't leave her mind.

That, plus the heady, disturbing fragrance in the black silk handkerchief in her hands made it abundantly clear that sleep wouldn't be possible. Logic said there had to be a way to get it back to him and she needed to think about it. Restless, she decided to treat herself to a final glass of champagne in the Rainbow Room on the top floor of the hotel.

The cream knit gown was too low-cut for her to run about unescorted, so she changed into her black cocktail dress and stepped into the elevator. On the top floor, the doors opened to a small foyer; on the left was a sign indicating the hallway to the cocktail lounge; to her right, she heard the voices. Alissa Bellemy and Thomas Saxon were having a rip-roaring, old-fashioned shouting match.

She followed the voices to suite 2600 and eavesdropped shamelessly.

"I don't understand why it's such a problem for you." Alissa was furious, her Texas accent heavily evident. "All you have to do is tell them you want me as Katherine in the damn movie! If you don't think I have talent, say so, but don't keep telling me it's out of your control!" Outuh yur controle.

Saxon spoke slowly, his voice thick with fatigue. "I'm not the producer on this one and you know that. How many times do I have to say it?"

"Yes, but you're big enough box office to choose your leadin' lady. It's not like you'll have to carry me. You're not the only one of us with talent, y'know. People in this business help each other all the time. I'd do it for you. Why is it you won't do it for me, I wonder?" Ah wundah.

"We've been going around on this for weeks, Alissa. Give it a rest! I'm tired and I don't want to fight about it again tonight!"

"I agreed to keep our careers separate, I know I did, but it isn't working for me this way. I don't know what we got here—you don't want to get married. You don't want to work with me. I don't know what you want."

The tirade built on and on. Marielle could listen no longer and crept away.

In the crowded Rainbow Room, the bartender brought her a tall tulip glass of house champagne and she dipped her head in a silent toast to her double in the dark bar mirror. The icy wine bit her tongue. She pondered her decision about not getting pregnant and realized she'd known months ago that Michael wasn't the one. She smiled at her rueful image; trying to ignore her own best judgment hadn't worked at all.

Michael Winston swept into the room like an apparition, escorting a woman she'd seen earlier at the party. The two settled at the far end of the bar, him leaning in too close for casual conversation. Cringing at her embarrassing error in judgment, Marielle decided she'd rather be in her room, in the lobby—hell, the bloody parking lot! Anywhere but here.

She signaled the bartender, calmly wrote Winston's name and room number on the tab, and added an outrageous tip before making her way out the door with her champagne. Everything was quiet in suite 2600 when she pushed the Down button. Good, she thought. Life was too short for 3:00 A.M. fights of that decibel.

It reminded her, uncomfortably, of arguments she'd had with Jeff. She hoped she hadn't sounded so strident and desperate but suspected she had in her pleas to start a family. He'd always convinced her to wait and made sure there weren't any exceptions despite her attempts at seduction. Well, she'd waited and now she was prowling the halls of a Palm Desert hotel with a glass of champagne in her hand and no child to go home to.

She decided not to disturb Shirley in New York, but a sleepy Rose was properly thrilled at her account of the evening, promptly considering the possibilities of what might have happened if ex-Ms. Willow Grove hadn't chosen that moment to declare her energy exhausted. After a rundown of the jerk-off behavior of Michael Winston, Rose struck him from the possibility list and signed off. Marielle stared at the clock and her empty glass. Truly, more champagne was the only thing that would lead to sleep tonight. A magnum.

The Rainbow Room was out. Sighing at the waste of a perfectly smashing evening, she went downstairs to the lounge. The door was closed but most of the lights were still on and the bartender was serving a man in one of the booths. Marielle tapped on the stained glass for the bartender's attention.

"We're closed," he called out to her.

Annoyed, she tapped again. If the man in the booth could be in there drinking, she had a right to be allowed in also. She was in no mood for male chauvinism.

The bartender came to the door. "I'm sorry, miss, but we're clos—"

"She can come in."

The young man quickly stepped aside.

Breathless, Marielle crossed the room. As she approached the booth, it was instantly clear that internationally famous Thomas Stephen Saxon was drinking like an ordinary man and a lot the worse for champagne wear.

Three-quarters was missing from a bottle of Cristal and it seemed Mr. Saxon was either an alcoholic or a man determined to get well and truly blitzed. In either instance, she was being invited to join him and her nervousness disappeared into an undertow of sorrow at her discovery.

She slid into the booth opposite the devastatingly handsome actor, who promptly filled her glass and ordered more champagne. The bartender obligingly jammed another very expensive bottle into the ice bucket and added a fresh candle to the table before accepting a hundred-dollar tip and an autograph for his girlfriend; then he turned off the lights and made a discreet exit.

Saxon saluted her with a silent toast and smiled, and for a long moment his eyes searched her face, seemed to examine her soul in their intensity. Their conversation was minimal but charged with that wonderful, indefinable something that conveys to two people that they are powerfully, chemically on the same wavelength, and, if undisturbed, destined to resounding, breathless impact.

In the wavering light of the tiny candle, his eyes were coffee black, penetrating, and somewhere between warm and sad; she sensed a vast tiredness in him, that he was terribly in need of recharging and lessening of pressure. However, his manner was teasing and light.

"I am just drunk enough," he said slowly, articulately, with careful chivalry, "to tell you how terrific you looked in that incredible dress this evening. I had this fantasy, you know, of licking that crème off your . . . landscape. Until this moment, I hadn't had quite enough champagne to do it." He paused. "Thank heaven."

"I don't know what to say," she began, hopelessly baffled by his drunken candor.

"Please don't be offended," he continued. "It's just that I found you . . . find you," he amended and bashed her with an incandescent smile, "very attractive. And that hasn't happened to me in a very long time." He studied her with total concentration and she felt caught in a spotlight. "Are you an actress?"

Flattered, off-balance, she spoke before she thought. "No, I'm a real person."

He stared at her a full moment, then laughed strong and loud with great enjoyment. "Yes, well. I used to be a real person, too." He took a deep swallow of the champagne and refilled their glasses and continued to chuckle.

She sipped the heady liquid, felt it disappear like smoke at the back of her throat, and wondered at his presence. "It must be hard to be so . . ." She thought about the ripples brought about by their exit from the party and searched for a word to describe his being on constant display to the world. "So public all the time. Do you miss being a private person?"

"Not anymore," he said thoughtfully. "Not most of the time, anyway. But it's sure not what I bargained for when I started out." He laughed and drained half his glass. "Turns out everybody wants something," he mused, eyes on her face. "Sooner or later, they always want something. Always."

He sat back in the booth and she felt impaled by his scrutiny, trapped under a magnifying glass, unable to defend some unnamed accusation. "They start out swearing they don't. Some of them refuse to take anything, at first. Then it starts. A little bit here, little piece there. You turn around twice and before you realize, somehow . . ."

As she watched, he drifted out and back in again, voice thick with disappointment. "Somehow, they're tearing whole chunks out of you." He paused, charm flooding in to replace the disillusion in his tired face. "And just what is it, pretty lady, that you want?" he challenged lazily, her examination somehow concluded.

I want your pain to stop, she thought suddenly. *I can't stand that you're so unhappy, and I don't want to be "Katherine" in your next movie, that's for sure.* But the honest champagne added a more basic truth. *I want to get into bed with you and make love. . . .*

"I want . . ." Her mouth opened to say it but she managed to stop her mind and sat wide-eyed across from him, terrified he could read her thoughts. It wasn't possible. Even if it was possible, it wasn't possible.

". . . you to stop drinking," she finished. "There's no way I can carry someone as big as you, and I'm not sure you can still walk." This was also true and she stared back into those mesmerizing, incredible eyes that made it impossible not to hope. But it was well after four and time to reenter the real world, Cinderella. A couple of hours behind schedule.

"My room is just upstairs," she continued breathlessly, "so we should take you back to your suite first."

"I say we finish this excellent champagne before we decide," he countered smoothly, openly testing her.

She bit her lower lip and thought it over, savored the idea, allowed herself to slip through the door of magical, illogical possibility. *You can't doooo thiiis,* singsonged the sober, logical part of her mind. *You cannot seriously consider getting in bed with Thomas Saxon!*

By the time they negotiated the first flight of fire stairs, halfway to the second floor and her room, they were out of champagne. Too, she'd managed to silence the nagging little voice and refused to listen to her conscience about what was right or fair or what the hell would happen in the morning.

He carefully placed their glasses and the emptied Cristal bottle out of harm's way in the corner of the landing, and they climbed the balance of the stairs to emerge into the hallway three doors from her room. She produced her key; the actor opened her door and walked inside. Afraid to speak, Marielle followed him straight into the tiny bedroom, helped him remove his clothing, undressed, and moved with him onto the bed.

This isn't happening, she told herself. He's not here and this is not happening. Then he kissed her and she tasted heaven. She kissed him back and heaven exploded into the universe.

6

Pausing to nuzzle her neck at the end of the second seventh-heaven kiss, Thomas Saxon sighed and his body melted heavily into inadvertent, blessed rest; one arm sagged across her waist, pinning her next to him, and a bony hip rested against her thigh. The tight curve of his belly warmed her skin.

Tracing patterns through the dark hair on his forearm with her little finger, Marielle gradually grew bolder, gave herself permission to absorb the masculine feel of him—a singularly amazing, marvelous symphony of sensation. Unfettered by what he might think or do, she pushed away boundaries of her own thought and convention to explore further, guided by her senses.

Under the bedsheets and warm to her fingertips, the thin skin on his belly was baby soft; elsewhere his muscular body was smooth and taut along the length of her, arms and shoulders hard and knotted even in sleep. She trailed her fingers through the light covering of hair on his chest to the hollow where his throat began.

Cupping his face in her hand ever so lightly—a lover's caress—she traced his famous chin and full lower lip with her thumb; the sharp grain of beard along his jawline was rough and scratchy against her palm.

It had been too much too soon after all, and not in

her makeup to do something so wanton. She tucked the top sheet lightly around his body, taking care not to disturb him; it was enough to know that his demons were at peace for the moment.

With a luxurious heave of a sigh, Saxon moved even closer and snuggled against her, crushed her body against his chest for a moment, then relaxed again into deep, even breathing.

She worked the pins from her hair, pulled it loose, and molded her body to his, then drank in the intense sensation of the full male presence of him, lightly moist and pressed against her thigh. Lulled by soft breathing, safe in his arms, she lost herself in all those grand masculine smells that are like nothing else on earth and gloried in her inability to sleep.

In the dim half-light of predawn, she memorized for always the angular, darkly stubbled face, the heavy brows, thick black lashes feathered against his cheek, and slightly opened mouth as he slept on; remembered the wet, intimate softness and the heat of his mouth when he'd kissed her. Sodden with champagne, dark hair tight with damp curls from sound sleep, he was still too bloody gorgeous for words. What a picture he'd make.

Her eyes drifted toward her camera even as her mind formed the thought, impossible to resist. Don't think about it, whispered her conscience. Just do it! When on earth would she have another chance? Taking infinite care, she inched herself free of his arm and away from his warm body into the chilled hotel room. Soft early light slid through the open window, almost on cue, to light his face as she began taking pictures.

He'd never have to know and the memory would be hers forever, she rationalized. Something to prove to herself that she'd spent the night with the legendary Thomas Saxon.

Suddenly he rolled onto his stomach, taking the bedcovers with him, and the full length of his bare body was exposed in the exquisite, crystalline light—so extraordinary that she forgot for a moment who it was as she took shot after shot of the perfect form. She crossed her fingers that slow exposures would capture the bas-relief shadows carved in his broad shoulders, sculpting the curves of his body in the dim room. At the last frame, he rolled back, dreaming, restlessly drawing the coverlet across his body and destroying the moment forever.

On an inspiration, she framed a close-up, placed the camera at the edge of the bureau and tilted it slightly with a thin magazine under the back; setting the timer, she slid under the covers. After an infinity, the shutter snapped with a dull, heavy click. She retreated to the bath and removed the film, tossed it into her makeup case, and inserted another roll into the camera. When she returned, the pure, delicious beam of light had moved on, taking with it the magic.

Content that the moment was past, she crept under the covers to be next to him again, longing to know how it would feel to make love to him, to have him kiss her and want it to be her. She settled her body against him, soaking in the touch of his skin. Maybe when he woke up and found her naked against him . . . Maybe. She dozed lightly, filled with hope and anticipation of what the morning would bring.

Two hours later he turned over and settled in back to back with her. Her mind had been weaving busy scenarios. Someone, not least the former Miss Willow Grove, was bound to look for him soon. What if he was supposed to be somewhere this morning? What if he had an important meeting, or an appointment—what if he missed his plane, or? . . . Or, what if she just let him sleep? God knows he could use the rest and someone as important as Thomas Saxon could reschedule a meeting.

Her dilemma resolved itself when the phone rang. She clamped her pillow over it and extracted herself from the covers. It rang again. Even under the pillow the sound was deafening in the still room. She picked up the receiver and dragged the phone the length of its wall cord, then the length of the receiver cord around the corner into the bath before she whispered hello. Reaching out the door, she grabbed his tuxedo shirt off the floor and struggled into it for warmth.

"Good morning. Did I wake you?" Shirley's voice boomed into her ear. "It's noon here and I'm leaving for JFK."

"No, I'm awake," she replied, sotto voce.

"Rose called this morning and told me about that toad, Winston. She said he gave you quite a hassle."

"We had a major fight—knock-down, drag-out. In a way, I can't blame him, but he wasn't even civil about it."

"I hope you decked him. Rose said you met Thomas. Isn't he a love? Did you tell him I said to say hello?"

Thomas Saxon came from the depths of much-needed sleep to hear a ringing telephone, and a few moments later, a woman's hushed voice. " . . . major fight—knock-down, drag-out . . ." Rustling bedclothing obscured the rest as he struggled to clear his head of the fog from too much champagne. He'd lived in a succession of hotel rooms for so long that it took a moment to realize he was not in his suite. And the woman talking wasn't Alissa.

Whoever it was apparently knew about their fight earlier that evening. Correction: last night, according to his watch. What was going on? He dressed quickly and padded to the doorway of the bathroom. A blond woman he didn't recognize was wearing his shirt and whispering into the phone. "He's here. I spent the night with him." An empty film carton was lying on the vanity.

The woman jerked in surprise as his hand came down

on the telephone, his thumb deliberately depressing the button to disconnect the call. He took the receiver and placed it in its cradle. "Aren't we being a little indiscreet this early in the morning?" His voice was thick with sleep, raw and taut with warning. "I'd like my shirt if you can manage it."

Marielle watched the angry actor disappear around the door frame, then quickly removed his shirt and wrapped herself in a hotel towel.

"Who are you?" His voice cut through the room.

Too taken aback by his attitude to reply, she followed him into the room and grabbed her robe from the closet. Loosened, the bath towel slid to the floor before she could stop it. He watched her angrily, eyes unamused as she struggled to wrap herself in the robe, blushing and highly embarrassed.

Appalled at how suddenly the improbable situation had gone from the richest of possibilities to the tatters of her dignity, her mouth would not obey her mind and produce speech—justification, explanation, anything.

"Do I know you?" He put on the shirt in a controlled fury. Slipping into his jacket, he prepared to leave.

She managed to shake her head. At that moment, the phone began to ring and, amplified in the tile bathroom, it shrieked into the silent room.

"You *do* have a name?" he demanded. "I can get it from the desk clerk." He opened her evening purse and searched through it as he spoke. The telephone screamed another strident ring.

"Marielle McCleary," she said, finally coherent. What was he looking for? The phone rang again, assaulting her brain.

"Thank you," he said without charm, then picked up her camera. "I think what's in here belongs to me." He slid it into his jacket pocket. "I'll see the camera's returned."

The door closed behind him and he was gone.

The telephone continued its mindless jangle.

She retrieved the phone and sat woodenly on the empty bed, noticed vaguely that the sheets were still warm from his body, then picked up the receiver to talk to Shirley.

Packing for home, she poked at the cartridge of film, rolling the disaster around in her mind. It had been her weekend to get pregnant, to change her life, to create a child. Instead, she'd met Thomas Saxon and shared an interlude in his life for the space of a few crazy hours—until his anger and suspicion had raked it over and destroyed the enchantment.

Shirley had assured her it could all be straightened out, that Saxon had overreacted, that everything would be resolved when he learned there was no "evidence" to be disposed of. But there was and it was here in her hand. An entire roll of Thomas Saxon *au naturel*. Impossible to explain. Admitting that she'd taken the pictures was out of the question.

Besides, whether or not it was straightened out held no importance. He'd walked out of her life and back into his, and she had no place in it. It was almost retribution for having taken the photographs. She'd known better. It hadn't been fair to him and she'd ignored her principles as well as her conscience. All the magic had gone.

That evening she unpacked her suitcase, put the roll of film inside her empty camera case, and stored it in her closet; she told herself she'd destroy it. Soon.

7

The huge arrangement of spidery, pale peach chrysanthemums and lavender baby orchids, topped with towering gold and white lilies, arrived just as she was leaving for work. It was a masterwork of design and color.

"Prettiest bouquet I ever delivered and I been doin' it fifteen years," said the man in her hallway. Consulting his route sheet, he produced an additional carton. Marielle had to sign twice.

"Must be the camera," she assessed from the carton's weight.

"Yeah, well, this ain't no camera." The delivery man tapped a small blue box from Tiffany's tucked into the top of the mass of flowers and winked at her. "Y'all have a good day."

Indeed, the second carton contained her camera, well padded against damage, and three rolls of film; inside the Tiffany box was a jewel case that held a delicate gold-and-diamond bracelet. The diamonds winked and sparkled, obvious in their value.

"What on earth?" Marielle stared at the expensive bracelet, then tore open the accompanying card to read a printed message:

Marielle—
The evening was lovely—
Sorry for the misunderstanding.
T.

"T" could only be for Thomas, as in Saxon.

"This is crazy," she muttered. "What is he doing?" Late for work, she locked the flowers and the bracelet in the apartment and got in the elevator. Flowers, an apology, *and* a gift? Something about the whole thing was beginning to make her angry.

She walked up little Santa Monica to the tall, glassed-in office building in Century City that housed her office. Did he really think he could absolve an implied accusation of blackmail with flowers and a bracelet from Tiffany's? Aside from the fact that the gifts were thoroughly ostentatious, they smacked of compensation and, worse, dismissal.

Aggravated, she punched the UP button for the elevator to the seventeenth floor. The more she thought about it, the more outrage she felt. Who the bloody hell did he think he was? A gold-and-diamond bracelet for a one-night stand? Or sleep, in this case. What was the price of a weekend—a necklace with matching earrings? And why hadn't he signed his name? "T," indeed.

The morning passed slowly. The usual post-weekend deluge of minutiae multiplied by the thousand-and-one documents required to shepherd law suits through a jammed legal system occupied her hands as a paralegal for Stern & O'Brien, Attorneys at Law, but her brain worked busily on. By noon, she knew what she would do. "T" could stuff it.

At lunch, she retrieved the bracelet from her apartment and without allowing herself to be tempted even to try it on, she marched seven blocks to Tiffany's, and insisted it be credited to Thomas

Saxon's account. The unflappable manager quickly complied but insisted that she accept a copy of the receipt of credit.

After treating herself to an expensive lunch at The Grill, she messengered the receipt to the Mason & Pearson offices with a printed note of her own, and the instruction that both be delivered as soon as possible:

Mr. Saxon:

I have returned the bracelet. Such gifts come from friends or loved ones and you are neither in my life.

Marielle McCleary

Milford Haygood called that afternoon. "We've received a progress report from England," he informed her. "They can't go forward without opening the envelope. They're pretty certain it's a key, possibly to a safe deposit box but it could be merely a keepsake. According to Woods's instructions, you're the only one who's permitted to open it."

"I have to go to London to open an envelope? That's absurd." Disappointed that returning the bracelet hadn't made her feel anywhere near as good as she had hoped, she wasn't in the mood for British eccentricity.

"The terms are quite specific. Burnside's checked the banks in London and Reading for a box in Jameson's name. They're waiting on an answer from three more banks in London, but, yes, unless they locate a safe deposit box it's pointless to continue adding to the cost of a search without opening the letter. They're sticklers for this sort of thing. Personally, I think you ought to be there. Who knows what the key is for. Could be quite valuable. Could be nothing. You'll have to decide."

A trip to London would require spending some of the baby's money with the possibility of no reward and she wasn't in the mood for that, either. Still, a trip to

London . . . Best do it now if it had to be done, before a pregnancy.

Marielle stared out the seventeenth floor view of smoggy Los Angeles and her thoughts took her to England. Princess Di. The Queen Mum. Tower of London. Crown jewels. Double-decked buses. She'd wanted to go for years, and after the double disappointment of this past weekend, and the annoying events of the morning, she deserved it.

"I have some vacation time from last year," she admitted. "If I can get one of those cheapie fares, I'll see if I can arrange it for next week."

"Good," said the lawyer. "I'll telex Burnside and let him know to expect you."

Eight-fifteen the following night brought a decisive knock on her door. She was fresh from a bath, securely wrapped in her white terry robe, and settled on the couch with a small glass of wine. The still-magnificent floral arrangement scented the room from its resting place on her dining room table. Having lost the debate with her conscience as to whether or not to order in pizza, she was surprised at how quickly it had arrived.

"Just a minute," she called out, wishing mightily she had more discipline. Pizza was one of those foods that Communists or someone could use to make her reveal state secrets. She opened her door to poke out payment and gasped.

Thomas Saxon in a charcoal suede jacket, white T-shirt and Levis, stood in the hall with a wry, half smile, dark eyes teasing but wary.

"I know I should have called," he said evenly, "but the tone of your note didn't leave much room for argument." He looked up and down the deserted hallway. "Is it okay if I come in for a minute?"

Dumbfounded, Marielle backed into her apartment. The tall actor stepped carefully inside.

"I don't normally offend attractive women," he offered, glancing around the airy apartment with approval, missing nothing, including the flowers. "It was rude to send the bracelet. I hope you'll believe it wasn't my idea. However, I'm responsible for the actions of people I employ and let's just say they've shown better judgment."

Uncomfortable in the robe, totally thrown that this man, famous throughout the world, was standing in her living room cool as a cucumber, and, if her mind wasn't totally gone, apologizing, she tried desperately to follow the words.

"And I'm sorry about taking the camera."

The doorbell rang and she jumped, startled. "Pizza," she mumbled, and edged her way around him to open the door again. She accepted the hot carton from the delivery boy, then started to hand it back to him to search in the pocket of her robe for payment.

"Here." Saxon dug in his weathered jeans to produce a slim billfold and extracted twenty dollars. He took the box away from her and handed over the money. "Keep it."

The boy's eyes widened and his mouth rounded into an O. "Whoa. Tom Saxon! Hey, how's it goin'? I watch you all the time." He was planted in the doorway. "Can I get an autograph? Man, no one's gonna believe this."

While Saxon signed the delivery slip, Marielle flew to the bedroom and pulled on the first thing she could find, jeans and a sweatshirt. Still barefoot, giving up her hair as hopeless, she grabbed the money from her robe pocket and returned to find Thomas Saxon in her kitchen, jacket off, fiddling with her stove.

"How do you turn on the oven?"

Disbelieving, she showed him.

"I hate lukewarm pizza," he said pleasantly. Then, seeing the bills in her hand, "Please. I consider this rock-bottom compensation for upsetting you. Besides, this way I can invite myself to stay for dinner—unless you were expecting someone."

Stay for dinner? Marielle stuffed the money in a pocket and managed to remember where she kept plates and napkins. Peering in vain into the refrigerator for soda, she held onto the door handle until she was calm enough to offer him a glass of wine. "I have a fair Bardolino, but that's about it."

Without her shoes, he seemed enormous; the top of her head barely reached his chin.

The burnt-toffee eyes twinkled down, sent static to the soles of her feet. "Bardolino's fine."

Oh, God, was he flirting with her again? Afraid to venture too far into unknown territory, she laughed and deliberately moved away from him. "I prefer Cristal," she said breezily, "but what I can afford is Bardolino." She poured the wine and he followed her into the living room.

Half a pizza later she found herself remarkably comfortable in his presence. In the hour that had flown she'd discovered that Shirley was right, the handsome actor was open and candid and had answered her questions with disarming honesty.

"It seems odd someone as nice as you isn't married," she asked, genuinely curious. His face changed slightly—a probing look for an instant, maybe more—then gone as quick as a wink, and she sensed rather than saw his caution.

"Relationships," he said slowly, "require major investments of time. And careers take more time than you'd believe. I'm a realist. I've only got a few years left before the face or the body, or both, give out, and I have to chase this particular rainbow while I can." He settled onto her sofa and stretched long, lean legs out in front of him. "I'm talented but I'm not brilliant. Two bad movies in a row and good scripts will start going elsewhere." She realized he wasn't being modest, merely honest, and she was surprised.

Someone as famous as Thomas Saxon had a biological clock, too.

"I've deliberately avoided getting remarried," he said slowly. "I love kids . . ." Something central, private, took hold in his face for a brief instant. "But I had to make a choice. This business demands two hundred percent of your life and I swore I wouldn't put a family second to a career. Not again."

He studied the wine in the bottom of his glass with a pensive smile before he went on. "It's going to take a very strong woman to withstand the kind of pressure that comes with my life. Even my parents feel the strain. People they've known all their lives treat them differently because I'm so well known." He sat forward and looked at her seriously.

"There's resentment if they're not available for every social invitation, or don't invite everyone over when I'm in town, or make donations to every cause that's solicited—or the donation's not big enough—the list is endless. It wears them down coping with it."

She began to get the sense that he wanted her to say something. "I assumed someone as famous as you would have more control. Getting what you want should be easier, not harder."

"You'd be surprised. Sometimes I get away with murder. Certainly I get all sorts of special treatment, but on the whole my life is chaotic, demanding, and very public." He paused and gave her the full force of his concentration. "I'm vulnerable to anyone who gains access. If my face winds up in the tabloids, it's costly—to my career and my folks and the people in my life who depend on me for an income."

His eyes searched her face. Seeking—what? Then suddenly she made the connection. There was indeed a secondary message in the conversation. He was asking in so many words if he could trust her and she began to understand why he was here and why he'd stayed to dinner. "You're talking about what happened in Palm Desert."

He seemed relieved to get to the point. "It's been a long time since I've had that much to drink and I got really paranoid waking up in a strange room. When I heard you telling someone I was there . . ."

"I assure you, you don't have to worry about it. I was talking to Shirley."

"She told me."

"No one else knows. No one I know would believe it anyway," she joked.

"You'd be surprised." His eyes were compelling, unsettling her again. "Anyway, I'm glad you understand."

Somehow she met his eyes and held her own for several seconds as they burned into her very being.

"You sure looked good eating strawberries," he said at last, turning up the volume. "And that dress was something else. I decided to see how I felt about you when I was sober." He smiled the slow, lazy smile that was understood by women around the world.

Marielle flushed at the compliments. There was no mistaking his intent this time. He was definitely flirting with her and her heart rate was going up a mile a minute. Determined not to let the situation carry the moment, she held his gaze and deliberately introduced the subject she wanted most to avoid. "What about Alissa?"

He didn't pause. "It's no secret. She's in my life, has been for a while." He looked away at last and sipped the last of his wine. Then, choosing his words carefully, he looked at her again with candor. "I care about her, but I honestly don't know where things will go with us. We've lasted this long probably because we're in the same business. We know what kind of pressures we have to deal with. Maybe we could beat the odds, maybe not."

He sat for a moment, contemplative. "I'd really like to see you again. I don't know what else to say."

"I'd like to see you, too," she said, heart galloping. Maybe, just maybe, fate had finally decided to deal her some cards she could get in the game with. She really did like him. Separate and aside from his famous face and chiseled chin and black-coffee eyes, she really liked him. He truly had some brains tucked up inside that head with its luxuriant hair and two silvers at the temple.

And maybe, just maybe, it would be possible that she, Marielle Tèa Lilia Jonas McCleary, could be the next woman in his life. Why not? God knows she'd be good for him. She didn't want his money. She didn't want to be in his movies; she didn't want anything on earth except to find out what it was like to make love with him and have as many gorgeous children as she and he could make before the biological frog died. Could a future with this man be possible? Fate only knew, and fate had managed to deliver him to her apartment until midnight this night.

For the first time that evening Thomas Saxon glanced at his watch. "I've got to go," he muttered. "Listen, I'm going to be on location in New York until Sunday. How about dinner next week?"

He was serious. "Great. Sure." She held her breath not to break the spell.

"I want to see you in that white dress again." On a small notepad inside his wallet, he wrote down her number. He tore off a second page and wrote his own. "Thursday night, okay? Call me here if there's a problem." He handed her the page, then propelled her rapidly toward the door.

"As I recall, I do like kissing you," he said, whereupon he took her in his arms with slow deliberation; it was a thoroughly unchaste kiss but not enough to get him arrested. "Memory serves," he said, and was gone.

Waves of light continuously skittered through her body. The kiss had been perfect. Absolutely perfect! Whatever happened, she'd always have that kiss.

Then reality hit her with a shock. She had a date with

Thomas Saxon. She went slowly through her apartment touching where he'd touched, sat on the couch in the imprint of his body, poured the last tiny drop of Bardolino into his glass and drank from it where his lips had been. Thomas Saxon! Holy shit.

8

The next morning, sipping coffee, watching Abernathy circle his bowl, Marielle weighed her options. She'd jerked awake at 3:00 A.M. with the realization that she had plans to go to England next week. London versus dinner with Thomas Saxon. No contest.

At nine o'clock she called Milford Haygood and exhorted him to use his influence to have the mysterious envelope mailed to her, whereupon she agreed to fly to his office in San Francisco and open it in his presence so he could advise the British attorney of the contents. Then she began counting down the seven longest days in the history of the world, interrupted only by the arrival at Haygood, Haygood & Buchanan of a heavily insured air express package from London.

Entering the lawyer's office with anticipation, she hoped she hadn't been foolish to give up her trip. It was five days since Thomas Saxon had kissed her good night and there'd been no word. According to the English lawyer, any wealth the Woods family might have enjoyed had disappeared at the turn of the century; the key, or whatever it was in the envelope, could well be something Jameson Woods had forgotten long ago.

Expectant, Milton Haygood positioned the packet on the broad expanse of his walnut desk. Yellowed and fragile with age, it appeared of unimportant size. He slid it across to her and provided his jade letter opener.

"To be opened by the last living heir of Jameson Woods." To Marielle, the spidery handwriting was almost illegible.

When she picked up the envelope, a key broke through the brittle paper and clattered onto the polished desk. Old-fashioned, ornate brass with a squared hole in the center, it had been hand forged for a gate or lock box and it was not at all the numbered metal key she'd expected. Inside the envelope was a single folded page of paper with more spidery writing. Marielle frowned in concentration as she deciphered the faint ink.

"What's it say?" The lawyer's curiosity had slipped its customary mooring and his hands twitched to examine the document.

"'You'll be . . . o-b-l . . .'" Suddenly it was clear. "You'll be obliged to visit Billy McCafferty to employ the key." Her puzzlement turned to curiosity and intrigue.

"That's it? That's all?"

"Read it yourself." She slipped the paper across the desk to him. "Looks like I'll have to go to England after all," she said pensively. "To see Billy McCafferty. Whoever that is."

"Maybe. If this McCafferty was alive when Woods died in 1945, forty-odd years later it's unlikely he's still living. I'll notify Burnside, send him a copy of the note. Maybe there's family somewhere."

Marielle picked up the mysterious key. "I want to keep this for a few days."

Haygood looked up at her with lawyerly caution. "It could be very valuable. I'd feel better if you put it in a safe deposit box or something."

"Trust me, I won't lose it. It's my ticket to London." She carefully wrapped the key in a black silk handkerchief. "Just for luck," she explained to the uncomprehending attorney. "I need all I can get this week."

The message light was winking on her answering machine. She closed her eyes in a silent plea and pushed the Playback button. The machine whirred and clunked and a few seconds later, Thomas Saxon's famous voice was speaking in her living room. "Hi, Marielle. This is Tom. I'm sorry I missed you. There's no phone on the location site and I've been working every night till midnight. I'll finish Thursday in time to catch a flight to L.A., so I'll pick you up for dinner about eight-fifteen. I hope that's okay. I'm looking forward to seeing you in that dress. 'Bye."

The machine beeped three times and clicked itself off. Ecstatic, she played back the message half a dozen times, memorizing every word. It was really going to happen.

The next two days were suddenly gone. From the moment of the message she lectured herself sideways about not counting too much on the evening, trying to convince herself that, for Thomas Saxon, this was just another page in an endless black book of pages and not to expect a repeat of the magical mystery evening of a week ago. Oh, but, hoping, hoping, hoping . . .

Both Rose and Shirley had been supportive, but carefully noncommittal about anything resembling serious involvement with the man. Shirley had gone so far as to point out that their worlds were pretty far apart, while Rose the realist had been uncharacteristically focused elsewhere. Inside her heart, Marielle knew she hadn't really listened to anyone, including herself.

Thursday night, nervously adjusting her black cocktail

dress, she listened for his footsteps so hard she could hear the tick of her watch. She'd tried to wear the requested white gown with its plunging décolleté neckline, and at the last minute hadn't been able to justify the expanse of chest it afforded. Somehow, wearing it in public had been less revealing than the one-on-one situation of this evening.

As a surprise, she'd labored over a simple but elegant meal; when he arrived she planned to offer the choice of eating in the privacy of her apartment where he could relax and unwind outside the public eye, or be off to anywhere he chose.

Abernathy circled his bowl and stopped occasionally to watch the black dress move restlessly from the white-on-white striped couch to the window that looked down at the street, to the desert blue-and-beige chaise, then back to the couch. He circled the bowl again and again. Finally, at eleven o'clock, he watched her walk into the kitchen and begin putting perfectly good food down the garbage disposal.

Marielle washed off her makeup and brushed out the expensive efforts of her hairdresser; finally she stopped avoiding her eyes in the mirror. "He could have called," she said out loud. "There's no excuse for not having the courtesy to pick up a phone and tell me he couldn't make it."

The admission made way for the tears that had been crowding her for the past hour and a half. She crawled into bed with a leaden body. He could have called.

When the phone rang, it could only be Thomas. Torn between joy at the sound and fury at the disaster of her evening, she forced herself to let it ring twice more before picking it up. "Hello?" The chill in her voice might have welcomed spring.

"I'm sorry." Thomas's tired but excited voice sounded through the receiver. "I really wanted to see you this evening but this is the first chance I've had to get to a phone. We got off an hour late in New York and I was just about to call you from the plane when we had to put down here in Las Vegas."

"What happened?" Fear for his safety flooded her heart.

"What happened is five-pound Zachary Thomas Alvarez. I helped deliver a baby!" The astonished excitement in his voice dispelled any doubts she might have had.

"She was in the seat next to me, the mother. Her water broke and before you know it she's in labor and there was just me and a stewardess and no doctor. The most unbelievable experience of my life. Marielle, I'm really sorry I didn't call you earlier but by the time we got down things were pretty hectic. I went with her to the hospital and left my address book on the plane. It went on to Los Angeles. The airline people found it about five minutes ago and just called with your number."

"Is she all right?" She made a mental note to have her phone number listed as soon as possible.

"There were a couple of small complications, but she's fine now. And the baby's fine," he said proudly. She heard exhaustion overtake the energy in his voice. "The hospital staff says we did everything right and he's healthy as can be. I'm the only one who's a wreck."

He was safe and while she'd come in second for the evening, it had been because of a baby—a pretty good reason, at that. While she felt immensely better, she couldn't escape the fact that she'd been cheated of her evening with him, and fought to hide her disappointment. She looked at the clock. Maybe he would catch a later flight, but she knew better. "I can imagine," she said carefully. "You sound really tired."

"More like destroyed. Listen, I will make this up to you, I promise. It's too late to take a flight out of here tonight and I've got a ton of things backed up for tomorrow—I don't know exactly when but I'll call you and we'll make a new plan."

A new plan. What a *wonderful* idea. "Get some sleep." A new plan made all the difference in the world.

"Thanks for understanding. You're terrific. Good night."

She got up to get some ice cream from the fridge and savor *a new plan.* Yes!

Late Saturday afternoon, her phone rang and she answered it with hopes flying.

"This is a voice from your past."

Her hopes crashed and burned. Past, indeed. She'd last heard from Jeff six months ago when he'd called to see if she had the key to one of his cabinets. She hadn't.

"You have plans for dinner? There's something I'd like to discuss with you."

"What is it?"

"I'd rather not get into it over the phone. Can you meet me at the Largo in half an hour?" The Largo was a tucked-away little coffee shop near his condo in West Hollywood.

"What about Jimmy's in an hour?" She deliberately chose an expensive, high visibility restaurant, convenient to her apartment. If she was going to meet her ex-husband for dinner, she at least wanted to enjoy the dinner.

"Sure."

He hadn't hesitated an instant. Whatever it was must be important to him, she mused. Perverse, and enjoying it, she decided to wear the black cocktail dress and brushed her hair into a gleaming airy mass before driving the three blocks to the fashionable restaurant.

Male heads turned at the bar as she approached Albert, the maître d', and she was delighted; the confidence of having the personal interest of Thomas Saxon must be visible.

"Oh, yes." Albert beamed at her. "Mr. McCleary called to let you know he'd be a few minutes late."

This was highly unusual behavior on Jeff's part. He'd never been on time in his life, but to make a courtesy call was unheard of. Particularly for her. She followed Albert to a secluded booth that was going to cost Jeff a generous tip and began to be curious about the reason for this meeting.

He arrived twenty minutes later, freshly shaved, hair still damp from a shower, in an aura of fresh cologne. She offered her cheek and he kissed her and sat down.

"I'll have whatever she's having," he told the waiter. "I've been meaning to call you for a while, but you know how things are." He paused in genuine appreciation. "You look great."

"Thank you. So how are things?"

"Fine, busier than ever, I'm happy to say." He studied her closely and she was glad she'd worn the dress.

Jeff was employed by a law firm whose practice was primarily divorce and personal injury. They'd met when she was hired as a paralegal. When their relationship evolved toward marriage, they'd decided working together on a daily basis was too much time together and she'd found a position at her current firm in Century City.

As dinner progressed from endive salad to Dover sole she reveled in feeling good and deliberately ordered a glass of champagne; she chattered on about inconsequential goings-on in her life through espresso and chocolate mousse. He became more and more impatient to get to the point of the meeting and, finally, she decided to give him an opening.

"So what's this about?"

"Nothing all that much. I was just wondering who you're seeing, you know, and stuff. . . . We haven't talked in a while."

She felt color move into her cheeks and looked at him, surprised he would ask about her personal life. He'd never shown an interest before. Realizing he probably wouldn't believe her anyway, she hedged. "I've met someone."

She couldn't help it. Jeff harbored this illusion that because there wasn't a constant man in her life, she was waiting for him to come back and it felt too good to let him know she was interested elsewhere. She allowed a generous helping of not-telling-all in her smile as she continued, "It's a little soon to be picking out the china. . . . Why?"

Jeff took the bait. "Anyone I know?"

"I don't think so. Since when do you care who I'm dating?"

"Since I play racquetball with Michael Winston and he's bragging about this great-looking blond he took to Palm Desert for the weekend and screwed her brains out. That's since when."

Her good humor came to a jolting halt. "He said what?"

"How could you do that? I mean, Jesus, Marielle. Michael Winston? I do business with him and you're spending weekends with him."

Marielle tried to hide her shock but a gorge of anger rose in her throat. Winston was a sleazoid scum. What did she care what he said about her? But logical rationale wouldn't work. If Jeff hadn't been so bluntly crass, if he'd been genuinely concerned for her welfare, she might have handled it better, but his focus was on himself and his accusatory attitude and outraged-ex-husband disapproval stung almost as much as Winston's lie.

"I take it you didn't defend my honor," she said stiffly. "Am I to understand that you're angry because I went to Palm Desert with him, or because presumably he got in bed with *your* ex-wife?" She gathered her purse and slid to the corner of the booth, prepared to leave. "Is this meeting to supply me with a list of your business associates, or to tell me to check with you before I make future social arrangements?"

Jeff had the grace to look embarrassed. "Wait a minute." He took her purse from her grasp and tried to apologize. "Don't get all crazy on me. I'm sorry. It's just that he's such a jerk. You're not the type to . . . I mean, I know you're got more class than that. I just couldn't understand why you'd see somebody like him, that's all."

"Of course. And it had nothing whatever to do with your ego." She managed to bring her biting sarcasm under control. The good news was that she'd had enough sense not to get into bed with Michael Winston, macho cretin that he'd turned out to be. She had a sudden chilling thought that if she hadn't met Thomas Saxon that night, it was entirely possible that she might have done so, and that she might have been pregnant with Winston's child at this very minute.

The idea shocked her into a conciliatory manner. "I'm sorry you were embarrassed. It was a decision I regret and I certainly don't intend to defend, particularly to you. However, who I see is my business and if that's all that you wanted to say, I'd really like to go home now." She retrieved her purse and forced herself to wait while he paid the check.

Michael Winston is an asinine, gnat-brained little creep who's not worth the trouble, babbled her brain. *You've got a date with Thomas Saxon and you've kissed him, drunk and sober, and you've been in bed with him, albeit chastely. Michael Winston can stuff a sock in it. If he can find it.*

Her confidence returned by the time she got to the door and she managed an honest smile at Albert and threw in one for two older gentlemen at the bar openly appreciating her with their eyes. While they waited for the parking attendant to retrieve her car, she was genuine in her thanks for dinner but just to be perverse and add a little icing to the cake, she gave Jeff a big, sexy kiss she knew he'd remember. He was clearly nonplussed.

She drove to her apartment in a jaunty mood and slept like a child.

"They've located Billy McCafferty." Milford Haygood's voice from San Francisco on Monday morning held no promise. "He served with Woods in the British campaign in West Africa, 1874. Died of yellow fever. He was born in Fishguard in southeastern England. Burnside's checking to see if there's any information to be obtained from the parish church there, trying to find a family. Unless he locates someone, it looks to be a dead end. I'm sorry."

Marielle turned the brass key over in her hand. "I had a locksmith look at it over the weekend," she confessed. "He said it was quite sophisticated for its day. Whoever had it made wanted to make sure the lock wouldn't be tampered with. That's why the teeth are so intricate. He told me it could only be duplicated by hand and the measurements would have to be precise down to the weight. He's a collector and he's only seen one other like it. Made in Ireland somewhere in the early 1900's."

"Ireland? Why would someone living in England go all the way to Ireland to have a lock and key made?"

"Who knows? Maybe an Irish locksmith living in England. Maybe I'm looking for reasons to go to Ireland, too."

"So, you're thinking about traveling to London after all?"

"Maybe, but I won't spend the money unless there's a pretty good reason to go. Besides, I want to stay in town for a while just now."

The lawyer clucked paternally. "Do I detect a young man in your life?"

"Maybe," she said again, twinkling. "Just maybe. Right now I have to get back to work."

* * *

Three more weeks elapsed and two broken dates: A two-hour interview with *Newsweek* had stretched into an all-day shoot, and a last-minute voice-over session had to be called to cover a production disaster on "Murder 101." Two incredible highs. Two unspeakable lows. She'd given it up as hopeless.

Jeff had called three times. Twice to apologize and invite her to dinner. The third time he'd offered choice seats to *Phantom of the Opera* with Michael Crawford. After much soul-searching she'd accepted and they'd actually had an enjoyable evening. He was clearly interested in reestablishing a relationship, and beside himself with curiosity as to whether she was still seeing Michael Winston.

Dinner had been a bantering inquisition and when she admitted there was someone in her life but wouldn't elaborate, he'd been openly jealous and proprietary in his behavior toward her.

"What's this about an inheritance?"

Oh, God. Michael Winston clearly needed a life.

"Investing in futures? You don't know anything about the stock market. Speculating in futures can be dangerous unless you know what you're doing. Who's advising you, Michael?"

It had taken a full half hour to get him off the subject. And she hadn't kissed him good night.

Finally, the phone rang and it was Thomas.

"This Saturday, hell or high water, what are you doing?" His deep voice still gave her the shivers.

"Laundry." It was true and a week overdue.

He laughed. "Not anymore. Where do you want to go? You name it."

From nowhere came the answer. "I have a cabin . . . near Malibu. We can disconnect the phone." She squashed the sneaky little part of her mind that knew full well Saturday fell squarely into the red zone on the September calendar. It was fate, pure and simple. "I guarantee no brand-new babies, no voice-over sessions, no *Newsweek* interviews. No lights, no cameras." She paused to avoid the cliché and potential curse on the day. "No acting," she finished lightly.

He laughed again, sending her heart soaring. "You promise?"

This time, supremely superstitious, she told neither Rose nor Shirley. If it was to be, it would happen, and she would tell them after the fact. Besides, all that had happened so far was three broken dates and two three-alarm kisses. If you didn't count Palm Desert, there wasn't much to build a dream on. To counter her conscience she included plans for birth control. Just in case.

9

September 27, 1989

Sitting behind the darkened windows of the huge Mercedes, the half-hour drive to her cabin sped by like a feather floating in the wind. Casually dressed in crisply pressed Levis and an oversize honey gold cashmere sweater, Saxon steered the car easily with one hand and glanced over occasionally to smile. And each time he did, she couldn't keep a grin off her face. She consoled herself with the knowledge that no woman in her right mind could sit next to him and be unaffected, he was that good-looking. And she had him all to herself for at least the next three hours.

After gales of indecision, she'd finally opted for a white cotton fisherman's sweater, her mother's heavy gold cameo locket, and an old pair of washed-until-they-were-butter-soft denim cutoffs, which she knew flattered her long legs. In a basket in the back seat, she had wine and tomatoes and fresh basil and grated romano and parmesan cheeses and enough fresh-made pasta for an army, as well as a salad and a couple of rum tarts for dessert.

Maneuvering the big black car through the heavy coastline traffic, Thomas described in hilarious detail the astonishment of the airline hostess when she discovered the woman next to him was not fat but pregnant, and the delivery of the baby. Then he filled her in on problems they'd encountered filming in upstate New York with autumn leaves on the trees in one shot, falling madly in the next, gone entirely after a night of pouring rain, so that even with twelve-hour days, none of the background shots matched the close-ups, and about the difficult guest star.

"So here's this guy, stewed to the gills, who's supposed to jump in to rescue me in the middle of a lake that's like ice water, and he won't do it. Says his agent told him he wouldn't have to swim. Meantime, I'm in a wet suit, freezing my butt in the lake. So, we got a stunt double to do the jump. Then we lower this guy into the water to get the shot of him saving my life. We put a frogman under him to hold him up and he says the guy's getting smart with him under the water."

"Was he?"

"Hell, I don't know. He stayed in the water and we got the shot, that's all I know."

He helped her take the groceries into the cabin and during a walk around the lake, she told him about the mysterious key. Talking about the key brought the inherited money and her plans for pregnancy too near the surface; she was happy to have him change the subject when they got back to the cabin.

"How long have you had this place?"

"Two years. Since my divorce. Are you about ready for dinner?"

"What're we having?"

"Pasta?" It hadn't occurred to her to check.

"Hey, I make great pasta. My ex-wife was Italian. You pour the wine." He tied a towel around his waist and began taking ingredients out of the basket; he found a knife in one of the cabinet drawers, thumbed its sharpened edge approvingly, and returned to the subject of her divorce. "Who's problem, his or yours?"

Marielle poured liberal portions of a good Bardolino into crystal wine glasses she hadn't used in years—wedding gifts to her and Jeff from Jeff's mother—and watched him work.

"Ours. Too many women. In the three years we were married, he was unfaithful to me at least twice. I didn't see any reason to get a specific count." She was suddenly curious. The Hollywood community was famous for its lack of fidelity. "How about you? Were you faithful to your wife?"

The question was rude and she was astonished at herself, but he lightly tapped her glass with his own and didn't seem to notice. The resulting double-*clunng* from the fragile crystal rang satisfactorily in her ears. A good omen? *Please, please, please.*

"Believe it or not, I was. When we got married we were two of the starving—also known as actors in Hollywood looking for work. We had a cheap apartment, a baby . . . a lot of money trouble. The standard problems."

The powerful fragrance of olive oil and sautéeing garlic filled the air.

"She went home to Italy to do a movie, moved in with the producer. Married him as soon as we were divorced. They live in Paris now."

Clearly, he didn't wish to pursue the subject. Marielle watched him concentrate on slicing half a dozen tomatoes, then dicing them into neat geometric squares before dumping them to sizzle in the saucepan with the garlic. She was glad she'd asked the audacious question. Then she tackled the really tough arena. "What about Alissa? Are things still the same with you?"

"Yes," he said, totally noncommittal. He stopped for a moment to take a drink of wine. She knew he was assessing her reaction and she paused. Asked and answered. Your move, Scarlett.

She elected to withdraw. “It’s getting cool. I’m going to light a fire.”

The debate began to rage the moment she left the kitchen. You won’t get another chance, her gut was pounding at her. She’s beautiful, she’s in first position; she’s got the public edge; she’s already career-acceptable and you’re not out of the starting gate. Don’t kid yourself, Marielle, you can’t think about this tomorrow. The calendar won’t wait. Do something about it. Now. And don’t change your mind.

She lit the fire, then slipped into the bedroom to contemplate the small blue container that held her diaphragm. It wasn’t as if he’d given her any reason to assume she’d have use for it. So far he’d proved to be an absolute gentleman. Not so much as a kiss. What if he didn’t want to make love to her?

Inside the container, wrapped in tissue, were four lucky pennies—every one she’d found with the head side up. Marielle tipped them into her hand, closed her eyes, and before she could lose her courage, walked to the back porch and tossed the blue plastic into the underbrush. Thomas stepped outside to join her and she began flipping the coins into the lake.

“What are you doing?”

She was able to answer honestly. “Throwing pennies, for luck.”

“Maybe I ought to do it, too,” he joked. “I need a hit movie in the worst way.”

“Be my guest.” She held out one of the two remaining coins.

Thomas glanced at the lake and sighed. “I wish it were that easy. I think people make their own luck. Most of the time, anyway.”

They tossed the pennies together then laughed as his, newly minted and shiny, bounced off hers in midair, and the two coins sparkled into the water in the late afternoon sunlight.

* * *

The pasta was excellent. The salad superb. Italian bread crisped hot, and soft in the center with melted butter, was delicious, and the wine was perfect, light, complementary, and heady. Marielle gathered their plates and silver and heard Thomas step outside. He'd left the kitchen surprisingly neat, and it took only a moment to wash the few dishes. When he came back into the cabin with a grocery bag, she joined him in the living room by the fire.

"I have a surprise for you," he said, flashing the wicked smile known around the world. Out of the bag came a carton of crème fraîche, a box of brown sugar, and a small container of strawberries.

"I couldn't find long stems so these will have to do."

Marielle looked from the berries to the crème and sugar, then blushed hotly to the roots of her hair as memory came jolting back. Something he'd said in the hotel bar that night—about licking the crème off her "landscape." Alone with him in the cabin, he couldn't possibly think she'd be willing to . . . The idea of him actually doing it tripled her embarrassment.

Innocence began to leave the room when it dawned on Thomas why she was suddenly flushed and self-conscious. It was his turn to blush.

"Hey, I swear I didn't have an ulterior motive. . . . Really. It was intended to be funny." Fire-warmed licorice eyes held firm to her own in denial.

She was instantly mortified at her assumption. Accusing him of lechery! What on earth was she thinking of? "Oh, God," she apologized. "It's just that you were the one who . . ." His eyes wouldn't let her go, assumed an air of intrigued speculation that charged the room with that indefinable something.

"It really didn't occur to me. Of course, if I'd thought about it . . ." He grinned at her and dropped his glance to her chastely covered chest, obviously intrigued. He reached across the space between them and examined her antique necklace; turning it over in his huge hand, he read the inscription on the back, ALWAYS, his face inches from hers. "What's inside?"

He held the locket slightly away from her, not touching her body. She could feel the heat from his hand and it was hard to think with his eyes penetrating her composure, refusing to let her regain her balance. "A picture of me," she said. "I think I was fifteen."

He smiled and his eyebrows raised with interest. "I'd like to see you at fifteen."

She'd been gawky and awful at fifteen. "It doesn't open." This was thankfully true. The clasp had been broken for years.

He let it slip back in place against her chest and his eyes roamed over her face and hair in the firelight.

"Beautiful," he said to her. "Very."

The air between them began to thicken, to dance and hum in highstrung, pulsing energy. He toyed with one of the berries and they both knew in one instant that it was going to happen.

"So what do you think?" he said quietly, eyes teasing, intimate, gently challenging her participation in the game. "Shall we?"

The decision was made; it was only a matter of how long from now. She wanted it to be a long time—as long as she could stand. She would have to remember it forever. She sought refuge in humor, heart hitting a rapping hammer beat, totally out of control. "After all the trouble I had learning to do this?"

Selecting a strawberry, she dipped it into the crème, then the sugar, and stuffed it in her mouth—then dipped another and held it for him to eat.

"My turn." He chose one of the berries and dipped it into the crème. Thoughtful brown eyes with astonishing reflections of the firelight, sought hers again; he offered the treat. She had the fleeting sense that it had been a long time since he'd had the privilege of chase. Too long.

Opening her mouth, Marielle felt a tide of long-forgotten emotion well through her own body, wash to her fingertips, distilling every sensation to an aching, raw essence. Warmth of the fire now infinitely warmer, the slow passage of time crawled exquisitely slower and darkened the room.

Soon she'd know the touch of his hands and the feel of his skin on her body. A mysterious bridge of new and intimate knowledge was now to be crossed, delightfully withheld promise—soon to be hers. He filled her mouth with sweet juicy strawberries mingled with crème and brown sugar, tasting of heaven to come.

Finally, there were no more berries and he carefully removed her necklace, took hold of her sweater, lifted the nubby white cotton smoothly over her head, unfastened the clasp of her bra and laid it neatly aside; he leaned forward so she could remove the rich, golden cashmere, caught her breasts in his hands, and cradled them, kissing them with appreciative deliberation before guiding her body firmly down beside him onto the thick, old-fashioned braided rug.

At last, Marielle was able to lose herself in the rich, sweet pleasure of his mouth and savor the taste of his gently probing tongue. She felt the hardness of his bare chest against her skin, her excitement powered by the knowledge that he wanted her, wanted it to be her.

Slowly undressing, sharing sweet-hot, unhurried kisses, they explored each other as first lovers do, caressing and teasing; their kisses melted into a fire that steeped and raged through their bodies, a burning continuum.

Sighing like a well-fed kitten, Marielle followed him with her eyes as he abandoned her for a moment to pick up the phone and punch numbers from memory.

"Marcy? I hate to bother you, but something's come

up and I won't be home tonight." He paused and Marielle, jealously curious, wondered who Marcy was.

"Will you call Breslaur? He's invited me to brunch tomorrow to pitch that Del-Fi investment again and I'm going to pass. Make my apologies? Tell him I got snowed in or something." Marcy apparently agreed to do so.

Supine, no longer warmed by the dying fire, Marielle marveled at the perfection of him as he positioned two new logs onto the grate. Black-topped embers, disturbed by his efforts, sparked to a deep red glow and created a faint roseate outline of his naked body. In the darkness, tiny flames began to lick at the wood. Her desire for him was so great she was momentarily frightened.

Satisfied the logs were secure, he returned to her side. "My secretary," he explained.

She reached for him, needing desperately the taste of his mouth, to touch him, to feel his skin against her own. His hands began smoothing the outline of her body, fingers carefully exploring the taut fullness of her breasts, lightly kneading her nipples, moving slowly down her rib cage to the hollow of her stomach, smoothly across her abdomen and up the insides of her thighs. "You're incredible," he told her. "I'm going to make love to you for a long time."

Carefully deliberate, he teased a fire in her, building it steadily onward, fueling it with the touch of his mouth and his skin and his fingers, with the skill of a man who took genuine pleasure in pleasing women. The flame advanced, danced high, went mad with greed, senseless with want, wild to be free.

"Not yet," came his voice, muffled against her flesh. "I'll tell you when."

Melting dollops of smooth butter-rich crème first on fattened hot-peach, then pale porcelain skin, and slowly, deliciously removing it with his tongue, he sent his voice humming through her body, "Not yet." He built the fire higher, set the flame dancing wilder, burning deeper.

Greed dissolved, hardened beyond want and ground into need, into desire beyond thought. His touch was all, his voice was all, taking her harder and further into waves of oblivion. At last she felt the fullness of him inside, driving her body, driving her existence and finally the words he'd withheld for hours.

"Now, baby. Now."

And her world turned inside on itself and exploded outward, incandescent, beyond control, white with heat and pierced with sweet agony, and again—and each time he joined with her, until she could bear no more.

10

September 28, 1989

Marielle woke to the deliciously pungent aroma of rich, brewing coffee; he was in the kitchen. She rolled over in a lazy new body, full and whole again. She hadn't realized she'd been walking around with so much of herself missing.

Molten sunlight edged over the sill and spilled a warm glow into the room. Supremely content, she arched her back like a lazy waking cat, then pounced on his pillow and slid it under the comforter to hug its softness to her sensitive skin. She held it fiercely, wanting his body in its place.

Nude and not in the least self-conscience, Thomas padded barefoot into the bedroom with two huge mugs of coffee. "Didn't find milk or sugar," he rumbled in an early-morning voice, "so I brought it black."

She punched his pillow back in place and made room in the bed while he put the mugs on the bedside table; then she watched with pleasure as he folded his long, gorgeous body in beside her.

After a warming kiss he reached for one of the mugs. "I'm a morning person. Plays hell with my social life." He sipped the scalding coffee. "But it's great for work. Sometimes it takes hours to get into makeup."

She motioned to let her coffee cool a bit. It sounded bizarre to hear a man discussing makeup.

He studied the room and began naming the places he recognized among the photographs on her picture wall. "China, Egypt . . . What's that, Kenya? These I don't recognize."

"Belize and Nepal."

"Quite the world traveler."

"Before I got married. Until I ran out of money."

"We've been to a lot of the same places."

They spent a lazy morning comparing their adventures in various countries, made love, mouths coffee-hot, then had rum tarts for breakfast and made love again.

Each time, ruled by his skill and her pleasure, she was driven to the end of her senses, convinced she could not, had no hope of withstanding another split instant of the precise pressure of his body and the pleasure he created in her.

His voice and his hands held her with him, controlled her rapture, prolonged her pleasure, then took her even higher, held her suspended, balanced on a fine, blinding edge of ecstasy until permission was given for the incredible roller-coaster plunge, deeper and more branding than ever before.

Each time, she learned new ways to please him, tease him, make him wait as she waited, eventually taking him with her on the same wild, joyous ride.

"No one's ever been so sexually in tune with me," he breathed against her skin. Tucking damp tendrils of her hair out of the way, he traced an outline with his tongue. "It's never been like this. Never."

Her body had never been so alive. The touch of his tongue and his warm breath in her ear caused spasms of splintered light to streak through her exhausted body. She was lost in him, unable to think, unable to know what was real and what must be some extraordinary, erotic, euphoric dream. How on earth could anything feel this good? It wasn't possible, yet it was happening.

Bodies entwined, glutted with each other, appeased beyond measure, eventually they dozed, finally slept.

She jolted awake with realization. Caught up in the incredible, endless pleasure of his body and the emotional and sexual roller coaster he'd created in her over the past several hours, she'd totally forgotten. What if she were to get pregnant? Any chance of a future with this man would be ruined if it happened now. Frozen with guilt, she waited until her heart stopped its erratic thudding and she eased her way out of the bed to confront her conscience.

She crept to the bathroom, hating to be away from him but needing some time to decide what to do. She ran a hot bath and lowered herself into the water, savoring the sensations in her tingling body. Her breasts, sensitive and achy from his bearded attention, had been a small price indeed. It was no use. Fresh little memories of licks and kisses to her body, firm lips sucking her nipples, rippled through her mind, clouded her determination, made it impossible to think.

He was waiting as she emerged in a towel and gave her a lingering kiss.

"God, I hate to do this," he said, opening the towel and wrapping himself inside next to her, "Mmmmm, warm. Some kind of witch, that's what you are. I can't believe I still want you." He kissed her again and crushed her against his body. "But I have to get back," he murmured into her hair. "I have a bloody meeting this evening that I cannot avoid. I hope you understand."

"I can leave whenever you're ready," she managed, shaken at the sudden shift to reality.

He left her to take his turn in the shower, and cold, chilling truth began its journey up the back of her neck as she dressed. And jealousy, incredibly, unbelievably bile, began dragging cat claws inside her stomach. He'd be gone from her in a few hours, maybe forever if she told him. And her heart closed up inside her chest.

She was silent much of the time on the drive back to her apartment. Once inside, he kissed her, reading her thoughts.

"I have a lot to think about," he said quietly. "You have a right to know where things stand between us and the answer is I just don't know." He pinned her gently against the door frame with his body, raised her chin with his fist. "I didn't expect this to happen." His sigh was huge, troubled. "You know that I have to consider Alissa."

What about me? she was screaming at him inside her brain. *What about me? I don't give a damn about Alissa. What about my share of your concern? I want my own rights. I have to be considered, too!*

But she stood mute with indecision, feeling every inch of his body, memorizing, committing to memory every instant.

During the numb ride home she'd split her mind into two people. One Marielle had laughed and smiled, joyous that his arm was curled around her shoulders and in the feel of the golden cashmere against her skin. She'd savored the heat from his body pressed to her side in the front seat of the car, while the other Marielle had come to a decision and knew that if she acted on it this night, it might well be the last time she would ever see him, feel his hands on her body, taste his mouth, run his hair through her fingers.

Finally, she broke her silence.

"You're right," she answered carefully. "I want to

know if you want me in your life. But you have to understand—I won't be the other woman. I can't. 'No strings' ends at this moment. If you call me, and I hope you do—"

He stopped her with a kiss, taking her breath away.

"It has to be with the absolute understanding that you're making a commitment," she continued doggedly, her body aching with the need to compromise, hold on to him at any cost, to ensure a nonstop continuation of the wildly ecstatic sexual fulfillment of the past few hours. "If you call, it has to mean that you want a relationship with me. Otherwise . . ." Her heartbeat thundered in her head and she forced the words into the open. "Otherwise, I don't want to hear from you."

He kissed her again, no longer gentle. This time his mouth was urgent and demanding, crushing her lips, and she kissed him back in kind, angry and desperate in her determination not to be swayed. Finally, he pulled away.

"I understand. I wish to hell I didn't, but I do," he said heavily. He pulled her into his arms, holding her gently once again. Working his fingers deep in her hair he held her face and searched her eyes, his frustration evident. Finally, he let her go, kissed the top of her head with passion. "Damn, I hate to leave you." And then he was gone and she was alone in her apartment.

Aching and empty, she was made of lead. A hollow feeling of loss filled up her body and she was seized with an empty, terrible loneliness. He was gone. She was terrified and it was all she could do not to frantically dial the number he'd left and rescind every word, take it all back, make no demands, say anything, do anything to ensure she'd see him again.

Then came the nagging ache of her conscience and she stifled the need to confess what she'd done—that she could be pregnant. That fear counterbalanced the need to compromise and she entered a never-never land of indecision. Intellectually, she knew she'd made the right choice, but emotionally she was in torment.

Two days later, a blinking light and a rumbling message on her answering machine lifted her from hell; hurried, immersed in business, it was Thomas: "Hi, it's me. I'd have called you sooner, but I've been buried in appointments—stuff I won't bore you with. The short of it is we've got a 'go' on the *Winter Love* project and I'm up to here testing costars. We have to be on location in three weeks due to the weather. I'll try to call you from Mexico City—I'm going down there tomorrow to see if I can help get through the red tape for some of the film permits. Public relations stuff."

At last his voice softened and became the man she'd made love with. "I remember our deal, and I want you to know . . . that I do want to see you. I miss you, more than I thought possible. I want to see you and I want to talk to you and I'll try to call later."

Her heart sang with hope. He'd called *and* wanted to see her. He'd said it twice. Life was beautiful. Fabulous. Wonderful.

When she was calm enough to go through her mail she found a letter from Rettig Burnside advising that no grave for William McCafferty existed in Fishguard but the firm had traced a great-nephew, William Townsend McCafferty, to the town of Westbury, some eighty miles east of London. They had contacted Professor McCafferty, who claimed no knowledge of Jameson Woods. Did she wish to visit Professor McCafferty personally to see if she could persuade him to part with information he might be unwilling to disclose to a law firm?

Marielle was too distracted to give it consideration. What did a key matter when Thomas Saxon wanted her in his life? Who knew or cared about anything else?

But there was no call that evening. Hope kept her

alive for four more days. She went to the market and came in the door just as he was hanging up. Frantic, she ran to the phone, but was too late to catch him. When she played the message back, his voice was different, distracted, careful. "Hi, again. I'm sorry I can't leave a number. I have a flight to Oaxaca leaving in a few minutes. I need to talk to you and I'll try to call you from the hotel there tonight."

She waited up until 1:00 A.M.

Another week crawled past with no word from him.

Then her phone rang Monday morning, early. Shirley's voice was somber. "How're you doing?"

"I'm okay. Why, what's going on?" Shirley was rarely awake at this hour of the day.

"God, Marielle, I hate to be the one to tell you, but it looks like he's getting married."

"What are you talking about?" It didn't sound like her own voice, even inside her head. She went rigidly calm.

"Jon Mason called me this morning, wants me to arrange a press conference. Alissa's been cast in Saxon's new movie." Shirley paused. "And she's wearing an engagement ring."

The funny thing was she didn't feel hurt. No pain, no sense of breakage. Not at first. Just a hard, nauseating vacuum where her mind had been, then a floating sensation with no air and no sound. She felt the blood drain from her face and reached into herself to find something solid, something tangible, anything to prove she was still there and capable of feeling.

Then it came in waves. Disbelief. Denial. Untrue. Not after the two days they'd spent together. No one could be that deceptive. Marry another woman? After the passion they'd shared in each other? The sexual oblivion? It wasn't possible. She struggled to keep the world in perspective.

"I don't understand. When did all this happen?"

"Over the weekend, apparently." She heard truth in Shirley's forced and painful words. "The deal with Melanie Salters fell through and the producer met with Alissa on Saturday. The contracts were signed last night."

Contracts were unimportant. "You said she was wearing a ring."

"Jon says it's a rock. Said she had it on when he saw her in Mexico. Asked me if I knew anything about it. I'm afraid it's true. It's why I called."

"Thanks." There was nothing else to say.

"Are you all right? You want me to come over?"

"No." It was a lie. "I'm fine." An even bigger lie. If it was true—and in her heart, she knew absolutely that it was—she was going to come apart. Badly.

"Really, I'm fine. I'll call you later."

She hung up the phone and walked to the kitchen, unable to remember if she'd had breakfast. What day it was. What she was supposed to be doing.

Then came anger. Was this the reason he hadn't called, hadn't faced her? The phone jangled again and she reached to the baseboard to remove the spring-clip from the jack, disconnecting the messenger, the bringer of hurt from the outside world, from her life. No more calls. No more messages. No more pain.

Silence. She wanted silence. Anything else at this moment and she would shatter and come flying apart like rotten glass, jagged and dangerous!

They'd made a bargain. He wasn't to call unless he was serious about being in her life. He'd called. Twice! Said he remembered their agreement. Said he missed her. Had to talk to her. Talk to her? *Talk* to her? Explain, maybe. Lie was more like it. Well, damn you, Thomas Saxon! Damn you, superstar! Superstud! Damn you to hell!

The tears were miserable, scalding as they coursed their way down her cheeks, ceaseless. The weeks of waiting; the hours of rationalizing, excusing, hoping, daring to believe, daydreaming about the surreal weekend they'd shared, reliving the passion—all useless now. Holding her breath, willing herself to be pregnant with his child, praying she was not, planning how and when to steal time with him again. Pointless! Waste! Folly!

He was marrying the woman she'd heard screaming at him in a Palm Desert hotel room, a shrewish, selfish . . . beautiful actress he'd made no secret of being involved with. Tears began to drain her defenses, dissolve her tirade, make room to accept reality. For whatever reason, he was marrying her. It didn't matter why. It was happening.

Leaden, she connected the phone long enough to call her office, told them she was ill and couldn't work. She ran another bath to soothe her stomach, aching from the wracking sobs. After a while, she walked to the local pharmacy and bought an early pregnancy kit.

When she returned, the kit was unnecessary. She'd started spotting. Distraught that she wasn't pregnant and relieved at the same time, she gave up her dreams to the empty, piercing ache of being alone.

The press announcement received extensive coverage: the local news at noon, newsbreaks between the soap operas, the early local news, the local news, the late local news, "Entertainment Tonight," "E," and a mention on all three networks as well as the cable channels.

"Thomas Saxon, world-famous bachelor, handsome star of 'Murder 101,' has become engaged to his longtime girlfriend, Alissa Bellemy, former Miss Willow Grove, Texas. The couple is expected to wed in Mexico where Saxon has just begun principal photography of his new movie, *Winter Love,* although no official wedding date has been announced."

Most of the local news agencies had included video footage of the press conference and a glowing Alissa, whose monstrous four-carat diamond engagement ring was very much in evidence. One of the reporters asked how long she'd been engaged.

"We managed to keep it secret until we went to Mexico," she'd answered. "I can tell you it's been quite a challenge. Now that it's out, I can have fun with it." Camera close-ups had magnified the huge marquise-cut diamond in its platinum crown setting, perfect for her hand.

Marielle snapped off the set and sat in agony. Why on earth had she watched this? And why had she taken Thomas to the cabin? At the thought of the cabin, a new slice of pain worked its way through her heart. She'd managed to eliminate her only place of refuge, her one escape. Now it was saturated with him—with the two of them and the perfection of their lovemaking. The new pain fed her anger and the circle of agony began again.

"He wants to talk to you," said Shirley, later that evening. "He's called me three times and says he's tried your office and there's no answer at your apartment."

"I disconnected the phone."

"Why?"

"Because it hurts too much the way it is! Why should I listen to an explanation? You don't buy a ring like that in twenty minutes—he's known for a long time he was going to give it to her." She threw herself on the couch. "He admitted he didn't expect us to happen. Obviously, he never had any intention of getting involved." She shuddered. "The whole thing was an ego trip and I bought into it."

"There has to be more to it."

"Like what? What could there be?" She couldn't bring herself to say his name. "He's one of the world's biggest stars. He does anything he wants. Forget it. I don't want to talk to him. I don't want to see him. Tell him I said congratulations on his engagement. As a matter of fact, tell him I went to Europe. It'll be true as soon as I can arrange it."

11

London, October 2, 1989

Sunlight filtered dimly through the soot-stained, tilted glass roof of busy Victoria Station. Marielle stepped from the train, sorting her way through scores of tourists mixed with sensible British commuters and homeward-bound students with backpacks of books. After the quiet train ride, flowing with the bustle and swirl of travelers out onto the historic streets of London was a welcome diversion.

Reckless to fill time, she'd thrown herself into a frenzy of preparations for the trip, rising early, working late, determined to eliminate any possible moment to think. Thought allowed feelings and feelings were cruel, and she simply refused to have them.

Yesterday had been a blur of luggage and porters and taxis and airplanes and an endless, miserably silent ride from Los Angeles across the pole to Heathrow. She'd arrived at the modest Hanover House, exhausted, amid London's late-afternoon snarl of traffic.

The Hanover was a converted mid-Victorian house straight out of "Upstairs/Downstairs"; the former parlor, now the lobby, looked out onto St. George's Drive while her room on the third floor had a chim-chim-cheree view of rows and rows of soot-blackened, bottle-shaped chimneys perched atop London's gray slate rooftops.

Her exhaustion, thankfully, had permitted dreamless sleep.

Early this morning she'd boarded a train to Westbury. The William Townsend McCafferty who met her at the rail station was fiftyish, reserved, tall and spare with ruddy English skin and wide-set gray eyes. They'd driven to his office at the local university where he'd plied her with tea.

Mounted in a display case on one of the bookshelves behind his desk had been a wonderfully interesting primitive statuette worked in gold. It was the focal point of his office and she remarked on its beauty.

"You're familiar with Asante artwork?"

"Not at all. I've never seen anything like it."

"They're a West African people. Ghana, now. It's an effigy representing a slain enemy. Came to me from my father's family. Everyone comments on it." Professor McCafferty eyed her, mildly curious, wonderfully correct, slow-spoken.

"I confess I hadn't pursued the inquiry from your solicitors regarding my great-uncle," he continued. "However, I've since spoken with my mother and family legend has it he served in West Africa in the late 1800s. Died of yellow fever. Buried at sea. This piece is a souvenir of sorts from the campaign, apparently quite valuable. I've never had it assessed, however. It's passed to each William McCafferty in the family. Rather ensures there is one," he said dryly. "There are currently two, my son and myself."

She smiled. "The instructions with my inheritance were to 'visit Billy McCafferty,'" she told him.

"And you're here in the hope that I'm the proper Billy McCafferty. I assure you I'm not. My son, William, is nine, so that would seem to eliminate him as a possibility. My uncle was William Albion McCafferty—never

'Billy,' I'm afraid. He disappeared during the war in 1943. I don't know what else I can tell you except William McCaffertys in this family don't seem to live to an age to die in their sleep and be buried. I do, however, have hopes of changing that situation."

William Townsend McCafferty had a sense of humor and she liked him. "It was foolish to come on such a slender chance," she told him. "I truly appreciate your giving me your time."

"Not at all. I'd be most pleased if you'd accompany me to lunch."

"Thank you, lunch would be wonderful. My stomach's in another time zone and I'm positively famished," she conceded. "I do want to catch the two-fifteen to Salisbury. I can't come this far and not visit Stonehenge."

William Townsend McCafferty was at once enthusiastic. "If you've not been there, it's not to be missed. I'd be happy to drive you. I take my students there at least once each term. We can have lunch on the way, I quite insist," he reached for his cap.

"Actually, I fancy myself an authority on the place. I used to play there as a child. You could do that then." He smiled broadly, with large equine teeth. "It's being given a great deal more care these days. Some moronic idiot carved his name on one of the stones and they've had to rope it off."

She caught her breath at the first sight of the monument; it appeared small at first for so celebrated a place, and isolated amidst the great Salisbury Plain. Highlighted against the pale hue of the midday sky, she watched it grow in majesty as the professor's car crested a sudden rise. Rich farmland surrounded the site, dotted with sturdy Shropshire sheep. Thickly white with unshorn wool, ears black as English coal, their long muzzles voraciously grazed the rain-green grass of the fields encircling the monument.

Professor McCafferty was properly livid that the public roadway had been cut so carelessly. It sliced through the ancient avenue leading to the circled stones and came so close to the canted granite heel stone that the center line in the highway was a mere fifteen feet from the ancient giant which had only the protection of an ordinary pasture fence. The monument itself was cordoned off by a thin strand of rope atop a row of stakes.

They traversed a tunnel under the highway and emerged onto the path surrounding the site. Along the graveled pathway the professor recited a bewildering array of statistics and explained that the mysterious circle of great sarsen boulders was in fact a reconstruction of the original design begun some five thousand years ago in prehistory. As they proceeded, the monoliths of mystical stone seemed to weave and dance and reform themselves into a series of beautifully patterned structures, each different from that visible a few steps before.

"They had only primitive tools to cut and shape these huge sandstones. The lintels are morticed-and-tenoned to the uprights—you might say 'tongue and groove'—and they're curved to follow the rounded circumference of the circle. Some quantity of mathematics went into this."

For a short while she and the professor enjoyed the luxury of being alone at the site. Standing before the immense, enigmatic work, it occurred to Marielle that human beings not dissimilar to herself had accomplished this amazing feat nearly two thousand years before the great pyramids in Egypt. A decision had been made, a goal decided upon, and ordinary people like herself had seen to its execution. If it could be done then, it could be done now. All that was required was a plan and a determination to carry it out.

Eventually, a large bus rolled up the road and turned

into the parking lot and soon a group of German tourists came straggling toward them along the path, ending their solitude. When they returned to the parking lot, Marielle left the professor briefly to walk down the highway to the heel stone.

Determined, she rested the weight of her body against the loose wire fencing and by leaning across as far as she could, she succeeded in placing her hand flat against the cool leaning giant, felt its weathered granite surface smooth and rough along her palm.

In that instant, a great weight lifted from her spirit. It wouldn't be Thomas Saxon's child; fate had been toying with her, but there would be a child. Whether or not it issued from her body was no longer important. The goal was to find and love and raise a child, and she would make that happen. She could feel it as certain and as strong as the granite under her palm.

The current William McCafferty deposited her at the Westbury station in time for the train to London with an admonition to let him know if there was anything he could do, and waited until the train pulled away.

Arriving at the hotel at last, Marielle went to sleep without dinner, exhausted again but secure in her decision to bring a child into her life. She gave up trying to adapt to the time zone until tomorrow.

She slept late and skipped breakfast in favor of lunch at Harrod's. There, she picked at a delicate shrimp salad with no appetite before wandering through the magnificent department store until time for her appointment with Rettig Burnside.

"Buried at sea? Well, that ends that." The fussy barrister didn't bother to hide his annoyance. "Much ado about very little, I suspect." He examined the intricate brass key. "I had thought . . ." Burnside declined to say further.

"Do you remember him?" she asked curiously. "Can you tell me what he was like?"

"Jameson Woods?" Burnside paused to consider. "Not a happy man in my estimation. My father knew him quite well, but we seldom had occasion to meet. There was some family quarrel, as I recall," he said delicately, handing her the hollowed book of poetry containing the wedding invitation. "He was ninety-one when he died. I don't think his daughter ever recovered from his death." He returned the key and she rewrapped it in black silk, closing her mind against its memory.

"I should like to visit his grave while I'm here."

"Of course. You'll want to see Father Derning, also. I'll ring him up and let him know you'll be by." He set about dialing the telephone. "I'm sure he can give you more information about the family."

Father Derning would return from a brief holiday on Friday, and a meeting was arranged for that morning through his clerk. She could leave for Heathrow directly from Reading on Saturday morning.

"You'll be staying in London till then?"

She nodded. "I'm on my way to Buckingham Palace," she said with more cheer than she felt. "I saw the changing of the guard on my way from Harrod's this morning. Big Ben this afternoon, certainly Parliament."

"Do see the crown jewels in the Tower of London. I'm told they're spectacular."

"You haven't seen them?"

The formal face broke into a brief grin at her aghast statement. "No, actually. But I'm assured they're there."

Marielle blushed. "I'll check and let you know."

"Do that. Enjoy your stay, and if there's anything I can do, please don't hesitate to ask."

For the next two days, Marielle worked very hard to play. Supremely conscious of her status of one in a world of twos, she toured the Tower of London with its grim Traitors Gate complete with resident arrogantly sharp-eyed ravens—which caused her to shiver in empathy for every miserable soul whose life and hopes had ended here—and viewed the displayed cases of jewel-encrusted crowns and golden urns, massive silver candlesticks and plate of every description. Trapped in their highly secured glass cases, the crown jewels were spectacular, but struck her as lifeless in their captivity.

On her way back to the hotel to rest, the battered red double-decker bus butted and bossed its way through London traffic like a grand old dowager. The weather was warm and Marielle sat on the upper level, listening idly to the peculiar, pungent speech of the local passengers as they maneuvered through street after street of Victorian, Georgian, and Regency architecture: stately palaces, cathedrals, art galleries, shops, theaters, a city firmly suspended in time, strewn with trees and garden squares.

Her lonely gaze invariably encountered young lovers, hand in hand, exuberant in their joy in each other. Each time she resolutely turned away her eyes, fought the overwhelming tide of emotion that threatened to sweep her away. She lost the battle with depression, and lectured herself repeatedly that she was spending entirely too much time sleeping in one of the most beautiful cities in the world; still, it was all she could do to summon enough energy to get up each morning. Despite determinedly tiring herself to be able to sleep, her dreams were haunted by Thomas Saxon's face and painfully delicious memories of their night together at the cabin.

At the end of the week she threaded her way once again through busy Victoria Station to board an early train for Reading. Rocking with the gentle motion of the train, pastoral English farms gliding past her window, she let herself slip into the quiet of the countryside and closed her eyes; this day had come at last and she was able to put the pain of Thomas aside and enjoy the peace of her mission to visit her great-great-grandfather's grave.

At the Reading Station, she secured a shiny black taxi and stopped at a local nursery to purchase two pots of cherry red peonies, certain to withstand cold English winters and guaranteed to bloom each spring. Then she called on Father Derning.

The middle-aged priest walked with her through the surrounding grounds of a modest church built with square-hewn granite alternated with blocks of local flint. The rough and broken stones caught the midday sunlight at a thousand points and gave a surreal quality to the afternoon.

Surrounding the church, the aging churchyard was crowded with ancient graves; centuries of weather had worn smooth their headstones. Some, barely legible, dated to the early 1700s. Parishioners buried amid now-stately elms and maples had suffered their capstones to be heaved askew, giant roots disturbing and displacing residents of two hundred years.

At the grave site, she saw that Jameson Woods had not been interred next to his wife, that Margaret Woods had contrived to be buried between her parents. Marielle placed the peonies on either side of Jameson's headstone.

"I'd like it very much if these could be planted."

"Ah, yes, I'll see to it." The priest seemed pleased at her gesture. "I can't say I approved of Margaret's treatment of her father," he said absently, "but she stayed with him, cared for him till his death. That's something in her favor, I suppose."

Marielle took a moment to utter a silent prayer of thanks to her great-great grandfather, truly grateful for the gift he could not have imagined.

"Did you know him, Father?"

"Not well." The priest furrowed his brow in thought.

"He'd visit us occasionally, but didn't attend services. Father Greystoke administered the trust. Spent a great deal of time together, they did, but he passed on two years ago. It's too bad."

Marielle stared at the stark slate gray stone marking her great-great grandfather's place of rest. Then more to further the conversation than anything else, she asked, "Which trust is that?"

"For the grave sites," he answered amiably. "Jameson was most particular about appearances. The McCafferty monument requires a great deal of care, and of course Elizabeth was laid to rest nearly sixty years ago. Now there's himself and his daughter, so that's four sites to be considered."

It took a moment to register. "Excuse me, Father, you said there's a grave for McCafferty?"

"Ah, yes. Has been for many years."

"Could I see it?" Her curiosity was skipping like a ten-year-old.

"Of course. It's right over here." He walked her to an adjacent limestone structure surrounded by a wrought-iron fence. At the front of the building, she saw that it was in fact a crypt and engraved in the soft stone wall was a fading legend:

> *This monument and grave shall be painted and repaired as often as need be to keep the soul of* BILLY MCCAFFERTY *safe within as well as that which remains on earth of his most worthy self.*
>
> *1850–1874*

Her thoughts skimmed excitedly through a series of oddities. A grave for a man who'd been buried at sea over a hundred years ago. Not an ordinary grave with a marker, but a crypt raised above ground and fenced to keep the curious at bay, with a trust provided for upkeep. Her imagination soared. "May I see inside?"

"Ah, yes, certainly."

The priest unlocked the gate and iron hinges screeched as he pried open the stout wooden door, swollen with the damp of ages. "I'll be in the rectory if you need anything."

"Thank you, Father." She stepped inside the dank, musty structure. In the center stood Billy McCafferty's coffin, constructed of stout oak and positioned on a tall bier of black marble; gaunt wrought-iron stands with massive candles, wicks black and twisted, stood guard at either end. To and from the coffin were dust-laden footprints.

Jameson Woods had died in 1945. Clearly no one had entered since. Settled into the footprints and everywhere in the room was a coating of fine dust from the past forty-odd years, creating a pale, monochromatic landscape in the dim, windowless gloom.

Her eyes adjusted to the vague light and she exhaled a sigh, uneasy at disturbing the record of visitations imprinted on the floor. The footprints were large, square-toed—her great-great grandfather's. She had a sudden sense of him: tall in stature, the slow step of advanced age, alone at the side of his former confederate, Billy McCafferty. What had passed between them that Jameson Woods would feel compelled to create a shrine for his friend, in a graveyard he would someday share?

She inspected the tiny enclosure. Just enough room for the coffin and bier, barely headroom for her. Nestled against the bier was an aged and mildewed leather strongbox, bound in dulled brass, no larger in size than a makeup case. She advanced carefully, her own footprints mingling with those of Jameson Woods placed decades past, and bent to examine the box.

She freed the small brass key from Thomas Saxon's black handkerchief and it opened the lock with smooth precision, as she knew it must; in contrast, the heavy lid of the strongbox scraped the bier in eerie, rasping complaint.

Inside, rolled in oilskin were several unused candles identical to those in the stands flanking the bier, plus a smaller beeswax candle and a warped box of sulphur matches. She struck a match and carefully lit the bier candles. In their uneven light she returned to her search.

Pulling aside the wrappings, she discovered among the oilskins a damp and cracking roll of leather; it was fragile but supple enough to withstand her efforts to unroll it. Unfurled, it revealed deep stains of ink:

> *If I be ded, my gold be that of J Woods if he promis to giv me a proper grav. Witnes my hand Febry 1874 Wm. McCafferty*

So there had been gold. Her mind threw up terrible images of Billy McCafferty's last moments on board his ship, ravaged with yellow fever, certain of death and fearful of burial at sea; of another man in attendance, her great-great grandfather, witness to his friend's last wish on earth. A promise kept.

"I think this qualifies as a proper grave," she whispered, and the echo of her voice carried back to her from the stone walls.

Laying the scroll and the candles carefully into the lid of the strongbox, she probed further among the documents inside. Atop a small mound of papers was a small leather diary. Under that, a tiny portrait of a beautiful woman, a miniature, framed in a slightly worn sliver frame, now nearly black with oxidation, and not much larger than an American silver dollar. She placed them carefully next to the leather scroll on the lid. As she disturbed the cache, the papers below began to crumble.

She lit the smaller candle, cupped her palm to catch wayward wax and held the flame close to the topmost paper. It was a bill of sale for a "Kumasi golden object." The date, except for 1938, was obscured and the fragile edges were too frayed to risk picking it up. The document visible underneath was dated December 9, 1937. War years in Europe. The same war that had claimed her grandfather Oldham.

Marielle blew out the small candle and replaced it inside the strongbox before she secured the lock. Then she wet her fingers and pinched out the bier candles and left as carefully as she'd come, her own footprints now on record in the dust.

Outside the crypt, she sought Father Derning in the rectory and showed him the leather writing from the strongbox, the diary and miniature portrait, and the inherited key. After a short telephone conversation with Rettig Burnside in which he confirmed that Father Greystoke's records were clear that the contents of the crypt were the property of Jameson Woods, the priest returned with her to the crypt and carefully lifted the strongbox from its dusty resting place and carried it to her waiting taxi.

That night in her hotel, Marielle first studied the face in the miniature, then spent several hours reading Elizabeth Woods's sad, erratic diary and the tragic story of her great-great grandfather's family.

> *My heart, my soul has died. My son is gone. The light has gone from my life and I do not know how I shall stand it. May she burn in hell that caused a father to turn against a son bare seventeen. Last night they came to blows over the whore, and I fear I shall not see Boyce again. If this be so, I swear on my life I shall never forgive Jameson. Never.*

The passage was dated April 6, 1895. There followed pages of recriminations against a woman named Lilia Foxworthy. The first time Marielle read it, the name gave her pause. Was it eerie coincidence that she, too, was named Lilia?

She continued to read through the diary. Rare days of hope were intermingled with months of Elizabeth's despair of finding her son; eventually a letter had arrived from America, and, according to the diary, Boyce had refused to answer her written pleas to return to her side. There was so little mention of Margaret that Elizabeth's daughter might not have existed.

Intermittent gaps of months, sometimes years, were followed by page after page of Elizabeth's virulent suspicions that Jameson was continuing to see "the whore," endless disbelief of his denials, culminating in an exultant entry in April, 1908. "The whore is gone. My prayers have been answered and she's gone from my life. Margaret understands the money was mine to give. I'll have peace at last."

The diary ended with a final, desperate entry dated on December 30 of that same year. "He married the whore. My husband's bastard has his name. I have no son. I have no life."

Try as she might, Marielle could not fix the words in the diary with the face in the miniature painting. She put them aside at last to sleep.

The following morning, dreading the flight, she busied herself securing the strongbox inside a sturdy carton and succeeded in receiving permission to hand carry it onto the plane. But once she'd boarded, nothing kept her thoughts from home and memories of the night with Thomas Saxon. And the baby that might have been.

She stared down at the shadow of the plane skimming across the great, glistening ice floes of the Baffin Islands, marking her progress toward California, and him. "I want to hear it from you, Thomas," she said to herself. "If you love her, I want to hear it from you. Then I'll get on with my life."

That resolved, she slept.

12

October 9, 1989

Jet-lagged but wide awake, Marielle insisted on having dinner the next evening with Rose and Shirley to persuade them that she'd regained control of her life. It was obvious that even Rose felt relief at not addressing the issue of Thomas Saxon, so she kept the conversation light and regaled them with details of her discovery of McCafferty's grave.

"A crypt? How absolutely Sherlock Holmes." Rose went to the essentials out of habit. "I can't believe you didn't look in the coffin. There might have been something left, you never know."

"I brought my pictures." Marielle took a handful of packets from her purse and placed them in her lap. Rose was still looking at her. "The lid was nailed down," she confessed, shamefaced. "When we went back for the trunk, I looked."

"It's not likely," said Shirley. "He'd certainly have kept it in a safer place after the war, if there was anything to keep."

Marielle decided that now was the time to dispose of the Thomas Saxon situation. "I want to see him," she said to Shirley. "I'm strong enough to do it now."

"He's asked about you every time I've talked with him. He's in town next week and I know he wants to see you." Shirley paused, her relief tempered with concern.

"But what? I have to deal with it sooner or later. Hiding didn't solve anything. He has a right to do what he wants with his life. So do I." She met her friend's questioning look with a great deal more bravado than she actually felt but her determination was absolute. "Besides, meeting him kept me from making an even bigger mistake," she justified. "So, in a backhanded sort of way, we're even."

Rose pushed past the subject of Thomas Saxon. "I can't wait to see the crypt."

The first three packets contained the usual glamour shots of London. Rose looked through each group and passed them on to Shirley.

Marielle groaned at the scant half-dozen prints in the next envelope. "Uh-oh." She opened the last packet and checked. "No, these are Stonehenge." She handed the photos to Rose and went back to the damaged group. "They all look underexposed. You suppose it's from X rays at the airport?"

The only thing discernible in each of the shots was a clear shaft of sunlight through an opened window and an ordinary bedroom lamp. Her memory suddenly supplied the details of the room—and the bed and the man laying across it. She stiffened, ill at ease at the forgotten episode. Somehow, the roll of film from Palm Desert had gotten mixed in with those from her trip and she was looking at Thomas Saxon's naked body.

"Who's that?"

Shirley's question startled her and she colored with guilt.

"Looks like a train station. Professor McCafferty?" guessed Rose.

She quickly slipped the incriminating pictures out of sight. "Yes, that's him. Somewhere in that group is the McCafferty crypt. I know it's on the Stonehenge roll."

Conversation drifted on to the strongbox and its contents and it wasn't until Marielle reached her apartment later that evening that she was able to give the pictures of Thomas closer inspection. The entire roll of photographs was not only underexposed but victim of a nervous camera and recognizable only by memory. The strip of negative containing the last three exposures resembled thickened, opaque plastic; not a single detail to help her imagination. She sighed at the loss, unsure whether it was relief or sorrow.

Before flying to San Francisco to meet again with Milford Haygood, she spent hours easing the top several sales documents out of the chest and into clear plastic sleeves. She and the lawyer examined each receipt and their results supported Marielle's opinion that the objects had been sold, one by one, to help Jameson's family survive World War II. Billy McCafferty's gold—whatever it might have been—was no more.

"It's wonderful to have the diary and the miniature. I don't know what I'd do with a treasure, anyway," she admitted. "I'd just have to sell it. It doesn't appear to have made anyone happy. Jameson's marriage was a nightmare, his relationship with his daughter was terrible. Even poor Billy McCafferty died bringing it home."

The rest of the week passed without event and she was calm until he knocked on the door. At the sound, her heart leapt painfully, hurting her chest. She realized that subconsciously she'd been waiting for the sound for hours. Weeks. Five weeks.

When she opened the door, the sight of his face sent a wave of uncontrolled emotions jerking through her body, but she succeeded in shutting them down in order to concentrate. His greeting was awkward and she noted with satisfaction that he was nervous. She'd dressed with deliberation; after pulling her hair back into a severe, no-nonsense twist, she'd chosen a teal green silk sweater and pale gray knit slacks that required high, high heels and brought her more equal to him in height.

Tall and lean in tan cords, a navy turtleneck, and a Polo jacket, his face was tight and drawn; tired circles had crept under his eyes since she'd said good-bye to him in the doorway where he now stood, uncomfortable.

"I don't want to talk here," she said stiffly.

"Good, I don't either. Maybe we could go for a drive. It's hard to find someplace—"

"Private. I know."

She threw on a light woolen poncho and they rode down in the elevator in silence. The clear California night was damp and she was glad she had the wrap. He guided her toward a blue Cadillac. "It's a rental," he explained. "Local photographers know my car and I didn't want to take a chance."

She said nothing and slid into the passenger seat.

He drove carefully through quiet Beverly Hills streets and entered Benedict Canyon. Stiff conversation extended from "You're looking well" to "Thank you" and died at the bottom of the canyon road. The silence was leaden between them. The Cadillac reached the crest of Mulholland Drive a few moments later and he pulled the car into an empty viewing site overlooking the lights of the San Fernando valley and cut the engine.

"She's pregnant." The words were terse, steeped in betrayal and rage. "I wasn't consulted."

Marielle was stunned. Her own near miss with pregnancy had obliterated any thought that Alissa might be pregnant. It simply hadn't occurred to her.

His voice was strained as he recited the details. "She called me in Mexico to tell me she was three months along. She wanted to come down to talk to me. I decided it was messy, but certainly something we could work out. The next day she showed up at the hotel with this engagement ring and told me she was going to announce to the press that we were getting married."

He twisted angrily in his seat to look at her. "I tried to reach you, I swear I did, more than once, but it's not the kind of thing you can leave on a machine. After that, things got a little crazy. Then you were gone and I didn't hear from you, I figured you'd written me off. When Shirley said you wanted to see me, I hoped it meant you were giving me a chance to explain my side of this."

Her mind was reeling and a dull ache began to pound its way forward through her skull. Pregnant. "You're going to get married?" she asked quietly, dreading the answer.

He paused a long time, his eyes black with anger. Finally, he looked away and stared out at the myriad lights in the wide valley stretching away before them. "In about two weeks. In Mexico. I'll stay with her until the baby's born. That's it. I swear it."

She turned away to look out at the valley. At the shimmer of lights, rows and rows of them crisscrossing each other to create acres of black space marked off with white and yellow, mostly, some red, in geometric street-defining patterns, swimming and blurry in her sight. "I don't know what to say." She felt airless, under water; she had to force her mind to go forward. "Are you in love with her?"

"I feel sorry for her, but I don't love her." There was a pulse in his jawline as he ground his teeth. "I cared about her, but not after this. Not after this."

"Then I don't understand your getting married." Her mind sought legal ground. "You could support the baby and be its father. Children aren't illegitimate anymore if their parents don't marry. I mean, they might be on some social level, I suppose, but not legally. . . . You know what I mean."

"She threatened to terminate the pregnancy," he said

heavily. "I'm convinced she'd do it. I can't take that chance."

Her stomach rolled over. "Three months—that's . . ." Surely no woman could be so vindictive.

"Sure it is. She's got me and she knows it. I couldn't stand to lose another child."

She looked at him and saw his handsome face twist in private grief. She remembered his mention at the cabin of a child from his first marriage. And a divorce. Apparently his son lived in Paris.

"Of course. I understand," she said lamely. But she didn't, and she knew it. "It would be very difficult."

He didn't seem to hear and continued his unseeing stare out at the valley of moving light. "I lost Noel when he was six. A bright, wonderful, loving child." He spoke with difficulty. "His mother had custody after the divorce but he knew who I was. He loved me. I saw him whenever I could." He paused in deliberation, then went on in his effort to make her understand. "I used up a dozen movie salaries in phone calls and plane fares to France. She and her husband took him to Spain on vacation and he was playing on the beach."

Oh, God. The chill that ran through her body hurt her heart so that she tried to shut out the words. Lost a child.

"He was helping some kids dig a cave in a sandbank. It collapsed. They didn't get him out in time. They saved the others. . . . He'd be fourteen." His eyes were dead and far away. "Eight years. It never gets better."

She felt a tremor roll through her body. Oh, God. He'd lost a child. She wouldn't cry about this, she wouldn't. Not more tears. She wanted to hear that he was in love and getting married and have it over with. Have it finished. This wasn't finished. This was awful. "You're getting married to make sure . . ."

"It's the only way I can keep an eye on her. She told me she had an abortion four years ago. She's probably lying, but who knows." His voice was careful, without emotion. "They're legal in Mexico after three months."

He turned to look at her again. "The lawyers are working out the papers. First, it was fire Melanie and put Alissa in the movie as Katherine, which I did. Now, it's marriage. I don't know what else she's going to want, but it's the only way I can be sure." He stayed carefully behind the wheel and made no attempt to touch her. She heard his voice change and tears welled in her eyes.

"I care very much about you and I don't want to lose you." There was a long pause. "But there's nothing I can promise until this is over."

And a hundred thousand things could change in the meantime, shrieked her mind. She forced herself to regain control. Anger solved nothing. Guessing solved nothing. There were no choices to be made here. She would have to wait and see what happened.

"I care about you, too," she admitted carefully. She took the black silk handkerchief from her purse and held it out to him, newly washed and pressed for its return journey. "I was going to give you this and wish you well with your marriage. Now I don't know what to do. I can't wait in the wings. I'm still the other woman. If you weren't getting married, maybe."

He cut her off. "I have to."

"I know, and I truly understand, but it is a marriage and until you're not married . . ." She laid the silk square on the seat between them. "I don't want either of us to make promises we might not be able to honor. If it didn't happen, I wouldn't be able to stand it."

Two carloads of teenagers pulled off the highway, one after the other, and parked on either side of their car to take in the view. One of the young girls did a double-take, staring hard at Thomas; Marielle realized it would only be a matter of seconds before he was identified and under siege for autographs and questions.

"It will happen. I promise." His voice held a quiet

plea. He reached for her hand but she pulled it out of reach.

"I'd like to go home now."

On the drive down the canyon, the black silk on the seat between them fluttered occasionally in the movement of air from the open windows, making no sound in the silence. It was there when she let herself out of the car.

He said good night, but she could only nod, unable to speak. She didn't watch as he drove away.

13

Rumors of rushed nuptials soon became lead stories in the entertainment sections of nightly news broadcasts speculating details of the upcoming "wedding of the year." The tabloid press rushed front-page headlines and the majority of the popular media worldwide featured special articles, "exclusives," and focused on little else until finally, from Mexico, came word that Thomas Saxon and the future Mrs. Saxon were to exchange vows at sunset on a beach at Cozumel.

According to Shirley, the date had been chosen so that everyone from local Mexican television stations to the international wire services could be invited to attend. After the brief ceremony with helicopters circling in dangerous, deafening arcs, technicians dribbled cables and interviewers clutched hand mikes to jostle paparazzi and magazine photographers for key positions along the beach while the newlyweds posed at a small podium for a press reception and pictures.

Radiant, Alissa, wearing an extravagantly embroidered satin empire wedding gown and an elegant pearl-encrusted headdress with a veil that billowed majestically in the tropical breeze, tearfully announced to those assembled that, "In addition to being the luckiest woman in the world—marrying Tommy—my husband's surprise wedding gift is the role of Katherine in his new movie." She paused while the crowd responded with polite applause.

A woman reporter with a clarion voice threw out an impertinent question. "Mrs. Saxon, isn't it true you and your husband are planning an immediate family?"

Another reporter chimed in. "How does this affect *Winter Love?*" More photographs and flashing cameras, and Alissa tossed her head. The pearls and sequins on the headdress bobbled and sparkled in the lights. Marielle's stomach turned over. She might be a scheming, manipulating bitch, but she was beautiful. There was no denying it. Her eyes filled with angry tears.

"Well, I can see it's no longer a secret. . . ." The actress paused to wait for a relatively quiet moment. "So I may as well tell you. Just this morning, my doctor confirmed that I'm expecting my first child." Mah firs chile. There was a renewed flurry of applause and a battery of strobe-lit cameras captured the announcement for interested parties around the world.

"But he assures me it will absolutely not interfere with my role. Truly, I am the happiest woman you can imagine."

Congratulations showered onto the beautiful couple. Thomas Saxon, severely correct in a black tuxedo, said merely, "Folks, we've just gotten married. I'm sure you understand I have a few things on my mind. Thank you all for coming." The reporters, satisfied, accepted his remarks with good humor and allowed him to escort Alissa from the podium without further questions.

Marielle switched off the television and dried her eyes. Since their conversation atop Mulholland Drive there seemed no end to the flow of her tears. Watching the press conference had been guaranteed to be upsetting but she'd been driven to see him, determined to make his marriage real in her mind. To that end, she'd prepared for the stinging hurt and certain tears with a box of tissues standing by.

But tears seemed to happen everywhere lately: love scenes in her favorite novels, silly sitcoms when lovers kissed and made up, terrible colorized movies at 3:00 A.M. with hissy soundtracks and actors with black teeth. Sometimes, nothing more complex than a melody line from a popular song evoked a sadness that would not be denied, provoked hot tears that slid down her cheeks. It had never happened before she met him and if this was being in love, it was tearing her apart.

By now, too many sleepless nights had convinced her that as a former love Alissa might at some point be omitted from his life—but as a wife with a "chile"? Marielle was nine times a fool if she thought the actress wouldn't use the existence of her child to remain Mrs. Thomas Saxon. To build dreams of a future on the thin possibility that it would all work out was being an even bigger fool.

The next morning, the L.A. *Times* ran an in-depth interview with the new bride. "It's going to be a girl and she'll be Katherine, of course. Due in April," she'd been quoted. "*Winter Love* will be released in May. Naturally, I'd hoped for the role of Katherine months ago, but he was saving it for a surprise. I've decided to use Alissa Bellemy-Saxon as my professional name from now on." The Saxons were honeymooning in Mexico.

Marielle turned the page.

November passed with infinite slowness. The announcement of Michael Winston's engagement and upcoming January marriage caused a mild ripple of interest in a month otherwise devoid of amusement. Thanksgiving was a listless affair, try as she might to invent an interest in the Minds' traditional dinner at Tonio's. When she admitted she hadn't heard from him, both friends admonished her not to permit Thomas Saxon to become an obsession.

The date circled in red on her December calendar

came and went and when the days of her cycle passed without incident, confirming Dr. Lanier's expectation that menopause was at her doorstep, her spirits sank dismally.

Unable to think about Christmas gifts, obsessed with another woman's husband, unable to concentrate, by day Marielle wasted hours of the firm's time double-checking the accuracy of her work, product of a distracted mind. At night she switched ceaselessly through the thirty or so cable channels on her television to avoid her bedroom and the visions that wormed their way into her brain, condemning her nightly to a wakeful purgatory.

Surely Thomas wouldn't sleep with her—or would he? According to the math, Alissa was four months pregnant. Her body, kept slender for the role of Katherine, would still be inviting. He was human, after all. They were married. She was already pregnant. Night after night, living in the same villa or hotel, or wherever, in Mexico, alone. There would be love scenes in the film.

Images of the two of them invaded Marielle's mind despite anything she could do to block it out. In refuge, she sought memories of their own mystical, sensual interlude and ached with want even as her mind tormented her. Would he make love to Alissa the way he'd made use of her own body?

Such imaginings drove her, stirred and sleepless from her bed, taunted her in patterns that evolved from heartache to jealous to pain at her loss, in endless cycles. In desperation, she sought something, anything, to take her mind to another place.

She called Jeff, invited him to dinner at her apartment with every intention of getting into bed with him. But the evening was a fiasco. She'd forced her actions every step of the way, and even the food had been mediocre. She hadn't been able to kiss him with interest, let alone make love with him. At last, she pleaded a sudden migraine, kissed him good night, and sent him home.

After he'd gone, she paced her apartment in frustration. Finally she took up Elizabeth Woods's diary and willed herself to reread it. This time she studied the violent pages with a new perspective on the bereft woman's rage.

As the pages ran on with year after year of recrimination for behavior Elizabeth either suspected or purely imagined, with no proof or actual knowledge of the truth, Marielle began to understand that Elizabeth, too, had been at fault. Her jealous fury had been as destructive as her husband's illicit affair. At some point, perhaps, it had driven Jameson back to Lilia's arms. Surely Elizabeth had extended her own unhappiness by her refusal to forgive her husband.

When she realized that to continue to rail at Thomas's decision to marry Alissa was equally harmful in her own life, Marielle began to regain a sense of peace. What was done was done. He'd made a choice not to risk the life of his child and whether that decision proved right or wrong, the world was going forward. Life continued. Making herself miserable about it served no purpose.

She closed the diary and was able to sleep.

The next morning, she set herself the task of examining the balance of the papers in the strongbox. By noon she had removed the last of the sales receipts and, with a great deal of care using flat philatelist's tweezers, she managed to encase the documents in clear plastic sleeves.

Under the last of the papers, at the very bottom of the strongbox, wrapped in oilskin, she found what she'd been hoping for: a letter addressed to Boyce Woods in the unmistakable spidery writing of her great-great grandfather.

* * *

Reading, England, May 7, 1945

There'd been a tightness in his chest these past several nights, an increase in the weight on his soul; Jameson Woods hadn't planned to live this long and was tired. He walked with the deliberation of his ninety-one years through the quiet house to a favored room. Margaret wouldn't like it but he'd decided to open the bay windows in the library this morning to allow in the fragrance of early purple lilacs.

She'll just have to be upset, he thought. It wasn't likely he'd see them again. Lifting the latches he'd cranked both windows open wide. A light spring breeze skittered into the room, riffling papers on his desk, threatening to spill them onto the floor. He removed a book of prose from a nearby shelf to secure the papers and a thick volume of Spanish poetry he didn't recognize tipped sideways on the shelf.

Later he would wonder at the workings of fate. If Margaret hadn't gone early to the market and it hadn't been a perfect spring day; if the lilacs had bloomed late instead of early; if he hadn't felt his age and gone against his daughter's wishes to open the window for their fragrance one last season, which allowed the breeze—he might never have seen the book, never have picked it up.

The unfamiliar volume slipped from his grasp and crashed onto the desk; an envelope addressed to him and his late wife spilled out of its hollowed cavity. As he read the invitation to the wedding of Caddie Lilia Woods, and the date, his old heart thumped ominously at the revelation.

He'd wondered endlessly what had happened to his child and whether Lilia had found with his son the happiness forbidden to them by his own marriage to Elizabeth. He hoped with all his heart that it was so, that her life hadn't been wasted, as his had been.

Stiff, arthritic fingers fumbled to extract the contents of the hollowed book. Inside he discovered his wife's diary and he sank heavily onto an ancient leather chair to read Elizabeth's words and understand at last why, and how, Lilia had been removed from his life.

Lilia. God forgive him, he'd been blind about her. In love with her from the moment they'd met, desperate to have her, he'd entered asylum from the wasteland, the emotional desert that was life with Elizabeth. He traveled to London to drown in the passion Lilia created in him, that fed his dreams and fulfilled his hopes, as often as he dared. He'd commissioned a friend, an artist, to paint her in miniature so he could see her always, carry her presence with him everywhere in his life.

Once, she'd tried to leave him, put an end to it, and had refused to see him for three months. He'd been desolate, suffering abominable despair at her loss. Boyce had been seventeen that year. By some hateful trick of life, his son had met Lilia, fallen in love with her, and they'd begun an affair.

Elizabeth had been relentless in her accusation and pain, and eventually obsessed, he'd begged Lilia to take him back. And she had. She'd told him straightaway about Boyce—that she'd discovered he'd lied to her about his name. How, appalled, she had broken off with the boy without explanation.

But Boyce, infatuated, heartsick, had refused to accept her decision and had begun to follow her; eventually he'd discovered them together. That same night, drunk, overcome with jealousy and rage, Boyce had confronted him and to his everlasting regret, he'd struck his son down. Mortified, determined to retaliate, Boyce had run away, taken passage to America.

Unable to give her up, unable to convince Elizabeth to divorce him, he did his best to protect young Margaret by denying all. To no avail. Over the next several years, his business suffered fatal reverses; Elizabeth was ceaseless in her rage and pain and his sole source of refuge was Lilia. *Lilia. My heart.*

Then the wonderful, devastating news. Lilia was with child. He was thrilled beyond delight and began to make plans to secure money for a life for the two of them. Unfortunately, her pregnancy was discovered and she was sacked from her position in London.

She'd been forced to return to Reading to take up residence with an aunt. Townspeople held little sympathy for unmarried women who were foolish enough to become pregnant; even so, speculation ran high as to the identity of the father.

She'd begged to go to Elizabeth to try to make arrangements for the child. He'd been adamant. "I have a way," he'd promised. "I'll have money soon." But an illness had intervened before he'd managed the sale and she'd gone before he could stop her.

Had he known where to follow, he'd have given every ounce of the gold for passage. But he did not. He could only wait and hope she'd let him know where to find her and the child.

The pain when he'd learned of the marriage could still pierce his heart. He well remembered the frozen day in December and the triumphant look on the old crone's face when she'd announced to the parish that her niece had married. He'd stood rooted, wooden, numbed to his soul with agony and disbelief, but Elizabeth had turned with a feral rage and backed the old woman against the rough stone wall of the church.

"Who'd marry a whore?" she'd cried, in full hearing of the parishioners.

"Who but your son!" The words were shot back at his wife with the dead aim of eternal malice, to shatter her pride forever. "Boyce Woods married Lilia," the old woman shouted at the passersby. "It seems my pregnant niece married well after all."

He hadn't known from that moment which hurt was the deeper, that Lilia would marry or the knowledge of it.

Elizabeth had gotten hysterical; he'd taken her home, called the doctor, who put her to bed. Unable to face his daughter, he'd gone to his office to drink himself into a stupor and had continued to do so without pause until his credit was exhausted with the local merchants, some six days later. To this day he had no memory of those hours.

The same feelings were at him now and his breath was ragged in his throat as he grasped the fact that the date of Caddie's wedding had been three months past the day of his wife's passing. The invitation and the knowledge of Lilia's daughter had been kept from him, not by his wife, who would most certainly have done so, but by Margaret. His thin shoulders sagged under the weight of new sadness and understanding.

Perhaps it is just, he thought tiredly. Any life her inheritance might have provided for Margaret had been taken away; an unjust price, indeed. A daughter should not pay so dearly for her father's obsession with a woman not his wife. Yet both of his daughters had done so.

Margaret's return didn't stem the flow of tears from his old eyes, nor the ache building in his heart.

"What is it?" she demanded. He saw her glance for an instant at the book now safely back in its position on the shelf. "Are you in pain?"

He couldn't bring himself to give her an answer.

After a sleepless night, he'd dressed for church and called a taxi in her presence. Each time she questioned his intentions he shook his head, knowing that, with Margaret, to answer one query opened floodgates to a thousand more.

Once inside the taxi, he changed his destination to the railway station and boarded the early train for

London. He waited in Rettig Burnside's office until the codicil was drawn and insisted on signing it that very hour. On the return trip to Reading, he wrote a letter to Boyce.

From the station he took a taxi to the church and met with Father Greystoke, who waited outside Billy's crypt while he placed Boyce's letter in the bottom of the strongbox, added Elizabeth's diary, and the miniature of Lilia. He locked the box securely and walked with Father Greystoke to the curb where the taxi waited patiently.

"There'll be someone coming, Father," he said.

Father Greystoke nodded in sadness and touched him on the shoulder.

"The trunk in Billy's crypt belongs to me. It's to stay here until it's given to my son."

"I'll make a note of it."

"It may be some time."

Father Greystoke looked at him kindly. "It will be here, my friend. You have my word." They shook hands in an unspoken understanding. "Good-bye, Jameson. Rest well."

A letter from father to son delivered in this manner was a private thing and not to be disturbed lightly. It was early evening before Marielle could bring herself to open it. She put the miniature, Elizabeth's diary, and the key to the trunk on the table in front of her. Then she lit one of the bier candles with a warped wooden match and placed it in a small holder. The smell of sulphur tainted the air for a few moments, then cleared.

Finally, she poured a small glass of Bardolino and sipped a silent toast to Jameson Woods before she inserted a letter opener with great care to cut through the envelope.

11 May, 1945

My dear son Boyce,

I learned yesterday that you named our daughter Caddie Lilia. It is a beautiful name. I hold the most profound sorrow that I am never to see her face or take her hand or call her name. If you have not done so, please do not reveal that I, too, am her father as I have no wish to disturb her life.

I will love our Lilia through eternity, but I hope with all my heart that you and she have found happiness with each other and that you have forgiven, and been forgiven, the heartbreak caused to those we love.

Having no desire to live more years on this earth, I wish to make peace between us before I die. I am leaving a key with Margaret in order that she will be obliged to contact you. I love you both. It is my deepest wish that with my death you can put the past aside.

The key has another use. Near my grave, in Billy McCafferty's crypt, inside the north end of his coffin, is an inheritance which I have this day decided to set aside for Caddie. In place of your share, I give you a portrait I have carried until this day of the woman we love.

Your father

In the soft glow of the candle, the beautiful face in the silver frame looked out at Marielle with a new light. No wonder she hadn't been able to make the connection with the voice in the diary. "Caddie was my mother's mother," she said aloud, and the resemblance became more fully apparent. Lilia Foxworthy Woods. Not a coincidence at all, but a namesake. Her great-great grandmother.

There was a terrible, final sadness in Jameson's words, unrelated to his impending death, which she felt he'd embraced. Had it been punishment to himself when he'd asked that Caddie not be told about him, perhaps? She couldn't decide. Whatever it was, there was a chasm between father and son that hadn't been crossed, at great and desperate cost.

Finally she considered the last paragraph. The north end of Billy's coffin. She gently tapped the key end for end on the tabletop and stared at the small portrait in the flickering candlelight. An inheritance intended for his child, her grandmother Caddie Oldham, daughter of the woman in the miniature. "Which would have passed with her death to my mother," she said to Abernathy. "And from Mom to me."

A voice which had never spoken to any of them reached out from the letter. It could not be ignored.

"I guess, technically, it's mine after all," she said quietly. Abernathy circled in silent agreement.

She blew out the candle and watched the smoke curl toward the ceiling.

14

December 19, 1989

This time her trip to England was fueled by imagination and anticipation of what might be found in the crypt. The day was overcast and gray with cold. She went by taxi directly from Heathrow to the Reading churchyard and enlisted Father Derning's witness at the crypt. Resigned to the destruction of her great-great grandfather's footprints, she helped the priest set aside the heavy wrought-iron stand at the north end of the bier.

Thereafter, close examination of the coffin eventually led to locating an entry for the key: a precise, oblong notch cleverly hidden in the grain of the wood near the bottom, just above the marble bier, and sealed with clay. Marielle closed her eyes and bowed her head as she turned the key and felt the mist of her breath drift back up into her face. Nothing happened.

She removed her gloves and placed her palm against the flat gray marble, cold and impersonal to her touch, and pushed. Spring locked, it gave inward no more than a fraction of an inch, then the entire end of the bier and the hollow coffin swung toward her on well-oiled hinges.

Marielle sank to her knees and held her breath at the sight of several rows of golden objects placed neatly on the shelving inside. "Oh, dear God," she murmured. "I don't believe it."

Dizzy for the moment, she leaned against the bier to allow Father Derning a look inside. Then she recovered herself. "I don't believe it," she said again. "After all this time." She stared at the cache and counted the empty spaces on the shelves. Fourteen. There had been fourteen receipts in the trunk.

She replaced her gloves on her freezing hands and one by one she examined the remaining objects. A magnificent ram's head of exquisite proportion as large as her hand was first. Its metal, icy cold in the December weather, had a wondrous luster, buttery orange in color, and was heavier than she expected. It scraped lightly against the opening as she removed it from the bier and created a small scratch on the underside. She felt terrible for causing the mark on the pristine figure, but realized that the gold must be quite pure to be so soft.

She was doubly careful with the rest: two wolf masks of equal beauty and weight; three delicate elephant figurines; four giant replicas of seashells; five stylized figures of cats, lions most probably. Then came a small gold object she couldn't identify composed of five finely worked birds, geese or wild ducks, grouped on a raised, hollowed platform; the bird in the middle was larger and protective of those surrounding it, whose heads were tucked under their wings.

Next were a series of gold bracelets, some with blue stones encased in delicately raised settings; these ornaments were unusually heavy. Then a dozen gold effigies, strikingly similar to the one she'd seen in Professor McCafferty's office, four and five inches in height, hollow upper torsoes with hauntingly regal faces resigned to their fate as slain enemies of the Asantehene.

Finally, a group of incredibly intricate thin golden discs each with a similar design in the center resembling a sun with twenty points, surrounded with a chased circle of flamelike images, filigreed and decorated with the skill of a royal artisan, timeless in their beauty. Seven gold necklaces, three knives with marvelous gold baubles attached, and a golden tobacco pipe completed the inventory.

Marielle was speechless, overcome with the enormity of the find. She and the priest closed the bier, and while Father Derning busied himself sending his clerk to the local dry goods store with orders to purchase six dozen linen cloths, Marielle walked humbly to Jameson Woods's grave site. There she sank to her knees, immobile, staring at his name on the headstone and the two circles of bare earth on either side where the peonies had been planted. She willed the old man resting there to hear her thoughts, understand her gratitude.

Eventually she felt the damp chill of the day move into her clothing and got to her feet. After calling Rettig Burnside to explain what had happened, she asked if she could leave the objects in his care until she decided what to do. He immediately agreed, counseling her to speak to no one else about the matter.

She and Father Derning returned to the crypt and wrapped the objects carefully in the linen cloths. The priest rounded up four battered leather suitcases for their journey to London and accompanied her on the evening train and to Burnside's office where the golden booty was safely ensconced in the firm's office safe with little room to spare.

The following Monday morning, on the express understanding that the objects were not for sale, Marielle agreed to have them examined by a gentleman from London's famous Museum of Mankind who enthusiastically declared every piece authentic; he explained that the article she could not identify was in fact a finial, an ornament designed to be placed atop a royal Asante umbrella. The discs were known as soul-bearer's badges and, according to the museum's expert, were of exceedingly rare quality. And the deep purplish blue stones were sapphires. Huge ones.

"The museum would be most excited to acquire the collection if and when you choose to dispose of it," the expert informed her, and harrumphed in resignation when she thanked him for his interest.

Her days were spinning out of control; things had happened so quickly she genuinely had no idea what she intended to do. Rettig Burnside had assured her the golden treasure was unquestionably her property under the terms of Jameson's wishes; however, given the objects' origin and value, he had also informed her that it would be wise to make a decision as to their future promptly, before anyone proposed an enquiry. Further, he'd cautioned her strongly about potentially brutal tax assessments to be expected and since she was not a British subject, requested a few days to look into the laws governing matters of this sort. "Quite beyond my experience, I'm sure," he'd said with a sniff, excited as a small boy at a new legal aspect to be solved after decades of practice.

Suddenly it was Christmas week with bakery smells and glowing golden lights from the pubs; gloomy rain turned to wet, sticky snow that feathered down onto busy London streets and bridges and formed droopy caps on bottle-topped chimneys and castle walls. It melted into the glossy gray water of the Thames, stuck churlishly onto the tops of the black beaver hats of the palace guard, and delicately outlined trees and statues and fountains in the parks, transforming the humblest of streetlights to the perfection of a painting.

The breath of bundled English shoppers puffed white against the cold. Not quite Charles Dickens, but charming just the same. Settled once more at Hanover

House in a cozy room with a warming fireplace, Marielle decided that spending Christmas in London was a proper gift to herself under the circumstances.

Energized with the snow and brisk cold, snug in ski boots and a warm down jacket borrowed from Shirley, she shopped at Harrod's for gifts to take home to her friends and people in her office. In a tiny antique store she found at last a delicate silver frame as a gift for Thomas and Alissa's baby. She surrounded herself each night with great quantities of festive paper and ribbons and took delight in creating perfectly wrapped packages. Bundled in a new pink flannel gown and wrapped in her white terry robe, she sipped steaming hot, cinnamoned cider in front of the fire and daydreamed about the golden treasure that had sprung out of the past and into her life.

Christmas Eve morning when she left the warmth of the hotel's old-fashioned feather comforters, she felt a bit peaky and even lost her breakfast. Convinced that she was victim of the excitement of the last several days and the rich lobster at Burnside's dinner party the previous evening, she climbed back into bed for a couple of hours, but later she rallied and was fine the rest of the day. However, when she lost her breakfast Christmas morning as well, another reason occurred to her.

It couldn't be possible. . . .

She counted the days. Eighty-six of them.

Elation slammed into her chest; afraid to trust the feeling, she paced the room on eggshells and went over the dates again. How could it be? She'd spotted in October. . . . Yes, but it hadn't been a normal period. Her skin prickled with hope. No period in November, which was usual and she hadn't questioned, but now December . . . and nausea two mornings in a row? It was too good to be true.

If she was pregnant, it was nearly three months!

Pregnant.

Suddenly she knew it was so. She stopped pacing and sat down, weak at the thought. If her legs refused her weight, her mind refused to take it in. It was too much. Tears of joy formed in her eyes and she blinked them away and hugged her abdomen protectively.

Now that she thought about it, there had been something different about her body lately. Things began to take on a wonderful kind of sense.

No wonder her breasts had been tender and achy. No wonder her zippers were getting balky. She laughed out loud at the thought. And she'd been blaming her smaller skirts on innocent British dry cleaners. No wonder she'd been dizzy . . . the sudden bouts of energy and the drops into sagging tiredness; the hours of insomnia, the tears, and all the rest of the strange behavior that had plagued her holidays. Raging hormones. She was pregnant!

"I'm having Thomas Saxon's baby." She said it out loud. There was no room in her chest to breathe in more air. She wanted to write it on walls and shout it in the streets and, suddenly teary, she wanted to tell her mother. More than anything on earth she wished her mother were here to tell. She fingered the ALWAYS inscription on the antique cameo necklace. She'd worn it that weekend. Life didn't always give you what you wanted, but this time it had. Somewhere during that magical night and the morning that followed, she had conceived Thomas Saxon's baby. She kissed the small oval locket and blessed her luck.

Somehow the day passed. When Shirley and Rose called that evening to wish her merry Christmas, she managed with a supreme test of will not to break the news. "I have exactly what I want," she trilled gaily. "I'm having the absolute best Christmas ever."

They assumed it was due to the discovery of the Asante gold and a late attack of old-fashioned Christmas spirit, which she did not deny, and promised she'd be home for a New Year's celebration to end all celebrations.

Early the next day she went to see Rettig Burnside. Nervously balancing a cup of Miss Gibbs's tea, she ventured the news. "I'm not sure I should tell you this," she said tentatively, "but I have to tell someone or I'll burst." He looked at her, mildly quizzical in his speculation, his look reflecting his opinion that Americans were generally given to overstatement.

"I have reason to believe I'm expecting." Once she'd said it out loud to someone other than herself, the huge weight lifted itself from her chest.

After an almost imperceptible pause, Burnside replied. "I see."

"If it's true, and I'm sure it is, it will make a difference in what I decide to do."

"About the inheritance?"

"Yes. There's no question that it's very valuable and should be protected, but I now have a child to consider. . . ."

His eyes disappeared under bushy brows and a deep furrow appeared in his forehead, giving her pause. "When's the, um, occasion?" His voice was noncommittal.

"Late June, I guess. I'm still figuring it out."

"If that's so, it's possible that the items in question might reasonably be construed to belong to your child."

"I beg your pardon?" What on earth was he talking about?

"It appears you are no longer the last living heir of Jameson Woods." The solicitor heaved himself out of his chair and stood facing the window with the bare lilac trees beyond, and contemplated the falling snow. "Word of the gold will get out, my dear. You may count upon it. While I have no question that you are entitled to it, it is, as you know, of incredible value.

"Therefore, it is entirely possible that there will be claims launched by various parties to gain an interest. If so, you might be called upon to prove valid ownership. Even if you were inclined to sell it, any legitimate purchaser will wish to have a guarantee that it is indeed yours to sell."

The point he raised became clearer. "You mean in order to do anything with it other than keep it, I'll have to prove I'm the last living heir"—she took a hoarse breath as the revelation assumed proportion—"and it will soon become obvious that there's another heir on the way."

"I wouldn't have stated it in quite that manner, but, yes, you've managed the essence. I've always held the opinion that only children who've arrived can qualify as heirs, however, I've never encountered this particular set of circumstances."

She could see he was genuinely intrigued by the legal ramifications of her situation and part of her mind found it odd, because her sole interest was whether or not there was a child. If there was, and she knew in her heart it was so, the gold could sit another hundred years so far as she was concerned. Unless she needed it for the baby's welfare.

As if reading her thoughts, he offered the opinion, "We are legally obliged to notify authorities that these items have been found and someone must be identified as the responsible party. Nothing can be taken out of the country until matters are settled, however I see no reason why we can't go forward naming you as trustee for a child yet to be born. When the baby's arrived, then we'll see what's to be done. In the meantime, I'd suggest you limit the number of people to whom you admit knowledge of this matter."

"I see," she said, not really giving him her full attention.

"I'll insist, however, that you obtain a safe deposit box—we'll arrange one this afternoon. I don't wish responsibility for these items, fabulous as they are, a minute longer than is necessary. You'd be best advised to keep everything out of sight until we're ready to proceed, in whatever fashion."

"That's fine," she agreed. "Oh, about the baby." She paused, struggling for a polite way to phrase her request. "It's not public, yet, and I'd appreciate your not saying anyth—"

"Of course," he cut her off. "The information is privileged between solicitor and client. You have my oath."

Two days later, safe deposit key securely dangling next to Jameson Woods's hand-forged key on a monstrous key ring she could not misplace under any circumstance, Marielle said good-bye to Rettig Burnside and boarded her taxi to Heathrow.

15

New Year's Eve, 11:56 P.M.

"Okay, what's up?" Rose studied her intently. "I know that cat-full-of-canary look. What is it?"

Marielle smiled benignly under her friend's inquiring gaze.

"Am I crazy, Shirley, or has she been glowing all evening? No margarita with dinner. Didn't eat enough to keep a gnat alive, no dessert." Rose cocked an eyebrow and declared, "You're holding out on us."

Marielle couldn't help it. She knew she was beaming but her happiness was so great she couldn't keep it in; it ran in her veins like liquid sunshine, leaked from her body at random. Wherever she'd gone that week, people had noticed.

Shirley, too, gave her a look of quizzical contemplation.

An expectant hum filled the room and conversations began to cease at table after table as people in silly hats turned their attention to the clock over Tonio's bar. Marielle, too, glanced at the giant clock. It was one minute to midnight. "I want to make a toast," she said, diverting them for the moment.

Her friends lifted their glasses and Marielle solemnly raised her ice water. "To the future," she declared proudly. "And to the baby. I'm pregnant."

Rose shrieked and both women did a fast inventory of Marielle's shape under her black cocktail dress, now a full inch thicker in the middle. They clinked glasses all around and drank the toast. Then Marielle grinned with glee at their scrutiny.

"When? Someone in London? And you didn't tell us?" Rose's questions came a hundred miles an hour. "It had to be the first trip, that's too much tummy for this last one."

"Congratulations." Shirley's eyes were misty. "I think it's wonderful."

"Dr. Lanier confirmed it yesterday," she told them. "I'm due sometime in late June as near as we can tell." She held up three fingers.

Shirley finished a lightning calculation and sat her iced tea down with a thump. "That makes it . . . October." She stared open-mouthed as voices throughout the restaurant began the ritual chant.

Six . . .

"Yes," whispered Marielle, between numbers.

Five . . .

"No." Rose breathlessly finished her own math. "I don't believe it."

Three . . . two . . . one . . . reverberated in the room around them but the three women at table six were already jubilant.

"Happy New Year!" Marielle shouted, beaming. "We're Mothers." Rose and Shirley joined the bedlam and the three women hugged and kissed each other with the exuberance of genuine celebration.

Nineteen eighty-nine was relegated to history and soon the majority of Tonio's patrons began their departure for home and hearth in the wee hours of the New Year. The women at table six sat in quiet excitement, making plans.

"My tenant gave notice," Shirley said. "The house will be vacant in March. The bedroom on the second floor is perfect." She paused, but only momentarily. "It was Jody's. It's next to the master and I'll have it painted any color you choose."

"White." Marielle was scheduled for an amniocentesis next week, but she had every confidence things would be fine.

"I'm in charge of wardrobe," Rose insisted. "Don't start wearing maternity too soon. You'll have a full five months of stretch fronts and support hose. It'll get boring. Trust me."

"Have you decided to tell Thomas?" To Marielle's surprise, Shirley asked the question she'd expected from Rose.

"I'm still on the fence about that," she admitted.

"What you do affects both of you, whether you tell him or not." Rose finished her drink. "I say it's totally your call."

Marielle looked at Shirley, who sighed, troubled. "I don't know. Personally, I wish I didn't know. My relationship with him is primarily business to be sure, but I also consider that we're friends of sorts. Right now it feels awkward." She looked at her watch, uncomfortable. "Plus, I know how he feels about you. I think he'd want to know. But Rose is right. It's your decision. I won't say anything unless you tell him."

"If Alissa wasn't pregnant, he wouldn't be married and it would be a hell of a lot simpler."

Her mother's voice came at her from within. If wishes were horses, beggars would ride.

Truth was truth. Wishing was pointless.

Amniocentesis confirmed all systems go. Dr. Lanier was pleased with her general health and issued instructions, prescriptions for special vitamins, and mountains of advice. Mostly to relax and enjoy her pregnancy until confinement. What a strange word, she thought, to describe the process of delivering a child as a living, breathing human. There was nothing confining about it to her way of thinking. It was an open door of possibility, a ticket to ride in life's adventure, her every wish come true.

If only she could decide about telling Thomas.

Shirley called to let her know he'd be in Los Angeles for the day to meet with the executive producer of *Winter Love* at the studio in Culver City. She offered to arrange a pass onto the lot if Marielle cared to "run into him."

After endless sessions of wrestling with her conscience Marielle finally decided to take him the gift she'd bought at Harrod's. If all went well and the status hadn't changed between him and Alissa, she'd tell him. He'd married that witch for the sole purpose of protecting an unborn baby, surely he'd welcome the knowledge of another child. Surely.

She drove through the studio gates and was cleared into the guest parking lot. From there she got on a tram full of musicians shepherding various instruments. They traversed the three-block movie lot, passing actors in full makeup and dressed in elaborate period costumes pacing outside huge soundstage doors, technicians standing by talking into headsets, and messengers flying by on bicycles. This was Thomas's world and she was fascinated with this bizarre arena that was his work. Nerves mounting, she was glad for the distraction.

The tram paused while the musicians departed at the site of the music stage and a few minutes later the operator directed her to the producer's building. She had no trouble finding suite 153 on the first floor. She'd stopped first in the ladies' room to confirm that her tummy, still ninety percent flat, was safely hidden under a billowy blouse and loose belt, but at the door to his suite she became edgy at the thought of seeing him and nervously fidgeted with a straying strand of hair. Her decision today affected several people's lives.

The silver frame, wrapped in paper printed with tiny booties sprinkled across row upon row of powder pink and white striping, had a small white rattle tied inside the bow, and thus was clearly identified as a baby gift; it was tucked in her purse. She'd decided to hand it to him as an opening line.

Inside the anteroom to the suite, she stopped beside an empty secretarial desk wondering how to announce herself. A young man wearing thin wire-framed glasses, a loosened tie, and dark gray jacket opened one of the inner-office doors and hurried past her.

"It's a damage control situation, Tom—the best we can do for now," he tossed back over his shoulder. "I'll be back in ten minutes."

Thomas's voice, lethal with fury, emanated from the inner office and caused the young executive to jerk to a halt on his way into the hall. "I don't care what it costs, just shut them up."

Marielle heard the obviously harried young man mumble under his breath. "Yeah, right." He disappeared down the hallway.

She ventured a glance into Thomas's office, all black-green carpet and beautiful art deco furniture with gleaming brass fixtures. A huge mirror framed in an ornate pattern of black lacquer and blond wood, inset with jade and mother of pearl, dominated the wall above a matching inlaid marble fireplace. He was alone, staring out a huge window, his shoulders set in rage.

"Hello," she said, attempting to be casual while her heart thumped heavily at the sight of him, slim and elegant in a gold silk shirt with the sleeves rolled back and black linen slacks. "Is it rotten timing?"

He whirled at her voice, his face showing astonishment before turning to stone.

"What the hell are *you* doing here?"

He charged around the desk and she thought for a

moment he was going to strike her. She backed up involuntarily.

"You've got some bloody nerve," he said, taut with rage. "I can't believe you'd do this. I'm some great fucking judge of character."

She stopped short. What was he talking about? How could he know she was pregnant? Only Rose and Shirley . . . "I thought we should talk," she began uncertainly.

"Talk about what?" Anger contorted his face. "You want to talk about my wife being in the hospital? You want to discuss whether or not she's going to lose the baby? What do you want to discuss?" He grabbed a newspaper from the desk and threw it at her. "This?" The pages flew apart as they hit her in the chest and scattered to the floor.

She stooped to retrieve the papers and her purse crashed onto the carpet; the baby gift spilled onto the green with the rattle clattering noisily, along with a lipstick, her wallet, and a pair of sunglasses. Everything was going wrong at once and her mind went blank at this totally unexpected reaction. How had it gotten into the papers?

Thomas retreated behind the desk to punch buttons on his phone while she scrambled for her things.

"Joe, I need you in here. Now."

He stared through her as he spoke, eyes black with frightening, righteous anger. The situation was surreal and she felt absurd on her knees in front of him, struggling with her things, clutching the newspapers. Plus, she was beginning to get angry. "Can't we talk about this?" Surely she was entitled to a hearing.

"No. What's going to happen is you're going to leave or this is going to get real ugly." He stalked to the door and opened it for her exit.

"I can explain." She placed the gift on his desk and juggled the papers, trying to make sense of things.

"Yeah? Well, I don't want to hear about it."

Marielle stared at him, totally confused. Alissa was in the hospital? The baby was at risk? Was this why he was so upset? Why was he holding her responsible? She scanned the print, searching for a clue to his behavior.

It was an issue of *ReVeel*, the newest in the tabloid press. The headline jumped out at her. "Mystery Woman in Saxon's Love Nest." Underneath, "Who's Bedding the Newly Wed?" She looked blankly from the page to Saxon's rigid face. He held his gaze in the middle range, refusing to see her.

How could anyone know? She skimmed rapidly through the accompanying article, trying to get a handle on what was happening. "Three weeks after movie star's marriage, mystery mistress tells all," the article said. "Shattered at his betrayal, she swears she'll wait for him as promised. Despite his marriage to pregnant Alissa Bellemy, 'I'll always love him,' declares lover."

Her gaze moved finally to the accompanying photograph of two people in bed together. Thomas's face was clearly visible; the woman's face was in deep shadow, but clearly not Alissa.

Joe stepped into the room, a vigilant, humorless man of huge girth. "You got a problem, Mr. Saxon?"

"She's leaving." Thomas Saxon's voice was ice.

"I had nothing to do with this," she stammered in confusion. "They've made it up. It has nothing to do with me."

He moved close enough to grab the paper from her grasp and stabbed at the photograph with his finger. "Take a real good look, lady." His eyes flashed hurt and betrayal, then hardened to disgust as he jammed the paper into her fingers. "Get her out of here."

"Come with me, miss." The big man's voice left no room for discussion. He interposed his large body between her and the furious actor. "Let's not hassle this, okay?"

"Wait a minute. This is crazy." Things couldn't be this

out of control. She searched Thomas's face for a sign of the man she knew and found only a remote, rigid stranger.

"She's leaving now, Joe." Thomas's voice was steel and final.

In seconds she was out of the building. Joe escorted her in silence to an electric security cart and drove her back through the maze of studios. She felt strangely cold and numb, unable to function. When they reached the parking lot he asked her to point out her car; she managed to climb out of the cart, still clutching the newspaper.

"He's got a lot on his mind right now, lady. I wouldn't bother him if I was you."

"There's been some misunderstanding," she mumbled.

"Just leave the lot, miss." Joe waited while she unlocked her car and got inside. "I don't know what they paid you for those pictures, but I hope it was worth it."

Shaking and fighting tears, Marielle managed to ease her car out the studio gate. A block away, she pulled to the curb and sat stunned. After a moment, trembling so hard the papers were hard to read, she leafed frantically through the pages to find the continuation of the story.

A full-length photograph of Thomas Saxon, completely nude, was sprawled across page seven. Some part of her brain identified it and a new wave of horror coursed its way through her middle. Oh, God. She returned to the front page and looked again at the huge, distorted photograph. It was her face in the picture. Blacked out in deep shadow for the rest of the world, but her face, nonetheless. Joe had recognized her. And Thomas.

She sagged with the weight of responsibility. The missing pictures on the roll of film! How? Finally her mind found the answer. From the lab where she'd had them developed. Obviously. Stolen and supplied to this rag!

Tears spilled down her cheeks. How could he believe she'd give them to this disgusting paper? How could he even think . . . The depth of the problem expanded, rippling in ever wider circles. What else could he think? He'd recognized her in the photo and realized it had been taken in Palm Desert. He'd suspected it at the time. He'd even taken her camera.

She slumped in misery. To admit she'd taken the pictures, to plead she'd been careless, wouldn't go far to convince him she hadn't given them to the paper. It was too late to explain, too late to expect him to believe her. The whole thing was hopeless. In ruins.

"My wife", he'd said. Not Alissa. My wife. Despair shot through her soul. If Alissa lost the baby . . . If her own pregnancy had been at risk . . . The mere thought of miscarriage took on terrifying proportions. Oh, God, what had she done?

Somehow she turned the key and started the engine. She managed to drive to her garage and park. Dragging her unwilling body into her apartment, she fell into bed fully clothed to try desperately to make it all go away. All she wanted was to wake up tomorrow to a world that had not witnessed the destruction of her hopes. A world in which her pregnancy was a joy to be shared, not something hidden and secret.

She slept until midnight. Thereafter sleep eluded her and she stared blankly at the ceiling light, tears leaking down the sides of her face onto her pillow.

Thin streaks of dawn eventually crawled into the eastern sky. She knew she had to get past what might have been and deal with the reality of the life within her body. In point of fact, nothing material had changed. Nothing in her life was different from yesterday morning when she'd gotten out of bed and eaten her breakfast.

Her pregnancy had always been intended as hers alone, not to be shared with the father. For a brief while she'd dreamed wonderful, magnificent dreams, but reality was the order of this day and those particular dreams were finished and had to be put aside. The child was hers. She would make plans for it, care for it, devote her life to it. The interlude had come to an end. Time to move forward.

So be it. With the strength of that resolution, she was able to go back to sleep.

16

February 14, 1990

Fair warning.

Barefoot, moody, wrapped in a kelly green robe, Thomas Saxon stepped onto his balcony to survey the twenty-second-story view that had prompted him to invest in expensive Beverly Hills "adjacent" real estate.

Half a million dollars had been pricy for a penthouse in 1983. Apartment properties had been depressed, but he'd just signed his contract for the starring role in "Murder 101," his future as an actor had turned around at last, and he'd been in the mood to celebrate. Now, according to his investment counselor and his tax accountant and his real estate agent, with the addition of the two condominiums on the floor below, at a cost of another $750,000, and knocking out the walls and connecting the three with a grand, circular staircase, the five-balconied complex was conservatively valued at more than four million and going up.

The year before last, he'd hired an interior designer and handed him the keys and a check for half the proceeds of *Shotgun Summer*, with the instruction to make it a showpiece. He'd moved into the Century Park Hotel.

When he returned, the original flooring throughout had been replaced with creamy Cararra marble. Each room now had deep pile, custom white wool Dalmon rugs; the living room, library, and den were furnished with oversize couches and chairs in cream linen, all hand-embroidered in silver, bronze, and coral silk passè plat; tall, airy fishtail palms and full-size ficus trees were planted in massive antique vases of delicate white jade and celadon green porcelain that he'd had shipped from mainland China.

Entire sections of glass walls in the penthouse permitted an unobstructed two-hundred-sixty-degree vista of Los Angeles and the surrounding minicities. The view began with the white-domed observatory in Griffith Park past the burgeoning steel-and-glass towers of downtown L.A., on to LAX, the muddy green Pacific that stretched beyond the horizon and Catalina Island, and ended at the north end of the Santa Monica Bay with its glorious late summer sunsets.

An eclectic assortment of Polini, Flores, and Chagall paintings and a magnificent de Monvel portrait dominated the white interior walls. During the summer, sunlight warmed the rooms from ivory in the morning to rich honey gold in the afternoon. This February morning, however, the sun was an irritable pale red eye above the downtown city skyline. He shifted uneasily in the crisp air and stared at the glowing orb.

Over the past nineteen years, he'd been with more women than he cared to think about. He'd married at twenty, divorced at twenty-one, lost his son at twenty-six. Once his celebrity status had been defined and particularly since the debacle of his first marriage, he had no trust in emotional involvement where women were concerned.

For nineteen years he'd faced relationships with a vague sense of disconnection, seeking an indefinable something that would lift an encounter beyond the physical and create a meaning in his life that he hadn't found—a solution to his puzzled soul and spirit. Something he'd decided did not exist until a weekend in a tiny cabin in the Malibu Mountains. It had turned into a lie all too soon, but for two days and a night it had been possible and he mourned the loss of it with the anger of enlightenment.

The red eye dissolved into the smog layer and emerged a dirty peach-colored circle. Last night he'd entered new ground; his body had functioned but his mind had been totally elsewhere. Apparently Alissa hadn't suspected.

How, he puzzled, as detached as if it had happened to someone else—how had he managed it? He'd been exhausted for weeks from work and lack of sleep. The rich red wine at dinner had hit him pretty fast. Despite California's protracted drought, he'd taken a long, hot shower and crawled naked into bed determined to get some rest.

Just at that place where his body was embracing delicious oblivion he'd felt her hands, warm and smooth with some kind of oil, stroking and teasing him into hardness, and his body, four months without a woman, had reacted. When she straddled him in the dark, hunched forward in her efforts, in his mind the thick warm hair cascading onto his chest and belly had been a mane of pale gold-and-silver blond.

It wasn't until she moaned in her orgasm that he rose to conscious thought and realized the hard round breasts in his hands were not those he remembered, but Alissa's, swollen in her pregnancy. At which point he'd gone soft.

In the jaundiced morning light he shook his head and paced the balcony. How in the hell had he managed sex with a woman he hated, by imagining she was someone else? Someone who'd betrayed him at that. This was indeed a first.

Thalia Barrett, a blessing in the form of housekeeper

and cook, stepped onto the balcony carrying a silver breakfast tray with a carafe of black coffee and a favored cup. She placed it on the patio table.

"Happy Valentine's Day, Thomas. Will you be having breakfast this morning?"

Damn. Valentine's Day. He hoped Marcy had thought to send Alissa some roses. Better that than another fight. "Just coffee. Thanks."

"What about Mrs. Saxon?" There was no change in tone, just a subtle shift to formal inquiry as she arranged a linen napkin and silverware next to the cup and uncovered a perfectly toasted English muffin.

Alissa had not made friends with Thalia and had not yet won the battle to have her replaced. Thalia, for her part, had patiently explained that while she had enjoyed working for him these past nine years, she wasn't sure she would be able, at her age, to take on the added responsibility of a baby. She had promised to think it over six weeks ago but had given no hint of her decision.

"She's still sleeping," he replied absently.

Thalia padded back inside and Marielle's face rose in his mind for the hundredth time, wearing the startled look he'd denied the day he confronted her about the pictures. It haunted him. It hadn't been the trapped look of someone caught, desperate to deny fact against evidence, nor the smoothly professional innocence he'd learned to unveil. In fact, she'd seemed totally bewildered; then—there was no other description for it—she'd looked betrayed. His mind could not reconcile the matter.

The beautiful silver frame was still in its box in the top desk drawer at his production office at the studio. Of all the gifts she could have given his child, a frame for a photograph seemed an incredibly poor choice. Was there some hidden message of guilt he was missing here or was he looking for something additional to add to his stock of anger?

He'd decide what to do with it when all the cards were in. At the moment the matter of the bedroom photos was in the hands of his lawyer, Barry Cooper. *ReVeel's* attorneys had taken the position that the photographs had been legally purchased but had been unable to come up with proof other than a check paid to someone named M. Bruckmann in the sum of two thousand dollars.

He followed the circle of logic he'd played out innumerable times. The pictures had been taken with her knowledge and permission. She'd been looking directly into the camera while some sleaze—maybe this Bruckmann jerk—was in the room taking pictures of the two of them naked in bed. A chill ran up his neck every time he thought about it.

He'd had a lot to drink that night, but he still had a clear memory of an empty film carton in her hotel room. It had prompted him to take her camera but he'd dismissed his suspicion when the film inside hadn't been exposed. He'd even apologized. She'd played it perfectly and he'd fallen right in.

He poured the scalding coffee and watched thin wisps of steam dance off its surface into the crisp morning air.

Why or how was unimportant. She'd permitted it. Caused it, perhaps. However it had come about, it had happened the first night he'd met her and everything thereafter was suspect. Even the perfect weekend.

The fact that his nude pictures had shown up on the front page of the tabloid rag was embarrassing but survivable. The fallout had been surprisingly limited. The general public seemed to recognize it as the scruffy exploitation of his name and career that it was, and while his parents had been mightily embarrassed, they'd taken it in stride. Alissa's rage and brush with miscarriage were now relegated to the past.

The coffee seared his lips and burned its way to his stomach. Thinking about it at all made him angry.

He hadn't had a decent night's sleep since the middle of January when he'd answered the phone in Mexico and a woman had babbled on in Spanish about having to change Alissa's appointment with the doctor, and an increase in the fee, which had to be in cash. It hadn't been difficult to figure out what kind of doctor.

Since their marriage, she had been practically phobic that her pregnancy would interfere with her role as Katherine. She'd wasted hours of production time and money demanding changes in wardrobe and lighting and camera angles, while the rest of the cast, crew as well, had cooled their collective heels. Costs had spiraled through the roof and he'd been forced to compensate the production company for the losses by giving up a share of his points in the picture. He'd flown to L.A. to negotiate the overage and, at the last minute, she'd decided to come with him.

Mason & Pearson had obtained an advance copy of the *ReVeel* issue and the firm was already hard at work on damage control. When he'd tried to discuss it with Alissa, she'd flown into a screaming rage. Later that night she'd started bleeding. Thalia had found her in the bathroom and called him and the paramedics.

The doctors at UCLA Emergency warned them that she might lose the baby if she didn't take better care of herself. They'd kept her two days and stabilized the pregnancy. She'd been meek and obedient in the hospital but the moment she was released she'd flown back to Mexico in a silent fury that she was still pregnant. The day before the nurse's call, she'd been suddenly calm.

At first he'd threatened to pay off the investors and walk off the film; Alissa had retaliated by swearing to destroy the child if he did such a thing and he realized he'd succeed only in bankrupting himself for no purpose.

"Did they tell you how dangerous it is?" he'd demanded, horrified that she would consider an abortion at this late date.

"It's my body and my child!" she'd hurled at him. "I'll do what I want!"

"Did they tell you you could die?"

She was stubbornly silent, refusing to hear him.

"You couldn't finish the picture then, that's for damn sure!"

He had her attention at last. "If you do anything to destroy this baby, I swear I'll take it public. You'll not only lose your career, but I'll have you prosecuted for murder, and I don't care if it costs everything I have in my life." He'd been deadly serious and apparently she'd believed him.

After that he'd watched her like a hawk but there'd been no further attempts to abort the child. Instead, she simply stopped eating. It must have been an incredible test of her willpower because he knew her pregnant body was demanding food. She began chain smoking to control her hunger.

After a week her weight began to come down rapidly and he suspected she was taking diet pills of some kind. She denied it to the wall and despite his efforts he hadn't been able to catch her at it. All he'd been able to do was watch her destroy herself and pray for the health of the child.

Thereafter production had resumed in a blurry nightmare of tantrums and thrown objects and delays as Alissa exhausted a thousand and one ways to demonstrate her insecurity. He'd been enraged and embarrassed another thousand times, furious with himself for creating the situation, determined to bring the insanity under control, only to encounter a new range of threats whispered at night on the phone, of suicide, of disappearing with the child. That the child was already dead in her body.

The location work had been interminable but had finally, mercifully, wrapped. When they returned to California to complete the interior scenes, Alissa's doctor, appalled at her weight, had furiously gone on record as recommending her hospitalization for the safety of the baby.

Frightened for the first time at what she might have done, Alissa genuinely tried to gain weight and succeeded in adding twelve pounds by the end of filming, but the baby was diagnosed as being severely underweight and her guilt was monumental. She was now obsessed with the baby's condition and monitored herself in an all-consuming effort to make amends.

The only diversion she allowed was the film. It's completion and release became equal obsessions in her mind, but separate and disconnected from the child. Her mood could swing in an instant from nurturing concern for the baby to scorn at an editing decision, then back to severe calm once an edict to re-edit had been acceded to.

Assistants cowered from her tirades, executives avoided her. Secretaries either quit or refused to have anything to do with her; business associates and friends were advised to steer clear or risk onslaughts of rage when Alissa's goals were unmet. She was a singularly focused soul, determined to be a star with the dedication of a moving freight train and woe to anyone who stood in her way.

He'd had fair warning. Since he'd known her she'd functioned with the precision of a computer. Despite the glamorous public image, stardom was a business and exceedingly hard work. In its money-driven, intractable world, survival was known as the bottom line, which had to be written in the black ink of profit.

"Murder 101" had made him a star, a household word, and identified him to the world, but the personal cost had been great. With no privacy whatsoever, his level of success had demanded a grueling five and a half years of six- and seven-day work weeks with eight- to ten-hour shooting schedules. There had been times he'd been tired to the bone, having nothing left, and she'd been there to help him pull it out of nowhere to charm the endless parade of names and faces at the umpteenth business function that week.

After the wrap party for "Murder 101" at the end of each season, he'd grab a couple of hurried weeks somewhere Alissa had arranged for supposed rest and a crash study of an upcoming movie script. The phone never stopped ringing. Friend after agent after business manager after lawyer stopped by for "five minutes" that inevitably turned into three-hour meetings and a call-back in twenty-four hours for an answer, an opinion, an agreement to go ahead with plans.

After these days of "rest," he'd fly off to meet a contract date for wardrobe fittings, publicity photos, and rehearsals, with a new group of studio executives, producers, directors, backers, cast, crew, and another hundred or so people whose futures would be affected by whether the public would pay to see him act in a film. And finish in time to meet his contract date for the fall shooting schedule of "Murder 101," and the beginning of another television season with its round of parties, premieres, and personal appearances.

There'd been a paucity of time to reflect, think, or implement career moves without a great deal of help, and she'd been there—not only sexually, but with scripts and ideas and plans. She'd been a valuable friend and ally, brilliant in her assessments and openly selfish in her purpose by seeing that he was well served by the support community she courted for her own career. Absolutely she had used him, with his knowledge and permission.

Somewhere in this mix she had deliberately gotten pregnant—she was too smart for it to have happened accidentally—in order to use it to get what she wanted. Unfortunately the studio's timing on the early go-ahead for *Winter Love* had put her pregnancy into direct conflict with the only thing in life she valued—stardom. With her growing belly now a burden and a threat to her career, she had turned on him and she was proving herself to be as brutal an enemy as she had been a friend.

Yes, he'd had fair warning.

But for a few hours before the nightmare of Alissa's pregnancy, the hours his mind refused to abandon, there'd been Marielle. And the bizarre, wonderful surprise of falling in love, probably for the first time in his life. Certainly the first time it had hit him from a blind side with the impact of a brick wall. Maybe Alissa had sensed the change.

Marielle. God knew he'd been full of her that weekend, a giddy, forty-year-old adolescent saturating himself with the feel of her, her smell, the incredible fit of her long, sensuous body, and absolutely the most incredible sex he'd ever experienced. Her presence had been an island of peace in a sea of offered bodies competing for his attention, his favor, his power to lift their lives to another plane. She'd seemed a haven in an ocean of hustle and distrust.

It was months now and he knew it was no longer simply the memory of an unusually special interlude. Admittedly the time with her had astonished and delighted him but it lingered in his psyche long past a normal high. Her essence persisted, invaded his thinking daily with a frustrating quality that eluded identification.

She'd made him laugh; she'd had an opinion that hadn't always agreed with his, straight-ahead manner of asking serious questions, and an ability to listen when he needed to talk. Try as he might, he hadn't detected flattery or guile. When she was angry, she'd been righteously honest about it and he well remembered the ice in her voice the night he'd called her from Vegas to apologize for standing her up. At his explanation she'd changed immediately to concern and understanding, with no coy verbal punishment games or demands for proof to hurdle in the interim.

When she returned the bracelet after the disastrous night in Palm Desert he'd been intrigued by her integrity; their hours on the phone and subsequent relationship convinced him he'd found someone with a genuine interest in him that transcended his celebrity. She'd nailed him down right up front—an "other woman" status was unacceptable.

She'd refused to see him while he was married, said good-bye. Then ran to the highest bidder with those stupid pictures? It didn't make sense. His inability to resolve it and walk away irritated like a thorn.

Why was it that opening up to someone always had a price?

Damn her anyway for seeming so perfect and being so full of deceit. What was it with him and women?

He forced his thoughts aside to deal with the situation at hand. Alissa clearly considered last night a signal that everything was forgiven. She'd been all smiles and delight this morning and determined to go to a party at the Breslaurs this evening. He didn't want to go and she knew it, but she'd picked up the phone and confirmed their attendance with Marian Breslaur in front of him before rolling over to sleep in.

He sipped now-cold coffee and longed for the day when there'd be light in this endless tunnel, and picked up the phone to check with Marcy about the flowers.

17

February 14, 1990

Marielle turned sideways to the mirror and assessed her middle. Absolutely three inches thicker, and growing. She giggled in delight.

Jeff had been making comments about her weight and she wondered if she'd have to tell him or if he'd figure it out. She was astounded he hadn't guessed already; her body had been puffing up like a toad for the last three weeks. Yet, knowing Jeff, it was all too possible. His preoccupation with his own life was so all-consuming, the reason for her weight gain probably hadn't crossed his mind.

He'd called last month and they'd met for a drink. It was the first time she'd seen him since their infamous dinner in November and he'd put on nearly thirty pounds. He was visibly embarrassed about it and openly relieved that she was no longer the slender reed he'd married. He'd made a passing reference to their both being a bit out of shape and she hadn't pursued the matter.

Jeff had practically begged her to accompany him to this evening's party and she hadn't had the heart to refuse when he explained. His contract with the law firm wasn't being renewed and he was hopeful of joining the team of lawyers at Martin Breslaur's investment corporation before his leaving became public. After weeks of consideration by the Breslaur Group, he'd been invited to attend a dinner party. Would Marielle please do him this one last favor and go as his date?

She turned before the mirror and smiled. Being tall worked to her advantage and the weight of her pregnancy was distributed well, but even a blind man would be able to figure it out soon. Rose had been working wonders with her wardrobe; still, there was a limit and she was reaching it.

Tying poufy black silk pajama slacks loosely around her thickened waist, she adjusted the blousy knee-length jacket over a black silk shell; the resulting line was pleasing and she felt frivolous and special. She gathered a mass of hair and clipped it behind one ear with a black-and-silver barrette and added outrageous marcasite earrings.

In two weeks she would celebrate the anniversary of five months during which time she hadn't gained an ounce over Dr. Lanier's recommendations; in two weeks she'd graduate into full-fledged maternity wear. Rose had promised.

Jeff was uncharacteristically early and anxious, bearing a long-stemmed red rosebud wrapped in a cone of shiny cellophane and tied with a white ribbon. A Valentine's gift. He looked her over and nodded in nervous satisfaction; he was pleased in turn when she complimented his suit and straightened his tie. In truth, he was attractive in a lawyerly sort of way and she was genuine in her hope that things would work out well for him.

They were the first to arrive at the Bel Air estate of the prominent investment counselor and Marian Breslaur showed them to the pool area where her husband insisted on Jeff's opinion about the design of a new cabana. Mrs. Breslaur left to shepherd her twin daughters off to bed and Marielle looked out onto the beautiful sculptured gardens and ornamental trees decorated with strands of glowing shell pink and matte gold lanterns; cupid cutouts and traditional red hearts were tucked into festive sprays of red and white carnations that adorned a score of scattered patio tables; the spicy scent of the flowers was heavy in the still evening air.

Mingling its marvelous fragrance with the carnations, graceful pale purple wisteria hung in profusion from the latticework of a lanai. Clumps of pungent English lavender and night-blooming jasmine acted as a hedge to the rose garden and dragged at the hem of her long silk jacket, adding their languid perfume as she passed by. The leaves of a pair of sprawling, majestic oaks buttressing the yard, were motionless, while heat from a dozen outdoor braziers warmed the area where she stood next to the pool. A perfect California night.

When she felt the baby move for the first time she froze, unsure that it had happened. But it was there, the slightest of sensations. Her joy was electric.

A bartender in a short white jacket hastened to her service. She sipped club soda and orange juice, supremely happy, every sense on the alert for the motion of life within her body. Guests filtered onto the patio in twos and threes and she smiled her way through introductions and polite greetings and compliments on her choice of wardrobe as she waited for Jeff to finish his conversation.

A troupe of musicians took up instruments nearby and she drifted with elegant chamber music and the small talk of strangers commenting on the house and grounds, the music, the weather. The baby moved again and she laughed delightedly at an idle remark. A stunning couple entered the patio from the main house and there was an instant change in the conversational hubbub. Marielle's laughter died abruptly in the ice-water shock of recognition.

He hadn't seen her as yet, but it would be inevitable.

Her mind locked onto Rick's famous line from *Casablanca*, subconsciously paraphrasing: of all the nights, of all the parties in all the homes in a city this size, Thomas Saxon had stepped into this one—and his baby had just moved inside her body. She was totally unprepared to see him. Or Alissa.

She moved a few feet away from the side of the pool and positioned herself behind a cascade of flowers, trying to think what to do. Jeff was in a secluded corner of the yard, deep in conversation with Martin Breslaur. It had taken six weeks since their encounter at the studio to work past the loss of Thomas and she was barely beginning to recover and feel like herself again. It was painful to know that just the sight of him could still derail her completely.

From her vantage point, she saw them clearly in the light from the house. They were a smashing couple and Thomas was smiling as he helped Alissa down the flagstone walk to the patio. Startlingly handsome as ever, he appeared very much at ease in an elegant regatta-striped black-on-gold linen jacket and a white silk shirt casually open at the throat. Alissa was rail thin, her pregnancy enhanced by a quilted green brocade maternity jacket that flared perfectly over pale gold satin jodhpurs tucked into black suede riding boots. She made a delicate, glowing entrance and immediately held court.

"The picture's coming along marvelously, thank you. So's the baby. We can't wait for the big day, can we, sweetheart?" She looked up with adoration into Saxon's face and moved her body under his arm, casually placing his hand on her shoulder.

Something's odd, thought Marielle, cutting through her initial shock and confusion. After a moment it came to her. When she looked past the padding of the carefully complementary outfit, Alissa didn't look seven months pregnant. She counted backward to the conversation in the car atop Mulholland Drive to confirm the number. If Alissa was four months in November, she'd be seven by now. The baby was supposedly due in April, but the actress didn't look much larger than she herself was at this moment.

Jeff arrived at her side, beaming, and she grabbed his arm with the determined strength of a drowning soul. "I'd really like to leave," she said fervently. "I know it's rotten timing. . . ." She searched for a viable reason. "I feel terrible and I need to go home."

"What's wrong? Migraine?" He pulled her into the light to look at her. "You are pale. Maybe you need to eat something."

"No, I need to get out of here." She freed her arm and started around the pool away from the patio, feeling Thomas Saxon's eyes on her every move.

Jeff hovered at her side. "Are you sure? Maybe you should just lie down for a while."

"Jeff, please. I know it's embarrassing. Can't you explain that I don't feel well and insisted you stay?" He paused in indecision, and she seized the opportunity to reach the safety of the house and find her way to a guest room to call for a taxi. The dispatcher promised a cab in twenty minutes or less. She looked in the guestroom mirror. "*Casablanca*," she said to herself with a wry laugh, and felt a bit calmer. "And I'm Ingrid Bergman." How fitting. An unmarried pregnancy had nearly cost the actress a career. Thank God for women's lib.

After splashing cold water on her wrists and flushed cheeks, she collected her shawl and ventured into the Breslaurs' huge, stainless-steel kitchen. Trays of foil-wrapped food lay in soldierly rows on the granite sideboards; the room bustled with the activity of a catering staff and various waiters. There she located Marian Breslaur and made her apologies.

"Certainly, dear," soothed her hostess with a knowing look at her middle. "I absolutely understand. These things happen. Now, don't you worry about anything. Just take care of yourself."

He saw her the instant he stepped onto the patio, exquisite mass of shining blond hair, sophisticated black-and-silver jacket. The lilting, joyous sound of her laughter had drawn his attention and the sight of her hit like a brick in the center of his stomach. She was radiant with a soft, ultrafeminine glow about her face. She'd seen him, too, he was certain, and he watched as she kept a carefully averted gaze. A man joined her after a few minutes, and they spoke briefly together before she made a sudden exit.

He knew immediately that she intended to leave without speaking to him and decided to prevent it. At least long enough to see her reaction to him. To see her face again without the look that was lodged in his memory. It had taken endless minutes to disengage from Alissa and find his way through the house, but he heard her voice in the kitchen, waited until she came out, then blocked her exit from the foyer.

"Leaving, are we?"

She lifted her chin and looked at him. "I'd like to explain about the pictures," she said steadily.

In the dim light of the foyer her eyes were shaded to a deep, dusky blue and her voice was low and musical to his ear. He set his jaw against his feelings. He didn't want to discuss the pictures; he wanted to upset her the way he was upset.

"It's history." He took a small measure of satisfaction in being abrupt.

"I should have told you," she went on, refusing to be stopped. "But you were sleeping. I was wide awake and I'd had too much champagne. . . . It seemed harmless, it really did."

"You took them?" He was genuinely surprised. He'd

been convinced there'd been a second party, but her eyes were clear and unguarded and her voice held a convincing honesty.

"And?" he prompted sharply, deliberately jolting her again.

"They got mixed in with pictures I took in London." The blue eyes faltered and almost dropped from his gaze, but did not. "The negatives were stolen when I had them developed. It was careless and stupid. I'm sorry."

He clenched his teeth in frustration. It was always something stupid that blew holes in your life. Always. Never anything intelligent. "How many were taken?" *Damn you.*

"There were twelve—three are gone. Negatives, everything."

Damn you, anyway. "You have the rest?"

Tears were gathering on her lashes. She blinked them back and nodded. Something finally deflected his anger—not the tears, certainly, but something. He martialed his concentration and was deliberately tough. "I want them."

"Of course, I'll . . ."

A concerned male voice from the next room ended their conversation. "Marielle?"

Thomas turned away before the man from the patio stepped into the foyer. He tried to ignore the twinge of territorial interest. So who was this guy? Lover? Friend? His jaw ached from tension.

"I've made our excuses. Are you feeling any better?" The guy recognized him but was refusing to give ground. "Hi," he said pleasantly. "I'm Jefferson McCleary." The guy took hold of Marielle's arm, establishing possession.

McCleary. Husband? Was that what she'd come to the studio to tell him? Why hadn't Shirley mentioned it?

He nodded curtly and stalked to the door. He

glanced at her again as he left the room. She looked fine. She looked terrific, in fact. *Damn.* Halfway through the house he realized he hadn't made arrangements for the photos and turned back to tell her he'd have Joe pick them up. Let her explain *that* to Jefferson McCleary—whatever he was in her life. Approaching the foyer, he heard their conversation a split second before he came to the doorway.

"I don't understand what's going on," the guy was saying. "You tell me you're sick, Marian Breslaur gives me a wink and tells me you're perfectly fine. What the hell's going on?"

"I'm not sick, Jeff, I'm pregnant."

She was standing with her back to the doorway and Thomas had a clear view of McCleary's stunned face; it was a picture in incomprehension, almost comical. The poor shlub had no idea.

"You heard me," he heard her tell McCleary distinctly, "pregnant. With child. Having a baby. Expecting."

The words stopped Thomas midstride and stayed with him as he retraced his route through the house and returned to Alissa's table. *Pregnant. I know just how you feel, pal.*

His public performance for the rest of the evening was worthy of an Academy Award; he was charming, witty, attentive to Alissa, and out of his skull with an impotent rage he could not shake and couldn't justify because Alissa, bless her little soul, was on perfect behavior.

"You heard me, pregnant. With child. Having a baby. Expecting."

Quiet footsteps sounded in the next room; Marielle turned in time to see Thomas Saxon's retreating back and felt the air go out of her body. There was no question he'd heard her angry announcement. She'd vented her frustration from the confrontation with Thomas on unsuspecting Jeff and it echoed as a ridiculous tirade in her head. When she turned back to Jeff, he was studying her stomach with enlightened, open-mouthed surprise.

"Oh." He slumped onto a huge gold brocade wing chair in the Breslaurs' foyer and said with wondrously self-involved candor, "They're going to think it's mine."

Hollow, she walked with him to the portico and waited while he gave the valet the numbered stub for their car. The taxi arrived. The driver accepted twenty dollars for his trouble and screeched his tires on the brick driveway in an irritable departure. She stared rigidly at the valet captain's box with its neat rows of numbered hooks, each with a tagged bundle of keys, determined not to turn around and hope to see him.

The drive home was exceedingly quiet. Jeff, for once, didn't babble.

"I got the job. I start next week."

"Congratulations." Her mind was vacant. Room for rent. She tried again. "That's good news. I really am happy for you."

"Thanks." He was quiet for three long blocks.

Huge pine trees whizzed by in an orderly fashion as they descended Stone Canyon, past the Bel Air Hotel, past huge gated mansions with dark windows, their inhabitants unconcerned about the chaos in her life.

"I don't suppose you'll tell me whose it is."

"No." She didn't want to have this conversation.

"It's not that hard to figure out, you know." His voice held an accusatory truculence.

She stared at him. He couldn't possibly have concluded . . .

"It explains why you were so upset when he got married," he continued decisively.

Her mind shrank from his knowledge. Oh, God, let this night end.

"It's Winston's, isn't it?"

She really tried to stifle her reaction, but the convoluted absurdity of it all built to uncontrollable laughter. The more she thought about it, the more she laughed and the funnier it became to her.

Michael Winston had been married in January, the week after her defeating encounter with Thomas. It had been a splashy society affair at the Beverly Hills Hotel and Jeff had been in the wedding party. The only thought she'd had about it at the time was that someone should have warned the bride.

She felt movement within her body once again. Jeff's guess had come so near and so far from the mark that she was helpless to stop her reaction. If she hadn't met Thomas that weekend, the moving child in her body could well have been Winston's. She laughed all the way down Stone Canyon Road, high, clear, crystalline laughter that echoed from the open car window through the quiet Bel Air streets, and tears ran down her cheeks.

18

March 24, 1990

March swept past.

A fire sprinkler malfunction in Neiman's on St. Patrick's Day brought a unit of the Beverly Hills Fire Dept. to Swimwear on the second floor. Thirty-three-year-old Calvin Logan had been the deputy chief in charge, strong and lean of body, boyishly clean-cut, attractive, newly divorced and vulnerable. Rose had taken one look and gone over like an oak.

Happily, cupid's arrows had flown in both directions; it was instant mutual attraction. Deputy Chief Logan in civilian dress had materialized in Swimwear two days later to ask Rose out for coffee and when she learned he had custody of Suzie, three, and Jennifer, six, things had moved very rapidly indeed. The weekend before, she'd met his mother, a retired widow who took care of Calvin's daughters while he was on duty at the fire station. Pragmatic, cut-to-the-chase, straight-ahead Rose had been as nervous as a cat on a bicycle.

Apparently things had gone well because Rose and Calvin were now officially an item. Marielle and Shirley took turns teasing Rose unmercifully that she was blooming with love. "Blooming lucky," she would agree and blushed each time the subject was mentioned. Marielle was thrilled for her. And envious, if she were honest, but thrilled all the same.

Rettig Burnside had written to advise that he was still investigating the manner in which the treasure should be declared in the English courts. There was a question as to whether the items would be treated as an addition to her previously acknowledged inheritance even though they would go to her child, or as a separate matter, which was his intention.

Either way, clearly the treasure fell under laws relative to patrimony—estate inherited from an ancestor; an additional problem was the difficulty of assigning value in order to reach a satisfactory conclusion with British authorities concerning taxes. The Museum of Mankind, while most cooperative about helping to establish their aesthetic value, had been very conservative in their valuation in real terms. The highest monetary figure they'd been willing to assign, and this based on the antiquity and art-object status, was, in his opinion, quite low at somewhat less than two million American dollars.

Burnside cautioned again that even if he managed a higher evaluation, and thus a higher residual after inheritance taxes were paid, any attempt to sell the pieces would prompt the necessity of validating provenance, or origin—in short, clear ownership. Any potential buyer would demand a certificate attesting that the pieces were newly discovered and not stolen.

He'd also received a second inquiry from the museum concerning their expressed interest in obtaining either the objects themselves or the right to exhibit them with their extensive collection. Did she wish him to pursue the matter? Solutions in the past had been reached by contributing portions of taxable inheritances to public institutions, thereby salvaging an increased residue of material for private sale and eventual income, he'd informed her.

The inventory of the gold pieces, the museum's evaluation thereof, and a statement for Burnside's services to date had been included with the letter. From the size of his fee, including the reduction he'd given as a professional courtesy, it was clear to Marielle that she would have to consider an income-producing solution within a very short period of time.

Jeff, after his initial shock at her pregnancy, had assumed an unexpected position of caretaker and protector. Despite her denials she knew he was still convinced that Michael Winston was the baby's father, however he kept his peace and did his best to be a friend. Somehow not bearing responsibility freed him to participate safely in the pseudofatherhood that her being pregnant engendered; he even mentioned on one occasion that, once, it might have been his child.

He was openly happy that it was to be a boy and showed up one Saturday afternoon with buckets of takeout Chinese and a giant brown-and-white floppy dog; thereafter on Saturday evenings Chinese food and a variety of masculine-oriented stuffed animals—bears, lions, pandas, gorillas—became a mild ritual that she began to count on.

For all his posturing and chauvinism, Jeff was reasonably handy with tools and there was generally something she couldn't quite manage: unsticking a frozen window latch, muscling a balky piece of furniture to a new position, dismantling and packing the stereo.

Eventually, she tentatively sought his counsel about the inheritance and he was astonished at the amount.

"A million eight! Are you kidding?"

"As soon as the baby's born I plan to set up a trust. That's when the taxes have to be paid. He says they could amount to nearly eighty percent and Haygood's checking to see how the IRS will handle it here in the States."

Jeff whistled through his teeth. "I didn't know English tax was such a killer. No way around it?" At her negative response, he began to tote up the additional costs. "Shipping the stuff over here until you can sell it, finding someplace to keep it, insuring it against theft." He stabbed his chopsticks in her direction with emphasis. "I'd check on the exhibiting situation in England if I were you. Let them handle the problems and maybe make enough to offset the expenses until you can find a buyer. Why don't you let me look into it?"

"I haven't decided what I'm going to do yet." Marielle moved her burgeoning stomach into a more comfortable position and the baby responded with a firm kick to her ribs.

"Unggh."

"What? Did he kick? Can I feel?"

"Here." She guided his hand to her stomach and they waited in silence. Nothing.

"What're you going to name him."

"Boyce Jameson."

"Boyce? What kind of name is that for a kid? Boyce? How about Jefferson Boyce." It was said in jest, but his look did not quite hide his hope.

"You had your chance, sorry." She moved again and the baby kicked a second time. "Uumph." She moved to a large pine rocking chair and sank gratefully into its blue plush cushions. "He's going to be a placekicker for the 49ers," she wheezed. "I wish he'd lay off practice."

Her co-workers had greeted the news of her pregnancy with a mixture of congratulations and awe, with the exception of her boss, who was thoroughly dismayed until she assured him that she intended to return to work as soon as possible after the birth.

Birth. Birth inched closer to reality on the calendar, in her mirror, and in her mind. Lamaze classes, while helpful in terms of knowing what to expect, had done little to allay fears that she might not manage it with the ease conveyed by the instructors. Rose and Shirley took turns practicing the breathing exercises with her and monitoring all the stretching and muscle preparation recommended. "You'll be fine," Shirley told her constantly. "Look around. Women have been giving birth for two or three million years, last count."

Yeah, right. But this is different, screamed her insecurities. *This isn't them, this is me.*

Birth. Her belly expanded rapidly and her breasts ballooned from D's to backachingly unbelievable, and she felt her body exploding out of control under the cute maternity clothes and support hose with expandable fronts. A faint brown line appeared on her skin, perfectly straight, bi-secting her navel and the basketball her abdomen had become.

She'd given notice to her landlady and spent two weeks preparing to move into Shirley's former home. The small bedroom on the second floor was indeed perfect and she decided on white with accents of crabapple green and sunny yellow with lots of active, normal-looking brown bunnies, even though babies were only supposed to be able to see black and white for the first few months.

Shirley and Rose had insisted on doing the painting and Shirley had seemed particularly pleased that her son's former bedroom would be occupied by a baby once again. "Life goes on," she'd said, and blinked back tears before fiercely attacking the Dodger blue wall with a paint roller. "Get outta here," she'd demanded. "Paint fumes and pregnant ladies don't mix."

Jeff gifted her with movers and had driven her with Abernathy perched atop the dome of her lap to his new home in her new home—a five-gallon glass bowl complete with castle, or condo, depending on your point of view, and a couple of friends, Mae and Edgar, to hang with.

* * *

"I talked to the museum. It's not good news." It was pouring California's brand of cold, miserable rain and Jeff stepped through the door holding a strange black-and-white penguin with a giant orange beak, wrapped in plastic; he handed her the usual buckets of Chinese and a dripping umbrella. "They'll only prepare the gold for display and go fifty-fifty on the sales of the exhibition edition of the book. It's sold in the gift shop while the gold's on exhibit to help defray their costs. They provide security, display cases, authentication, restoration, stuff like that."

"Restoration?" She shook the umbrella out the back door and left it to dry.

"Hey, I don't know, I haven't seen the stuff. Maybe some of it needs cleaning, polishing, touch-up work. They'd have to decide." He centered the cellophaned penguin on the dining room table. "I thought he'd look good in the menagerie. What do you think?"

She surveyed the monstrous bird with a baleful eye, trying to see it from a baby's point of view. If he kept this up, she would need more and larger shelves in the baby's room. She decided to put the bird discussion on hold. "Did they say how much money it would make?"

"Your share could come to fourteen or fifteen thousand dollars. That would pay a few of the expenses until we can figure out something else." He made himself at home in the living room and poked at the wood burning in the fireplace. She got down plates from the cupboard and retreated to the dining room while the microwave zapped the sweet-and-sour chicken and moo shoo pork. She'd been ravenous for sweet-and-sour lately. She put the penguin on one of the dining room chairs and it immediately toppled onto its beak.

"I've talked to a couple of museums here in L.A.," she told him, "but they don't have the kind of extensive collection that the one in London does so they're not really interested in displaying it. One of them's hinting at donation."

"Sure, like you're going to donate two million dollars worth of gold." He joined her in the dining room, righted the penguin, and sat at the table while she served from the heated cartons.

"It is one solution," she said pensively. "At least I wouldn't have to break up the collection and they could pay the taxes."

"I think you should agree to the exhibit in London and if it goes okay, look around to see what else you could do with it. There's got to be something besides exhibition to earn money with. What-all's in it, anyway?"

She handed him Burnside's letter and watched him review the inventory. He whistled in astonishment. "Seventy-two pounds of solid gold estimated to be at least twenty-two karat?" He sat silent for a moment, calculating. "That's half a million at bullion prices alone. Too bad you can't use that as the tax base."

"Mr. Burnside said by the time I pay taxes, I might come out with a couple hundred thousand, at most."

Jeff was appalled. "No way. We'll figure out something. I'll steal it before we pay that." He continued reading the list and whistled again in amazement. "Seven torques? What are torques?"

"A necklace design: like a horseshoe with the open side in back. They're beautiful. Wait till you see them."

"Three small knives with gold sheaths and attached gold castings of cowrie and cockle shells, ground-nut flowers, stars, aya leaves, and assorted fetishes. A tobacco pipe? They smoked tobacco?"

"European influence. Portuguese or Dutch, maybe both."

Jeff got to the bottom of the list. "Thirty soul-bearer's badges—thirteen of excellent quality, one of exceptional quality. What the hell are soul-bearer's badges?"

"According to the authority from the Museum of

Mankind, soul bearers are innocents the king keeps in his presence to remind him to rule with a pure heart. Some of the badges are used as visible indications of importance and rank within the king's representatives."

"Half this stuff is jewelry. What about a jewelry company? Maybe you could sell the designs. Better yet, sell copies of exclusive African jewelry." His excitement carried her along. "Here's what we'll do. I'll go to England, take pictures of all this stuff, then make arrangements with the museum to have it exhibited like they want. In the meantime we can start shopping it with jewelry companies. Can't hurt. What do you think?"

The phone in the living room interrupted their conversation. It was Rose.

"Are you watching TV? Turn on channel five. It's been on about thirty seconds."

Marielle picked up the remote and turned on the set. A young blond newswoman was front and center with a picture of Thomas and Alissa framed over her left shoulder.

". . . hospital. The Saxons have been married since last November and the baby was not due until May. Our prayers are with this beautiful couple tonight." The anchorwoman's voice droned on with other news.

"The baby's premature," Rose's voice spoke in her ear. "I thought you'd want to know. Shirley says she's at UCLA."

Marielle's shoulders began to ache. "Thank you, Rose." She flipped through the channels looking for another news source. There was none. She turned off the set and returned to the table, thoroughly distracted. Her eyes encountered the awful penguin. "He's got to go," she said absently.

"What was that?"

"Nothing. One of Shirley's clients . . . Never mind." She picked at the sweet and sour chicken, appetite destroyed. Alissa's baby was two months premature.

Protectively, her hands sought her protruding belly. Two months. The knot in her shoulders would not ease. With today's miracles . . . UCLA's medical facility was recognized as one of the best in the country. Surely the baby would be all right.

She sent her thoughts in the direction of the hospital, hoping to connect in some way with Thomas's child inside the huge facility. *Hang on,* her mind willed the tiny life. *You're going to be fine. You're going to be okay. Just hang on.*

"Hey." Jeff's voice intruded into her concentration.

"I'm fine. I'm just tired."

"Maybe I'd better go." Jeff got to his feet and grabbed the offending penguin. "Listen, I'll draw up a proposal and you give me power of attorney to handle this stuff until the baby's born. You can't travel until then anyway."

"All right. Whatever." *You're going to be fine. Just don't give up. Hear me. I send you strength. Use me and hold on.*

"I'll go to London in a couple of weeks and make arrangements to take some pictures. Can't wait to see this stuff. You sure you're okay? You better lie down."

She retrieved his umbrella and walked him to the door, anxious to have him out so she could focus on Thomas's baby. "Photograph it?"

"Right. I'll be personally responsible. Safe as a babe in its mother's arms. Trust me."

He and the penguin disappeared into the rain and she was alone at last.

19

March 25, 1990

"I don't know what to tell you, Mr. Saxon. We're doing everything we can. She's holding her own. That's a very good sign. We're running several tests, however it's too soon to predict much of anything. The next twenty-four hours will give us a better reading." Dr. Goodin glanced away to ask the question. "I take it the amniocentesis was late?"

"About six weeks ago." Thomas heard his own voice as a hollow sound. There'd been no need for the procedure. Alissa had been concerned at the baby's lack of movement and had insisted on the test.

"If it's going to happen, that's usually when they become sensitized," said the doctor. "It's a good thing it wasn't longer. We've replaced the baby's blood. That should bring the Rh factor under control. We'll just have to wait it out."

Thomas listened to the doctor's words, acutely aware that he couldn't feel. The numbness seemed to spread from his insides to every nerve ending in his body. His sole sensation was that of having enormous, unnatural weight; he was composed of foreign material, dense beyond flesh and bone.

When he was eleven, his father had tossed him a small black rock that had come to the surface in the backyard when they'd turned over a line of sod. It was an asteroid fragment and weighed ten times more than it should have. He still had it somewhere. He was the human equivalent. An A-negative asteroid.

"Your wife's awake and asking for you. She handled the surgery pretty well but, as you know, they had to give her a couple of pints of blood."

Funny the manner in which life lets you in on dirty little secrets. The short of it was that Alissa's blood type was A-negative and the baby's was AB-positive. Thalia and Marcy were both O, universal donors, and had roused themselves from their beds to make themselves available early that morning. He was also A-negative. Two negatives don't make a positive in blood.

There was no reason on earth for him to know about blood types at this particular point in time, except that he'd overheard a couple of the nurses sharing the information. Stretched out on the waiting-room couch, exhausted from a tense flight in from New York and consumed with worry for the baby, he'd been waiting for Dr. Goodin; the words were spoken before the duty nurse had been able to shut them up.

Oh, the lack of preparation for this new chapter in the nightmare surrounding this child. He'd feigned sleep, desperate not to have something else to deal with, but the words wouldn't leave him alone; they looped repeatedly on some kind of crazy echo, mocking and indelible.

"Did you see him yet?"

"Yeah, he was here earlier."

"I wonder what the kid'll look like."

"With those parents, what are you, serious? She'll be great looking."

"Don't be too sure." A nervous giggle.

"Why? What?"

"It's not his."

The twitter of laughter.

"Get outta here. Whatchyoo talkin' about, girl?"

"Check the blood types."

A rustle of papers. The sound of an indrawn breath.

"Oh, my God . . . is Goodin going to tell him?"

"Would you tell him?"

"Not me, honey."

More nervous laughter, and the scrambled sound of departure as the duty nurse descended into their conversation with admonitions to find something else to do and to hush up, followed by terse, whispered advice that the matter was "not your business."

They were right, of course. He'd turned his life upside down for a child that wasn't his.

Dr. Goodin had answered his questions with a welcome brevity. It had taken about three minutes to absorb a lesson in Rh factors. Two negative parents do not produce a positive child. There had to be a third party, the positive factor. The father.

Further, when an Rh-negative mother becomes sensitized by the Rh-positive blood of her unborn baby, her body begins manufacturing antibodies against the blood of that child, in effect attempts to destroy it as an alien substance in her body, and will be equally destructive to a subsequent Rh-positive pregnancy unless there is medical intervention.

In Alissa's case, fetal cells had either entered her bloodstream at the time of the amniocentesis or somehow mingled through the membrane separating the placenta and uterus. Either way, the baby had undergone something called hemolysis in which its tiny body had been forced to replace red blood cells destroyed by the antibodies in its mother's blood. The doctors had detected severe fetal distress and had performed caesarian surgery to deliver the underweight female child.

This information burning in his brain, he'd gotten

into a hospital gown and Dr. Goodin's nurse had taken him to neonatal intensive care to see the little girl that both Alissa and her body had tried so hard to destroy. He was unprepared for the unit and its array of blinking, humming machinery, the hanging garden of intravenous bottles and tubes, the beeps and voices and telephone noise, the nursing staff in constant motion as they circled a dozen Isolettes. Expecting a hushed quiet, it assaulted his ears like a foundry.

In her Isolette, the baby's tiny skull was covered with a miniature ski cap to capture and hold in body heat; her eyes had been blindfolded against a bank of fluorescent lights to combat jaundice, and an intravenous tube fed silently into a matchstick leg. She was a painfully thin, naked creature with ruddy skin so transparent he could see through to her veins and arteries.

At the sight of her, something hard squeezed his heart until he couldn't breathe; when he did at last, huge waves of emotion spilled over and moved across the space between him and this strangely inert child. He knew at that moment it would not be possible to leave until he could take her with him. Turning his back, walking away, abandoning her to Alissa's care would ensure only that her life would be a living hell.

"Can I touch her?"

"Certainly," said the nurse, a bent, gray-haired black lady who was probably a grandmother and couldn't have cared less that he was famous or who had what blood type. She guided his hand through the opening in the side. "You put your hand in here. Mind the monitor leads. They're just fastened with electrode jelly and come off easy." She kept a close eye and eventually nodded in approval and, after a few minutes she got up to leave. "I'll just get a cup of coffee. You take your time, son."

Inside the see-through plastic compartment with its radiant heaters and fluorescent lights and monitor lines and beeping attachments, he patted and stroked a tiny arm with an infinitely gentle touch, painfully aware that his scrubbed hand was almost the size of her lax body.

According to Dr. Goodin, the baby was in drug withdrawal; she quivered and jerked intermittently, her little chest heaving with effort and her mouth stretched open in a silent cry and Thomas could literally feel her pain. He lifted a miniature hand but the perfect fingers refused to cling to his finger; her body was too exhausted to move. Tears ran from his eyes and he struggled furiously for control.

"Hang in there," he whispered tightly, and the blinding tears washed down his cheeks. "I'm here and I'm not going anywhere, so you stay with me, you hear? You're going to be okay. I may not be your dad, but I'm going to see to it."

He remained at her side as long as they would allow, then sought the doctor to learn what to expect. Dr. Goodin was, again, direct.

"Right now I give her a twenty-five percent chance," he said bluntly. "A hundred things can go wrong and, normally, we can fix about seventy-five percent of them, but she's got an extremely low birth weight and is already in chemical withdrawal. We've ruled out amphetamines. Was your wife taking thyroid medication, perhaps?"

"Not to my knowledge," he answered honestly. "I'm pretty sure she was taking something for weight loss but she's been denying it."

"Unfortunately, withdrawal uses up energy the baby needs to fight off infection, jaundice, brain-bleed. As I told you earlier, we have to give her oxygen and there are risks of scar tissue that causes blindness."

The doctor sighed.

"It would help if we knew what your wife's been taking. Look, I don't want to scare you, but I don't want to give you false hope either. The truth is it can go either way and it's pretty much up to the baby right now. We'll do the best we can."

Alissa was asleep when Thomas looked in on her; the night nurse told him she'd been sedated. He was vastly relieved, because in his present frame of mind had Alissa uttered one wrong word, given him one wrong look, he wasn't sure he wouldn't have strangled her among the baskets and vases of flowers.

He found a phone and called his agent and his attorney to have them advise the network that he wouldn't be reporting for work until further notice. "Just hammer out whatever it takes to protect the show. Hire another actor, revise the rerun agreements, I really don't care. Just do it."

He went home long enough to shower and shave, then drove back to the hospital and went directly to the fifth floor. He approached the door to Alissa's room with resignation. Dr. Goodin was due on duty again at ten and the head nurse had assured him the baby hadn't lost ground during his absence.

Alissa was awake and questioning her surgeon. "Will it go away or do I have to have plastic surgery?"

"It should all but disappear within several months, I should say. You have very fair skin and this could be a problem, but I promise it will be a very small scar," he told her kindly.

She saw Thomas and immediately changed the subject. "Did you see her? Is she perfect?"

"She's got all her fingers and toes," assured the surgeon.

Thomas shook the doctor's hand and searched his mind for the man's name. In the midst of chaos, Alissa had demanded her own surgeon. McElvain. "We appreciate your making yourself available this morning, Dr. McElvain."

"That's why we're here," the surgeon said modestly and looked at his watch. "Besides, my wife's a huge fan of yours. She'll shoot me if I don't get an autographed picture."

Thomas nodded an acknowledgement. "I'll take care of it."

Dr. McElvain smiled his appreciation, somewhat embarrassed. "I'll check in on you later," he said to Alissa. "Right now, I'm due in surgery."

Thomas closed the door. When he turned, Alissa had closed her eyes. "Is she gonna live?" she asked.

"They don't know yet."

"It's not my fault. Don't start telling me it's my fault."

"I don't have much of anything to say to you, Alissa. I want to know what kind of drugs you were on and I'm not in the mood for bullshit. It'll help if they know what they're dealing with."

She told him and he left to tell the baby's doctor.

20

Saturday, April 2, 1990

With Jeff in London, Marielle was at loose ends. She'd stayed abreast of Katherine Dana Saxon's condition through daily bulletins from Shirley and the past week had been a day-by-day affair of "she's holding her own," and "it's too soon to tell." She battled massive guilt that publication of the nude pictures had put a strain on what had obviously been a precarious pregnancy for Alissa and had a clearer understanding of Thomas's anger.

Shirley told her that he'd put his life and career on hold to spend most of his time at the hospital. She mentioned Alissa's room number in case Marielle wanted to send flowers. Driven by a need to see him, to see how he was holding up, Marielle drove to the UCLA Medical Facility in Westwood. She told herself she'd just stop by Alissa's room and if he was there, she'd offer congratulations and inquire about the baby.

Due to the celebrity status of the parents, the volunteer at Patient Information could not release specific information on the baby's prognosis. Marielle took an elevator to the fifth floor to find room 505 empty.

"She checked out a couple hours ago, honey. Are you

family?" A tall, broad-beamed nurse with friendly features smiled and sized up her pregnancy. "Four months?"

"Five and a half."

The nurse registered her approval with raised brows and a generous grin. "Lookin' good. Wish I'd carried that thin."

"How's the baby. Will she go home soon?"

"Naw, honey, not that baby. She's still in intensive care. Will be for some time, I hear." The nurse looked at her carefully. "You a friend of hers, or friend of his?"

"His."

"I thought so." The nurse gave her a speculative glance.

Marielle shot her an indignant look. "He does have friends and I'm one of them."

"Oh, I don't doubt that," said the nurse, good-naturedly. "I didn't see none but his friends all the time she was here." She moved with Marielle down the hallway. "He's one good-lookin' white man, that's for sure." The nurse laughed at herself. "Hell, he's good-lookin' enough for any color. He could put his shoes under my bed," she teased with a bawdy grin.

Marielle smiled in agreement but her mind was elsewhere. "Are they with the baby?"

"He's down there. Every day since that chile was born." The nurse pursed her lips in disapproval. "His wife went home." She stopped at a patient's door. "Neonatal's in the basement, honey, but you cain't go in without a parent's permission." She disappeared inside the room.

Thoughtful, Marielle continued down the hallway to the elevator. Visiting Alissa in her hospital room was one thing. Hanging around outside the neonatal unit was a little more difficult to justify. She returned to the first floor and found a cafeteria. There, she bought a carton of chocolate milk, heated it in a microwave, and took a minute to collect herself. Perhaps it was best. To show up uninvited when he was probably exhausted . . . He had no reason to be charitable toward her anyway.

She was halfway through the hot chocolate when a woman across the table from her gasped and nudged her companion's arm.

"It's him. I told you that baby was still here."

Marielle couldn't stop herself. She turned to follow the women's gaze and met Thomas's dark eyes. In jeans and a gray-green sweatshirt, he had a cup of coffee in one hand, a newspaper in the other. When he saw her he immediately changed course and approached her table; the two women retreated into a breathless silence and hung on every word exchanged.

"What are you doing here?" His voice was hoarse with tiredness. He'd lost weight, looked haggard with lines under his eyes, needed a shave, but otherwise he was unguarded and the sight of him shook her heart, as always.

"Shirley's been telling me about the baby and I guess I was concerned." She had no idea what she was saying. "Is she going to be all right?"

He sat in the chair next to her and fingered the paper cup of black coffee, finally shoved it away. "I'm coffeed out, I guess." He got tiredly to his feet. "I'm on my way down. . . ."

She was conscious of his dark eyes searching her face in the pause.

"Would you like to see her?" he offered.

"I'd love to."

"We're praying for you," said one of the women.

He glanced at the women and acknowledged the statement with a nod of thanks. Marielle felt his eyes appraise her pregnant body when she stood to follow him, but he said nothing and she did not want to break the silence. It was enough to have regained this small friendship. She copied his actions at a wash basin and scrubbed her hands twice before putting on the requisite mask and gown.

Inside the busy neonatal unit he led her to a brightly lit Isolette with a large placard taped to its side. Stress Precautions was written on the card in large bold lettering. Marielle cringed inwardly at her first sight of the tiny, tiny infant, eyes wrapped, all the tubes. . . . Inside her own body, Boyce Jameson was larger. She felt lightheaded at the thought.

"It's okay," Thomas whispered. "She's awake. They've just changed her and we have about two minutes." He reached inside and held his huge hand against the baby's body.

Thrilled that he would share so brief a time, she brought her fear for the child under control and reached into the opening on the opposite side; she brushed the infant's cheek with the gentlest possible touch. "Hello," she said softly to the unnaturally still child. "You're beautiful and wonderful and I'm so glad to see you."

She willed toward the incredibly small being all the caring and strength she could muster, sent it coursing through the tips of her fingers and into the immobile fragile body. Katherine Dana yawned and put infinitesimal pressure against her fingers, then she made a few sucking motions and was quiet again.

Thomas looked across at her, eyes bright above his mask. "That's the first time she's done that," he whispered happily.

After four minutes a nurse approached. "Sorry, Mr. Saxon, you'll have to let her rest." She was professionally apologetic but no-nonsense; he and Marielle obediently withdrew their hands from the Isolette. While Thomas took a moment to speak with the nurse, Marielle left the unit, removed her gown, and waited for him outside, so shaken at the condition of his child that her hands were trembling. A chill of dread for Dana's future ripped through her body. A child that small . . . A moment later Thomas joined her in the hallway.

"She's got a fifty-fifty chance now, they tell me." His

voice was drained, the energy from a few moments ago depleted. "Still hasn't gained any weight, but hasn't lost any."

She walked on leaden feet with him to the hospital exit, consumed with fear for his child. A fifty-fifty chance.

"I can see her again in two hours. They let me sleep in one of the doctors' rooms when it's available." He gave her a thin smile and suppressed a yawn. Amazingly, he didn't appear to realize that Dana might not survive and her mind hurt at the thought of what the loss of another child would do to him.

"I'm glad to see you." He hesitated, and she saw him change gears. "I got your note and the photographs. I'm sorry about the way I treated you. I should have known you wouldn't . . ." Whatever else he might have said was lost in a tired sigh.

"I understand. You have every right—"

"No, I don't," he interrupted. "I could have listened to you, at least I could have done that."

She opened her mouth, having absolutely no idea what she was about to say. She could barely concentrate on his voice. His tiny daughter was two hundred feet away and literally fighting for life; it was all she could think about. Maybe it was all he was thinking about, too.

"Anyway," he continued, not letting her speak, "my lawyer had an investigator look into it. The woman in the photo lab sold them to the magazine. We got them back and she's been fired. I'm not going to proceed against her. I don't have time for it anymore." He yawned, unable to prevent it this time and she ached for him.

"I'm too tired to talk really, but I appreciate your coming by. Is everything all right with you?" His gaze crept briefly to her puffed-out belly, concern in his handsome face. "Are you taking care of yourself?"

His look was too direct. "I'm fine. The doctor says everything's fine," she told him distractedly.

Exhaustion was overtaking him at a rapid pace and he blinked to focus. She could see he was close to falling asleep on his feet.

"You really are?" His concern overrode his drained body for the moment, his intensity frightening. The condition of the gaunt infant they'd just left in ICU rose in her mind and she understood his fear for the child she carried within.

"I promise." It was the truth and she managed to convince him at last.

"Keep it that way." His body sagged tiredly and he moved toward the bank of elevators. "Listen," he called out. "Dana won't be released for a while. I'll be here. If you want to see her. Just let me know."

She said good-bye and fled to her car.

In London, Jeff answered the phone expecting Marielle.

"You don't know me, Mr. McCleary, but I'd like to introduce myself. I'm Kathy Elwis with Elwis Galleries and I have your name from a gentleman at the Museum of Mankind. He indicates that you represent a collection of Asante artworks for exhibition. Can we meet to discuss this further?"

"Absolutely."

"Good. Do you have plans for lunch?"

He didn't.

The maître d' of the Marland House showed him to a preferred table where one of the most beautiful women he'd ever met smiled up at him with perfect red-glossed lips and handed him a richly embossed business card, and under her name, Katarina Elwis, he read:

Elwis Galleries
Bruxelles/London/Paris

Slender to perfection, jet black hair smoothed back from a sweet, heart-shaped face, she had flawless skin, velvet eyes, and lean, gorgeous legs; she was nothing short of stunning in a black-and-white check Chanel suit that he recognized as exceedingly expensive in its tailored perfection. He'd done a bit of homework on jewelry in anticipation of the trip and eyed her casual mixture of necklaces: long chains of open-worked and probably 18 karat gold beads, well-cut jets, and a marvelous double strand of luminous black pearls that he was pretty sure were real. They slid carelessly on her wrapped white silk blouse. A deep open collar revealed moderately sexy cleavage while the silk softly outlined firm, full breasts.

In law school, he'd taken it upon himself to devise, for the edification of his fraternity brothers, the definitive test for a perfect female breast. Size and shape were preliminary: Minimum B cup, C's were preferable, D's were ideal. The nipple had to be high and facing front with a slightly upward tilt. But the true test, the pass-or-fail bottom line, was whether or not a pencil placed horizontally underneath would fall to the ground or remain in place from the sag of the breast. A firm breast would allow the pencil to fall, and was therefore graded perfect. Perfect breasts required no bra.

When he'd married her, Marielle's had been close to perfect D's, the hardest to find. With her pregnancy, they'd expanded to double D's, and double D's, barring silicone implants, which automatically ruled them out, were never perfect.

Kathy offered her gloved hand and the smooth fabric of her blouse shifted to press lightly against her body and he discerned the least hint of nipple, small with a full upward tilt. C's, he judged, and perfect indeed.

A row of three round, brilliant-cut diamond post earrings, from a full carat to three-quarters to a half, sparkled from her right ear and a full two carat stone shone wickedly from the other; in addition to the short black gloves, she wore a slender gold Cartier watch, and nestled next to it on her wrist, a tangle of gleaming, delicate gold bracelets. He calculated that she was wearing easily ten to fifteen thousand dollars worth of jewelry and at least another three thousand in clothing; the Chanel purse alone would clock in at a thousand.

Wonderful perfume rose from her body like an aura and he could have sworn her ebony eyes held a moment of distinctly feminine interest. She glanced away and when she looked at him next she was absolute business in her manner.

"I've ordered champagne. I hope you don't mind."

He didn't.

Lunch was inexpressibly wonderful. Jeff set himself the task of making it apparent that any personal interest she might have would be absolutely and enthusiastically welcomed. At the same time, he was careful not to go too far in case he'd been mistaken. She kept him delightedly off-balance when she did not acknowledge his efforts.

"Unfortunately . . ." She was looking over his shoulder, but her voice came at him in a low, European manner that could have been construed as either provocative—or simple sincerity. "I have a flight to Paris this afternoon so I'll be brief." She fixed him with direct eye contact at last. "Elwis Galleries is prepared to offer one hundred fifty thousand dollars American for the exclusive right to exhibit the Asante materials for three years. Those items the museum has authenticated, that is."

When he made no immediate response, she smiled and added with a small look of chagrin. "Plus, of course, a percentage of the admission gross, which we are willing to negotiate."

"I'd be willing to consider such an offer," he answered carefully, feeling at that singular moment the luckiest lawyer alive. He'd had absolutely no idea that a percentage of the gross could be had and hadn't thought of introducing the idea until she brought it up. "Provided we can agree on the percentage, of course." He swallowed the last of his champagne and felt like shouting Hallelujah.

It was, by far, more than he'd hoped for and, at the moment, meeting her ambivalent gaze, a hell of a lot less than he wanted. He forced himself to proceed casually and wondered mightily what she looked like without the designer clothes and jewelry, and that wonderful sassy red lipstick. Just the perfume and those perfect breasts would do fine.

"We are also interested in an outright purchase of the entire collection and would make the right of first refusal a part of the deal."

He brought himself back into the conversation. When he looked up he caught the glance again and there was no doubt this time; she was attracted to him. He couldn't believe his luck, or how good it made him feel that she had a similar interest.

"Of course. However, at the moment, a sale is not possible," he said with renewed confidence.

She leaned forward and he felt the physical impact of her concentration like a magnetic force. "Let me give you a figure to consider in the event it becomes possible," she insisted. She held her position and her focus on him while the tireless waiter refilled their glasses. He focused back with every ounce of energy he could manage. "We'd be prepared to offer the sum of three million dollars, providing the collection remains intact," she said, finally.

Jeff exhaled slowly and looked away for a moment to sip his champagne, damned and determined not to let his excitement show. Three million dollars. "It's been evaluated at somewhat less," he hedged, when he could look at her safely. Three million dollars! Who would have believed that an offer of this size was possible.

She laughed at him, eyes sparkling. "By the museum, of course, but they have to live within budget constraints, and it's in their best interest to keep the value down." She paused significantly. "Until they acquire it."

They worked their way through the balance of the champagne, and he explained that the gold was to go into a trust, and when that happened it could not be disposed of without a great deal of legal complication. Difficult, but not impossible.

"It's not in a trust, yet, is it?" Kathy drained her glass, which retained a glossy red imprint of her mouth. Her liquid eyes were direct for the first time with more than business as usual.

"No." My God, but she was beautiful, and interested. It was one of the three most excellent days of his life, and just at the moment, he couldn't remember the other two.

"Then my offer's open. If it goes into a trust, we'll have to reconsider, you understand."

"Of course. How is it you can offer so much more?" He usurped the waiter's domain and poured more champagne.

"When items such as these are made public, potential buyers can have access without exposing their interest. Elwis Galleries purchases a collection, makes arrangements to tour it for a few years in exhibition at several reputable institutions, museums, and so forth. This provides free publicity, and approval in these arenas tends to raise the value. We invest and wait, sell it off piece by piece if necessary, and hope for a suitable profit."

They finished the champagne and she put her hand lightly on his wrist.

"This is my business. I'm set up to do it with safety and, generally, individual owners are not. I provide a service and I'm very good." She smiled, obviously recognizing the double meaning in her choice of words. It was possible she was blushing, but he couldn't be sure.

"I'm sure you are," he answered intently, prolonging the supremely enjoyable moment.

Abruptly her smile faded and she struggled to resume an air of business as she looked at her watch. "I assume you'll want some time to make a decision and I've stayed much too long. I'm about to miss my plane."

He signaled the maître d' and took her hand. "Are you sure? Couldn't you manage a later flight?"

For a split instant she gave it thought. "I have an important meeting tonight. I really can't." Her liquid eyes were warm and willing, but she held firm in her decision.

"When can we talk again?" Damn business. Damn plane flights everywhere.

"I'll be back in London on Friday." She smoothed the impeccable gloves along her slender hands and stroked the fingers. "Will you be here?"

He made an instant decision that it would unquestionably, absolutely take at least until Friday to find a suitable photographer—maybe longer—and smiled casually. "Those are my plans."

"May I call on you for a decision?" She waited until he nodded in agreement then stood, and after briefly shaking his hand, she left the restaurant. He noticed the men at the surrounding tables discreetly watch her exit, then glance at him to fathom their relationship. The touch of her hand lingered on his wrist. He couldn't remember the last time he'd been so instantly attracted to a woman.

The maître d' arrived.

"The check is paid, sir. The lady made arrangements when she came in." The man was a model of rigid discretion who understood these things. "I do hope everything was to your satisfaction, sir."

He openly tipped the man fifty dollars, and felt superb doing it.

Later that afternoon he went through all the

required identification procedures and preparations with bank authorities; around four o'clock he got his first look at the gold. He'd expected to be excited by the sight of it but had been unprepared for the extent of its power. Piece after piece of it came out of the vault and thrilled his senses as no woman had ever done. Even Kathy Elwis. No wonder she wanted it.

Stroking the beautiful pieces, reveling in their beauty and exquisite workmanship, fully enjoying the sensation of nearly pure gold under his fingertips and its peculiarly smooth texture appreciated by every culture in the world, he wondered at Marielle's cavalier attitude. To her, ownership of these pieces was some bizarre fluke in her life, a puzzlement, something to be dealt with; she clearly considered her pregnancy of far more importance.

To him, however, the surrounding pieces of art represented something of infinitely more interest. Barring wealthy and financially secure executives, this was more raw power than he'd ever experienced in one sitting; their power had been on paper, in banks and printed money—this was real and tangible and sparkling at him. Three million dollars' worth.

Enlightened by his luncheon conversation, Jeff was satisfied with the insurance estimator's precision in carefully weighing and calculating the value of the treasure. He watched the man create constricted rows of numbers across a notepad with an inexpensive automatic pencil, with no discernible change in expression.

Thereafter they agreed upon the tally and the terms of an interim premium that provided for three million dollars in insurance while the gold remained in the safe deposit boxes, with provisions for riders to go into place should it be removed for display and the manner in which it could be transferred to another place of safekeeping.

In the event of theft during shipment to the United States, another rider would go into effect, doubling the amount. That accomplished, Jeff returned to the hotel. After a courtesy call to Rettig Burnside, who'd left for the day, he phoned his office and left word with the answering service that he'd be staying a few extra days in London. Probably a week. He'd call Marielle first thing tomorrow.

He'd touched three million dollars in gold, and Kathy Elwis, in one afternoon. It had indeed been a perfect day. He dreamt extremely well.

21

Sunday, April 3, 1990

"I think you should take the offer. It's a hundred and fifty thousand plus a percentage of the gross. I'll ask twenty-five, accept twenty. You want me to go ahead and set it up?"

Marielle sleepily switched Jeff's voice to her other ear before she answered. It had been worth his trip after all. "When do they want it?"

"All that has to be worked out. Probably pretty quick. I'll let you know. I'm meeting their representative again on Friday. There's also an offer to purchase the whole group."

She didn't let him finish. "We've never talked about selling it. It belongs to the baby."

"Marielle." His voice assumed that be-patient-with-her-she's-pregnant tone that so annoyed her. "It's considerably more money than the appraisal."

"I don't care what it is. I can't sell it until it's set up in a trust, anyway." Discussing the specifics of a potential sale was the last thing she wanted to concentrate on just now.

"We could make the deal now and worry about it wh—"

She interrupted again, her own patience at an end. "Did Burnside say I could sell it? Why are you asking me about a sale when you know nothing can happen until the ownership is settled?"

She could tell by his silence, typically Jeff, that he hadn't cleared things with the English lawyer; besides, anyone who wanted to buy the treasure would still want to buy it ten weeks or ten years from now, when she'd be in a better position to make decisions. She'd had nerve-wracking nightmares all night and had just fallen asleep when his call came through from London. She'd answered the phone in a grumpy mood that wasn't improving with his insistent tactics.

Jeff must have gotten the picture, because he backed down. Sort of. "I'm going to pursue the offer anyway and we'll talk about it later. I've had everything insured and just to be on the safe side, I'm going to take pictures before anyone has access. I'll take care of it before I leave."

The mention of photographs shut her down. She'd had enough of photographs to last a lifetime. He had everything under control and she wanted to go back to sleep. "Whatever you say. Just try to have the money by the end of June." Boyce Jameson was due the twenty-ninth.

He rang off and she restlessly fought the covers, chasing the safety of sleep. She'd had a perfectly hideous night filled with dreams of a slender white coffin centered on a giant black marble bier with warped, gaunt candle stands at either end. Please, God, let it not happen.

Sleep would not return. She gave up and grabbed her white robe to go into the living room; the front of it barely met to cover her middle these days but it was warm and soothingly familiar. The smell of fish food was unutterably vile as she sprinkled it into Abernathy's bowl.

Her encounter with Thomas at the hospital rolled to

the top of her mind and added its guilt to her exhaustion. That he thought she was pregnant with Jeff's baby made her crazy. Each time she allowed herself to consider it, the question of whether or not to tell him the truth gave rise to a growing list of ripples that would be created if she did so. His life would be affected in a very public way, personally, professionally. A hurried marriage followed by a pregnant "friend"? She cringed.

Part of that admission would have to be that she, too, had gotten pregnant on purpose; that she, too, was presenting him with a child he hadn't been consulted on. In the midst of the crisis that was Dana's survival? Was she crazy? Her mind rebelled at the very idea.

Exchanging one lie for another gained nothing. Boyce would be born soon and sooner or later the dates would give her away. Did she really expect Thomas to choose her and his son over Alissa and poor Dana?

Not only was there no way to predict how he would react, but she was forced to admit that she had no clear, firsthand knowledge of his current relationship with Alissa. According to Shirley, they were still together. Until she knew where he stood with Alissa, it was foolish to do anything she might live to regret.

Eventually, she managed to push the dilemma out of her mind and was dozing by the pool when Shirley dropped in to share a light lunch. Their conversation centered around the advance word on *Winter Love*, which wasn't positive, and on Thomas and Alissa in general. "They have the top two floors." Shirley leaned back in her chair and pointed out the tall residential building a few blocks away. "I understand the view is spectacular."

Shirley left to spend the afternoon with a client and Marielle could think of little else except Thomas living so close by—with Alissa. She'd had no idea. It was hard enough walking past his picture with those laughing brown eyes that seemed to be on every magazine cover she saw these days. Her bedroom closet was stuffed with them.

Abandoning the facade of not giving a damn, she positioned her lounge chair so she could lie back and study the row of balconies clearly visible from her position next to the pool, and wished Shirley hadn't told her. If she ever saw him standing there, she knew she'd spend all her time looking up. The doorbell rang and she was glad of the distraction.

Rose had mentioned that she and Calvin might stop by with Suzie and Jennifer on their way back from the beach, but when Marielle opened the door she found instead a slender, elegant black woman who introduced herself as Meta Kates. "Can I come in, please, Miss McCleary? I've come quite a distance to talk with you."

Marielle grasped instantly the woman's importance. Strength of purpose emanated from her heart-shaped face and her regal bearing sent a clear signal of authority. She wore a wrapped native dress and matching turban made of an exquisite burnt umber fabric with a striking African design woven in gold thread; suspended from a thick gold chain around her neck was a small soul-bearer's badge with the same configuration as those in the Asante treasure. The gold work in the fabric and in the badge danced in the sunlight.

Marielle invited her in, offered a glass of iced tea, and they settled beside the pool. Meta's speech was free of discernible accent and her large dark eyes seemed never to leave Marielle's face. Since there was nothing to be gained by pretense, Marielle chose to come directly to the point.

"It's about my inheritance, isn't it?"

Meta's ebony eyes were unwavering. "Word of this matter has reached the Asantehene," she acknowledged. "He has asked me to talk with you to see how we may come to agreement where it is concerned." Meta sipped her tea and Marielle felt herself being openly appraised.

"You are making arrangements to exhibit the royal treasure," Meta continued.

Marielle voiced her surprise. "I'm looking into it, yes. How did you know?"

"When valuable items such as these come to light governments impose taxes, which must be paid. Most people do not have money available in anticipation of such occasions. Therefore you must either sell the treasure or exhibit it for a fee."

Marielle felt outflanked. "I'm giving it consideration."

"I'm sure you've had offers of purchase. Are you also considering to sell?"

The open appraisal continued, not unfriendly but disconcerting all the same. She returned the woman's gaze.

"Not at the moment. I hope I don't have to," she responded honestly. "It was my great-great grandfather's wish that it go to my son when he is born. I plan to keep it until he is old enough to make that decision." As soon as she said it, Marielle realized her intentions ran directly counter to this woman's purpose. Meta Kates wanted the gold returned.

"Let me tell you about my people," Meta said to her. "We are a matrilineal society. Kingdoms pass through our daughters to their sons. My great-great grandmother was sister to King Kofi Karikari and pregnant when the British burned Kumasi and . . . acquired this treasure," she finished delicately.

"Her son was my grandfather and my uncle is now the Asantehene. He is old and ill and will die soon. As I have no children, my sister's son, Osei, will be Asantehene after him.

"It is my sorrow that I could not myself provide an heir, but my dream is to return to my nephew that which is rightfully his." Meta's eyes burned with commitment and her voice gained passion. "These things of which we speak are not art objects or antiquities.

They are sacred items of the Asantehene and belong to the Asante people. They are no different to us than the icons in the Vatican are to the Catholic Church. What words can I say to convince you of this?"

Marielle held her ground. "I don't doubt you, but surely you don't expect me to give up two million dollars' worth of gold. I have to provide for my son. He'll be born soon and I have his life to consider."

Meta dismissed the rationale. "Your son has nothing to do with it," she said softly.

"Wait a minute," Marielle flared. She tapped her fingers on her belly in emphasis and the baby inside responded with a small startled movement. "We are talking of this child's inheritance," she said firmly. "If he were not in here the gold would have come to me and I could decide without considering him. I don't know what decision I would have made in that instance, but I doubt if I'd simply hand it to you."

Meta rose to her full height and began to pace the narrow path next to the pool. "That I do not have a child does not mean I cannot understand his importance to you." She walked in heavy silence for a full minute, her beautiful costume shining in the thin afternoon sun, the soul-bearer's badge glistening against her breast. She approached Marielle once more.

"Before you decide what to do, you should know that the true value of what you have lies in its return to its rightful owners," she said earnestly. "These masks and icons have much significance in the Asante world. They are instruments of spirituality, like prayer, and serve as windows into the lives of the gods and the afterlife.

"Before their creation, souls were cleansed with fasting and prayer. Guidance was procured from the gods for the benefit of the king. An Asantehene is deity on earth, the most powerful living being for us. He is exalted, protected—the object of offerings. Think of it as no different than if Jesus Christ were returned to earth to a Christian believer. Such is the power of our faith."

Meta's words were spoken with a quiet passion; they surrounded Marielle like a fine mist, obscuring response. She could not deny the truth of them. And she could not agree.

"What things—not persons—what things do you hold most dear in life?" Meta demanded suddenly.

Marielle's thoughts went immediately to her mother's cameo locket and her father's wedding band. He'd been killed in the Korean War before she was born and the damaged ring had been returned to her mother, and treasured by her. She'd seen them all her life in her parents' wedding portrait; both had come to Marielle on her mother's death seven years ago.

"Suppose an enemy came into your life," continued Meta's voice in appeal. "Came into your most sacred place to steal these things, defile them, by offering them for sale in the streets. If your son discovered these treasures in some future instance, would he not want them back? Would his pain be different from my pain?"

There was a long, uncomfortable silence as both women examined these concepts. Finding no adequate response, Marielle felt trapped.

"Think of these objects as you would your child. They have a rightful place with the Asantehene just as your child's spiritual place is with you."

"I'll think about it," said Marielle finally. "That's all I can do right now. I won't make you any promises but perhaps we can work something out. I don't know." She shifted to relieve her back and glanced upward at Thomas's penthouse for strength. "Under British law, the objects belong to my son as soon as he is born. Nothing can happen until then."

Meta returned to her chair and took from her purse a necklace with a tiny black wooden doll suspended from it. "This is for you." She handed it to Marielle. "An

Asante woman would wear this to assure the birth of a healthy and beautiful child. A perfect son from a strong man."

Marielle flushed at the thought of the baby's father and bent to examine the gift. The doll had a flat disk for a face and a modified cylinder for its body with beautifully defined arms and legs and penis; it was perhaps two inches long and attached to a strand of perfectly matched, white cowrie beads and decorated with tiny, iridescent turquoise and carmine feathers mixed with gold and black beads. It was an exquisite piece of jewelry.

"It has been given strong powers by the Asantehene and will protect your son," Meta informed her quietly, eyes still watching her carefully.

"Thank you. It's a lovely gift and I will look forward to wearing it." Marielle could feel tiredness creeping into her body, from lack of sleep, from her pregnancy, from the exhaustion of her energy during this troubling meeting.

Meta rose to leave and Marielle saw her out. The two women paused in the doorway. "I had a lot to consider before you came here," Marielle said warily, "and now things are even more complicated. I have no idea what I'll do, but I am willing to keep in touch with you as things progress. Please believe that it's not my intention to do anything damaging to the Asantehene."

"I am sure of that," said Meta and offered a small card with a hand-written number. "You can call me at this number. They can always find me. I hope you decide well." She paused for a moment on the walkway. "Thank you for talking with me."

Marielle closed the door and sighed. "Word has reached the Asantehene," she'd said. How? Not only was she uncomfortable with the knowledge that Meta had known about the treasure and her plans to exhibit it, she'd also known that Marielle was pregnant. More than that, the woman had come prepared with a gift depicting a male child, which, she conceded, could have been coincidental, or cultural, certainly. Could Meta have known she was expecting a boy? She dismissed this last thought as most likely a fluke, but the entire incident made her uneasy.

However, going over every aspect of their conversation again in her mind, Marielle could find no threat, not even a hint of one. As vital as her mission had been, Meta had been serene, pleasant, and concerned. She felt certain Meta Kates was genuine in her attempt to convey the importance of the gold resting in the safe deposit boxes in London, beyond its value in money. Still, the entire incident left her disquieted and she decided to talk to Rettig Burnside about it.

In Monday morning's L.A. *Times,* on page seven, there was a small report attributed to Reuters, entitled "Gold Icons Come to Light in London". She read through the article with lightning speed and cringed at the amount of information. "Large cache of Asante gold icons," stated the article, "with an estimated value exceeding £1.3 million has been recovered from a crypt in Reading, England, by a Los Angeles woman, Marielle McCleary." *Oh, dear God,* she thought, and picked up the phone to call London.

Rettig Burnside came on the line in high dudgeon. "It's been reported quite thoroughly in every paper in London," he complained. "It was most unwise to release this information, Miss McCleary. I do wish you'd consulted me."

"I have no idea where it came from," she informed him, "but I've already had a visit from a woman representing Asante royalty. Yesterday."

"Oh, dear. Need I ask her purpose?"

"She wants me to return it."

"Not surprising, considering its source. How did you handle the matter?"

"I told her about the trust and that I'd think about it."

"The documents are on file and the trust will become active upon the birth of your son. I don't anticipate that this current wave of publicity will create difficulties at this time as we're unable to proceed until then in any case. However, since the source of this information saw fit to supply your full name, at some point you can expect a barrage of well-wishers and hucksters appearing at your doorstep to have a go at getting a finger in the pie, as it were."

"Surely the museum wouldn't give out this information. If they're trying to buy it from me, it would only lessen their chances that I'll sell it to them."

"What about your representative? Are you certain he's reliable?"

"Jeff?" She knew instantly it was his doing. "I can't believe he'd do something so . . ." She struggled for a descriptive word.

"Lacking in foresight?" supplied the wry barrister.

"Yes!" She was exasperated. Why would Jeff open this can of worms without telling her? "Is there anything for me to do?"

"Just keep a very low profile, my dear. That's my advice. Since it's gone public at three million it's going to be more difficult to keep the lower valuation at this point. Might have been, anyway," he said consolingly, "but we'll never know. The barn door's ajar."

She hung up the phone and searched for Jeff's number in London in a fury. What possible reason could he have for doing such a thing? A few moments later a defensive Jeff admitted he'd deliberately released the information.

"The tax value's already been established at a million eight hundred thousand, Marielle," he explained patiently. "Newspaper stories won't change that. This was intended to raise the exhibition value. It's free publicity and sets up an interest in the viewing public at the minimum, but more important it opens the bidding to buyers around the world."

She was so furious with him she nearly threw the phone. "And why on earth didn't you warn me you were going to do it?"

She could tell by the long pause that he was getting angry. "Correct me if I'm wrong, but you gave me specific authority to handle this." His voice took on that patient quality she hated. "Releasing this information increases the perception of value, therefore increases the exhibition fee. If I have to check with you on every detail, I'm reduced to errand boy and there's no point in my being here. What's the problem? Is there some harm done that I'm not aware of?"

She read him the article and told him about Meta's visit. He was rattled for a moment. "I did provide proof to the reporters that I represented you. And the power of attorney is on file at the bank, but that was specifically off the record and didn't appear anywhere in print here in London because I deliberately left you out of it." He began ticking off possibilities.

"There are easily a dozen people who know about this now, including executives at the insurance firm, surely half a dozen secretaries, a bunch of bank officials and the guy at the museum who took a look at it in December, right? Not to mention Burnside and the priest, whatshisname, and who knows how many people in Reading."

"Father Derning and his assistant," she conceded uncomfortably.

"Right. It's a small town and these people talk to people. It could have gotten to any good reporter in any number of ways."

"And how many others?"

"Relax. So your name's in the paper. Who was it who said everyone's famous for ten minutes? Warhol?"

"Fifteen."

"So this is your fifteen minutes. It's all handleable. I'll be back on Sunday. You tell anyone who approaches you to talk to me, including this Meta person. Your life's not going to change. You just relax and concentrate on having the baby. I'll take care of everything else."

She hung up the phone in frustration and found a pair of scissors to cut the article out of the *Times,* then took a shower and fixed her face. By the time she got to her office calm had returned. In actual fact, nothing had changed except that the gold was public and she was now identified with it, which, as Jeff had pointed out, might have happened anyway. She would simply have to chalk it up as the cost of accepting free legal representation by an ex-husband who had reverted to his old habit of making decisions without consulting her.

But later that morning and several times that afternoon, whenever she had a break in her work, flashes of her nightmare about the white coffin crept into her thoughts. Suddenly supremely superstitious, she decided to wear Meta's necklace until Boyce Jameson was born.

After work, she was drawn to the hospital to see Thomas and Dana, to try in some way to defeat the specter. She waited in the cafeteria reading her baby book without any real concentration, too distracted by the events in London and her determination to ask about Alissa. She found herself glancing up often in hopes of seeing him. Around seven o'clock, Thomas stepped inside long enough to scan the room.

He saw her instantly. His grin of welcome quickened her pulse. He was looking for her. He was clear-eyed but a day's growth of beard was evident; he apologized and explained that he'd been sleeping in the doctors' lounge and forgotten to shave. The fear about the baby that had been on hold in her stomach melted away. If Dana were worse, it would be written in his face. She was able to relax a bit. Now, if she could just be more certain about Alissa. He was sleeping in the doctors' lounge with a penthouse fifteen minutes away? Her mind leapt with joy. Maybe, maybe, maybe . . .

He sank onto the chair next to her. "It's good to see you," he said, and a warm feeling settled in her chest. "It's true what they say about pregnant women. You look great."

Both Alissa and the botched mess in London receded in importance, then left her thoughts entirely. She floated on air for a few moments while Thomas brought her up to date on Dana.

"She's gained a couple of ounces, but there's a new situation. She's got what they call brain-bleed. Dr. Goodin keeps telling me he thinks it's going to be all right." He moved about in irritation. "I don't want her on any more medication than is absolutely necessary, but I don't know what's best any longer. Goodin says to wait it out."

"I just read that it's not uncommon in preemies and it usually goes away." She slipped the baby book into her purse and changed the subject. "Are you working at all?"

"Not yet." He fingered the feathered necklace in curiosity and smiled at its odd appearance against her maternity smock. "What's this?"

Not working *and* not sleeping at home. Another good sign. Alissa might be in the penthouse, but odds were beginning to look like she was alone. "'This' is a long story," she said gaily, buoyed by her discoveries. "It's supposed to have magic powers and protect my son." At that moment, Boyce Jameson began kicking up such a storm that she winced. "Uohh."

Thomas put his hand on her belly and waited. Her heart picked up a beat. "You know it's a boy or are you guessing?" he asked.

"A boy for sure. State of the art and all that." The urge to tell him beat against her brain. No, countered reason. Not with his child's life so uncertain and *not* until she knew about Alissa. She suppressed the impulse and contented herself with the warmth of his hand on her belly.

After a moment, the baby moved again and Thomas smiled as he shared the sensation. "I'd give a million dollars if Dana could do that," he said thoughtfully. "That's a healthy guy, all right. Keep him that way."

"I call him the placekicker." His hand was hot against her skin through the thin cotton dress. Soon, she decided. If they're not living together, I'll tell him the second Dana's released from the hospital. She concentrated on his handsome face and allowed her hope to expand.

Thomas sat smiling with his hand pressing lightly upon her stomach until the baby quieted down, then glanced at his watch. "We can see her in about five minutes. You can leave your things in the lounge."

This time in the preemie ward, Marielle was prepared and she was able to move smoothly to Dana's Isolette. She slipped her hand through the opening without hesitation and placed her thumb under one of the baby's tiny hands. The minute fingers moved only slightly but made no motion to grasp. Thomas took his place on the other side and at his touch, Dana briefly waved her arm and tried to cling to his finger. "She knows you," whispered Marielle.

"I think she does," he answered softly. "The nurses say she's different when I come in." There was pride in his voice.

After a few minutes, they were required to leave and Thomas walked with her to the doctors' lounge to collect her purse.

"How often do you see her now?" she asked, bidding for time.

"About every three hours. In between I sleep and eat, mostly. I'm getting pretty good at dropping off on cue. Do you have a few minutes?" He smiled and lightly tapped the wooden doll on her necklace. "I want to hear about this magic."

He wanted to talk to her. Her heart rate elevated again and his tone convinced her it would be something positive. She settled onto a chair and dug in her purse for the *Times* article. He was full of questions and soon she was describing finding the treasure and Jameson Woods's legacies and Thomas was smiling at her descriptions and listening to her adventures with fascination, eyes on her face. Finally, she told him about the visit from Meta Kates and the gift of the necklace.

He examined the necklace carefully. "You have to be careful about this," he said soberly.

"Committed as she is, I don't think she'd do anything dangerous," she assured him, filled with joy that he was worried enough to issue this gentle warning.

"Not her necessarily." Thomas dropped the necklace into place against her chest. "The problem I see is that you've been identified. You could have all kinds of kooks and crackpots at your door. Separate and aside from the folks who will try to hustle you with business propositions, there are people out there who are nut cases. They see you with found money and decide you can make their lives wonderful by giving part of it to them. It happens all the time in this business. That's why we live behind gates and with bodyguards." He sat forward, intent on his lecture, his concern for her safety evident. She savored his interest, glowed at being the center of his attention.

"The more it's worth, the bigger the problem you'll have. Ask any lottery winner. People smell money and they come out of the woodwork like cockroaches," he said sadly. "It sounds like you have an excellent counselor in London but if you want additional advice, I'll introduce you to someone who has a legitimate career based on experience and reputation. In the meantime, just use reasonable caution."

"It's getting more and more complicated every day," she confessed, pleased to be saying it to someone who genuinely understood the complexities and didn't consider value the primary concern. "I know giving it back sounds crazy but it might be the simplest solution. It's beginning to create more problems than it's solving. I would never have thought of it as stolen property if she hadn't come to see me."

"Well, stolen today and inheriting it as booty taken during a war a hundred years ago are hardly the same thing. I'm not really up on the moral versus the practical issues of something like this, that's something you'll have to decide."

Marielle glanced at her watch. Two hours had flown past and it would soon be time for him to return to Dana. In her delight in answering his attentive questions and enjoying being able to entertain him, she hadn't been focused on introducing conversation relative to him and Alissa. She was frustrated with herself for getting so caught up in his attention that she'd lost track of time.

There was a sudden rush of silence and she knew her interest in his situation with Alissa was written in her face. For the first time in two hours, Thomas turned away, avoiding her eyes, and she absolutely hated what she was beginning to suspect. He looked at his watch and said nothing. He was going to leave it to her to bring up Alissa's name and she realized suddenly that she'd built her whole case on supposition and might well have misjudged the situation entirely.

Absolutely, he'd sworn to her that he would only stay with Alissa until the baby was born. Dana was now thirteen days old. At the time that pledge was stated, neither he nor she herself had known that she was pregnant. Fool. Idiot. From his point of view, her pregnancy changed everything. Just as Dana's birth and brush with death had changed everything.

Tell him it's his child. Do it now, urged her brain. *Dana's getting better, she's going to be fine, even if he's angry at first, he'll understand, he'll—*

His voice broke into her thoughts. "We haven't talked about Alissa." He still wouldn't look at her. His agitation and the look on his face took on a terrible significance. There was a black pit opening up at her feet and it took all her concentration not to fall into it.

"Are you going to stay with her?" she said stubbornly, fighting the maw. With a supremely difficult effort she managed to sound equally casual. They *were* still together. Had Dana's birth brought them closer after all or was it a reason he didn't want her to know? Warning bells went off in her mind as he took a few moments to reply.

This time he resolutely met her eyes. "Yes," he said flatly. His jaw was tight. "I have no idea what will happen with Dana." She waited, but he added nothing. Clearly he wasn't going to elaborate and she was suddenly afraid. He nodded at her pregnant belly. "How's Jeff handling all this?" His eyes held her on the edge of the pit, searching, unyielding.

At his deliberate change in subject, the black pit widened. "He's been very supportive," she said carefully, on slippery ground and supremely cautious. There was a brief pause while she searched inwardly for something else to say that would not further Jeff's identification as the father of her child, and found nothing to fill the silence. She felt leaden and stupid. The earlier joy of the afternoon was long gone and her mind was tired. "He keeps buying stuffed animals," she finished limply.

"So he's jazzed about the baby?" Thomas's face was unreadable and the deep brown eyes had gone carefully neutral.

"Yes," she admitted, increasingly uncomfortable with the direction he was taking the conversation. Where was he going with this? She had to turn it around, to talk about him and Alissa, but his next question tossed her into further disarray.

"Are you two thinking of getting remarried?" His voice was completely casual and offhand, with no discernible emotion.

"We haven't discussed it yet," she hedged with a technical truth, and cringed at the edge to her voice. This was game playing and she hated it, and she hated not being able to fling herself off the cliff of caution and into the unknown, to tell him and be damned for it.

Staying together. Of course they were staying together. That's what he hadn't wanted to tell her. There was a shortage of air in the room and energy drained from her body. "I'm sorry," she said in sudden exhaustion. "I'd love to stay and see Dana again, but I'm a little tired and . . ."

He was instantly on his feet and concerned. "I understand. Are you okay to drive?" She assured him she was and he walked her to her car and helped her inside. "I enjoyed talking to you tonight," he said awkwardly. "It's the first time I've been able to get my mind off Dana's problems long enough to get some perspective. Thanks for that." His face was still closed against her but he leaned in the window and kissed her cheek. "If I can help, with anything, just say the word," he said. "Don't forget what I said about being careful."

Staying together. Nothing else penetrated. Nothing else was important.

The scent of his aftershave lingered on her skin and she saw him in the rearview mirror, watching her drive away. When she looked back from the tollgate, he was gone.

At home, her answering machine was blinking furiously: Two calls from Rose; four messages from people she didn't know introducing themselves and asking for meetings; two people she'd forgotten she knew, plus a reporter from the *Valley Sentinel.* She erased the tape and went to bed.

Staying together. She'd been a fool to hope.

All that night when Thomas and Alissa were not making love next to her in the bed, the ghost-white casket infiltrated her dreams. She woke at 4:00 A.M. in a cold sweat with a horrible fear that it might not be Dana at all. What if it were her own child? A rush of icy terror streaked through her body so great that she sat bolt upright in fear. It was a long time before she went back to sleep.

22

Noon, April 6, 1990

"You want to do what?" Jeff was aghast. His voice jumped half an octave.

"I haven't decided to do it, I just wanted to talk about it." Marielle held her ground. She was tired and not in the mood for lectures about money and taxes.

"You can't possibly be serious. Nobody gives away three million dollars' worth of gold!"

"Three million? When did it become three million?"

"I told you I had an offer to buy it, you didn't want to hear about it!" He was furious.

"I'm sorry. You did mention it." Her head was spinning. From a million eight to three million was a pretty good jump. "I just want to know how far along you are in this exhibition agreement and whether or not it's too late to change my mind."

"There's nothing signed yet, but I have to proceed in good faith, and for all intents, I've indicated we're willing to make the deal," he said stiffly. "You change your mind and we look like *idiots.*"

She knew what would come now. First disbelief, then anger, followed by exasperation. Next would come a conversational seesaw that would begin with laborious explanation that a five-year-old could follow, would swing to exasperation then back again, and so on until she was exhausted in her argument. Funny how the pattern, so apparent to her now, had eluded her during their years of marriage. She brushed away the thought and returned to the defense of her position. The amount of money had nothing to do with it. Even if it was ten million, she wanted things to slow down until she was convinced she was making the right decision.

"I'm just not sure I have the right to do this. I want more time to think about it."

Jeff, equally resolute, stuck to his pattern.

"There's nothing to think about. This stuff is over a hundred years old. Even if it was stolen, anybody it belonged to is dead and buried, and who knows who this woman is who's trying to claim it. It's like selecting an Indian and giving him the deed to Manhattan. It's crazy! Why can't you see that?"

"Stolen is stolen," she said stubbornly. "What if I steal your car, sell it, and keep the money. Is there a time limit on your wanting it back?"

"Yes. Before I'm dead," he exploded. "After that I don't give a damn! Marielle, don't do this. Even if this woman is legitimate, governments rise and fall over there like yo-yos. How do you know this stuff won't end up in some guy's bank account?"

"I have the feeling she's legitimate. Certainly, I'd look into her credentials. It's not like I'd be taking it entirely on faith." It was now a battle of wills and even if he was right, she was tired of bending.

"Three millions dollars' worth of faith?" Jeff was frothing, beside himself with impatience with her. "You want to give away three million dollars' worth of gold and you don't want any guarantees?" Exasperation had pushed its way to anger.

"Lawyers need guarantees. All I need is a decent life for my son." Apparently she'd been waiting for something to allow her to blow some steam, because she took the opportunity. "Money from stolen treasure won't ensure that. My phone hasn't stopped ringing for three days. You wouldn't believe the things people have said to me. It's been a mess! If having this gold is going to bring this kind of hassle, if it forces me and my child to live behind locked doors, it's not worth it. Hear me, Jeff. It'll go back and good riddance! All I'm doing at the moment is thinking about it!"

When she found herself shouting back at him, which was *her* old pattern, she gave herself abrupt instructions not to continue. "Other than change my phone number, I don't know what I'm going to do, okay? This is taking too much out of me and I don't want to fight about it. Just please don't lock me into an agreement until I'm sure what I want. I'll call you with the new number."

"Just promise you won't make any decisions without letting me explain things to you first."

Another wrong button pushed.

"I promise to listen to any explanation you think I should hear," she said tersely. "Just not now."

"Fine."

Both phones hit their cradles with a bang.

Jeff ran his hands through his hair in frustration. "She's like a mutt with a bone," he muttered to himself. "Once she's latched on to something, it takes an act of Congress to get her to change her mind. So she's had a few phone calls. You'd think Quasimodo was waiting in the woodwork." He picked up the phone and punched out the number for Elwis Galleries. "All the time we were married, she wanted to get pregnant. Well, she's finally pregnant." What was her problem?

The gallery answered on the first ring.

"I'd like to leave a message for Katarina Elwis," he

said to the disembodied voice. "Have her contact Jeff McCleary at the Leveque Hotel. Tell her I have an answer. Thank you."

That accomplished, he spent the balance of the evening planning appointments with various photographers and locating a security service. A short visit to Seneca Security the following morning and a cash payment later, he secured an armored truck and the services of two armed guards with the location of material to be supplied at 8:45 A.M. Friday morning for a 9:00 A.M. pickup, destination to be advised.

The next two days were spent visiting various commercial photographers' studios. There were not great disparities in their prices and he finally selected Duncan Portraits for its proximity to the bank. No point in moving the gold all over town just to take a few pictures. He persuaded the owner to rearrange his schedule for an all-day shoot and explained that he had a large quantity of modest estate jewelry that he wished photographed for insurance purposes before he left town.

The Leveque concierge gave him two messages Tuesday afternoon. Marielle had called with her new phone number and Kathy Elwis had returned his call but hadn't left a message. Still irked, he avoided the first and was frustrated by the latter until that evening when Kathy called again.

"Where are you?" he asked, more than casually interested. "Can we meet for dinner?"

"I don't think so, I'm in Stockholm." She laughed and went immediately to business. "You said you had an answer. Your buyer's considered our offer?"

"Well, to tell the truth there's a small glitch, but nothing that can't be worked out. I spoke to the owner yesterday and due to events I'm not able to disclose at the moment, she's rethinking her decision to exhibit the material."

"I see."

He felt the gravity of her pause and was prepared.

"What is there to be worked out?" Kathy asked coolly.

"Your offer to purchase. She's taking it under advisement," he said truthfully but with a hell of a lot more confidence than he felt. Marielle could be stubborn to a fault, but he'd always managed to handle her difficult moods when they were married. Still, this would take a pretty good effort unless it was a sure bet. If he got the sale, it shouldn't be too hard to convince her that a million dollars net profit was in the best interests of her baby.

Kathy's mood changed instantly. "That is good news. When do you expect her response?"

"I told her I was meeting with you on Friday. I expect to have an answer by then."

"That's wonderful." Her voice took on the texture of warm honey.

"I'm having the material photographed. I thought you might be interested in inspecting it." He threw the offer out with supremely casual confidence.

"Our insurance company will require it at some point," said the charming voice, "and it would save time—unless you plan to stay in London for a bit. Perhaps I should bring an expert to look it over as well?"

"I'd rather you didn't." Jeff paused, savoring the tasty hint of personal interest in her question. "There's plenty of time to verify authenticity once we agree to agree. Besides, I was going to take you to dinner."

She didn't hesitate. "I'd love dinner, thank you. And where do I meet you on Friday?"

"I'm still working on arrangements," he instinctively lied on the side of caution. It was nice to have her off-balance for a change. "Can I call you tomorrow?"

"I'll be traveling to Budapest tomorrow and from there to Rome on Thursday, but you can leave the information with my office. Better yet, I'll call you

Thursday night. I'll be arriving back in London about ten o'clock. Will that be too late?"

"I'll be waiting."

Marielle borrowed two lunch hours from later in the week and left her office at three o'clock to drive to UCLA, this time with a double purpose. Thomas had left a message on her answering machine asking her to meet him at the hospital around six. He'd given no hint of his purpose and still aching from her painful lesson in jumping to conclusions, this time she absolutely refused to speculate.

She parked in the hospital lot, then walked slowly across the beautiful campus toward the main library, aware of the extreme youth of the students. *I must be getting old,* she thought. *They look like high school kids.*

Then she smiled. This time last year she'd been sitting in Tonio's with the Minds to determine a suitable male with the goal in mind of getting pregnant. Now she was rotund with a baby by a man she loved even if she couldn't have him, and had a three-million-dollar tax problem. If life was nothing else, it was full of surprising change. She paced the campus in the afternoon sunlight and entered the college library with a determined step.

A computerized system of locating books and information simplified her task and within twenty minutes she'd found enough books on Asante history to keep her busy for a week. Each contained material that supported Meta Kates's position; indeed, the British had mounted a punitive campaign against King Kofi Karikari in 1874 and burned and looted the king's palace. Jameson Woods and Billy McCafferty had taken part in the history written down in these volumes; it gave her a less than comfortable sensation to read of a city's devastation at the hands of a man directly related to herself and the child in her body.

With every piece of corroborating information, her indecision increased. If only Jameson Woods had bequeathed a cash legacy. Money would have had no moral strings attached and there wouldn't be a question in her mind about accepting it and investing it on behalf of her son. But the dilemma of having highly valuable religious items that were obviously stolen . . . She closed the last book with an irritated snap.

Still, three million dollars.

Except it wasn't three million dollars. It was a wonderful, golden, thorny burden. A fabulous goose that promised great riches for her son but had to date managed to eat legal fees and insurance fees and maintenance fees and banking fees and fees for advice and information and the cost of hotels and airfare from her cash inheritance, but had yet to lay a salable egg. And, thanks to the British tax system, in order for it to do so she would be forced to sell most of it to salvage anything at all—and even that wasn't possible unless she shut her mind against what she knew to be right and fair.

Frustrated, no answer in sight, she left the library and began her return trip across campus to the hospital to wait for Thomas, unsure for the first time of her feelings about seeing him. Distracted, it took a few moments for her to recognize that she was being followed. Thirtyish, of modest size and carrying a small leather pouch, the man had sparse light-brown hair and a round, bland face with a weak chin; dressed in a nondescript beige suit, he wore his tan shirt open at the throat and his shabby loafers had run-down heels. He'd been in the library at the next table. Now he was walking a parallel path through the grounds.

Marielle stopped, pretended indecision, and sure enough he stopped a few feet farther on and studied his watch. Her pulse rate increased perceptibly and she swallowed, not looking directly at him at any time. What could he want? She had only a few dollars in her purse. There were hundreds of students about. Granted her pregnancy made her a slow, clumsy target, but surely he wouldn't attempt a theft among so many people.

When a group of students caught up with her, she walked as a part of their number until they stopped at a bus shelter. The beige man followed casually, walking on the opposite side of the street.

From the bus stop Marielle angled across campus toward the hospital as quickly as she could walk, glancing back now and again to see if he was still following. Unfortunately, shrubbery and campus landscaping with new spring leaves shining in the oblique afternoon sunlight obscured the winding sidewalks and she could not be sure. Finally, she reached the side entrance to the hospital and was relieved to be safely inside the building. She went directly to the cafeteria.

After heating some chocolate milk, she found patio seating with her back to a wall and sipped the hot, soothing liquid until she was calmed. Feeling slightly foolish, she waited for Thomas and chided herself that she'd been imagining things.

Getting up to discard the paper carton, she started. The man had seated himself directly across the patio behind a woman in a wheelchair. His jacket was off and he'd been so inconspicuous that she hadn't noticed him come in. He was shadowed by the cafeteria's plate-glass window and was surreptitiously taking her picture. Suddenly she was violently angry. How dare he invade her life and take pictures without her permission!

Realizing he'd been seen, the man abandoned any pretense of subtlety and openly aimed the camera at her face. She heard the camera's professional high-speed advance whine and click in rapid succession as she left her table and started toward him. He immediately turned and walked smoothly through the revolving door and had disappeared out another exit by the time she got inside the cafeteria.

The encounter left her with a major case of paranoia. She returned to her seat to retrieve her purse and several of the cafeteria patrons openly stared in curiosity. She was being followed for some reason, and photographed. Why? How long had he been watching her before she'd realized it?

People in the patio quickly lost interest and returned to their food. Marielle sat, unnerved, trying to sort it out. If it had to do with the inheritance, a single photograph would be sufficient to identify her. This man had taken dozens. Perhaps someone had connected her to Thomas because of her visits to Dana. Maybe it was as simple as some sleaze magazine lying in wait for a picture of the two of them. Her pregnancy would make a wonderful smear campaign after the January mess. She quailed at the thought.

That her baby was in fact Thomas's child only compounded the potential horror. If that were to become public, it was the kind of thing that could be thrown up to her son by ignorant and destructive people for the rest of his life, not to mention the damage to Thomas and his career. The thought pulled her to her feet and she walked cautiously down the hall to the information counter. The man was nowhere in the waiting area.

"I was supposed to meet Thomas Saxon," she said to the woman volunteer, "but I can't wait any longer. Will you give him a note for me?"

"What's the name?" said the woman.

Marielle identified herself.

"He came in about three minutes ago." The woman slid a pink message slip across the counter. "Ask Miss McCleary to come to the doctors' lounge," it read.

She found him pacing in the hallway outside the lounge. "Hi." He gave her a lingering kiss on the cheek, glad to see her but clearly distracted. "It's best we meet here from now on," he said evenly. "Upstairs is a bit—"

"Public. I'm sorry, I should have realized it." She dreaded telling him about the photographer. "How's Dana?"

"She had a good night. Dr. Goodin says the brain-bleed looks like it's going to disappear without medication. He's given me a slight increase in her odds. She's up to fifty-five percent now."

"That's wonderful." She felt genuine exhilaration and saw pride and emotion in his eyes.

"I can't tell you how good it is to see you." He gave her a gentle hug and put his hand on her taut stomach. "How's the placekicker?"

"He's sleeping right now." She felt her curiosity leap to the fore and forced herself not to allow any more conclusions.

"Would you be able to have dinner with me?" Thomas asked. "I miss talking to you. Maybe we could pick up a few things at the market and I could cook at your place." He looked at her with an intensity she hadn't felt since the night at the cabin. "We don't have much privacy here but I'll understand if you'd rather not," he finished, glancing at her in silent assumption of the other man in her life.

She bit her lip, hating to destroy a moment she'd prayed for, but he had to be made aware. "I was photographed in the cafeteria a few minutes ago," she told him.

His reaction was immediate. "Damn!" He paused for a moment to let the initial anger pass. "Part of the trade-off in my life," he said tightly, "is lack of control. The press considers me and anyone connected with me as public property. Someone's probably seen us together and made some sort of connection. Did he talk to you, threaten you in any way?"

He looked so upset that she decided not to tell him

about the library and shook her head. "I got scared, but I'm over it now."

"Well," he told her levelly, "the only thing that changes is, we'll have to be more careful. "You and I know there's no harm in our relationship, but, depending on who's paying this jerk, they could make a mess in our lives. . . ."

"No harm in our relationship" dampened all expectations.

"We can still have dinner," he said thoughtfully. "I'll get the food and meet you at your place. I know when I'm being followed and if I have to, I'll order in pizza and come in as the delivery boy. I'm an actor. I can do that," he joked lightly.

"That would be terrific."

"Let's go see the kid." His good humor returned and they moved through hand-scrubbing procedures and put on their green gowns. "Let's see what she thinks of this whole idea."

Inside the ward the nurses nodded hello and went about their rounds. Clearly in this room Thomas Saxon's world-famous presence was accepted as merely routine and was second in importance to the needs of the infants under their care. Marielle placed her hand inside Dana's Isolette, resting her fingers lightly against the baby's tiny arm. This time she was convinced that Dana reacted to her touch with a small gesture. There were definite sucking motions with her mouth.

Marielle thrilled at the idea that this miniature being could identify her touch among all the others. Thomas's eyes above his mask were warm and caring and he gave a small wink that signified he, too, had noticed the baby's reaction. When he placed his hand inside, the baby's attention was instantly withdrawn in his favor and her tiny fingers curled tightly around his thumb, her perfect cupid mouth opening in wide, clear greeting and acknowledgment of his presence.

There was a sudden loud disturbance in the ward. A woman's harsh voice cut the air, followed immediately by a frenzy of hushing commands from the nurses.

"I want her out of here," the woman demanded, ignoring the staff.

Thomas's head jerked up instantly and one of the warning signals began to flash in the battery of machinery attached to his daughter. Marielle looked from his angry eyes to Alissa being restrained in the doorway by the head nurse.

"You heard me, out of here! I'm that baby's mother and I don't want her here!" Alissa's voice raked heavily through the room.

Marielle carefully withdrew her hand and hurriedly threaded her way through the machinery toward the door. Any unnecessary disturbance to the infants in the Isolettes was dangerously stressful, potentially lethal to those clinging to life, and her only thought was that the sooner she left the ward, the sooner Alissa would quiet down and cease her upheaval.

The stocky head nurse who had Alissa's progress blocked was using her ample frame physically to force the actress's backward exit; two additional nurses joined in the fray and prevented Alissa from passing on either side. The combined barrier of all three firmly ejected the thin woman into the hallway. Marielle followed them outside in rigid silence, embarrassed for Alissa and angered that her selfish tantrum clearly lacked judgment or concern for the infants in the ward.

The two neonatal nurses immediately returned to check on the infants under their care and the head nurse remained in the hallway to prevent Alissa's reentry. Alissa fixed Marielle with a deadly glare and turned on her. "Whore!" she raged. "How dare you come here."

The head nurse reached for an emergency phone. "Mrs. Saxon, lower your voice and behave rationally or

I'll be forced to have you physically removed from this area," she warned.

Alissa ignored her. "Whore," she screamed again and Marielle began to back down the hallway as Alissa moved toward her. The head nurse started punching numbers into the phone.

Marielle's thoughts were frantic as she looked for an exit. How to quiet this woman? How to get away from her? "I'm sorry," she offered quietly. "I know she's your child. I was only trying to help."

Her attempt to placate Alissa showered gasoline on a three-alarm fire. "You're never going in there again," Alissa shouted at her, voice shrill and ragged. "I don't care what my husband wants, I won't have his bastard around my child! You hear me? I won't have it!"

Marielle, unable to get past her to the doctors' lounge, looked in vain for an elevator, a stairwell, an escape of any kind.

"You'll never have him. Never! You hear me!" Alissa was totally out of control and advancing toward her.

Thomas came flying out of the ward and grabbed his wife. Pulling her forcibly into his arms, he picked her up like a little girl and Alissa went mad with rage. He carried her kicking and shrieking down the hall to the doctors' lounge. She struck at him and one of her expensive pumps flew against the wall and went skittering on the worn green tile along the baseboard. Marielle picked up the fallen shoe and followed, aware that she had to get out of the hospital for her own safety. Clearly, Alissa wasn't rational.

"Stop it," Thomas thundered at his wife. "Stop it right now!"

Alissa glared at him defiantly but lowered her voice. "I know about her. You think you have me fooled, but you don't." She whirled like a cornered cat and raged at Marielle. "I know all about the two of you and I tell you right now, I'll never divorce him. I won't give him up and I won't give him grounds, you can bet on that one. I'll be the most perfect little wife you ever saw."

She straightened her clothing and wrenched her shoe from Marielle's numb fingers. She held it by the vamp with the high heel exposed like a weapon until Thomas grabbed her wrist and gently loosened the shoe from her grasp. When it had dropped safely to the floor, Alissa acknowledged his precaution with a spate of fury and savagely kicked it aside. "I'll see to it your precious pregnant bitch never goes near my child again, Thomas. I'll get a court order if I have to. Don't you think I can't."

"That won't be necessary," Marielle said evenly. She picked up her purse and walked toward the door. "I won't come here again."

"You're damned right you won't." Alissa's vicious voice racketed down the hallway after her, echoing into the elevator. "You don't come back here, ever!"

Marielle shook uncontrollably all the way home. It took hours to get warm and even longer to fall asleep. God, what a nightmare. God help Thomas if that was a sample of his life with Alissa.

And God help Dana.

Whatever her fantasies of Thomas leaving Alissa might have been she knew there was no possibility that he would abandon Dana to Alissa's care. Not now, not ever.

23

April 7, 1990

When a conciliatory Jeff called from London, she told him about being stalked by the photographer. He was concerned and genuinely apologetic. "Jesus, Marielle, if I caused it, I'm really sorry. I never dreamed anything like that would happen. The last thing you need is additional stress. I was just trying to protect your interests here and get the best possible deal. It's what you sent me here to do."

"I know," she agreed. "It's all getting a little beyond me, I guess." She told him about the letters she'd been receiving. Her mail had tripled since she'd changed her phone to an unlisted number, and it contained proposals for everything from investment schemes to marriage to indecent suggestions. When she was centered and in a positive mood, the more absurd of the offers were good for a laugh, but on the whole, the letters were pathetic and difficult to assess. All were passionately determined to gain her sympathy and attention, and all made mention of the treasure. Some were positively frightening in their intensity, and reading them alone in the house, she was mightily aware of her single status and occasionally got the shivers. Most, thankfully, bore out-of-state postmarks.

"Maybe it's better just to sell it. Now, hear me out," he said before she could enter an objection. "I don't see why we can't make an arrangement now with Elwis Galleries, get all the negotiating done and an agreement in place by the time the trust goes into effect. As trustee, you have a duty to proceed in the best interests of the beneficiary and as long as you pay the taxes, I don't think any court in Britain would complain that selling this gold to the highest bidder is contrary to that directive.

"Then all you'll be involved with is money and someone else can deal with the morality of the situation, and the hassles and headaches that come with it," he concluded.

Marielle listened patiently. What he said had some merit. She wasn't sure she was up to making a proper decision where the treasure was concerned and handing the decision to someone else sounded wonderfully tempting. "I'll talk to Mr. Burnside about it," she conceded.

"Great. Now, you're tired and I've got to get to the bank to get this stuff packed and ready to travel tomorrow so I'll say good night." Jeff signed off.

Long after she hung up the phone, worry pervaded her thoughts, corrosive and uncomfortable. The more she considered it, the more she realized the gold would have to go. Even if she sold it for a million dollars over the taxable value in Britain, she'd be liable for more than three hundred thousand in American income taxes, and assuming she didn't have to defend a lawsuit to have the gold returned to the Asantehene, by the time all the expenses and legal fees were paid, Burnside had been right—she'd be lucky to have two hundred thousand left.

Two hundred thousand for something that was not only stolen but sacred; she knew she'd never be able to do it. Besides, as Thomas had pointed out, there were too many people out there who acted irrationally and if she were this frightened by a pushy photographer and a couple of pounds of unsolicited mail, how on earth would she handle someone who became abusive or aggressive?

First thing in the morning she would call Meta and Burnside and see how she could go about returning the gold and requesting reimbursement for her expenses to date. Jeff would just have to understand.

Tea drinkers at heart, the British were unjustly proud of their coffee, Jeff decided. He sipped his fourth cup of the morning and alternately paced the length of Duncan's studio, going over everything in his mind, trying to think of anything he'd overlooked. Fortunately, things had proceeded as smoothly as clockwork but there was still a lot to accomplish before Kathy Elwis arrived at two o'clock.

Good beginnings always made him nervous. He'd spent half the night planning his strategy and he wanted the sale a fait accompli before Ms. Elwis knew what had hit her. Then he planned to go to dinner with the beautiful lady at an intimately exclusive little Chelsea restaurant he'd learned about and concentrate on what the evening might bring. His reservations were for eight-fifteen and he'd been gently advised by the concierge to be punctual.

It was another gray London day but the persistent drizzle had ceased. Barclay's bank officials had been crustily cooperative about packing the items and permitting him to store the cartons in their main vault overnight. The blue Seneca armored truck had arrived in the underground access on schedule. The Seneca guards, two alert black men in their late twenties in identical blue uniforms, each with a convincing sidearm and a belt full of bullets, had worked in easy concert with bank security to transfer the cartons from the vault to the waiting truck. Four blocks of London's busy Friday morning traffic from the bank to the studio had been uneventful.

Big Ben's famous chimes had sounded for the tenth time a few minutes ago; the armored vehicle was parked squarely in front of Duncan's Portraits; the front door to the studio had an On Holiday sign taped in the window. With the help of a dolly, the guards had quickly moved the heavy cartons into the larger of the two portrait studios and Jeff stationed one of them immediately outside the doors to prevent entry and the other a few feet down the hall to watch the rear exit.

Everything was ready at last and he finished his coffee. It was time to get this show on the road.

He opened the first carton and placed the exquisite solid gold ram's head, on the black velvet cloth to be photographed. The look on Duncan's face was priceless and he grinned at the photographer's reaction in satisfaction. Once the lovely Ms. Elwis saw these pieces of gold, she didn't have a chance.

The sniffy Englishman walked around the table with his mouth hanging open in awe. "It's the bleedin' African stuff that's been in all the papers. And I'm to photograph it?" The little man's face closed in sudden suspicion. "You can't use my pictures for anything commercial without an agreement, you know."

"The pictures are for insurance purposes and you can't sell them without *my* permission," countered Jeff. "Of course, depending on their quality, we might be willing to make other arrangements."

Duncan, pacified, began to hum as he set up his lights and adjusted his camera equipment with care. Too much care, as it turned out. By noon, he'd only completed photographing the series of soul-bearer's badges.

"I only have one day, man," Jeff complained. "Can't we hurry this up a bit?"

"Not if you want quality, we can't," said a huffy Duncan. "If you wanted trash you should have gone to Lamont's. I do a first-class job or not at all."

"All this has to be back in the truck by four o'clock. The bank closes at five. I think you'll agree that it's in both our best interests to have everything on film by then."

Duncan said nothing, but after a brief lunch there was a perceptible increase in his pace. Thereafter, the gold pieces flowed smoothly from carton to black velvet for the camera's flashes: front, side, side, reverse, then back to carton.

A few minutes before two o'clock, Jeff informed the patient security guards in the hall that he expected a visitor shortly, a beautiful young lady. "No one else is to be admitted," he cautioned, just in case she'd decided to bring her expert after all.

The guard touched his cap in acknowledgment, exchanged looks with his partner, but otherwise had no comment. He walked to the front door to wait.

Promptly at two o'clock Kathy arrived in a swirling black cashmere cape; its hood, edged with delicate gold threadwork, floated lightly over her hair like a monk's cowl. Scores of gold bracelets jangled pleasantly at her wrists and trios of golden bangles swayed delicately from her ears. The Seneca guards snapped to masculine attention when she removed the cape to reveal a smashing black silk jumpsuit that flattered her lovely body to perfection. This time the looks exchanged were rife with male envy, pure and simple.

She moved into the studio, a fluid force, and was instantly drawn to the gleaming icons aligned on a side table, awaiting their turn in front of the camera. Jeff saw that she wanted them and that she made no effort to hide her interest from him. It wasn't going to be that hard after all, he realized. He threw out any plans to sell as unnecessary. Marielle's golden treasure was selling itself.

A great sigh escaped Kathy's lips and she lightly touched each of the small golden visages with gloved fingers. "Slain warriors," she said at last, breathing the words like a mantra. "They're absolutely wonderful." When she glanced at him there were tears on her lashes.

"Would you like to see the rest?" he offered, pleased at the visible impact the icons were having on his prospective buyer. "We've already photographed the badges and sword decorations. They're in this box." He stood aside and studied her body language as she knelt to examine the contents. It was clear she'd move heaven and earth to own the lot and he alone held the key to a sale. It was going to be a good day. And hopefully a good night.

Duncan continued to photograph the gold as Kathy examined the articles in each of the other cartons. Her perfume was as wonderfully exotic as he remembered and Jeff allowed himself to appreciate again her slender figure while she stooped to pick up the ram's head mask. She turned it over in her hand and laid it briefly against her breast.

"That one's particularly fine," he pointed out.

"Yes," she agreed, "I think it's probably the best piece in the group." He decided to move things forward. Marielle could be stubborn, but she'd already agreed to explore the possibility with Burnside. She'd come around. Particularly when he surprised her with the full three million. Her son would be born a millionaire. No mother could say no to that. "I've talked to my client and she's definitely willing to consider a sale if we can come to terms," he told Kathy confidently.

"What terms?" Her voice was professionally casual. Her eyes did not leave the mask, but he knew he had her full attention. She wanted to buy and he wanted to sell to her.

"I'm reasonably certain we can come to an agreement that can be concluded within, say, three months, but it would have to include a provision that the sale would take place after the trust is in place and taxes have been paid." He studied her as she processed this information, her eyes still studying the golden ram.

"I explained that we would have to reconsider our offer if a trust is involved," she answered silkily.

"Yes, but you didn't say why."

She replaced the ram carefully in its carton. "Because we are then dealing with courts and lawyers and things become difficult and expensive. We have to employ our own lawyers to participate in the negotiations and everything bogs down at the least complication."

"There won't be complications."

"Of course there will. In that event, I withdraw our original offer and reduce it to two million five." She was serious. She wasn't going to bend in spite of her desire to own the gold that surrounded her. Jeff was annoyed at his miscalculation.

"Half a million for lawyers?" he chided.

"No, half a million for aggravation." She looked at him wickedly, and he realized she was doing some very skillful negotiating. He decided to be more careful.

Marielle's baby would arrive sometime in late June and the trust would immediately go into place. Three months from then would be September, October latest. Plenty of time. "Three million," he insisted, laughing at her implication. "If the seller causes complications that extend the closing ninety days beyond the date we set, we'll take the lesser price. On the other hand, if the buyer creates problems, it's still three million."

"Done." They shook hands, hers lingering in his a fraction too long. "Let me call my office and have them start on the paperwork." She gave him a brilliant smile, full of promise.

"Use the phone in Duncan's office," he offered. "It's too early in California to confirm with my seller but I'm certain she'll agree. Then I want to take you out for the best dinner in London to celebrate."

When she returned a few minutes later, he looked up with the satisfaction of a done deal. "All set?"

"I'm afraid not," she said. She seemed distracted and his first thought was that it was another ploy.

"Why? What happened?" Instincts on the alert, he tried to determine what could possibly have occurred in the last three minutes to cause her to change her mind. Something he'd overlooked? What else could she want?

She moved through the room with purpose, picked up her huge leather purse, gathered her cape and walked to the door, prepared to leave. "I've been advised not to proceed. There's some question about the ownership," she said abruptly, not looking at him.

"Wait a minute," he challenged, unable to comprehend. "You're rescinding your offer? What question? What's the problem?" He stopped her at the door. If this was a ploy she was playing it to the hilt. "The ownership is clear," he insisted. "We have a deal."

Unfazed, she opened the door and spoke to the two guards.

"Gentlemen? Will you come in please. Mr. McCleary and I will want you to witness this." Her voice was crisp and authoritative, with an edge of irritation.

Still trying to process her shift in tactic, he was a beat late in recognizing that something central had changed in the situation.

"I have something to show you." She searched in her purse for a moment, then paused to hold the door for both men to enter. "It's in here somewhere." When she turned back to the room he saw the heavy automatic in her slender fingers.

"Oh, no." He felt the dead weight of helplessness settle into his shoulders, an iron-clad revelation that he was entering a nightmare. "No," he said again in denial. "This isn't happening."

The guards spun in unison at his words and froze in response to Kathy's pointed gun.

"You're not doing this. Tell me you're not doing this. . . ." The thought kept repeating itself in an absurd attempt to stop what was going wrong until he could figure out how to fix it.

"You gentlemen will please be seated, you here, him over there. Place your hands on your heads and don't do anything foolish." Kathy was polite, but no-nonsense.

The chagrined guards sank slowly to their assigned places on the floor; hands raised to the tops of their caps, both men's eyes betrayed embarrassment and anger. The photographer immediately pushed his hands high in the air and sought refuge behind the large immobile camera but Jeff stood frozen in the middle of the room, refusing to accept what his brain told him was taking place.

"You can sit down, too, Mr. McCleary," she directed. "Duncan, you remain standing. We're all going to have a little chat for a few minutes and no one will get hurt if you do as I ask."

There was a light tap on the rear studio door, then three more taps. Kathy directed the photographer to open his back door to two thin black men in impeccable business suits, gloves, and white ski masks. One held a sleek automatic pistol, the other carried a roll of duct tape. Jeff would remember later that it was at this point that he abandoned any hope that the theft wouldn't happen.

The first man stood watchfully in the doorway to the studio; the man with the tape moved silently into the room, quickly disarmed both guards, and efficiently wrapped their wrists and ankles with the tape, adding a small strip across each man's mouth to ensure silence. Duncan was similarly immobilized while Jeff sputtered in appalled frustration. "I trusted you. I can't believe I was so stupid."

In the next instant the silent black man used a minimum of motion and energy to tape Jeff's mouth and wrists and ankles. He sat without choice in an impotent rage as the bright golden objects began disappearing into the cartons, a sight he would see in his dreams for years. Everything, all three million dollars' worth, was packed within an incredibly brief period of time and the boxes disappeared one by one out the exit door to the alley.

Then it was very quiet in the studio. The only sounds Jeff could discern were the swoosh of blood as his heartbeat crashed in his ears, the breathing of the three immobilized men on the floor around him, and the clinking of glass on metal preceding the splash of liquid as Kathy emptied various bottles of developing chemicals into the darkroom sink. In the next few minutes she methodically immersed all the film from Duncan's efforts that morning in the destructive bath.

When she opened the back of his camera to expose the film within, Duncan moaned in professional agony while Jeff seethed at his own stupidity. He'd breached his own security. There was no one to blame but himself. The tape on his mouth pulled against his skin and a sick, blinding fury at his own foolishness filled his throat. He'd turned his head for an attractive woman.

The two men returned for the last of the cartons, then disappeared, never having spoken a word.

Finally, Kathy stood in the center of the room and began to undress before the four totally astonished men seated on the floor.

"One thing I've found in life, there are always lessons to be learned." She directed her comments to the two watchful guards. "Let me tell you something about trust. Portuguese sailors arrived in Africa in the thirteenth century with some very interesting cargo." She unbuttoned the jumpsuit, slid it off her bare shoulders, and let it drop to the floor. She stepped out of the shiny black pool of cloth. "They had all this money, lots of pretty beads and mirrors, and in the holds there were hundreds of huge stones nicely cut into squares. Used it for ballast."

She nudged the silk into a pile with her foot. She turned to face Jeff she stood with her bare back to the two trussed guards. The briefest of black lace panties and her black silk gloves shone dully against her skin. As furious and crazed as he was, a part of Jeff's brain couldn't help verifying his first assessment of her body. The boys in the frat house would have agreed. She was braless perfection, category C. Bitch.

"They approached the tribal leaders in the towns along the coast and explained that they had masons and holy men on board and requested permission to build churches. Great big ones," Kathy continued, unperturbed that she was nearly nude and undisturbed at the men's absolute attention. The bracelets came off her wrists and she unclipped the earrings and created on the rich black silk a gleaming pile of gold that winked and gleamed in the bright studio lights.

"In exchange for land for the churches, the ship captains promised they would have their holy men perform great and wondrous blessings on the people." She took a pair of athlete's socks out of the purse and balanced gracefully on one foot, then the other, delicate as a dancer, while she pulled them on. Then she dug in the bag for more clothing: a worn pair of jogger's pants, a baseball cap, and a man's faded blue sweatshirt.

"The chieftains would agree after payment of a suitable tribute and I don't know for a fact, but I have to assume there was always a measure of trust involved that the blessings would indeed take place. There was certainly negotiation for the purchase of slave labor." Finally, she produced a pair of running shoes.

"Eventually trust was given, agreements were

reached, land was set aside, and the slaves they'd bought unloaded the stones and hauled them to the land involved."

Despite their indignity, her audience was entranced as she slid her lithe, braless body into the running gear and picked up the shoes.

"And don't you just know it, once those churches were built and the people of the village had been blessed as promised, the buildings were armed as fortresses. It's true," she told them pertly. "But you won't find anything about it in history books because history is always written by the victors."

She looked at Jeff and shook her head sadly as she slipped her feet into the running shoes. "So let's you and I discuss trust," she said to him. "I told you I planned to invest in the gold and make a profit with publicity and public display. You used that information for your own benefit. You went against me within twenty-four hours." She positioned the cap on her head and tucked in her hair, ebony eyes gleaming in her beautiful face.

He stared at her, unable to deny the charge.

"Don't talk to me about trust," she said and smiled at him. Still wearing the gloves, she carefully tied her shoestrings. The gold jewelry, the black silk clothing, and her sandals were whisked inside the bag as the phone began to ring.

"Time to go, my dear."

Helpless, Jeff watched her approach.

She bent forward to put her gloved hands on either side of his head and held his face as she kissed him through the tape that sealed his mouth—a long, lingering kiss. "Bless you, my son," she said clearly, liquid black eyes triumphant. "What goes around, comes around, and you had this coming."

Then she picked up the bag and walked on silent cat feet through the door; it closed and they heard a solid click as the lock turned on the other side.

They were found three hours later by a curious London bobby checking up on the security truck parked after business hours.

24

April 8, 1990

Life in hell continued. Thomas's T-shirt was wet from an exhausting workout on the rowing machine. When he stepped out onto the far corner of his balcony to look out at the city of Westwood, moisture in the fabric began to evaporate and created a bracing cold against his skin. He located the giant red brick UCLA complex that housed the neonatal ICU where Katherine Dana lay sleeping. He was frustrated that she was still there, frustrated that her existence was the key to the one dilemma in his life he couldn't solve until she was released and at least had a shot at good health.

He shifted his gaze to the roof of a small house on Villa Rosa Drive, part of a small residential pocket that had survived developers in the area. It belonged to Shirley Canfield, and according to Shirley, Marielle had taken up residence there last month.

Once in a while he'd been able to get a glimpse of her in the backyard by the pool. On rare occasions he'd watched her take a walk and followed her progress for a few minutes before losing sight of her among the trees that lined the street. The distance was mere inches in his sight line, not more than four and a half city blocks in real space from where he stood, but either measure of distance translated into an insurmountable obstacle that all his power and all his money could find no way to cross. Yet.

Until he could manage, she was there and he was here and the baby they'd watched and worried and cared about was about three miles from them both, separating them as surely as a chasm. He welcomed the ache of his tired body and returned to the punishment of the machine as his mind sought a solution.

He hadn't been able to say or do anything to convince Alissa there was nothing between him and Marielle. His refusal to identify her by name had confirmed in Alissa's mind that he was hiding something. They'd had another furious confrontation that morning.

"I have pictures of her and if she shows up there again, I'll have her followed. I'll find out who she is," she'd threatened.

He'd been confounded at her admission. To discover his relationship with Marielle, Alissa would have to have spied on him first. His singular lack of reaction to this logic brought home to him that nothing she did surprised him anymore.

"Is it yours?"

She'd thrown that one at him again with eyes narrowed to slits of suspicion.

"Jesus Christ, no," he'd shouted at her, out of patience at the ridiculous accusation. "She's a friend who happens to be pregnant. There are women who manage to get pregnant without my participation, you know." He'd glared at her, all too aware that he was being reckless and walking on thin emotional ice, dangerously close to nailing her about Dana's paternity. Knowing that once that box was opened there'd be no going back, he'd shifted ground. If she left, Dana would go with her. As always, the price was too great.

"What do you want, Alissa? Let's get to it."

"Swear you'll never see her again," had been the first demand.

"I agree that I won't see her as long as you don't pursue the situation."

"You'll never see her again, period. And I want a restraining order against her. She's never to go near Katherine again."

"That's ridiculous. She has to have our permission to see the baby. The hospital wouldn't let her in anyway."

"I want a restraining order!"

The thin hold on his temper had snapped. "Then call a lawyer and get one! Go through my Rolodex and put all my friends' names on it while you're at it!"

"You're right," she said maddeningly. "I want a letter from the hospital stating that no one will be admitted to see Katherine without my written permission."

"Barring my family, okay. Whatever. What else?"

At his cooperation, she began to calm down. "I want you to come home nights."

"I'll start sleeping here again. What else?"

"Stop saying 'what else.'"

He ground his teeth to keep silent.

She switched to a wheedling tone. "Thomas, I don't want our life together to go on like this. Can't we work this out? Can't we start over? You never make love to me, you look right through me when we talk. No wonder I'm upset."

He waited in silence, doing his best to placate this woman he no longer knew. She waited him out, determined to get his agreement. He gave ground to break the stalemate.

"It's going to take a while, Alissa. You can't expect me to overlook everything that's gotten us to this impasse."

"Yes, but that's all over. I did some things that were wrong. I admit it. But I didn't mean to and it's all been fixed. The doctors say she'll be able to come home in a few weeks. She's gaining weight and she's going to be okay."

"I hope so." He'd rubbed his forehead to ease the perpetual headache he seemed to have these days. She'd always been selfish, but when had she entered this total self-preoccupation? Was it new since her pregnancy or had he overlooked it somehow? He didn't know anymore. She'd become a black hole. Everything in, nothing out. Events either pertained to her or they didn't exist. If it wasn't for Dana . . .

"I have to go back to work tomorrow or they're going to sue me for breach," he reminded her, "maybe cancel the series. Right now I'm going to put in an hour on the rowing machine and then go to the hospital."

"What time will you be home?"

"I don't know, late. I can see her at six and again at nine. You want to go?"

"No. I'll wait up for you." She'd stopped at the door. "I do have someone watching. I'll know if she's there." She'd turned and walked from the room. He'd picked up the phone and called Barry Cooper.

At six o'clock, he spent his allotted ten minutes with Dana, then drove to the Mandarin Garden to meet Barry for an early dinner. Cooper, trusted friend and longtime attorney, had vehemently warned him against the marriage. Thomas knew he sorely needed his friend's advice once again.

Barry was waiting in a booth by the restaurant's trademark water fountain where they were unlikely to be seen and could not be overheard. Thomas ordered a drink and quickly got to the point. "I intended to stay until the baby was born. I never anticipated this kind of complication." He downed the last of the Finlandia double, his first drink since Dana's birth, and gritted his teeth at the raw bite of the vodka. "I know you don't think she'd have done it but you don't know her like I do."

The lawyer sighed, commiserating. "If it's any consolation, now, I think you were right given what you've just told me."

"So what's your advice, counselor?"

Cooper sipped his wine. "She never signed the prenuptial. Even if there weren't a child to consider, a divorce is going to be quite expensive."

"Expensive is rapidly becoming a relative term."

"Without the agreement, I figure you'll sustain heavy damage," continued Cooper, "but you can withstand it financially. We can make the case that what you had before you got married is your separate property, which we'll agree to place in trust for your daughter in the event of your death, but you'll have to give up at least half your income from *Winter Love* to Alissa. Your fee was four and what?"

"Four million flat. I had to give back the points. I won't argue with her about money. What else?"

"Certainly it's going to be personally and professionally painful. Considering the medical condition of your daughter, no jury in the world will grant you sole custody unless you're willing to get really messy. You'd have to prove Alissa unfit or dangerous to the baby. Very public, very destructive. I don't see that in you, my friend."

"Don't be too sure." Thomas studied the ice in the bottom of his glass. "Hypothetical question," he said carefully. "Just for the sake of argument, what about custody, if Dana weren't my child?"

He saw Cooper's eyebrows lift slightly and felt his friend's open scrutiny for a few moments. The lawyer shifted his gaze to the graceful fountain and Thomas waited while one of the best legal minds in the country filtered through the legal ramifications. Finally Cooper framed his professional opinion.

"You haven't a chance in hell, my friend. You'd have to prove Alissa was an ax murderer in front of thirteen witnesses, and there still wouldn't be any guarantees.

Dana comes with at least two million dollars attached to her mother—probably closer to five by the time we fight this out. More if the movie's successful overseas. Even if you succeeded where Alissa's concerned, there could be a carload of relatives *she* never even heard of filing suits for custody."

"That's what I figured."

"Is there anything you want to tell me?" Cooper was doing his best to be discreet.

"No." Thomas changed his mind. "Yes. You're going to think I'm certifiable, but there's another woman."

His friend's glass of wine stopped in mid-air.

"She's a friend," Thomas justified. "Well, she was more than that but right now she's truly a friend. She's really special."

"Hell, Thomas, given your situation, it's purely understandable."

"I met her last year and we had a . . . I don't know what we had. Some kind of crazy, off-the-wall thing, before this whole fiasco started. She called it off when I married Alissa."

"Oh?" Cooper was surprised again. "Another woman's hell on juries," he warned. "Hard on careers, too, if you're not careful."

"It's not like that. I was seeing her at the hospital with Dana, until Alissa found out." Thomas started to order another drink, then changed his mind and waved the waiter away. "I can't stop thinking about her. The crazy thing is—and you're really going to think I'm nuts—she's pregnant. Very."

Cooper lost his customary cool. "Don't tell me it's . . ."

"Oh, no," Thomas said absently, distracted by the thought. "Alissa sure thinks so. I think it's her ex-husband's. I was planning to broach the subject the other night at the hospital but then Alissa came in—and I already went through all that. It doesn't matter, really. I don't care if it's his." Thomas paused. Truly, the paternity of

Marielle's child held no importance, and the admission sat well with him.

"Anyway, the reason I mention it is she's tangled up in a really bizarre kind of inheritance situation and she may need some legal help."

"I'll be glad to see her," said his friend. "Besides, any woman that walked away from Thomas Saxon, I want to meet. I'll even charge half my usual fee. I take it you want me to put it on your tab?"

Thomas nodded soberly, then laughed.

The lawyer released his breath in a long sigh. "I have only one question and I won't bring it up again." Cooper chose his words very carefully. "Are you absolutely committed where Dana is concerned?"

Thomas felt no hesitation in his being and answered immediately. "Absolutely," he said, knowing that it would continue to cost him dearly in human terms.

"Well, my friend, you've got a royal mess on your hands. Let me know what you want me to do." Cooper signaled for the check.

"As soon as I figure it out." Thomas reached for the tab. He gave his credit card to the waiter and Cooper conceded the check. "I appreciate your friendship, Barry," Thomas said gratefully. "I really needed someone to talk to and friends in this business are hard to find."

He was back at the hospital by nine o'clock and into his green gown. This time when he put his hand in the Isolette, Dana's little fingers grasped his thumb and held on for several seconds before she grew tired. "You just hang on, sweetheart," he said, fighting the emotion threatening to close his throat. His pride in her came to the rescue. "If you will, I will. First, we get you out of here, then we worry about the messy part."

When he got home, Alissa was waiting. "How is she?"

"She's getting stronger. Dr. Goodin says she's passed the brain-bleed problem. They didn't have to give her medical treatment, which is a good sign. There's some concern about all the oxygen."

"I know about the problems." Alissa was impatient.

"There's not much else to say. She's getting better."

"I want to talk to you about *Winter Love.*"

Ah, the real reason she'd been waiting.

"What about it?" He dropped onto a sofa in front of the fireplace and dug in his briefcase for tomorrow's "Murder" script. He had an early call and there'd be complicated material with a stunt double, plus hours of makeup for the fight scenes.

"They're releasing it next month," she said, watching him closely.

Somewhere he'd known that. Some conversation with his agent between visits with Dana in which he'd been advised of his upcoming schedules and commitments. "Murder 101" had been on the brink of defending legal action by the network. He'd agreed to return to the series based on his expectation of Dana's continued improvement, and four scripts were waiting, the first one in his lap.

The movie's release date had been mentioned but hadn't stayed with him. He was surprised it was so close, but not particularly worried. His agent had assured him that the studio probably wouldn't require much involvement on his part.

Plus, he knew in his heart that the film was fatally flawed. He'd tried everything to call up enough talent, skill, or pretense to transcend his rage and frustration with Alissa. But it had permeated the film, poisoned his performance, and he remained convinced that no audience in the world would overlook it.

Obviously, the studio smelled disaster and had gone with a presummer release; in all likelihood, the movie was doomed to an early box office death. He felt bad for the rest of the people involved with the film, but for Alissa's hopes for stardom he felt nothing.

She sat next to him on the sofa and placed some documents across his open script, demanding his full attention.

"The studio wants to open it here in Los Angeles," she said to him. Her entire body was engaged in a tension that related solely to her career. "They're giving it the full premiere treatment."

"Since when?" There'd been no mention of this to date. Why suddenly a premiere?

"I've been doing tons of public relations," she pressed on insistently, "and there's really a lot of interest in the film. With the baby's birth and all, there's a very high awareness rating across the country. Demographics are wonderful." She indicated the report in his lap.

He looked at her. Dana had come in handy in her life after all. The situation was getting clearer and he could see where it was coming from. She'd been lobbying, no doubt using his name for leverage, and the studio had decided to ante up and keep her—and ostensibly him—happy. They'd hype the movie out of the gate, throw a premiere to promote media attention; if the first weekend was slow, they'd drop their support like a hot rock. A moderate opening would buy a couple of weeks of newsprint and a few TV commercials. After that, it was anybody's guess.

He picked up the report. Awareness ratings were gained through recruited screenings and questionnaires to theatergoers. They indicated whether or not target audiences knew about upcoming films and listed their reasons for wanting to see them. Demographics, or demos, as they were called, were broken down into male and female age groups.

Good demos from the studio's standpoint were those patrons who would spend immediate dollars at the theater backed with an interested group that would wait for videocassette release. The report was mediocre at best but Alissa either didn't know it or didn't care.

She moved closer to him on the sofa.

"I want your agreement that we'll go to the premiere together."

"All right." It might help the film and he owed the studio and the rest of the talent that much. With a little luck it would keep peace in his life until Dana was released and he could decide what to do.

Apparently Alissa had expected resistance and when he agreed, she broke into a radiant smile. For a moment she was genuinely attractive.

"Good," she said excitedly. "That's terrific. I'll start setting up publicity and promotion for us." She ran her hand up the inside of his thigh.

His reaction was immediate and profoundly negative. "You. Not us. I'll go the premiere but I won't have time for anything else," he cautioned her. "I can't do publicity and catch up on four 'Murder' episodes, and see Dana."

Her hand stopped abruptly and the smile vanished. He saw her girding for battle and drew a hard line. "I'll do the premiere. That's it, take it or leave it." He laid the demos aside and began studying his lines.

She was undecided for a full two minutes. He felt her energy reaching out, clawing at him. Then, abruptly, she got to her feet. "Of course. I understand. The baby's welfare always comes first." She picked up the papers and stalked out of the room with her victory.

Marielle knew that somehow she'd weather this new crisis. Inside her heart she had confidence she'd survive but at the moment there was this gigantic lump of something cold in her stomach that had lain there for two days. On the phone, Jeff's voice charged stridently on, still justifying his fury at Kathy Elwis, who'd calmly stolen every piece of the Asante treasure with his inadvertent help.

His words continued through her fog as brick after brick in the wall of grim reality was stacked neatly into place. Despite the expensive business card, London police had informed him Elwis Galleries was nonexistent in Brussels, Paris, or London; there was no record of anyone named Katarina Elwis anywhere, barring a deaf, aging dowager named Catherine Elwis who lived near Covent Garden. The gallery phone number was registered to a man who'd been killed in a plane crash four months ago; the address, a vacant office in a run-down warehouse in the Soho section of London. The police were attempting to locate the printer of the business cards.

The museum, too, denied any knowledge of the woman. It was strictly against their policy to give out information of this nature; too dangerous to irreplaceable artifacts, a breach of ethics, against their best interests as they still had hopes of acquisition, foolish to alienate a prospective seller, and so on, and so on.

The maître d' at the Marland House remembered Kathy Elwis very clearly and gave a sworn statement that she'd paid for lunch in advance with a great deal of cash and had not returned to collect the excess. He had no idea of her name; she'd walked in from the street and insisted on being seated at that particular table. He hadn't seen her since.

"She always wore gloves," Jeff rambled on furiously. "I remember thinking how unusual it was for a woman these days. We don't even have fingerprints," he raged.

Marielle was silent. Still too stunned by the turn of events to protest, she watched Abernathy and friends swim aimlessly in their glass bowl and heard Jeff's voice from a small distance, strained in anger and apologetic.

"I don't know what to tell you except I was a monumental fool and I'm sorry. I know it doesn't help, but I can't think of anything else to say." He paused and waited for her response.

She tried to answer but her entire being was still spiraling downward, approaching zero. It was some kind of lingering nightmare. This sort of thing happened to someone else, to people like Thomas Saxon. People who could afford it. Newspaper reporters asking for information and mentions on television news programs didn't happen to ordinary persons who lived in borrowed homes in Beverly Hills and were seven months pregnant.

She felt like a curiosity in a fishbowl. She had a sense of the vulnerability of Thomas's life that she'd never been able to appreciate before. Jeff's persistent voice came at her from the phone. "Marielle?"

She released her breath and was able to speak. "I'm here. I'm just trying to understand, I guess." It was gone. All of it. The likelihood of recovery was next to nil according to the investigators in London. "What is there to say, Jeff?" she said vaguely. "They'll either find it or they won't. What did the insurance company tell you?"

The leaden silence on his end of the line bumped her heart against her ribs and squelched any hope she might have mustered.

"They're still dancing around me at the moment," he confessed finally. "I think they're going to try to step out of the deal. They want their own investigation, which isn't unusual in itself, except I can tell from their attitude they're suspicious."

"Of you?" This was new and completely unexpected. In all the chaotic phone calls and exchange of information, he hadn't said anything about being under suspicion. Her heart galloped full speed and she sat back in her chair to calm down. "Why?"

The admission came slowly. "I didn't notify them that I was taking the gold out of the vault and they're hinging their position on a provision about adequate precaution. And being advised in writing that it was being removed from the bank," he added at last. Fear shaded his indignant voice.

"You're not saying . . ." She knew what it meant and couldn't believe it.

"They may not honor the claim, is what I'm saying." His voice dropped to a lowered register. "And if they don't we'll have to sue them." His joking statement about stealing the gold before he'd agree to pay the exorbitant British tax streaked through her mind. She firmly suppressed the thought as ridiculous but there was a sour taste of bile in her mouth. To sue an insurance company would take months, perhaps years. And a great deal of money. With no guarantees that an English magistrate or a London jury would agree with their position.

"Is that provision in the agreement?" Of course it was or he wouldn't have said it. Her mental reflexes were at half speed; her questions faster than the obvious answers. She felt as if she were talking through two feet of water.

Again, his hesitation, then a faint but fatal, "Yes."

Her heart sank. As a paralegal she'd had enough experience with law to know that a contractual arrangement with anyone included all the provisions. You couldn't abide by some and not others.

Everything in the agreement was in full force and effect from the time he'd taken the coverage and if there was a provision that the insurance company was to be notified, she didn't have a leg to stand on. Claiming ignorance of the provision wouldn't hold up in court. Unless the insurance company had inserted the provision after execution, which could not possibly have happened, she was bound by it. As a lawyer, Jeff, of all people, should know that.

Anger filled her chest and threatened to spill over and she fought against hurling accusations at him: Why didn't you follow the agreement? After all your lectures to me about verifying credentials, how could you be so foolish? How could you let this happen to me?

But the answer to each question was the same and kept her silent. What difference did it make now? What earthly good would it do to scream at him long distance? It wouldn't restore the baby's lost inheritance. It wouldn't make everything all right again so what was the point? Besides, yelling at him would probably make him feel better and she didn't want him to feel better. She wanted him miserable.

"I'll fight this, Marielle! There's no way they can get away with this!" He was baying at the moon, tilting at windmills. "They can't arbitrarily decide I wasn't properly cautious. I had armed guards and a security truck. We'll let a jury decide!"

Jeff the lawyer talking. Jeff the lawyer, who'd let one small detail slip by. One small detail that had cost her a million eight hundred thousand dollars. Or was it three million?

Whatever it was, it was gone.

"I don't want to talk about this anymore, Jeff." She was suddenly unbearably tired of the whole thing.

"Do you want me to stay on in London and pursue this?"

"I don't care what you do. I'm too drained to deal with it right now."

Jeff was suddenly worried. "I know it's been a hell of a shock. Is the baby all right?"

"The baby's fine. Just say good-bye and let me get used to this."

"Jesus, Marielle, I feel like a total jerk. Can't you just scream at me or something? Call me an idiot. A moron. Anything. I feel so rotten I can barely function."

"Okay, Jeff. You're an idiot. And a jerk." She paused to let the anger pass. "It doesn't make me feel any better to say it, so please just let me get off the phone and try to adjust. If I need to talk to you I'll call you back."

When she hung up her hands were shaking and her mind began its race with restitution and denial. Maybe they'll find it. Maybe the insurance company will be forced to honor the policy after all. Yes, and maybe it's all some gigantic bad dream and it hadn't happened at all. *Like I'll wake up in "Dallas" and it'll be two days ago and everything will be back to normal,* she thought with supreme sarcasm. At least she could still call up a shred of humor for the occasion.

Her phone rang again and the bad news multiplied. It was Scotland Yard. An unctuous Inspector Morrissey.

"What can you tell us about this, Mrs. McCleary? Your husband went to great lengths to make the gold public, meeting with the reporters and all. Did you ever meet this Kathy Elwis person?"

"Mr. McCleary is my former husband, Inspector," she clarified wearily. "We've been divorced nearly five years." Her humor disappeared.

"Beg pardon," he said quickly. "It was my understanding that you were expecting a baby."

"Uh, yes, but . . ." She abandoned the explanation. "I've never met the woman."

"Ah, that would make more sense, then."

"I'm sorry?"

"Well, from all accounts we've received, this woman representing herself to be Kathy Elwis was quite an attractive young lady. It makes more sense now that Mr. McCleary might have been drawn in a bit."

"Sounds like someone who knows him," she said with the bitter edge of experience, angered and hurt that Jeff would be careless with her life over a woman. Again.

"We're not ruling it out, ma'am," said the Inspector. "It's entirely possible that you've both been under surveillance. It's not unusual in matters of this sort. It is unfortunate he invited her to the portrait studio, however. Might not have happened otherwise."

Her anger hammered to a boil. Jeff had neglected to mention that the woman had been young and attractive. The situation was becoming clearer. He'd been set up all right. And too embarrassed to admit it to her.

"Did you discuss Mr. McCleary's plans with anyone? It's not likely she was acting alone."

She told him about the incident at the hospital and described the photographer, as well as the meeting with Meta Kates. "She assumed I'd be exhibiting the material but we had no conversation pertaining to when or what preparation would be involved. I couldn't have told her where he was going to have it photographed, because I didn't know. She did have quite a bit of knowledge about me, however." She gave him the phone number from Meta Kates's card and he rang off after promising to keep her informed.

A few minutes later the inspector called again to let her know that the number was valid, confirmed by an officer in the Ghanian embassy in London. Meta Kates was a highly placed representative in the Asantehene's staff. Apparently her exploring the return of the gold pieces had been legitimate.

The rest of the morning was a blue haze of anger and regret. While the actuality of the gold had never reached a reality larger than solving the problems it had caused, part of her had embraced its existence with joy. Meta's intervention, her own acceptance of its origin and the resulting dilemma aside, having a desire to return it and enjoy the moral reward of doing the right thing was half the coin. To have it ripped from her life, taken without a thought to the hurt and destruction it would cause, was outrageous.

Little by little, however, she began to understand that her rage and sense of betrayal was no different than that of the original royal owners. Theirs was the seminal pain. Their rights of ownership had been ignored when their sacred articles had been taken without regard for the suffering that ensued. Her loss was not the first. Perhaps it was some elliptical justice that these things had been taken from her hands, as well as the decision concerning their return.

If she were honest, she didn't know whether or not she could have given back objects of such beauty and value. Something in her psyche would have screamed in the night for the rest of her life that she'd made a desperately foolish choice.

Then came another realization. This, too, was the kind of loss that had happened to Margaret Woods. Margaret's mother had rescinded an inheritance she'd promised to her daughter, disregarding any wish Margaret might have had, trampling her hopes and her future in the process. As a result, Margaret had evolved into a bitter, hurtful person.

If I hadn't discovered Billy McCafferty's crypt, she thought, *the gold might not have been found for another hundred years and I'd have gone through life on a different path.* Certainly not the path Margaret Woods had chosen. No amount of money was worth a life of anger over what might have been.

In truth, the loss of the gold had done little more than restore her life to its original course. She'd manage just as she would have had the whole thing never happened. This resolved, Marielle was able to put an end to her anger and move on.

25

May 22, 1990

Half of her wanted to go to the premiere, and the other half, the secret half concerned with vanity and insecurity, the half that considered her pregnant body huge and unattractive, was in full rebellion. The Breslaur Group, which had several major investors in the film, had invited Jeff, and after a great deal of soul-searching these past weeks and a couple of shouting matches, she'd agreed to accompany him to the screening.

Chastened and humbled by what had happened in London, Jeff was truly a changed man. He'd confessed to her at last that he finally understood that he'd messed up both their lives by adolescent, macho fantasies and had asked her forgiveness. For this most costly transgression as well as for those in their marriage. His admission, for the first time since they'd known each other, was honest and not directed at excusing himself and she hadn't the heart to deny him solace. Gone was gone. Over was over. It served no purpose to look back with anger.

She'd agreed to accompany him to the premiere, but she knew in her heart that it had nothing whatever to do with Jeff, that the sole and exclusive reason was to satisfy her need to see Thomas.

She hadn't seen him since the unnerving incident with Alissa at the hospital and she had gained nearly fifteen pounds in the interim. Her body was burgeoning out of control and her ankles puffed to the size of baseballs on a regular basis; she practically lived in the bathroom from the pressure on her bladder, and no matter how much she ate, being hungry was a way of life.

Her sensible self reveled in the wonder of it all, fully aware that her body might never produce another child, and celebrated her son as a joy of joys. Most of the time she sailed on, flags flying, secure in her maternal position.

The progress of her pregnancy had filled her days but no amount of activity had filled the void that not seeing Thomas had caused in her life. He had called twice to share the baby's progress and for that she was grateful; in the past month Dana had passed one grueling complication after another with flying colors and she, too, hallelujah, was gaining weight on a regular basis.

In London, the investigation dragged on with no discernible progress. There was no trace of Kathy Elwis or the gold, and Jeff, contrite and immersed in a vast guilt, had vowed to handle the matter with the insurance company. She'd written a letter to Meta Kates explaining that the theft had removed any possibility of acting on her decision to return the gold, and had banished the matter from her mind to concentrate on her pregnancy.

When news that the treasure had been stolen appeared in the newspapers, her unsolicited mail abated to an occasional anonymous letter of snide and dimwitted congratulations on successfully "cheating the tax man." She no longer read anything from anyone she didn't know and had been forwarding all matters pertaining to the theft to Jeff.

She turned in front of her bedroom mirror and saw

yards and yards of Mediterranean blue crepe. Once again doubt sneaked in and perched on her shoulder. Maybe black would have been a wiser choice. Rose came in to sit on the bed and commented on the dress, swearing it made Marielle's eyes twice as blue. While Marielle agreed the color was flattering, she'd have felt a whole lot better if there wasn't so damn much of it!

"I feel like a swimming pool," she muttered, torn with indecision. As badly as she wanted to see him, she wasn't entirely sure she wanted Thomas to witness the extent of her rotundity.

"What do you expect?" Rose hit her with an unusually sharp confrontation. "You're eight months pregnant, for God's sake. Don't expect sympathy here. You have exactly what you want. You're healthy as a horse. Your baby's healthy." Rose slipped off the bed and started toward the door. "Some people would kill to trade places with you."

Marielle stopped her. "Thank you. You are absolutely right." She was surprised to see uncharacteristic pain in her friend's eyes and realized Rose was frightened. "What's the matter?"

Rose's face clouded in misery and she came unraveled. "His ex-wife's back in the picture. She had a big fight with the new husband and came home from Rome. She wants to get back together with Cal and the girls."

Occupied with her own vanity and insecurity, Marielle hadn't realized Rose was mired in problems of her own.

"Wait a second." Determined to bolster her best friend's courage, Marielle ticked off Cal's ex-wife's transgressions. "We're talking about a woman who walked out of her marriage, right? She married some guy for his money, left two small children emotionally screwed up and unable to deal with the situation while she played Miss, excuse me, Mrs. Jet Set? And you're telling me Cal's dumb enough to let her back in his life? Give him some credit."

"She's their mother," Rose reminded her sharply. "Don't tell me it doesn't make a difference, because you know it does."

Somewhere in her heart, fear struck deep at Rose's accurate assessment. She and her best friend were aligned in a similar war. They were both in love with men battling the wrong side of motherhood. And motherhood was a primal force to be reckoned with.

"What does Cal say?" Marielle insisted.

"I'm afraid to talk to him. I'm afraid of what he's going to do."

"If he was willing to take her back, you wouldn't want him anyway, and you know it."

Rose looked at her with stricken eyes. "That's easy to say, but I love him," she said simply. "If he goes back with her, I'll die. I know I will."

Marielle sat next to Rose on the bed. "This isn't like you," she challenged gently. "When did all this happen?"

"He called me last night," Rose admitted in a whisper. "I'm scared to death he'll do it." Her tears moved closer to the edge.

"Do what? Tear up four people's lives again? Five, counting you, to say, 'hi honey—welcome home' and, 'oh, by the way, did you and whatshisface have fun on the Riviera while my seventy-year-old mom was up nights taking care of our kids?'" Marielle put her arms around Rose and held her tightly, defying anything to go wrong in her life. "I don't think so," she lectured. "His daughters were basket cases three months ago. Nightmares every night. Wetting the bed. All that's gone. Besides, I've seen you with them and you're terrific. Cal knows that. Trust him."

Rose shuddered and pulled herself together. "Oh, God, I hope you're right. Some mother I'll make.

One move from the ex and I'm ready to crash and burn."

"Well don't do it just yet. Give the cavalry some time to arrive, okay?" Marielle heaved her blue body to a standing position and examined her friend. "Do you want me to stay with you tonight?"

"Oh, please! Like I need a babysitter." Rose was her old sardonic self again. "You are a fabulously pregnant, seriously gorgeous lady."

"As a matter of fact, I am." Marielle gave her another hug. The dress was suddenly fine and she felt marvelous.

"Don't you dare stay home, and you look terrific in that color." Rose peered nearsightedly in the mirror and began to repair her face. "What happens if Miss Ex-Texas sees you at the theater and goes off the edge again?"

Marielle sat heavily on the bed. Her one remaining raw nerve about this evening had taken a direct hit. All things aside, it was an unpleasant thought and she'd been avoiding it.

After a moment's consideration, Rose answered her own question. "Not while there's a spotlight, she won't. You two could turn somersaults tonight as long as she's on camera—just don't talk to her, whatever you do," she cautioned.

Marielle maneuvered her clumsy body off the bed one last time and headed for the bathroom. "I couldn't do a somersault if the fate of the western world depended on it. Unless they're screening it in the ladies' room, I probably won't see most of the picture anyway."

Thomas paced his bedroom balcony absently fingering the black silk handkerchief in the breast pocket of his tuxedo jacket. Shirley had confirmed to him earlier that Jeff McCleary was on the Breslaur invitation list and would be attending the premiere this evening with Marielle; she was checking to see if he thought there might be a problem with Alissa if the two women met.

Shirley assured him that she intended to be at Alissa's side at all times and they agreed that Marielle was entitled to attend the same public function without becoming a red flag. Still, he was apprehensive. You never knew with Alissa. He and Shirley finally concluded that in all probability his wife would be too preoccupied with her career and the press to make a scene. All the same, he'd be very careful not to talk with Marielle in her presence.

This was Alissa's night. When he thought of what it had cost in human terms, of how much she'd sacrificed to gain a foothold on stardom, his stomach recoiled. She'd moved a mountain to make this night happen and nothing, not another living soul, had better get in the way.

Somewhere inside the apartment she was changing her gown for the fourth time. The studio had assigned a hairdresser and a makeup man for her use, charging their fees to the premiere, and thus to the picture. The two men were passing the time with fashion magazines and bottles of Evian in the living room.

Thomas paused to look down onto Villa Rosa Drive and located the familiar rooftop of Marielle's house in the early twilight. Jeff's gray Porsche was parked in front at the curb, as usual. Street lights came on as he watched; it was still daylight, but their timers had not yet been adjusted to the later darkness of spring evenings.

After each day's shooting and his visit with Dana, he'd driven past Marielle's address every night for the past several weeks on the pretext that it was a shortcut to his apartment. At that time of night the house was usually dark but once he'd seen her silhouette framed in a bay window, seated on a couch, book in hand, and once in a late-night embrace with her ex on the front steps as he drove by. Since McCleary was the baby's father and there was obviously a continuing relationship, he was curious as to why they hadn't remarried, and perversely pleased they had not.

He hadn't stopped to say hello on the chance that Alissa had acted on her threat to have Marielle watched. If it was true, the last thing he wanted was a casual conversation antagonizing Alissa into breaking her truce with him; plus, it was entirely possible that she would take it into her head to retaliate.

She'd been gone the past three weeks on a whirlwind tour of personal appearances throughout the country. For him the time had been a nonstop spinning wheel of work and snatched visits with Dana, and blessedly quiet nights in the penthouse. He'd finessed Marielle's new number from Shirley to bring her up to date about Dana's progress. Alissa had returned unexpectedly last night from Atlanta, the last stop in the publicity barrage of television and personal appearances set up by Mason & Pearson to call attention to the opening of *Winter Love.* Stalking in well after midnight, he had the feeling she was disappointed to find him home and alone. Her manner left him pretty certain his instincts about being under surveillance were accurate. He knew she was angry and suspicious that he hadn't accompanied her, but he didn't care. It couldn't have been otherwise and he was through fighting about it. Life with Alissa was purely a matter of time and he was determined to be patient.

He'd been welcomed back to "Murder 101" and all threats of legal action had disappeared in a round of back-slapping visits from the president of the network, the vice president of the program department and two or three other VIPs of stature, each of whom had taken him aside to assure him that all had been forgiven, that it had all been purely a matter of business and nothing personal.

The show's producer and the series writers had been

kind enough to alter the plot location of two of the show's episodes to a college, and UCLA had granted permission to shoot on campus in exchange for a modest donation to their theater department. Thomas had been happy to pay the fee from his personal funds. Thus, he'd been able to continue seeing Dana on a relatively uninterrupted schedule. The power of celebrity. For the first time in his life he was profoundly thankful to have it and vowed never to abuse such privilege in the future.

Dana continued to be a marvelous living jewel in his life, uncorrupted and pure in her reactions to him. Still in her Isolette, she'd been declared free of withdrawal symptoms this past week, and was slowly gaining weight. She waved her fists in the air each time he saw her.

She was still too young to see him clearly, but sometimes now she had a smile that wasn't gas, and was growing a head of thick dark hair with red highlights. He didn't think much about her paternity anymore. There was no point. On those occasions when she flailed at the world and kicked with fierce determination, he wouldn't have given her up for anything.

Now when he touched her hand she immediately curled surprisingly strong little fingers around his thumb and would hold on for dear life. He'd been obliged to apologize to more than one director and crew for being late to a scene because he couldn't bear to unfasten her tiny hand from his. It may as well have been his heart. To keep him on time, the production company provided an electric cart for his use. Each day a group of students with walkie-talkies worked as volunteers to clear a path for the "Dana Express" so he could careen across campus from the shooting site to the hospital between scenes, for which he would be eternally grateful.

His housekeeper Thalia, had fallen in love with the little girl and had taken Marielle's place in the preemie ward on those occasions when he couldn't be there. When she'd agreed to stay on he'd kissed the sprightly woman's cheeks until she was bright pink with embarrassment. He'd handed her his credit card and a handful of cash to fix up the guest room nearest his bedroom as a nursery.

Alissa had refused to create a place for Dana, citing her concern that it might be "premature." There had been a massive group of baby gifts, of course, from his and Alissa's colleagues, friends, co-workers, and their various professional relationships; many of the toys had company logos affixed somewhere or other. Most of the gifts were still in the boxes they'd been delivered in and remained stacked in one of the guest rooms. Thalia had written thank-you notes and Alissa had signed them.

His mother, wheelchair bound and railing at her doctors in Colorado, had crocheted a beautiful cotton blanket in an intricate pattern of pink and white wild roses, with a matching layette. It had probably taken a hundred hours to complete. Alissa's sole comment had been, "Nice." They'd been returned to their box and stacked with the others.

Alissa's widowed father had called once from Texas to offer his congratulations; conversation with the man had been strained and mercifully brief.

His parents had flown in from Denver immediately following Dana's birth and had departed tearfully after a row with Alissa. His mother lived for the day that Dana would be released from the hospital; her failing health made travel difficult and Thomas had promised to bring the baby to see them for an extended visit as soon as he could get permission to take her on board a plane.

Booties and bibs and mittens still arrived from his mother every other week with notes to him containing no reference to Alissa; she and Alissa continued at swords' points over the baby's health. His father refused to speak Alissa's name and Thomas battled his anger over the unhappiness his marriage had visited upon his family.

Despite his previous experience at fatherhood, the entire area of baby things remained bewilderingly complex and involved decisions he was uncomfortable making without a woman's judgment at hand. With Thalia's guidance, he unpacked the gifts, kept appropriate gowns and blankets, and she exchanged duplications of strollers and diaper bags. Within three days they managed an abundance of clothing, a supply of proper-size diapers—Thalia insisted on cloth—and, built around his mother's gift, a wonderfully feminine room furnished in a warm mix of rose-and-white ruffled chintz and white pine. A fairy princess would have been right at home.

Once, late at night, he'd gone in and sat for a long while in the antique white pine rocker, studying the flounces and laced ribbons of Dana's bassinet. May thirtieth would be fifteen years since Noel had been born and Thomas was heavily aware of the vast difference between this beautiful room and the blue denim niche he and his wife had carved out of their shoestring Hollywood apartment in 1975. He'd searched his soul to determine if he felt differently about this room created for a child not his own, and had discovered he did not.

On the sidewalk at street level, two dots, one black and one blue, miniature people from his twenty-second story view, caught his attention. Jeff was escorting Marielle to the gray Porsche and settling her inside. Her baby was due in a couple of months. Unquestionably, she knew Alissa would be at the theater tonight and he wondered if she was nervous.

When the Porsche's taillights disappeared, he paced the balcony, impatient to get the evening underway. He checked his watch for the fortieth time and realized they were going to be very late. Joe had been waiting downstairs in the limousine for a full hour.

He reentered the living room as Alissa came flying in to demand an opinion of a stunningly low-cut Versace gown, bodice elegantly shirred in emerald satin and a gracefully belled black chiffon skirt that flowed to the floor. Her hair was rolled in huge curlers, massive diamond and emerald earrings swayed from her ears, and she held a matching necklace with a large emerald drop in place around her neck.

The two men in the living room were discreetly silent.

"Okay, what's wrong?" she challenged.

The makeup man tilted his head. "Well, the color is lovely," he commented, not unkindly, "but greens are so hard on redheads, don't you think? It won't leave me much time to redo your base. I really thought the Mackie made a much better statement, particularly with the sable."

"The Mackie," purred the hairdresser. "With your hair color, yellow makes a much more striking entrance."

Veterans of *Winter Love,* they'd worked with her long enough to know which buttons to press to make her nuts.

"I'll have to change stockings, purse, earrings, everything," she wailed. "Thomas, help me. I can't decide."

"This one looks fine, Alissa," he told her truthfully. In fact he didn't care what she wore so long as they could get started. She'd do what she wanted anyway.

At the disinterest in his voice she fled the room to find the Mackie gown. Her tormenters exchanged Cheshire cat smiles and settled themselves for another few minutes wait. He resigned himself to the delay and went back to the balcony. Thalia was standing by at the hospital, filling in with Dana until he could get there.

Restless, he adjusted the beeper at his waist. Borrowed for the evening, it was the latest in quiet technology. In the event he was paged, a message would move silently across the screen to let him know who was calling and where they could be reached. No disruptions in the theater during the film. He checked for messages, knowing there were none, and rehooked it to his belt.

Alissa didn't know it yet, but he'd already informed *Winter Love*'s producer that he wouldn't be attending the gala after the screening. It was a private party, purely industry oriented, and there would be no press coverage to be gained for the film; at best, it would be an evening of overt speculation about himself and Alissa that he could just as well do without.

It was her party and her premiere, let her go and enjoy it. The producer and his wife had understood about Dana and agreed to stand by to escort Alissa across the street to the huge tented complex that had been created for the postpremiere get together.

Eventually Alissa was ready. Coiffed and made-up to her satisfaction, volatile and wired for sound, she fastened a pair of brilliant Harry Winston canary diamond earrings in place. The makeup man and the hairdresser took turns tucking her, the yellow Mackie gown, and a new ankle-length sable coat Thomas had yet to see the bill for, into the limousine with care.

During the short ride to the theater, she lit a cigarette with nervous concentration, pooched her lips to keep damage to her lipstick to a minimum, and took precisely three puffs. She stabbed it out and checked her compact to see if repair was necessary. Forty-five minutes late, she was rigid with tension by the time they approached the theater, and Thomas was almost sorry for her. Almost.

At the sight of the traditional rotating searchlights throwing huge beams of light into the night sky and illuminating the surrounding buildings, Alissa finally smiled.

Joe maneuvered the big limousine to a stop directly under the marquee. A valet helped Alissa out of the car and only when she heard screams and applause did she seem visibly satisfied with her splashy entrance. Transformed, energized, she poured it on, playing to a large group of noisy fans who'd been cordoned off at the street. They in turn rewarded her with a frenzy of flashing cameras and pleading requests for autographs, which she briefly obliged, pulling him along as she performed the ritual.

Shirley materialized at his side to whisper that Marielle was already comfortably seated inside the auditorium; the thought eased his concern and he was able to concentrate fully on working the gauntlet of press and media crews jammed along the red carpet from the valet station to the theater entrance, without glancing about to find the one face he was interested in seeing.

Studio publicity personnel, conscious of their very late arrival and the magnitude of personages who'd been kept waiting for his and Alissa's entrance, tried to hurry them along so the screening could begin. At each media grouping, however, there were the inevitable questions about the baby, and each time Alissa assured the interviewer that she was leaving the premiere as quickly as possible to check in on her at the hospital, that she was here to show her support for her husband and the many people who had worked so hard on *Winter Love*, but her heart was really at the hospital with her Katherine.

The film crews ate it up, and Thomas hated her as much for the deception as the exploitation of her child. She'd been to the hospital precisely twice.

Inside the theater, Marielle glanced at her watch. The screening was to have started nearly an hour ago and she was very happy to be seated. Boyce had been unusually rambunctious until she sat down; standing with Jeff through professional hellos and prolonged political networking caused by the delay would have been impossible. Actually, considering the situation, she was remarkably calm.

Shirley had assigned her a seat at the rear of the theater with easy access to the exit as well as the ladies' room. If all went as planned, Thomas would pass directly in front of her to get to his seat and she'd be able to feast her eyes on him a full five minutes before the screening began.

She knew from Shirley that he planned to slip out to the hospital as soon as the lights went down, and from her position she'd know when he left the theater. Watching two hours of Alissa and Thomas together on screen, with an inevitable love scene, would be more than she could handle, thank you very much, and she had warned Jeff that she planned to go home early. In fact, she intended to leave as soon as she was sure Thomas had gone.

The premiere audience had drifted with professional slowness into the auditorium but eventually the rows set aside for notables had filled with members of the cast, the producer, director, their wives, the writer, composer, cinematographer, as well as celebrity guests and stars and studio executives, agents, managers, and the massive retinue that represented the creative team responsible for the picture. Finally she saw Thomas and Alissa move quickly into the theater and begin working the room. Shaking hands and greeting people they knew, being introduced to others, they moved down each row of seats as host and hostess.

Within moments, she saw him identify her location. He sent a mischievous smile and a slight wink in her direction; she returned the smile and basked in the warmth of his acknowledgment. He was wearing the same white silk Armani jacket he'd worn in Palm Desert the night they'd met and she bit her lip to hold back a smile when she recognized the black silk handkerchief in his breast pocket. She suspected he'd worn it on purpose.

Thomas continued to work the room with ease, glancing up occasionally to meet her eyes between handshakes and hugs and slaps on the back. The electricity of his charm was magic with each person he met and she felt privileged to be his friend.

She also kept watch on Alissa's progress, being careful not to make eye contact, trying to understand what had drawn him to the thin, tough woman holding court as executives and well-wishers made their way to her side. Shirley was glued to Alissa, laughing and chatting and introducing her, without once glancing in Marielle's direction. Shirley deserved an award for this, Marielle decided.

The lights dimmed in warning that the screening was imminent and people immediately sorted themselves into their proper rows. Latecomers were tucked into corners and last-minute seat exchanges were arranged. More important personages changed places with less important folk. Celebrities took seats held for them by studio-employed shills. There were half a dozen people still to be seated and ushers were rushing up and down the aisles, checking for available space.

Marielle saw that opening the door to leave the darkened theater might call more attention to her departure than she had anticipated. She signaled an usher that her seat was available and asked him to notify Jeff, seated with the Breslaur Group. A grateful guest stood by to claim her vacated seat and Jeff got to his feet to escort her to the exit as the lights dimmed a final time for the screening. Thomas was seated next to Alissa and in animated conversation with the producer, and didn't see her leave, but she didn't care. It was enough that she'd seen him and it was time to go.

In the lobby, she convinced Jeff to return to his seat. "There are a dozen cabs standing by," she pointed out, "and I want to visit the ladies' room before getting into one of them. Please don't wait for me." He accepted her decision, kissed her good night, and disappeared into the darkened theater as the music over the opening credits began to play.

When she left the theater a few minutes later, she passed a small woman engaged in a heated exchange with one of the security guards.

"I tell you I'm his housekeeper," the woman insisted. "I came here from the hospital and I have to see him!"

One of the television crews had taken notice and was standing by with a camera, just in case.

"And I'm his secretary," said a large, middle-aged woman whose ample hips had been squeezed into a gold sequined minidress. "He told me he'd leave a ticket at Will Call and they won't give it to me without identification. Does this look like its got room for identification?" She brandished a small beaded evening purse in front of his face.

The security guard held firm. "And I'm telling you that I spoke to Mrs. Saxon," he said to the first woman, "and she said she would take care of it."

"I'm not leaving until I speak to him," the small woman said firmly. "You take him this note."

"If she goes in, I'm going in, too," said the woman in the gold dress.

"Ladies, please." The guard refused to give ground. "I personally spoke to Mrs. Saxon," he repeated. "I told her you wanted to see her about the baby and she said to tell you she would talk to the hospital. Now that's all I can do. I'll lose my job if I let you in there. You know it and I know it."

"I don't believe they're out of seats," grumbled the gate-crasher. "They'd let Julia Roberts in, I can tell you that."

"There must be someone here who will listen to me," insisted the first woman, agitated and determined to go inside. "Get away from me," she admonished the large gold person at her side. "Thomas Saxon's secretary is Marcy Fercano and she's half your age!"

Marielle cautiously approached the group. Thomas's secretary's name was Marcy. "Why do you want to see Mr. Saxon?" she inquired of the small woman.

"I'm his housekeeper. He's not answering his beeper. I've just come from the hospital and they need to speak with him right away. I want someone to take a note to *him*, not Mrs. Saxon." She threw the guard a disgusted look. "You tell him it's Thalia."

The camera crew edged closer.

"Wait here." Marielle returned to the lobby and gave the note to one of Shirley's assistants. A few minutes later, Shirley emerged from the darkened theater blinking in the strong lobby lights. She took one look at Thalia, waved her inside the ropes, and went immediately back into the theater. A few seconds later, Thomas emerged.

"What is it, Thalia?"

"It's not an emergency but they need your permission to give Dana some medication."

"Where's a phone?" he demanded. "Why didn't you beep me? That's why I wore this damned thing."

He and Thalia followed Shirley into an office to make the call to the hospital and, not wanting to see Alissa, Marielle retreated to the valets' booth. She watched the theater entrance, worried that something had happened to Dana. Shirley came outside to ask the valet captain to call up Thomas's limousine.

"She's okay," she said to Marielle. "It's something about medicine to help her breathe. Thalia tried three times and when Thomas didn't respond to the calls, she was smart enough to realize something was wrong."

Marielle relaxed a bit. Dana had a history of being a period breather—a version of apnea. Once she'd gone ten seconds without breathing and the warning lights had come on with a light hum. Thomas had tapped the Isolette to get her attention and it had caused her to return to normal breathing. There'd been discussions of giving her a caffeinelike substance to stimulate respiratory brain centers responsible for breathing. Since treatment involved another drug, Thomas had asked that it not be given without his permission.

Thomas and Thalia came out of the theater to wait for the limousine and the camera crew began to set up for pictures. Shirley went over to explain that Mr. Saxon was leaving for the hospital and didn't wish to be photographed. The crew complied with obvious reluctance.

"Joe says he'll be ninety seconds, Mr. Saxon." The valet captain went to the curb, motioning away vehicles to clear a space for the limousine.

Thomas kissed Marielle's cheek, then took her hand. "Thalia told me you got her in. Thank you." He regarded the beeper in his fist. "Technology. I had the damned message button on Hold. I owe you big time for this one." His eyes held immense gratitude that gave way to concern. "Why are you leaving?"

"The placekicker's insisting," she said, resting her hand on her stomach.

"I'm glad you listen to him," he said circumspectly. "I'm sorry we won't have time to talk—"

Shirley moved quickly between them. "Alissa's coming out of the theater," she said quietly. "Marielle, get behind me."

Thomas turned immediately and moved to intercept his wife. The television crew and interviewer stepped quickly forward also, camera lights blazing. "Mrs. Saxon! Is the baby all right? Why are you going to the hospital?"

Alissa stopped to answer their questions and Marielle moved behind the valet podium. "I'll need a taxi," she told the captain.

"Yes, ma'am." The savvy young man hadn't missed her conversation with the famous actor and he immediately threw up his arm to signal a bright green Beverly Hills cab.

At that moment, Joe squealed to the curb in Thomas's limousine. He jumped out and flew around the car, opening the doors. The captain rushed to the curb to assist.

Thomas joined Alissa in front of the television camera to stop the interview.

"We're just going to the hospital to be sure everything's all right, aren't we, darling. Katherine's having a little trouble sleeping," Alissa was saying. "They tell me there's nothing to worry about but I just want to see for myself. I wouldn't be here tonight if I wasn't certain she was getting the best possible care. I'm sure you understand why we can't stay. Thank you."

The television crew, satisfied with its exclusive, shut off their lights and began breaking down their equipment as Thomas hurried Alissa toward the limousine. Joe got in the driver's seat while the valet helped the actress into the car. Thomas paused briefly to look at Marielle over the top of the limousine before he, too, disappeared inside. "Thank you," he mouthed.

Then they were gone. Marielle watched them drive away, then got in the lime green cab and went home.

26

June continued its slow crawl across the calendar.

Thomas no longer allowed himself to drive past Marielle's house in his commute to and from the studio. He stood on his balcony, drinking coffee and debating whether or not to phone to let Marielle know that Dana had been released from the hospital and decided to do it the next day from the set. No point in allowing her number to show up on the phone bill. Alissa's behavior altered from minute to minute and he'd have to make a decision soon.

From the night of the premiere, she'd been wild with fury, determined that the call from the hospital had been orchestrated in some vague scheme or other designed to allow him to go back on his word about attending the premiere. She remained convinced that permission for drugs could have been given on the phone or have waited another two hours. From the minute they'd gotten into the limousine and he'd reached for the car phone to talk with Dr. Goodin, she'd raged, and all the way to the hospital while poor Thalia cringed in the seat between them and pretended not to listen. Joe had rolled up the glass partition.

"I saw you talking to her!" she'd accused. "She's as big as a barn!" This with vicious satisfaction as she smoothed her own flat stomach in the shiny yellow gown. "What was she doing there? I know damned well I didn't invite her. You can bet sure as hell I'll find out who did!"

Her tirade continued well into UCLA's parking area. She shut it down long enough to accompany Thomas and Thalia inside the hospital and simmered with frustration during the thirty-three minutes it had taken Dr. Goodin to make himself available from the treatment of another newborn. Refusing to sit in the expensive gown lest it sustain damage, unwilling to be placated, she continued to repeat her opinion through clenched teeth that "this all could have been handled with a phone call."

During the meeting with the doctor, however, she switched gears; she was attentive and focused and nodded in agreement that the recommended treatment was necessary. She hadn't gone into the unit, however, choosing instead to wait in the doctors' lounge with Thalia. Thankful Alissa had elected not to participate, Thomas stripped off his jacket and slipped into the now-familiar green cotton gown in order to sit with the baby as the medication was administered.

Dana clung tightly to his finger and he talked to her all the while, aware of the irony that this was the longest time he'd been allowed to spend with this child since her birth. The medicine dripped slowly, methodically, into the intravenous tube and forty-five minutes later, both he and the doctor were satisfied that her breathing was improved. Dr. Goodin returned his attention to other patients and Thomas stepped into the lounge to report to Thalia and Alissa.

He'd barely finished when she resumed her attack.

"I know that cow's having your baby. Why can't you be man enough to tell me?"

He refused to continue the denials. She was obsessed with the idea and primed to fight about it.

"She was there with her husband. I saw them together."

The word *husband* slowed Alissa's momentum, but only for a moment. "Where was he, then? What was she doing outside with you?"

"She said she was going home. Her baby's due pretty soon, maybe she was uncomfortable. I don't know, she was just standing there. I was waiting for Joe." His patience perilously thin, he ground his teeth to avoid being baited further. "Look, I don't know how we managed to come out the door together and I don't know why her husband let her leave alone. I don't know anything except you have a child inside who's very ill and I'm tired of trying to understand why you won't even go in and look at her."

"I'll look at her when she comes home." Alissa's shrill voice was suddenly small and frightened. "I'll see her when she's normal." For that instant she was the woman he'd met seven years ago, approachable and in pain, but the moment disappeared and a curtain descended on the admission so suddenly that seconds later he wasn't sure it had happened at all.

One thing was crystal clear. Alissa was riddled with guilt for having delivered an "abnormal" child.

"That'll be soon," he told her gently. Grasping at the curtain, he struggled to restore their connection. "Dr. Goodin says she can come home next week if she gains a little more weight. She's already past the critical mark but he wants to keep her a little longer to be sure."

It was no use. He saw instantly that it was more than she could handle. She looked at the clock, picked up the fur, and edged toward the door of the lounge, nervously stroking the sable.

"I'm going back to the premiere," she announced. "The screening will be over in a few minutes and there's no point in staying here." She opened the door. "Let's go directly to the party. If we hurry, we can be there in time to greet everyone."

"I want to stay here for a while. You go on ahead."

"Thalia can stay. You've got a beeper."

"I'd rather stay."

"I'll send Joe back for you."

"I'm not going to the party, Alissa."

At the finality in his voice, her face closed like a steel trap and she escaped down the hall, gold high heels tapping a quick hollow rhythm on the green tile of the empty corridor; yellow fringe swayed wildly and shimmered in shining layers with her rapid movement, the glass beads glistening cold and vacant in the fluorescent lights. He watched her flee the reality of the hospital in her expensive Mackie gown, canary diamond earrings, and huge, ankle-length golden sable coat.

When she disappeared around the corner a weight lifted from his shoulders. He felt a profound sorrow at her decision, even as he understood. It was her night, after all, and there was nothing she could manage here. An imperfect child could not hope to compete with a party she'd worked and waited for half her life.

He called a limousine service and sat with Thalia in the cafeteria until the car arrived; he sent her home to get some rest with instructions to the driver to return for him at one o'clock. Restless, needing to think and work off some of his tension, he walked the busy streets of Westwood past the record shops, theater marquees, and fast-food joints, all brightly lit and buzzing, loud with the energy of college kids. He longed for their youth, the open promise of their lives and an end to the compromise that was his.

He was recognized in front of a pizza parlor and he forced himself to sign half a dozen autographs; moving on, he was identified again. Congratulations on his marriage and questions about the baby came pouring at him from every side and he reached inside for the lies and the charm, as always.

Somewhere among the smiles and the thank-yous,

somewhere midprocess, he was suddenly stricken by the realization that he no longer thought about his interaction with the world, that answers came out of his mouth as reality, and lying about a woman he hated and a child that wasn't his had become his life. Finally, he ducked into a theater and asked the manager to let him out a side entrance.

He cut across a parking lot and followed an alley. Three blocks later he entered the silent UCLA campus. Walking the grounds, anonymous at last, he passed the time deep in thought. He was able to see Dana again at 1:00 A.M. She was asleep and breathing normally. Convinced at last that he'd made the right decision about the medication, he found the limo and returned to the apartment and was able to sleep.

He was about to leave for an early call to the set when Alissa came in with a group of her friends, all of whom were still in a mood to party at 5:00 A.M. Joe, dog-tired and looking like death warmed over, insisted on driving him to the studio before going home to get some rest. Thomas had given him a week off with pay, but he'd come back a day early to drive Dana, four ounces heavier, home from the hospital.

At the moment, the baby was asleep in her rose chintz nursery and attached to a sensor device that monitored her breathing. Thalia was supervising the needs of an around-the-clock nursing staff. Alissa had made no comment about the converted bedroom and had spent the week on supremely good behavior. Conversation had been normal for a change, and even productive. She was good, even attentive, toward the baby and his concern lessened. Perhaps things would normalize after all and he could begin to think about sharing Dana's custody.

That morning she was leaving to resume her personal-appearance tour in support of *Winter Love* with no apparent regret at leaving Dana behind. She was serene and life was civil and Joe was busy loading her luggage into the limousine. He had another "Murder" script to prepare. The end of the series was approaching and as soon as it was in the can, he'd have five minutes to think about his life and what to do about this farce of a marriage. In all likelihood Alissa would demand to stay here in the penthouse and he'd have to think about buying another home. He'd have Marcy call his real estate agent tomorrow. With a last glance at the roof of the house on Villa Rosa Drive, he went into the study to get down to work.

Two weeks had passed, and he hadn't called.

"Boys carry in front," Shirley told her. "Girls give their mothers big hips, but boys carry in front." When she stood, her feet disappeared from view entirely and her stomach took on the appearance of a dirigible. Definitely a boy.

Boyce did relentless tap dances on her kidneys morning, noon, and night; sometimes she wanted to move her life into one giant bathroom and be done with it. Her bra size hit triple digits. Sleeping was uncomfortable, standing gave her a backache, and everything except floating in a swimming pool, which was forbidden, was inclined to make her cranky. Occasionally she gave in and enjoyed being out of sorts.

Despite the gala premiere, *Winter Love* had been savaged by the critics and public reaction at the box office was lukewarm, but Marielle had been unable to stay away. Two days after the premiere found her sitting through the film in a sparsely filled Westwood theater; she had to agree with the critics' assessments. The film throughout was fatally flawed by Alissa's over-the-top performance; the love scene in particular, which was pivotal to the plot, had been embarrassing and Marielle's opinion had been shared by at least two other women who'd laughed out loud in the middle of the movie.

Alissa's characterization of the heroine had been heavily inconsistent from one scene to the next and Thomas's performance, while technically valid, was clearly not his best work and even his good scenes had gotten lost in the muddle. When the two were on screen together, they seemed part of two different movies.

Marielle sat through it twice.

Then, from England, without warning, the tax statement for Boyce's inheritance had arrived. Theft or no, the British government expected payment of four hundred thousand dollars in inheritance taxes based on the treasure's valuation weight in gold.

Stunned to her socks, she met with Jeff.

"How can I pay this?" she pleaded. "I've already spent nearly twenty thousand dollars of the baby's money. This will take everything that's left."

"I'll look into it." Jeff tried to calm her down. "Technically, you would have inherited the gold in trust. Burnside managed to get it evaluated based on its bullion weight rather than its value as antiquities, which is good. However, since there's not going to be a trust, apparently they've decided to pursue you as an individual. If they get by with it, at least there will be less tax to pay. Let me give him a call."

"I can't believe there isn't a way out of this. How can they make me pay four hundred thousand dollars for something that was stolen?" The thought of losing all of Boyce's money made her crazy.

"Please let me worry about it." Jeff moved her from the dining room to the couch and sat next to her, waiting until she was able to put her attention on what he wanted to say. "This isn't the best time to ask, or maybe it is, I don't know, but I want you think about something else."

"What?" She stared at his serious face, forcing herself to listen.

"I want us to get married again."

She was taken by surprise. He'd been abject about the theft since his return from London and on ultragood behavior, even for Jeff. But, marriage?

"I'll take care of the taxes, but I want to take care of you and the baby, too." He was watching her carefully, absolutely sober in his intent.

"Jeff, this isn't realistic," she began tentatively, but he wouldn't be denied.

"I know we didn't make it once. I know it was my fault. I was an idiot and I didn't have a clue what I had with you—and I blew away the best thing in my life. What happened in London finally made me see what a fool I am. I've never had a clearer understanding of how much I took you for granted. I've had a lot of time to think about this and I want you back. I want to provide a future for your child. I lost it for him and the only way I know to make up for it is to be the best father I can."

She looked at him, most of her mind still reeling from the tax situation. The idea of marrying anyone had been so far from her thought process since getting pregnant that she was at a total loss as to how to answer him. All she could think about was that if the money was gone, she'd have nothing to secure the baby's future. She wouldn't have gotten pregnant if she hadn't had that money.

"Because you feel responsible is no reason to get married," she began wanly, feeling her way into the situation with care.

"It's more than that. I think you know I'm serious. You could have destroyed me over what happened. Personally, professionally, you could have wiped me off the map and you had every right to do it—but you didn't, so I know you care about me, maybe more than you think. I don't expect an answer right now or tomorrow. I'll take it whenever you want to decide. No pressure.

Either way, I'm responsible for the tax situation so that's the last thing you should worry about."

"How?"

"It's no longer your problem, it's mine. Let me handle it." He kissed her and walked with her to the door. "I know you'll need some time to decide about this but I've given it a lot of thought and I am prepared to wait. Just promise you'll think about it."

"Okay, I'll think about it." Marriage to anyone was the last thing she wanted to add to her agenda.

"Promise," he insisted.

"I promise," she said honestly. "I really will."

"Maybe we can talk about a brother or a sister for this one," he said quietly. "I'd really like that." He kissed her again and said good night.

She knew in her heart he was serious, that the old carefree Jeff had disappeared forever. In his place was this new, dedicated version. A man ready to accept the responsibility that came with marriage and a family and the million-and-one situations that constituted parenthood. Someone who knew all her foibles, someone she had a history with—some of it unpleasant, but some of it good. There were fond memories mixed in with the disappointments and the failures. Logic said that most marriages were a mixture of good and bad anyway, and so long as the good outweighed the bad . . . She'd have to think about it.

At the next meeting of the Mothers, Rose exuberantly announced her engagement to Deputy Chief Fireman Cal Logan and exhibited a modest but beautiful diamond solitaire in a simple gold setting.

"When his ex-wife found out he proposed, she tucked her tail and split," crowed the joyous Rose. "She tried to put a first-class plane ticket to Italy on his credit card.

She wanted to get to Rome to reconcile with the playboy before he got the divorce papers started. But the airline wouldn't take the card and she had to ask Cal for the money. He told her he'd pay for a one-way ticket in economy as a late wedding present." Rose slapped the table. "Little Miss Ex-wife took it and ran."

Marielle laughed at the glee in Rose's face. "Did you drive her to the airport to make sure she got on the plane?"

"*He* did!"

They all laughed at this picture until tears ran down their cheeks. Marielle had to leave for the bathroom.

"We've decided on October," Rose announced when she returned to the table. "It'll give the kids some time to get used to the idea and I'll be able to take a couple of weeks off. He wants to go to Yosemite. We've already booked the Ahwahnee Hotel."

"What a wonderful idea," Marielle told her. "It's beautiful up there at that time of year. The leaves change color, it'll be a true fall wedding."

"From there we'll drive to San Francisco and fly on to Paris. I can tie the whole thing in with a buying trip for Neiman's and save one airfare. My boss says it's fine with her."

Eventually the conversation came around to the subject of the devastating tax assessment, and Jeff's surprising proposal followed in its wake around the table.

"He was a major jerk, he was careless. Okay, so the British government would have taken most of it anyway, he still cost you a lot of money. Why the hell wouldn't you marry him to complete the package?" Rose was sarcastic. Jeff still had a lot of ground to make up where she was concerned.

"What am I going to do, Rose? It's gone. Nothing I say or do to him will change anything. In order to hate him or make him miserable indefinitely, I have to stay angry and I don't want to do that. Life's too long. If it would make a difference, maybe. I don't know. But it won't."

"I know you're right, but it still makes me gag. As your friend and godmother of your forthcoming child, I'll support you in whatever you decide." Rose held her hand so the light from the restaurant candle sparkled in the facets in her engagement ring and laughed. "I'm too happy to make anyone miserable. If he pays the taxes, okay. Otherwise, you're on your own."

"I have to admit he sounds like a much better risk than he used to." The inevitable Shirley question arose. "What about Thomas?"

"He's got enough to handle with Dana's problems and Alissa being so screwed up," Marielle said painfully. "She'll never give Dana up. Eliminate her only hold on him? She'll never do it. Plus, she is seriously unstable. If anything were to happen to Dana . . . with me in the middle? Hell wouldn't have her. The baby's going to need special care for years and someone who's as dedicated to her as he is won't phone in fatherhood. I have to accept that as a fact and make decisions based on what's best for my son."

The truth came to the surface at last, surprising her. "I want my baby to have a full-time father. Even if lightning struck and Thomas and I were able to get together—whether he knew about his son or not, a child of his would go with Alissa and I'd be the reason. He gave up custody once and lost a son."

She fingered the wooden doll on the cowrie-shell necklace. "I see no reason to tear him in two with decisions about how to handle having another child who, God willing, will be whole and healthy when he gets here. The best I could hope for would be a weekend father and I want more for this guy." She put a protective hand on her front.

"So you're really considering this thing with Jeff?"

Marielle looked at Shirley, surprised that it was true. "Yes, I am," she admitted. "I hadn't realized it but I guess I'm giving it serious thought."

The idea of marriage to Jeff, that had been so bizarre and so left field at the time, had assumed new proportion somewhere in her subconscious and she was genuinely surprised that it had eased into her reality so smoothly.

"I'm as astonished as you are," she said uncertainly. "I had no idea I was going to say that, let alone believe it."

At home that evening, getting ready for bed, she turned to Jeff's proposal, rolled it over in her mind. Certainly people grew, matured, learned from their mistakes. Life was a process of change, after all, and adaptation. Anyone who tried to live otherwise was whistling in the wind.

Finally she crawled into her blessedly firm bed, her body tented in her comfy pink flannel gown. She tucked a pillow between her knees to ease the ache in her back and studied the miniature of her namesake, Lilia Foxworthy Woods, staring out lovingly from the fragile silver frame on her night table. As she met the eyes in the portrait, she wondered at her grandmother's decision to marry a man who was not the father of her child, and acknowledged that at some point soon she, too, would have to make the decision that would affect the course of her life.

San Francisco, California, September 15, 1908

Lilia stepped off the train into the moist coastal twilight, exhausted and lightheaded from the smell of coal dust and smoke. Grateful to be free at last from the endless rocking motion and the mindless chuffa-chuffa of the coal-fired engine, she sought her land legs and tottered to a nearby bench.

Groups of passengers, lean men of desperate spirit,

miners, prospectors, some mere boys not more than twelve, descended hungrily from the train and leapt off its roof onto the wooden platform to catcall at hard-eyed young girls and fondle heavy-faced women of questionable intention waiting at the station. Within a few minutes the crowd had dispersed in a flurry of tied bundles, carts, and carriages, and Lilia was alone except for railroad personnel tending the motionless train.

From where she sat on the station platform, her view of San Francisco reminded her of a wondrous water color: beautiful tiers of mauve hills lined with hundreds of ornate cheek-by-jowl pastel-colored gingerbread housing, with a fine mist slowly drifting in from the bay that made them disappear, row by row.

Damage from the catastrophic earthquake that had made headlines in the London papers two years ago had all but disappeared and the life of the city seemed centered in the pounding of nails and sawing of wooden beams. Great teams of draft horses labored up the hills pulling heavy wagonloads of lumber and merchandise under the cracking of whips and the shouts of drivers, fueling the noise and construction.

"Here's your luggage, ma'am." An ancient Negro porter deposited at her feet the thin carpetbag that contained all she possessed and touched his cap out of respect for her condition. "You 'specting someone, ma'am?"

She shook her head and welcomed the kindness of his interest. "I'll need a place to stay the night, possibly a few days. Can you direct me?"

"You best get yourself a room at the Rigsby, ma'am. It's real clean and they serve a right good supper. You tell 'em Eddie Macon sent ya up and they'll treat ya fair."

"How far is it?" she asked.

"It's a pretty good piece. You oughten' to be walkin' it this time o' night. Fog'll be in soon." He signaled a pony cart, carefully helped her aboard, and put her worn blue bag under the seat. He accepted her coin with thanks, negotiated the driver's fee, and gave him the hotel's address before heading back to the train. "Eddie Macon, ma'am. Don't forget."

The streetwise pony trotted confidently into the traffic, picking its way through the chaos that was San Francisco and she watched their progress without fear. She was here. And Boyce would find her. Tonight she would eat well and sleep in a real bed and look her best for him tomorrow.

The stormy passage to America had been ghastly. Seasick from the rolling ship and nauseous in her pregnancy by turn, too ill to eat, her dresses were inches too large by the time the HMS *Marabelle* sailed by the huge French Statue of Liberty in New York's famous harbor. She had feared for Jameson's child. Halfway to her destination, she was too exhausted to continue.

It had taken a few days' rest to get food to stay down. Finally, she felt well enough to cable Boyce that she'd arrived. She struggled with her conscience for hours, then decided to bare it all beforehand:

> *Am alone in New York* stop *Am with child* stop *Jameson is father* stop *Do you wish to see me* stop *Harbor Hotel 135 Harbor Blvd* stop *Lilia.*

Thereafter a thousand doubts assailed her nights as her money rapidly disappeared, and fear that he'd gone from the address on the letter received so many years ago. Perhaps he'd moved after the monstrous quake and no longer lived in San Francisco at all, had even been killed. Had she made a mistake telling him about the baby? She had waited, her life balanced on the reply, and a few days later his answering cable had arrived.

> *Must see you* stop *Am sending money for train* stop *I love you* stop *Cable arrival time* stop *I love you* stop *Boyce.*

She'd been reduced to tears in the hotel lobby.

The traveling funds had arrived a few days later and the last of Elizabeth Woods's money changed hands when Lilia paid her hotel bill. She took a hackney to the New York train station. Once on board, she cried again in profound relief when the engine gave a tug on the line of cars destined for Chicago and began its long pull toward the bridge spanning the Hudson River. She sank into blessed sleep before the bulk of New York City slid past her window and woke only occasionally to eat or change positions to ease her back.

The next several days had seen a nightmare of delays due to fall storms and a flash flood that necessitated a multitude of train transfers. It had been impossible to notify Boyce with any accuracy of her arrival time.

Eddie Macon's name secured a clean, reasonably priced room at the Rigsby with a lock on the door and a bath down the hall. The following morning, she woke late and fussed nervously with her hair. She disguised her pregnancy as best she could with her finest dress and a colorful shawl. Crossing her fingers for luck, she sent the pony cart driver to Boyce with the address of her hotel. He was on her doorstep within the hour.

With an older, wiser face of the youth she remembered, at thirty-one Boyce Woods stood six feet tall with a grand lion's mane of hair, a large, bushy mustache, and a full and newly barbered beard. His body under the proper gray suit was hard and muscular. She was shy with him at first, embarrassed at her great protruding belly and ample bosom, but he seemed to take no notice and crossed the room to kiss her. A great, hungry, loving kiss it was and she kissed him back with gratitude and an outpouring of emotion she hadn't suspected she possessed.

"It's a dream, that's what it is," he told her. "I had no hope to see you again and here you are, beautiful as I remember."

All the right words, all the right gestures. Tears filled her eyes as she allowed herself to believe him. "Go on," she said chidingly. "I'm as big as a cow and you know it."

"Beautiful." He took her face in his hands. "And you'll be a beautiful mother, as well." He kissed her again, tumbled her carefully back on the bed and buried his face in her bosom. "I can't believe you're here."

His hair against her breast was rich chestnut in color and his face tanned from work in the sun; his big hands bore heavy calluses. She stroked his head and marveled at her fortune.

After a moment, he sat up and looked in her face.

"I own my own house, I have savings and a good trade. I'm a wood carver," he told her earnestly. "Since the quake and the great fire, I've more work than I can do. You wouldn't believe what people are willing to pay for cherubs and eagles."

"I can't imagine," she told him, emotion thick in her throat. His speech was so Americanized, she had to listen with great attention to understand.

He left her and walked to the center of the room, not looking at her this time.

"Is my father all right?"

"Yes," she assured him. "He's fine."

"Does he know there's to be a child?"

"Yes."

"And my mother?"

"She knows as well."

"Do they know you're here?"

"No."

He returned to her side and they sat holding each other for a long time before he said, "I think it best that we not speak of this again."

She nodded in silent agreement and he paused for a long time.

"I've always loved you. Will you marry me?"

Surprised, she said the first thing that occurred to

her. "It'll be half kin."

He kissed her again. "Married or not, it's to be half kin. Will you?"

Two weeks later, they stood before an altar he'd carved for the Church of St. Anthony's and said their vows in front of the cross. Jameson Woods's daughter, Lilia's first and only child, was born ten days before Christmas and marked the saddest and most joyous day in Lilia's life.

On that day, she wrapped in a square of silk and put aside the necklace and the cameo locket that contained the miniature of the baby's father she'd worn next to her heart for more than seventeen years. He was destined never to know his child and it was best to break all ties. She recognized this winter day as an ending and a beginning.

27

June 25, 1990

Marielle left work the week Boyce Jameson was scheduled to make his appearance to finish last-minute details of his nursery and stock up on diapers. And go window shopping for clothes she hoped to be able to wear at some point soon. But most of all to concentrate on herself and focus on every waking minute before he was born so she'd always remember this very special time in her life.

In southern California, as a general rule June was overcast in the mornings, the cloud layer taking until noon to burn off, and the afternoons were warm and breezy, melting into cool, moist nights. But these particular days were crystal clear from morning to night. Late-blooming jacarandas along her street rained purple blossoms onto the green lawns and quiet streets, and the magnolia trees perfumed the night with their huge white flowers, mingling with the marvelous jasmine. Each morning the doves sounded plaintive cries and the mockingbird on her block set up noisy territorial song just outside her bedroom window. Sometimes he sang all through the night.

Los Angeles and its surrounding cities were experiencing what inhabitants referred to as a Santa Ana condition. They said it as a single word: Sant'Ana. It was a reverse wind pattern. Warm, dry air swept in from the deserts through the Santa Ana Mountains toward the Pacific Ocean instead of away. In so doing, the wind generated an electric charge that affected the air and at night it transformed street lights and traffic signals and the lit windows of office buildings into scintillating, magical light shows. From a distance, red taillights of freeway vehicles seem to trail on the highway like molten flares and oncoming halogen headlights burst into star filters.

The line between magical and disturbing depended on point of view. To transplanted Easterners accustomed to moist spring weather, to cabbies and truck drivers and commuters hacking the freeways for a living, it was a short-lived irritation to be endured. For people who loved warm, dry, breezy weather, who'd had a good day, gotten a raise, had moved to California for year-round vacation resort weather, it was great. Desert hot met ocean cool.

Marielle Tèa Lilia Jonas McCleary was mellow. Serene, never happier, in tune with her body and the child inside, in tune with her life, she was about to give birth and the Sant'Anas were wonderful. It was as if her entire body was rewired for life.

Shirley called, inviting her and Rose to a last "pregodmotherhood celebration" lunch. Tonio's was closed for his annual trip to Mexico so they decided on the Fleurette Room in the posh Peninsula Hotel.

"It's your last chance to party without a little someone in the next room," Shirley teased knowingly.

Tuesday was chosen and they agreed that she and Rose and Marielle would meet at the Mason & Pearson offices, next door to the hotel. "That way if I'm running late they'll have to let me go," Shirley plotted.

"The old pregnant-lady excuse, eh? I can do that,"

Marielle waddled across the room, exaggerating her swayed back. "Check this out."

"You'll do. See you at twelve."

Struggling into support hose, Marielle convinced the reluctant stockings to stretch over her middle, which was substantially lower than it had been a week ago. "Pretty soon, kid," she said to her stomach. She'd noticed the gradual lessening of her baby's activity and knew he was running out of space. "Can't be too soon for my money," she told him. "You either, I'll bet."

She fixed her face with care and slipped into her favorite periwinkle silk maternity smock and a pair of matching stirrup pants and flat silver sandals. She'd never thought she'd see the day, but in truth she was actually looking forward to wearing high heels again. The white cowrie-shell necklace went smoothly in place around her neck and she tied a portion of her hair atop her head in a Pebbles ponytail and let the rest trail lightly down to her shoulders. She topped it off with a sassy silver shawl against the inevitable air-conditioning, dumped a generous portion of fish food in for Abernathy and company, and left to meet the Mothers.

As she anticipated, Rose was late and Shirley was still in a meeting, but since she'd gotten there a bit early she settled in to wait. Shirley's secretary, Louise, made her comfortable in the reception area. A few minutes later, the door to Jon Mason's office opened and he and Thomas Saxon walked into the reception area. They were engrossed in conversation and didn't see her right away.

She felt her face flush at the sight of him. He was casually dressed in white leather tennis shoes and faded Levis, and she recognized the gold cashmere sweater he'd worn to the cabin that weekend. Her pulse did a leap into fast-forward at the memory and an unsettling shiver dived to the base of her spine. Had it really been nine months ago? She looked down at her belly and stifled a chuckle. Boy, talk about living proof. She sat rabbit still and listened as Mason put forth his argument.

"The public doesn't pay attention to reviews," he was saying. "They decide what they like and don't like at the box office. I personally think Alissa did a terrific job, being pregnant at the time and all. Both of you were terrific. It's gonna build as a word-of-mouth movie, wait and see."

"I hope you're right, Jon," Saxon replied. "I wish I could do more to help."

The movie's a dog, thought Marielle. *A real arfer. Alissa's horrendous and you, Jon Mason, are a liar. I know because I'm the public and I've seen the movie. More than once.*

She searched her mind for something, hopefully inspired, to say about *Winter Love.* She struggled to formulate a kind comment to have on the tip of her tongue when Thomas noticed her. What could she say that was positive, and not a lie?

The two men turned in her direction and Thomas's face creased into a smile of greeting. He excused himself and crossed the room to say hello, doubling his long, gorgeous body to stoop next to her chair so she wouldn't have to stand.

"This is certainly a nice surprise," he said, and brushed his lips against her cheek.

Kneeling next to her, his face inches from hers, he was so incredibly handsome that it still took a moment to get used to. Without thinking, she put her hand on his forearm. The smooth golden cashmere beneath her fingers and the scent of his cologne sent her mind crashing back. Masculine in every sense of the word, his drop-dead good looks and intelligent eyes that missed nothing, that body, the faint cologne—it had all been hers for a night and a day. For an instant every atom that made up her being ached at the loss of him.

She was almost grateful when Jon Mason strolled over for an introduction. Thomas helped her to her feet and kept a steadying hand at her back. Mason gave her a jovial greeting and shook her hand, clearly uneasy with her pregnancy. “So, have you seen *Winter Love?*”

“Twice,” she said brightly and closed her mouth tight as a clam.

“See?” said Mason. “The public speaks. Nice to meet you, Mrs. McCleary.” He excused himself to confer with his secretary.

“Twice?” Thomas’s famous brown eyes sparkled and he gave her a liberal helping of the dazzling Saxon charm. “What were you, trapped in the theater?”

Caught, she had to laugh at his candor. Stuck for a follow-up line, she struggled for sincerity. “Really, I . . .”

“You’re ahead. Stick with it,” he advised, smiling, and indicated that she should sit down. “I know how bad it is. Jon thinks he has a mandate to keep me happy.” The charming facade melted into genuine warmth. “Are things truly well with you?”

Her feelings sprang up again; the heat from his body, the look in his eyes, and his undivided interest in her welfare were tipping her sideways. She felt her psyche drink it in like a starving child. Defenseless, she realized she had to be very careful or her secret could come spilling into the open in the middle of a business office.

“Very well,” she said quickly, determined that whatever else happened she wouldn’t go near the subject of Boyce Jameson’s birth. “So, Dana’s home now.”

“She is.”

There was a father’s pride in his voice and his face radiated a new and subtle quality she hadn’t seen in all the time they’d spent together, a quiet joy in his daughter. She refused to allow a reaction on behalf of the child in her body. Dana was entitled to his love.

"Gaining weight like a champ," he bragged shamelessly. "I wish I had her with me today so you could see her. She's still a handful and I've been chasing myself in circles catching up with the series." He glanced at Jon Mason, who was now on the phone. "Now they're pressing me to promote the film."

He studied her with care and she was supremely conscious of her size. "I'm here to lunch with Shirley," she explained. "A premommy thing. I had no idea you'd be here. Shirley didn't mention it."

"It wasn't a planned meeting. I decided to drop by on my way to this afternoon's location. We're shooting the L.A. skyline, taking advantage of this gorgeous weather." He put his hand on her belly. "How's the placekicker? Looks like you're due, what, next month? You look great. Terrific, as a matter of fact."

His eyes never left her face and the full force of his charm washed over her mind and emotions started rolling around like loose cannons.

He tapped the cowrie necklace. "Still wearing this, I see. Anybody that looks as good as you do ought to be pregnant all the time."

All the right moves, all the right feelings even if her belly was out to there and back again. He was genuine in his caring and nothing else mattered. She was getting giddy.

"You'd best lighten up or I'll go into labor a little early."

"Hey, I've helped deliver one," he reminded her. "And I have one at home. I'm a pro with diapers. That ought to qualify me for some sort of certificate, don't you think?"

Jon Mason finished his conversation with his secretary and started across the room toward them. An elevator chimed gently before opening its doors onto the suite. Alissa Bellemy-Saxon stepped forward, svelte and beautiful in a stunning moss rose Donna Karan suit. Mason turned smoothly midstride and met her at the elevator door.

"We didn't expect you until tomorrow," he admonished her. "Why didn't you let me know?" He kissed her on both cheeks and escorted her into the reception area.

"This weather is abominable and I'm dying of thirst." She was petulant. "I'd like an ice-cold Perrier and I have a tape of one of my interviews I want you to look at."

Mason snapped his fingers. "Right away."

Marielle watched from the corner of her eye as the actress crossed the room, bone thin and beautiful in three or four thousand dollars' worth of clothing, and felt a raw, stabbing envy. She didn't have to examine her feelings to know that it was not about Alissa's thin body. Or her beauty. Or her career or her clothes or her face. The only thing she coveted about Alissa's life was Thomas. As all-consuming as it was undeniable. And unalterable.

Thomas took advantage of Mason's greeting to Alissa to stand and he put his hand on Marielle's shoulder. "I'd better go," he said quietly. "I'm really glad to see you. Will you let me know when the baby arrives?"

She nodded and watched him walk away. Alissa greeted him with open arms and a very public, very possessive, lingering kiss. The three entered Mason's office while secretaries scrambled for ice and cold bottles of Perrier. The door swung closed behind them and Marielle released her breath. Alissa hadn't missed her presence. She knew it like she knew grass was green, and it made her uneasy.

Louise pointed out the ladies' room and Marielle lurched to her feet to make the journey. Anything not to be sitting there when Alissa came out, and Marielle was certain she would. She assured the secretary that she was fine. "Just let Shirley know where I am," she requested and moved quickly out of the waiting room.

As she'd anticipated, three minutes hadn't elapsed

before Alissa stepped into the lavatory; the beautiful actress positioned herself just inside the doorway and stared at Marielle and the cowrie-shell necklace, saying nothing, her face reflecting distaste. After a few moments, she reached into her purse. Retrieving a lipstick, she removed the top with great care and moved to the mirror where she took an inordinate amount of time applying color to her lips. Marielle was fascinated: Alissa's perfectly manicured nails were the precise color of the lipstick; never in her life had she managed that close a match.

On the ring finger of Alissa's left hand, the huge, four-carat diamond from Mexico flashed to a fiery brilliance in the makeup lights surrounding the mirror; next to the massive marquise solitaire were two flanking rows of gleaming diamonds, a double-circlet wedding band. Shafts of light from the two sets of rings, one on Alissa's hand and another in the mirror, danced and glittered as the actress used her left hand to apply lipstick she didn't need.

"You do get around, don't you? How's your husband?" Alissa said at last, and shifted her eyes pointedly to Marielle's belly. "All geared up for an heir?" Anair?

"He's fine." Alissa's behavior was clearly designed to create intimidation and Marielle wasn't sure what to expect.

"I know who you are." Alissa guided the lipstick into its top with deliberation. "And I know you're in love with my husband." Husbin.

"So's half of America." It was flip but Marielle didn't care. The situation was ridiculous and she felt absurd.

"Cute." Alissa threw the lipstick into her purse with a quick, impatient motion and searched inside until she located a cigarette. Between her lips, the filtered tip was instantly stained bright red and it, too, matched her nails.

Marielle smiled and gathered herself to move past the woman to the exit.

"You look pretty ratty, actually. Can't imagine what he sees in you." Alissa casually dropped her purse onto the counter and felt for matches, her gaze once again on Marielle's face. "Babies do that, I suppose. Mine nearly killed me." Kilt me.

Her eyes moved to her svelte image in the bathroom mirror and she struck a pose, surveying her thin figure in the expensive suit with its small waist and tight miniskirt. She tilted her head and prattled on. "Took two months to get my figure back. No way I'd do it again. Wouldn't do it again for a million dollars. But then"—she found the matches and tore one out, scratched the book with it to light the cigarette— "I don't have to, do I?"

The thin odor of sulphur flared, then disappeared from the room. The smell of burning tobacco remained. A rope of smoke curled upward from the actress's mouth and separated into her nostrils; the sight was harsh and unpleasant. More important, it was unhealthy for a child.

Marielle held her breath and moved toward the door. This was over the edge and she saw no reason to put up with it. "Excuse me," she said calmly.

Alissa deliberately exhaled smoke into her face as she passed and Marielle almost smacked her.

"Class act," she said, smiling. "Not." She saw the remarks hit home and opened the door to fresh air.

Shirley was immediately outside, about to enter. Rose and Thomas were standing side by side in the reception area with matching sober expressions. When he saw her come out of the lavatory, Thomas gave her a quick grin and returned to Mason's office.

After he'd gone, Rose broke into a salacious smile and poked her thumb upward in the air. "Wow," she mouthed soundlessly. Seconds later, she and Rose and Shirley got into the elevator.

"He's bleedin' gorgeous!" breathed Rose. "How on earth did you stand it?" She bit her knuckle in mock pain. "Aieeee!"

Marielle laughed out loud from tension, relief, joy, a combination of all three. She felt terrific and she didn't care who knew it. "I managed," she answered, and tossed her head, frisky as a colt.

"I'll bet you did," Rose said lasciviously. "I want to hear about it sometime. Not the good stuff, just . . . oh, hell, anything you want to tell me. I'm not proud."

Shirley was still too wired to join in the fun. "I didn't know they were coming in today, I swear it."

"What were you doing, checking on me?" Marielle laughed at her friend's concern.

"If I hadn't gotten out of my meeting just then, I think he'd have been in there with you," Shirley answered nervously, still jolted. "What on earth was going on?"

"She was making sure I knew she intended to stay married, I think. I really don't know," Marielle said honestly.

"What? What'd I miss?" yelped Rose. "I always miss the good stuff."

Marielle told them about Alissa's strange behavior.

"Sounds like she's wrapped too tight. You be careful, you hear?" Rose was serious.

Shirley nodded in agreement but Marielle just laughed. Like it or not she had to accept the fact that Thomas and Alissa were still together. That was the way life had turned out. But Thomas still considered her a friend and so far as she was concerned, Alissa had blinked. She'd attacked for no reason and had stooped to boorish, juvenile behavior. Therefore, she'd lost.

Besides, Boyce Jameson—Thomas Saxon's child—was due soon and life was wonderful. And life was moving on, taking her with it. They were given superb seating in the Fleurette Room and lunch was wonderful.

Rose had the proofs for her wedding invitation and the women were soon mapping out plans to travel to Yosemite in October; they decided to drive up on Tuesday, the eleventh, with the ceremony on Wednesday at two o'clock, the warmest part of the day. The Yosemite chapel was situated near the Sentinel Bridge; the Merced River flowed through the valley floor with El Capitan, the gargantuan monolith of stone that identified the park to the world, towering less than a mile away and dominating the valley.

"It's going to be a very small ceremony, just close friends and Cal's mother," she told them. "I don't really need invitations but I wanted something official that'll look good in the wedding book. Suzie and Jennifer are all excited about being flower girls in their daddy's wedding and my godson will be four months old by then. You don't think it's too much for a baby that age, do you?"

Both women looked to Shirley for confirmation.

"You can take him anywhere," she said with the authority of motherhood. "I took Jody to Europe at that age."

"I'm sure he'll be fine." Marielle gave her an evil grin. "I'm not about to miss your wedding. I want to take the picture his kids send to his ex."

"Besides, he'll have his godmother to help watch after him," assured Shirley, good-naturedly, "while his other godmother is getting herself married."

"Here's to marriage," proposed Marielle to her friends. "And to making decisions and getting on with life."

"You've decided about Jeff?"

"That's what the 'making decisions' part was for." She sobered and drank her juice. "After today, I'm getting closer."

Jeff stopped by on Wednesday after baseball practice. The Breslaur Group sponsored a team and anyone in the firm under fifty was expected to participate. He sat gingerly on her couch in his dusty uniform and meandered through a vague account of the game. Eventually he got to the point of his visit and gave her his earnest attention. "I don't want an answer if you're not ready to give me one, but I need to know whether or not you're taking me seriously."

She nodded that she understood and avoided telling him again that she hadn't as yet come up with a definitive answer.

"Whatever you do, don't be 'kind,'" he pleaded. "I'll handle whatever decision you make. So long as you're giving it genuine consideration."

"I assure you, I am," she said to him candidly. "I admit I didn't think so at first, but I really am."

He was happy with her answer and instantly curious. "Are you leaning?"

"Leaning? What's that," she teased, "some new kind of legal term?"

"You know what I mean," he urged. "More positive than negative? More negative than positive? What?"

She got serious. "Jeff, I'm not leaning as far as I know. This is too big an event in our lives and I'm not willing to do it without being absolutely sure. If I say 'I do' this time around, I'm going to understand and honor the meaning of it. It'll really be for better or worse, richer or poorer, death do us part. It'll be written in cement as far as I'm concerned or I won't go through with it. It's not just you and me this time, there'll be a child to consider." She shifted in the chair to relieve her back and smiled at the utter concentration in his face.

"I will say this," she finished hesitantly. "If it was no, I'd have told you already."

"That's leaning," he said triumphantly. "That's what I want to hear." He scooped up his glove and baseball cap, kissed her, and headed for the door. "Now I can start making plans."

"It's not yes," she cautioned. "Not yet. Probably not until the baby comes, so don't do anything serious, okay?"

"Can I trade the Porsche for a town car?"

She had to laugh. "Yes, that you can do."

"Thank you. You got any color preference?"

"No." She threw a stuffed monkey at him.

28

June 26, 1990

At 3:00 A.M. the night nurse called to Thalia on the intercom system and woke her from a sound sleep; Dana was feverish and wet with perspiration. The nurse took a temperature reading and put a cool compress on the infant's forehead while Thalia knocked on the door to Thomas's bedroom. He was instantly awake.

The baby's temperature was spiking and by the time they got her to the hospital, she was having trouble breathing. Dr. Goodin was standing by to admit her into Intensive Care. Thomas recognized one of the nurses on duty. She nodded to him in acknowledgment and he saw a flicker of fear cross her face before she looked away.

"I'm afraid Dana has pneumonia, Thomas," the doctor said a few minutes later. "It's nothing you did wrong. Unfortunately, it's a common complication with premature infants." He paused before he added the warning. "It doesn't look promising. Please be prepared."

Thomas heard his voice answer, "I understand," but inside his skull he was screaming in rage and he wanted to hit someone. When was it going to be enough? How much hell did this child have to pay? His anger building, he challenged his beliefs. What was the purpose in giving a life if you were going to snatch it back, and take your bloody sweet time about doing it?

He placed a reluctant call to Alissa in Houston and convinced the hotel operator to override a Do Not Ring notice on her room. There was no answer and the phone seemed to ring forever. Finally the operator came back on the line and Thomas left a terse message that Dana was ill and a number at the hospital where he could be reached.

And waited.

He paced the doctors' lounge and tried to relax, the inability to do something physical, to have some impact, some choice, preyed on his mind. Helplessness where his daughter was concerned was one of the few things his celebrity couldn't surmount. All the money and the power and the stature in the world could only go so far, and at some point life took over and chips fell where they were going to hit.

Thalia sat with her head bent in prayer, a rosary slipping endlessly through her fingers. Her peace in her belief did little to comfort him; he felt too pent up and frustrated to focus on chanting prayers to a Creator who seemed intent on sending destructive forces into his daughter's life.

His daughter. He realized suddenly that he had no hesitation about this identification. Until this night, each time she had crossed his mind there was always the vague but distinct knowledge that although he loved her, Dana was not his child. Not his blood. The line of separation had disappeared with this new threat to her life. Perhaps there was a greater purpose here, after all. He left Thalia in the lounge and, pointing to his empty cup, went up to the cafeteria.

There, with too much coffee in his system and too much time on his hands, he replayed the chance meeting with Marielle at Jon Mason's office. The sight of her, healthy, plump with her baby, aglow with pending motherhood, had been light in the middle of the dark tunnel that was life with Alissa. It had taken an enormous effort to be casual. Mason was no fool and he'd had to use a great deal of care not to arouse Jon's suspicion.

He'd sensed her discomfort in his presence and had tried very hard to put her at ease. Why pregnant women considered themselves unattractive to men eluded him. She was not only beautiful as the woman he'd once made love to, she was beautiful in the largest, most all-encompassing sense of the word—she had a child in her body, a living human being who was a part of her.

Partly the father, too, he conceded, but in sum a totally new person in his own right. This ability to gestate, to create, granted solely to women, was a mystery to every man on earth.

Simply being in her presence had been intensely personal and had gone to the most basic of his instincts, possession and protection. He wanted her. Round and soft and pregnant with another man's child, he wanted to wrap a sign around her that warned Hands Off to the rest of the male world. And it had never been more clear to him that he had no rights in her life.

With that knowledge strangling his instincts, he'd still had a hard time keeping his hands off her. He'd touched her belly, her body, her shoulder. All the time that her hand had rested on his arm a sense of light had traveled through his body. He'd wanted to strangle Jon Mason for interrupting and breaking her apart from him.

If Alissa hadn't chosen that particular moment to get off the elevator he wasn't sure he could have kept up the charade. He knew she'd seen them together and when she left Jon's office to go to the ladies' room, he knew she was looking for trouble. He'd been terrified something stupid would happen and so wired that he'd been twenty seconds away from crashing in to check on her when Shirley had come out of her office and grasped the situation. If Alissa's mood was any indication, Marielle had held her own; even Mason had been rattled at her demeanor when she returned, irascible and venomous, to continue the meeting.

His beeper went off and he returned to the lounge to meet Dr. Goodin, who told him that Dana had not improved. It was 6:00 A.M. and the doctor looked haggard.

"Can I see her?"

"You can, but don't disturb her rest."

"I've sent for her mother."

"I think that's best. I'm going to get some sleep. They'll let me know if there's any change." Goodin stretched out on the bed and was instantly asleep.

Thomas left the tired physician alone in the lounge, checked for a message from Alissa—there was none—and, unable to stay away from Intensive Care, spent a few minutes with Dana forcing himself to watch her labored breathing.

At eight, he sent Thalia home and stationed himself at a courtesy phone and made the requisite calls to the studio and production staff informing them of this latest crisis and alerting them that he would not be reporting for work until further notice. This week's episode was ninety percent complete and the producer assured him they could work with his stand-in to put the rest of it in the can. He agreed to shoot scenes they couldn't fake with a double at the next opportunity.

There was still no word from Alissa and no answer at her hotel. Finally, he called Marielle. Dana's condition had not improved; eventually it would reach the press, and he did not under any circumstances want her hearing the news from another source. He tried to prepare her for the worst.

"I'll be there in a few minutes," was her sole response.

She found him in the doctors' lounge watching the

sleeping Dr. Goodin. Without a word, he folded her in his arms and clung to her. His fear for Dana, the living thing in his gut, tore at him despite her touch. They went immediately to ICU.

At first Marielle was astonished at how much Dana had changed in so little time. A full five pounds, she'd filled out and looked more like a full-term baby. A fringe of dark hair framed her wistful little face as she lay pale and limp in the Isolette, struggling to breathe. Marielle put her hand inside and pressed it lightly to the side of the baby's chest for a moment. With all her might, she willed strength into the little body and listened closely with her heart.

"She's going to be fine," she whispered to Thomas. "I don't know how I know, but I think she's going to be fine."

He looked at her with immense hope and put his hand in the other side. Intent on the baby's labored breathing, they sat quietly on either side until she went to sleep.

The news that Dana had been readmitted to the hospital was too late for the early edition of the newspapers, but there was mention on radio and television morning news programs. A profusion of concern and good wishes accompanied by flowers and baby gifts for Dana began to pour into the hospital: infant toys, balloons, good-luck charms, clothes, blankets, all accompanied by cards and prayers for the baby's health. Well-wishers and the merely curious filled the lobby.

The hospital staff made arrangements for a room to be used as a storage area and every three minutes brought another mail cart of gifts into the room. Sprays of baby roses and baby motif floral arrangements began to line up in the hall; the combination of flowers and fragances began to remind Thomas of Noel's funeral and gave him cold chills.

While they waited for word, Marielle helped sort

through the gifts and made arrangements to distribute the flowers to older children in the hospital. The clothing and toys were directed to Sojourn, a battered-women's group in Santa Monica, and any food was set aside for the homeless. Somewhere, she found a folder to keep the names and addresses of the senders. Thalia returned at noon with a basket of sandwiches and freshly baked cookies; she took over sorting the gifts and shooed them out for lunch.

Thomas picked up a couple of cartons of milk from the cafeteria and they laid out an impromptu picnic on a table in a secluded courtyard. He rolled his jacket and put it in Marielle's chair behind her back, satisfying himself that she was reasonably comfortable before settling nearby. They made short work of Thalia's chicken sandwiches and started on the chocolate chip cookies.

"I wanted to ask you the other day about what happened with the inheritance," he said to her. "I almost called you when I read about the theft."

She gave him the details and he was astonished to learn the British government was demanding taxes on the stolen inheritance. After learning of Jeff's challenge to the insurance company, he gave her Barry Cooper's number and insisted that she contact him for help in sorting out the mess. "Barry has two specialists in international law in the firm. It can't hurt to make sure all your bases are covered. I'll talk to him today and tell him to expect your call."

A shy aide stepped into the courtyard with a note, distracting him. Marielle watched his face change as he read the information.

"Alissa's on her way from Houston. She called from the plane." He automatically consulted his watch. "She'll be down in twenty minutes."

Time suddenly became a very precious commodity for them both and they returned to the lounge.

Dr. Goodin came in while Thomas was on the phone instructing Joe to meet Alissa at the airport; as Thomas hung up, Goodin's beeper sounded and he moved toward the phone.

"She's stabilized," the doctor announced. "There's been a small measure of improvement. Not out of the woods by any means, but I think I can safely say she's no longer in immediate danger. You're very lucky. It could have gone either way." The doctor picked up the telephone with one hand to answer his page while Thomas pumped the other. A moment later Goodin was out the door and they were alone again.

"I had a feeling," she said happily. "Whether it was right or not, I'm going to take credit for it and get out of here."

"I feel like I'm always saying good-bye to you." He held her shoulders and bent slightly to kiss her mouth, surprising her. "I can't tell you how much it meant to have you here this morning."

She was flustered for a moment then kissed him back. He put his hands in her hair, held her face, and it was a warm, sweet kiss. They were both swept into an unnerving silence.

"I love her, too," Marielle said simply, and glanced at the clock. "I think I'd best be on my way. Let me know how things are going when you have a chance."

"Promise me you'll see Cooper," he pressed, determined to hang on to a few seconds more. "He's the best around and it can't hurt to have him look into it."

"Good-bye." She disappeared down the hall and the lounge became a terribly empty room.

He sat back in the chair she'd used and savored the scent of her that lingered lightly in the air. Bracing himself for Alissa's arrival, he was glad he'd finally kissed her again. And that she'd kissed him back. He thought about the taste of her mouth and the disarray of her hair. In her haste to come to the hospital she had pinned it carelessly with a couple of tortoiseshell combs. Its color had always fascinated him and the silky feel against his fingers stayed in his mind.

In the firelight at the cabin it had been an exciting combination of silver and honey blond. He remembered it as sweet smelling and fragrant. He'd delighted in wrapping his hands in it when he'd kissed her that night, holding her head while he explored her mouth, tasting the salt on her throat and in the sweat on her skin. He'd been perfectly in tune with her body, long and smooth against him on the rug in front of the fireplace with those incredible breasts.

He hadn't gone to the cabin with the intent of seducing her. Certainly it had crossed his mind, more than once, if he was honest, but he'd been far more interested in whether or not she was genuine. If they made love, that was okay, too. Thinking back, he could not imagine not making love to her.

The berries and crème had been a joke, something to tease her about. After all, the bigger joke had been on him; he'd been the one who'd passed out in her bed in Palm Desert. More than any single thing, the look on her face when he'd brought out the strawberries had convinced him that he wanted her in his life. She'd looked at him with such guilt. And she'd blushed. Blushed!

When he realized why, and thought about it for an instant, at that moment he'd wanted to make love to her in the worst way and then somehow she was his. All the time it was happening, a part of him had been hopelessly mesmerized, hadn't wanted to stop. He'd never made love with anyone the way he had with her those two days. She'd turned his head around.

He wanted her. Not pregnant, certainly. But soon. As soon as she'd let him in her life. He wanted to take her back to that cabin and start on the floor again with strawberries and crème. The thought made him ache and he shifted in his chair.

Stop this, he demanded of himself. *You better figure out how to get discreetly laid. Someone other than the wicked bitch from the great state of Texas.* He struggled to return to a normal state of mind and body. *She's eight months pregnant, for God's sake.*

He forced himself to think about Jeff and her relationship with her ex-husband. Jeff, who was fair with dark brown hair. He wondered if her baby would be a blond like her or . . . The idea rose from the depths of his being like a physical force, and he denied it at first. It was impossible.

He'd never been particularly good at remembering names or dates, but his mind insistently worked backward from the night in Mexico when Alissa announced her pregnancy and told him he was the father. That had been September of last year. The 31st. That date he wouldn't forget if he lived to be two thousand.

That night would have been less than four days from the weekend they'd shared together. September. Starting with his thumb, his fingers counted it out and June wound up on his ring finger. Nine months from September was June. Still he denied it. It couldn't be.

But the feeling in the pit of his stomach told him otherwise.

'Could be' is a far cry from 'is', he cautioned himself. *You were there when she told McCleary she was pregnant. You saw his face when it registered.* He counted the months again. Ring finger, every time. She'd disappeared from his life the week of the October press conference.

He'd always assumed that's when she'd slept with her ex-husband. But the math was beginning to add up badly. If she was nine months, instead of eight, she'd gotten pregnant within days of their weekend together.

Either he had experienced the best sex of his life with Marielle, already pregnant with her ex-husband's baby . . .

Or, it was his child.

29

July 1, 1990

"He'll be here when he's ready, Marielle," said Dr. Lanier confidently. "There's nothing irregular so far as I can tell. Heartbeat is strong. Position is excellent. It'll be any time now."

"He was due two days ago. I keep having this urge to move furniture and scrub the carpet. Something to get this process started."

"Just be—"

"Don't say 'patient.' I'm through with 'patient' already." Grumpy, uncomfortable in the ninety-degree weather, Marielle scowled at her ever-smiling doctor with the urge to tell him to stuff it.

"All perfectly normal." He beamed at her. "Give me a call when your water breaks."

"Right. Like I'm going to call someone else. My luck, he'll wait three more days and you'll be somewhere skiing over the holiday."

She maneuvered her body out of his office and waited at the curb for Jeff to pick her up in his shiny new BMW. Driving had become all but impossible; the baby had dropped so much that her stomach bumped flush with her steering wheel. Standing for any length of time sent shooting pains up her back; sitting gave her leg cramps; lying down, she felt like a beached whale, and the baby's weight shifted painfully against her diaphragm. Moving from one position to another seemed to be a way of life and being comfortable was a memory.

Jeff was late and she had laid plans to nail him on it as soon as he arrived. She gave his long face a sideways scowl and settled into the passenger seat of what she privately called the ugly green car. The new smell of the leather set her teeth on edge. "You better have a good excuse," she warned, in no mood to grant favor.

Jeff spoke in resignation. "I may as well tell you. Rettig Burnside passed away."

"No." Her personal misery was set aside. "When? How'd it happen?"

"We got the call about twenty minutes ago, that's why I'm late. Quietly, in his sleep. Day before yesterday."

"Thank God for that, I guess," she said slowly. She thought of the kindly old solicitor with his quirky eyebrows, who'd been so taken with her legal dilemma, and was saddened. "I can't believe he's gone." Her physical discomfort receded and she regarded the bulk of her body with a renewed appreciation. "You forget just how fragile life is."

"The funeral's tomorrow. I have the details at the office."

She busied herself the balance of the morning arranging flowers for Rettig Burnside's services and writing a note of condolence to Miss Gibbs. The rest of the news that Jeff eventually passed on to her was that with the solicitor's death the status of the taxes would undoubtedly take a difficult turn. The assessment was currently under review, and without Burnside's intervention, in all probability the assessment was going to climb much, much higher.

The news prompted her to call Barry Cooper, who cleared his schedule at four o'clock the following day in order to meet with her. After listening with some astonishment to her explanation about the discovery and subsequent loss of the inheritance, he asked one or two pointed questions and gave her astute and generally favorable opinions about Burnside's handling of the matter. He agreed to look into the situation on her behalf but cautioned her that he didn't see a great deal of leeway in the situation.

"I assume you know I'm divorced," she asked him.

"I believe Thomas mentioned that, yes," he responded carefully.

"I assume they'll proceed against me as trustee once my baby's born, but if I were to get married," she asked him, "would my husband also be responsible for payment?"

"No. Certainly not. If the man in question has concerns, I could prepare a prenuptial agreement specific to that point. This is clearly a debt of a prior nature and would not flow to the marriage contract unless specifically undertaken by your husband. Are you planning to be married soon?"

"I have to consider the baby."

"Of course." He didn't pursue the matter.

That evening she told Jeff about the meeting.

"Barry Cooper," he exclaimed with a lawyer's admiration and a peer's acknowledgment. "How'd you get a meeting with him? He's the best legal mind in this town. Talk about fire power. You sure went to the top of the ladder."

"He says I'll probably have to pay, but he'll look into it."

"If there's anyone that can do something about it, it's Cooper. I think you were right to see him. We need the best we can get." He shook his head and sighed. "Damn. If he says it's got to be paid, I don't know . . ."

The first contraction twisted its way through her body and all consideration of taxes left her thoughts. She waited on tenterhooks all evening, prepared for the slightest signal that Boyce was about to arrive, but there were no further signs the rest of the night. The following two days were free of symptoms and she lapsed into resignation that it had been a false alarm.

The heat continued and she was bored with waiting. Beyond bored. At noon, she picked up her telephone and ascertained that Dana was still in the hospital. She was about to call a taxi when a second contraction rippled through her body, then quickly subsided. Two hours later another cramp told her this was most probably it.

She alerted Dr. Lanier, then called Rose and Shirley and Jeff with the news. She was more excited than scared, and flushed with expectation. However slow, the baby's birth was underway at last and it was now a matter of time until she could see the person who had been making her life a wondrous hell for the last few weeks.

She was a racehorse at the starting gate, tight as a windup toy and, more than anything, incredibly happy. She could manage whatever happened from this point forward. Her water broke at five o'clock and a couple of hours later labor began in earnest. Dr. Lanier gave the word and Jeff took her to the hospital.

About ten o'clock things started to get really tough. Every time she thought she couldn't stand any more, a new wave of pain fought its way through her body, splintered her concentration, and caused her to grind her teeth. Despite her best intentions and all her training with Rose and Shirley, the one person she least expected was the person who held her together. Jeff's voice, his face hidden behind a ridiculous mask, was the voice she could hear and focus on.

He took over as coach, talked to her, made her listen while he kept her in rhythm, helped her concentrate on the pattern of her body's demands. Eventually she learned not to fight the pain but to flow with it and make it work for her.

After that, things went more smoothly but it wasn't a day in the park: eventually she gave in to the use of a minimum of painkillers. All thought was set aside and her existence centered around the primal urge to expel the child within. Jeff and Rose and Shirley took turns in the delivery room and two minutes after midnight, Marielle delivered perfectly gorgeous, perfectly formed, seven-pound-six-ounce Boyce Jameson McCleary.

Dr. Lanier uttered the traditional, "It's a boy," and after clearing the infant's nose and throat and making sure he was breathing properly, laid him on her chest. Marielle took one look at her naked son and the unmistakably dark hair crowning his head and promptly burst into tears.

Everywhere he went, driving home at night, in the middle of complicated scenes, in strained conversations with Alissa, his concentration would suddenly wane and questions about the paternity of Marielle's child would nag at him like a fishwife. "Whose child? Mine?" Not the kind of question you ask a mother about to deliver.

As often as he reviewed the dates, as endless as his speculation, even the allowance of a growing conviction, could not dismiss the possibility that the baby's father was Jeff. *His or mine?* The fishwife would not be satisfied. Thomas swung between exhilaration at the thought and a fear of being drastically, devastatingly wrong.

Maybe she didn't know. Maybe she was waiting until the baby arrived to assess its features or check its blood type or count the days as he had. Maybe that's why she and Jeff hadn't married. For the past week his focus had been split, his sleep disturbed with the implications in either instance. He'd held imaginary conversations with her as he shaved in the mornings, brushed his teeth. *His or mine?*

Finally a phone call to Barry Cooper had thrown new light on the subject. The attorney admitted he didn't think there was much he could do about her tax situation—he had a few contacts in London and would pursue the matter, but at the moment it looked as if she would owe the British government their normal inheritance assessment of eighty percent.

The firm's inquiries about the basis of the assessment in light of the theft had been met with the view that there was no trace of the thieves or—this was considered particularly sticky—the lack of evidence to prove that it had not been an inside job. The resultant suspicion that the gold had not actually been stolen at all had caused a closer inspection than normal of the handling of the matter and until his death, Burnside's reputation had worked in their favor. Now that he was no longer available to vouch for the woman in question, the minimal support for the lesser assessment had melted away in the fog of English suspicion.

"I can see why you found her attractive," Cooper admitted. "She's a beautiful woman. I didn't get the sense that she's angry at the loss, which frankly amazed me. The thing that seems to upset her most is that she stands to lose the cash she inherited which she needs for the baby."

"The baby's the most important thing in her life," Thomas acknowledged. He didn't add, "Maybe in mine," but the thought was there.

"My bill for her legal work in London could go as high as thirty thousand, plus the prenuptial. I'd have to do some research on the tax aspects, but otherwise, it's a pretty simple agreement. She's going to let me know."

This last information was jarring. A prenuptial agreement indicated marriage. Why hadn't she said anything? Thomas wrestled with his conscience but could not stop himself from probing further. With full knowledge that Barry had no idea that he was sharing a professional confidence, Thomas commented carefully, "Not a great way to start a marriage."

"You ought to know," Cooper responded. "You're a veteran of marriage without one."

He tried again. "Seems a little late to be checking into Jeff's liability." When Barry volunteered no further details, Thomas gave it up. "Of course, it's a recent development," he ad-libbed lamely, and the conversation turned to mundane matters while the knowledge of her impending marriage swirled in his mind.

He hung up the phone with the vacant feeling that he had just missed the last train out of town. Marriage. It took every ounce of his concentration to focus on work the rest of the day. The tricky shooting required for the missing scenes kept him occupied for the duration of the necessary dialogue or action, but whenever there was a lull he found himself revisiting sore territory.

She had every right to get married, he acknowledged. She would soon have a child to consider and an uncertain financial future. The imminent birth of the baby was apparently tied to her marriage decision, which meant that contrary to his reading of the situation, the child was most probably Jeff's and the wedding wouldn't be too far distant.

The next morning he stood on the balcony and looked down at her home in the early morning light and noted with satisfaction that Jeff's new BMW was not at the curb. *Winter Love* was limping badly at the box office and Alissa was sleeping off a bad night with the bottle. For a few days, when news of Dana's health had hit the wire services once again, there'd been a flurry of interest in the film and a small rise in sales at the box office which he attributed to sympathetic patrons.

Alissa had clung to the numbers, phoned the studio research offices daily for their tabulation of the cumulative box office totals, and called every executive who would talk to her; she'd sent thousands of dollars' worth of scotch and roses to the distributors. When she wasn't pursuing the picture, she was lobbying the producer of an upcoming film in which she desperately wanted the leading role. She'd begun losing weight again and was painfully thin.

Her moods were swinging dangerously from defiance to paranoia to misery. Each evening she would wait for him to return from the day's shooting and be well into her fourth snifter of cognac by the time he arrived. Drinking openly, belligerent, caustic, she demanded his opinion of the chances that *Winter Love* would be pulled from exhibition. If he answered honestly, she was moved to rage. Ignoring her was equally exhausting and he'd soon learned to wait until the liquor moved her to lethargy and eventual sleep.

He had every intention of being gone before she woke up this morning. He'd looked forward to the Fourth of July holiday for a week. Dr. Goodin had indicated that Dana could come home today, and he would have three full days with her before going back to work. Thank God for unions. He called Marielle to give her the news, planning to steer the conversation in the direction of her marriage. But his well-laid plans were thwarted when there was no answer.

He hung up each time the answering machine clicked in and eventually tried Shirley Canfield. No answer there, either. He was left with a decidedly twitchy feeling.

Sure enough, at the hospital later that morning three different nurses mentioned to him that Marielle had given birth; her baby had arrived a little after midnight and neither had suffered any complications. While the nurses were preparing Dana, he beat a path to the maternity ward on the fifth floor. Marielle was sleeping, so he asked the nurse in charge to point out the baby to him in the nursery. She indicated a squalling, wrinkled, red-faced bundle with a smattering of dark hair, and his emotions were hard to define as he failed to recognize himself in its little features.

Disappointment, certainly. And, if he was honest, a little relief as well. Children were insatiable in their ability to alter your life. They drained your defenses and created a space of their own, engineering whole new vistas of love and emotion in your heart in the process. He'd been owned, totally and completely, by his son, Noel. And the pain from the loss of his firstborn had translated to a heightened fear of losing Dana.

To have known that pain, the desolation and despair of senseless tragedy, was to know that the loss of another child would do equal damage, and it haunted him. If indeed this newborn had been his child, and if he were to allow himself to continue falling in love with Marielle . . . he was asking for more pain than he could handle.

He switched his train of thought. If she and Jeff were planning to be married, apparently the paternity had been decided. He couldn't conceive of her willingly entering into a marriage with a man not the child's father, so the matter was settled. He would see her with a clear conscience, wish her well, and put the fishwife to rest.

Returning to her room, he saw Jeff, laden with dozens of red roses, just ahead of him in the corridor. He followed to the doorway and peeked his head around, unable to resist observing their greeting. He watched Jeff sit gingerly on the bed and kiss her. The roses obscured her face but Thomas heard the unmistakably intimacy of tone as Marielle greeted her future husband.

"Hey, partner," she said in a sleepy, husky voice.

"How do you feel, sweetheart?" Jeff asked.

"Marvelous. Exhausted. Wonderful. Isn't he perfect?" She eased herself into an upright position. "The nurse is bringing him in and we're going to try breakfast."

"I feel like a daddy." Jeff leaned forward to kiss her again. Thomas stepped backward into the corridor feeling like a voyeur, uncomfortably aware of their obviously private moment. He moved aside for the nurse carrying Marielle's baby. The woman recognized him and he was about to leave when he overheard her whisper to Jeff and Marielle, "I saw Thomas Saxon outside."

Having little choice, he stepped into the room and inspected Marielle's little boy as if for the first time. He scanned Jeff's face in comparison and was convinced he saw a resemblance as he turned to Marielle. "You make good-looking children," he said honestly. "You ought to make a dozen."

"I'd love to." She laughed and shifted most of her attention to the baby in her arms in preparation for his breakfast. "How's Dana?"

"I'm taking her home today. They're amazed—we're all amazed at her."

After a brief reintroduction and a formal handshake with Jeff, the conversation evolved into one of those awkwardly polite exchanges of all the proper good wishes and congratulations, and he used the first opportunity to escape so she could nurse the baby. He waited at the elevator, supremely aware that Jeff had remained in the room, and after an unbearable wait, took the stairs all the way to the basement and Intensive Care.

An exquisite bouquet of red and white baby roses, delicate baby's breath, and blue cornflowers arrived before noon. Marielle knew the minute she saw it that it was from Thomas and she had a sinking feeling when she read the card: "Best wishes and congratulations to you and your family." There'd been something in his face that morning, an aloofness, withdrawal even. With Jeff in the room, they'd been unable to connect, about Dana, about anything, even the infant—his child—at her breast. She knew he was cutting the fragile cord of their connection, disengaging himself from her life and she was powerless to stop it.

The recent kiss she'd so treasured, hadn't dared believe was a sign of his renewed interest, had been a farewell after all. Dana was going home to her mother. There'd be no reason to meet from now on, no life outside his life as a celebrity to share. It was over.

That evening there were tears in her eyes as she nursed her son. From her window in the hospital built high in Westwood's hills, several displays of holiday fireworks were visible over the various southland cities, great sprays of reds and hot pinks, sizzling whites, glowing bursts of greens and blues, crackling with incandescent light; dazzling displays that plumed for a magic moment in time then fell, melting into nothingness.

A visual statement of her moment in his life.

She felt more alone than ever. Nursing the baby, feeling the milk flow from her breast into his greedy little mouth, the joy and the terror of the first day of motherhood mingled with the pain and the loss of Thomas.

30

July 31, 1990

"The revised assessment from London is brutal." Barry Cooper took a huge bite out of his cheeseburger and delayed having to expound on the bad news as long as possible.

Eventually his friend would have to swallow and Thomas waited impatiently.

"Between the size of the policy her husband took out on the gold," the lawyer continued, "and the insurance agent's notes, which were quite extensive, they justified an evaluation of three million dollars. We got it dropped to two. They didn't like it, but they bought it. Taxes will be a million six." Barry Cooper wasn't happy. "Technically, we saved her eight hundred thousand. That and a bus token will get her across town."

"A million six. Sweet Jesus." Thomas could only shake his head. "How'd she take it?"

"Believe it or not, she laughed." Cooper was philosphical in his admiration of Marielle. "As she rightly points out, once what she has is gone, there is no more, so it really doesn't matter how much they assess. Her fiancé, ex-husband, whatever, was horrified. He insists on filing an appeal. Since you're footing the bill here, I need some guidance." Cooper took another bite of his lunch.

Thomas stared out the restaurant window onto Beverly Drive. "Go ahead and file it. Do whatever they want."

Barry signaled the waitress for another beer. "I have to point out that the fees to date amount to somewhere in the neighborhood of thirty-six thousand. That's a couple of trips to London, roughly seventy hours of legal time, research, and various out-of-pocket expenses. If we were talking real money here, you'd have a bargain." He tapped the table impatiently while the waitress conferred with the bartender.

"An appeal is going to run into a triple digit figure in a hurry. I don't want to brag, but I run an expensive shop and you can get the same result a whole lot cheaper from a firm that specializes in this sort of thing."

The waitress returned with the beer and smiled shyly in recognition of Thomas. He smiled back automatically and tapped his cup to signal for more coffee. "I want you to handle it."

"Okay. You're writing the checks but I think you ought to give it some thought, anyway."

"I'll think about it. It's going to be expensive for them to try to collect. Any possibility of cutting a deal if England doesn't have to sue her for it?"

Barry paused to look at him. "Very probably. Why? Are you thinking of paying it for her? I would most strongly advise you against such a thing."

"Why?" Thomas held his cup for the nervous waitress and waited patiently for a warm-up.

"Because even you don't have that kind of money available. You'd have to liquidate some assets, for one thing. And for another, you can't write it off. It would be a dead out-of-pocket loss."

"Did you do the prenuptial?"

Cooper sipped his beer. "Actually, yes. It was a very simple agreement, the cost was minimal."

"Maybe she'd decide not to get married."

He felt Cooper's incredulous stare.

"You got it that bad?"

Thomas didn't answer.

"Sweet Jesus." Barry ordered another beer.

Due to the size of his personage, "Boyce Jameson" was soon shortened to "Jamie." Marielle sat rocking her son, her new most favorite occupation. He'd finished his night feeding and was soundly asleep in her arms, limp and supremely content. She contemplated his angelic little face and thought about her future.

It would be a matter of time before the money in the savings account would have to be returned to England. It had never been more than numbers on paper after all, and it had been a mistake to build her life around it. Somewhere in the very near future, she would have to find someone to watch the baby so she could go back to work. Her office's policy regarding maternity leave was a maximum of three months and October would be here before she could blink twice.

Without going overboard about the baby, Jeff had blended seamlessly, insistently back into her life. She knew she was balancing on the wire of indecision and would have to get off soon. On the one hand, her sensible side made the argument that Thomas was gone. She could no longer hide in the fantasy of being in his life, and Jeff was someone she could build a life with; on the other, the hopelessly romantic, wishful-thinking half of her knew that if she remarried Jeff there would never be the kind of magic in the bedroom she'd experienced the night Jamie was conceived. Her sensible side prevailed. Thomas was gone.

She knew she was "leaning" or she wouldn't have had the prenuptial agreement prepared, but still she avoided broaching the subject and the commitment itself wouldn't form into words.

Jamie sighed and shifted gently in her arms. She had Thomas's child, maybe anything more had been too much to ask. As she'd expected, there'd been no word from him since the flowers. She eased herself out of the rocking chair and placed Jamie in his bassinet and he settled peacefully under the pale blue comforter she pulled lightly over his body. In love with this child, she understood at last how Dana had pulled Thomas and Alissa together despite the extent of difficulty in their marriage.

She turned on the monitor and tiptoed out of the room, pausing at the door for one last look. She could not stop herself from coming in at night three or four extra times just to reassure herself he was breathing and really there.

Finally, she joined Jeff in the living room. He'd opened the bay windows and the balmy California night was pleasant against her skin. He greeted her with a kiss and she settled in his arms on the sofa.

He had kept his promise not to pressure her for an answer, but seeing his face daily was pushing her to make a decision. With Thomas out of her life, what was she waiting for, damn it?

The grosses on *Winter Love* had taken a disastrous turn downward and for a week Alissa had been a holy, screeching terror. Dana had burst into tears every time they'd been in the same room together.

Today, however, Alissa was humming and bustling about, choosing first one then another of several exquisite outfits she had selected for Dana's debut photograph. Finally she chose a delicate christening gown and handed it to Thalia with instructions to have the baby ready in fifteen minutes, then disappeared into her room to dress in a matching antique cream lace gown.

The photographer and his assistant had been busy in the baby's room all morning, setting up lights and rigging an impromptu set for the occasion. Thomas had been instructed to make himself available for the entire day and was wearing the first in a series of color-coordinated shirts and ties that had been designated as his contribution to the project.

Alissa returned, resplendent, with Thalia and Dana in tow. He took his place next to them and the photographers fussed and fine-tuned their cameras, pronounced the family portrait "beautiful" and "perfect" and flashed away with their strobes. Dana had only recently opened her eyes and Thomas was concerned about the lights. He watched his daughter's face anxiously and was pleased to see that she was not being upset by the process.

While Alissa went to change, he asked the photographer to take a picture of Dana propped against a huge lace pillow, and again when the lights flashed in her face, she made no reaction. Thalia's face, wreathed with pride, took on a quizzical look about the same time that he, too, realized something was odd. He moved his hand slowly from side to side in front of the infant's face and spoke to her. She moved her head and looked in his direction but her wide open eyes never wavered, never blinked, gave no indication of sight. He sank to his knees.

Dr. Goodin's recommended specialist at the Jules Stein Eye Clinic made himself available Monday afternoon to administer tests and at the end of the session Thomas's worst fears were realized. Dana was blind. "It's too soon to know how seriously impaired she will be, but the possibility is there that she'll never have sight," said the specialist. "We'll have to wait. I wish I could give you a better idea of what to expect, but at the moment . . ." He shrugged, at the end of his ability to provide hope, and Thomas bowed his head in resignation.

He had been aware that there might be damage. Dr. Goodin had warned him from the start that there could be complications at some point as a result of the use of oxygen when she was hospitalized and in the preemie ward, but even being prepared didn't rule out despair at the unfairness being visited on his tiny daughter.

When the proofs arrived from the photographer, he chose only the photograph of the baby against the antique pillow and had it placed in the silver frame Marielle had brought from London. The family portrait was released to the press. It was used widely in the print media but this time there were no offers to Alissa of personal appearances.

The role she coveted and had worked so desperately to be considered for was awarded to Melanie Salters with major fanfare and a barrage of publicity. The studio sent word that *Winter Love* was being pulled from the theaters and would go immediately into the foreign and videocassette markets in hopes of making back some of its cost.

Alissa began drinking in earnest, prowling the apartment throughout the night with the insomnia of an alcoholic, miserable and irascible. Thalia became a lifeline. Without her there to be certain Dana was being well cared for, he couldn't have continued working. When two feature deals that his agents had worked on for four months fell through, he, too, was shaken. The final straw came the night he found the silver frame and the portrait of Dana destroyed in the fireplace.

He worked the blackened metal out of the ashes and, his mood growing from angry to ominous, he wrapped it in plastic and put it in his briefcase. He had very little hope the frame could be salvaged; it was more an automatic gesture stemming from his inability to accept it as a total loss and throw it into the trash. A buying of time before accepting the inevitable. His store of patience and willingness to purchase time was suddenly bankrupt.

Thalia, silent as a wraith, served dinner. Ignoring the food, Alissa sat at the table with a dull green bottle of Remy Martin at her right hand, replenishing a large crystal brandy snifter regularly as she stared at him; her mood was ugly and destructive. "I'm never going to deal with a blind child," she announced. "It's bad enough she's sick all the time, but blind? My God, what are people gonna say."

Bile rose in his throat. He had never hated anyone in his life the way he hated this woman, steeped in self-concern and drunken self-pity. Dumping caution, his rage ran away with him and he scraped his chair away from the table. "How much will it take to leave my life?" he challenged her. "Name the price."

"You'd like that, wouldn't you?" Alissa's speech was slurred and the Texas accent grated on his nerves like fingernails scraping their way across a slate.

"Yes. I would." He held very tightly onto the arms of his chair because he knew he wanted to hit her, to punch her face with its gaunt cheeks and perfect capped teeth. He wanted to wipe the drunken smile off her silicone-injected, pouty lips and make her see reason.

"You can' afford me," she threw back at him. "Y'lose any more movies and you won't b'able to buy mah groceries."

"Just how much?" he ground out at her, loathing the conversation and welcoming it at last.

She studied him with red, half-closed eyes, pig-greedy and narrowed with suspicion. "Ten million," she said clearly, malice in her face and voice. "Anytime you wanna pony it up."

"Five," he countered. "I can have it in a week."

The offer took her by surprise and she couldn't hide her interest. "I'll think about it." She was openly taunting him.

"The offer's good for two weeks," he warned. "After that, it'll take lawyers."

"They gonna have to be magicians to getchoutta this one." The snifter slipped from her grasp and rolled onto the table, splattering everything in its path; the heavy smell of cognac sprang into the air and surrounded him with an unpleasant aura of evaporating alcohol.

Thalia came in from the kitchen with a towel and swabbed at the sticky liquid while Alissa pushed herself away from the table and swayed toward her bedroom. "Five million? We had relations exactly once since we got married. Makes me th'most expensive wife in town. I guess that's somethin'."

That night Thomas sat in Dana's nursery, reassessing his actions and trying to determine his future. At the sound of his voice the baby turned her head in his direction and he stared into her sightless eyes. "You're not my daughter," he told her. "You're not my daughter, you're blind, and my life is in chaos because of you."

Then he made the hardest decision of his life.

The next morning, Alissa faced him grimly across the breakfast table, smoking a cigarette. Without makeup, puffy from the liquor and the hangover, her face was squeezed in pain.

"I want you to put me in 'Murder' next year," she said thickly. "It doesn't have to be co-star, just a good solid supporting role as your assistant or something. And don't tell me you won't do it," she finished belligerently.

He stared at her, ignoring the demand. "The only thing I'm willing to do is give you a divorce," he told her. "The offer stands. Five million to get out."

"I have no idea what you're talking about," she said sullenly and walked to the liquor cabinet to open a new bottle and pour cognac into her coffee.

"We can do this hard or we can do it easy. I'm going to have Barry draw up an agreement and you have two weeks to make up your mind."

"Do whatever you want. If you were gonna divorce me, you'd have done it. I'm not going anywhere and you know it."

"Two weeks," he reminded her. "You'd better take the money while I have it because my contract's up on the television series and I'm not going to re-sign."

"What is this, some kind of bluff?" She stared at him, eyes glittering with suspicion. "I happen to know you're in the middle of negotiating your new deal. I keep track of things like that, remember?"

"I'm giving you fair warning."

"I don't believe you."

"Watch me." He felt her eyes follow him from the room as he left for the studio.

"I've changed my mind. Tell the network I'm not interested in doing another season," he said to Barry later that morning. "I'll do three specials a year, but that's it."

"If this is a ploy for more money, tell me now because the deal is ninety percent closed and it could blow up in your face." His friend and attorney was worried.

"I don't care. I'm tired and I've paid my dues. There are more than enough episodes for syndication, no one's going to get hurt financially except me. The show's tired. Probably only good for one more season anyway. I want to get out while it's still in demand."

Cooper shook his head in disbelief.

"And I want you to draw up an agreement between me and Alissa. I don't care what you call it, but she divorces me and I give her five million dollars to do it."

"Is that why you're dropping a bomb in the middle of your career?"

"I told you the reason. I'm tired. I'm tired of the show, I'm tired of the character, I'm tired of the grind. I want to take some time off and look at my life. What I want right now is out of this marriage."

"She'll never go for it. You're worth ten times that to her, particularly with the baby."

"I want custody of the baby. Total. She's to have no further interest in Dana's life. It's part of the deal."

"You've lost your mind. No way in hell she's going to buy this."

"Just do it, okay? As a friend? Just draw up the papers and leave the rest to me."

When word reached the executives at the network, the phone calls began, and the lunches, the dinners, the persuasions, the gifts, the offers, the cajolery, the upped antes, titles, and salary. He was amazed at the additional amount of money that suddenly became available for his services. Meanwhile, the final "Murder" episodes were prepared, rehearsed as usual, and put in the can. His decision to leave became public and the flow of fan mail doubled with pleas not to stop the series.

Through it all Alissa remained a tight-lipped malignant volcano of anger, refusing to erupt, refusing to believe he was serious, waiting him out.

Scripts began to be slipped under his door and offers to do similar series began to filter through his agency reps, who began their own round of calls, dinners, and drinks to review his career. Mentions of not having discussed a decision of this magnitude with them before making it final filtered through the conversations.

Despite the pressure he remained adamant. He checked with Cooper daily on the progress of the agreement with Alissa and did his best to use his influence to see that the show staff was placed elsewhere. The wrap party was held at Chasen's and after a shaky start, members of the cast and various crew members began to offer genuine good wishes for the future. Professionals all, they knew that nothing in the entertainment business lasted forever and the old-timers were pleased that the show was bowing out like a classy lady while it was at the top of the charts, and not a down-at-heels series that had been sucked dry creatively and lost its public appeal.

Alissa put in an appearance halfway through the party. He had genuinely hoped she would stay away as he was pretty certain she'd show up drunk. She was not. But she was angry, and she went to great lengths to make it clear to anyone who would listen that she was in total disagreement with his decision to retire the show. Within an hour, however, she'd had too much to drink and he forced himself not to interfere with her behavior in front of his peers. Jon Mason did his best to control the damage, but Alissa was determined to be heard.

"My husband didn't want me to be here tonight," she announced to the embarrassed crowd. "And I want you to know that he thinks quitting this series is going to change my mind. But it's not. So you're all out of jobs for no good reason."

She rambled on and remaining members of the cast and crew began to seek the exits. Those who were forced to pass him on the way out either pretended not to see him or deliberately sought to wish him well without mention of Alissa's presence. He was grateful for both.

He signed all four copies of the agreement and he forced a confrontation the following day. "Time's up." He tossed them onto the table next to her lunch. "Five million dollars. Let's approach this like the business deal it is."

She picked up a copy and read it with maddening slowness. Finally she put it down and looked at him with relish. "This says you get Katherine. I didn't agree to that."

"You don't want her. You've never wanted her. You're ashamed of her. Why prolong a bad situation?"

"Where's a pen?"

He knew in his gut it was too easy, but he handed her a ballpoint pen and watched her sign. She reached for the other copies. When she reached the fourth document, she began striking out portions of the agreement. Methodically, she located the same paragraphs in each of the preceding copies, crossed them out, initialled each deletion, then calmly pushed them back across the table.

"You want her, it'll cost you another five million dollars."

He knew her well enough to recognize she was negotiating, as always. And after that, what? Another five million? If he gave an inch the demands would never cease. "No deal," he said in cold resignation.

God help him, there was another way.

31

September 29, 1990

Omens.

Rose's wedding was ten days away and the Mothers were deep in preparation. Marielle stood in her living room on a small stool while Rose and a seamstress borrowed from Neiman's measured the hem of her pale peach bridesmaid's gown. She waited immobile on her pedestal while a postal delivery woman admired her gown, then crossed the room to get her signature for a registered letter from London. She signed the requisite form still perched on the stool and stared with dread at the stiff, official envelope.

The British Exchequer's emblem was expensively emblazoned on the upper left-hand corner. She had so hoped it would not arrive until after the wedding. Glancing at it without interest for Rose's benefit, she tossed the envelope onto her heap of bills. She refused to think about it for the next two days.

When she got up the courage to open it, the last thing in the universe she anticipated was a terse notice from the British government that all assessments relative to the trust of Boyce Jameson McCleary had been satisfied. She read it several times to be certain she understood the content, then placed an excited call to Jeff to find out how on earth it had happened.

Jeff was equally amazed. "I have no idea," he admitted. "I had nothing to do with it."

Barry Cooper denied any involvement as well, and offered relieved congratulations. Avram Halkin in Rettig Burnside's office in London was equally mystified. Further inquiries by both firms were met with deadlocked British silence. Beyond confirming that the debt had indeed been satisfied, no additional information was available. Finally, Miss Gibbs, through a private and therefore unofficial conversation with a friend of hers in the Exchequer's office, had been able to ascertain that the assessment had been lowered by half and paid in cash; a condition of anonymity had been imposed and that under no circumstance were the terms to be made public.

Marielle was totally flummoxed, refusing to believe in her good fortune. She turned it around and around in her mind trying to come up with a reason why anyone would do such a thing. For what purpose?

"Maybe it's as simple as someone over there finally realized the gold was really stolen and there was no possibility of collecting the money. Maybe they were afraid it would get into the papers. Proceeding against a three-month-old baby would make them look like vultures. Beats the hell out of me. Maybe that's why they don't say it's paid, they just say it's been satisfied. All I know is, it's no longer due." Jeff was watching her nurse the baby.

"Don't say 'hell,'" she said automatically. "Are you absolutely positive."

"Absolutely."

"Then the money I have for Jamie is safe."

"Yes." He studied her closely. "That means you're not going to marry me, doesn't it?"

* * *

"Well, are you?" Rose was back in form. It was the Meeting of the Mothers that same night at Tonio's, and the baby was asleep in his bassinet on the fourth chair at the table. Josef brought a round of iced teas on the house.

"I don't know," she responded. "One of the reasons I wasn't sure was that I didn't know how much of marrying him was based on security for Jamie. But if the money's safe, then I have to think about it without security being a factor."

"You were really considering getting married, then?"

"Yes, I was. And you know what's weird? It's almost like an omen. Since I don't need financial security for the baby, marrying Jeff no longer seems like a compromise." Marielle jiggled the ice in her tea and said it out loud. "My periods have started again. And Jeff keeps talking about brothers and sisters for Jamie. Maybe it's the right thing, after all."

Rose gave her a fish-or-cut-bait stare. "You know everyone I know. You and Jeff are already planning to be at my wedding, aren't you?"

Marielle met her stare. "Yes," she agreed slowly, the idea taking shape in her mind. "It's less than eight days from now," she cautioned. "That's not a lot of time."

"You can have a dress in twenty-four hours, a license in three days, and a double wedding in Yosemite a week from Wednesday, if you're up for it."

"I have no idea what Jeff would say," she hedged, but the idea of a wedding in Yosemite, one of the most beautiful sites in the world, was building. In truth, she'd been envious since Rose had revealed her plans. They'd had a traditional church wedding when she and Jeff married the first time. If she married him again, it had to be a rock-solid decision. The symbolic strength of the granite monolith was appealing and the simplicity of an outdoor ceremony would be wonderful.

"If I knew for sure we could make it this time . . ."

Shirley took her hand. "There are no guarantees, Marielle. The only way to deal with life is to get into it with both feet," she said. "It's messy and it's terrifying at times, but what of value isn't? Bill and I nearly didn't get married and God knows we had our problems, but we had fifteen good years before I lost him and Jody." The death of her family was a very real presence in the room. "Children make all the difference. They're the only thing that's worth it."

"Don't look at me," Rose warned. "Everything I want comes with marrying Cal so I'm not remotely unbiased. If I were you, I'd ask myself three questions." She ticked them off on her fingers. "Does he love me? Does he love the baby? Do I want him in my life? If the answer to all three is yes, get off the dime and make a decision. He's not going to wait forever."

Marielle found she could not in all honesty answer no to any of the questions.

Jeff was waiting at the curb when she got home. They went inside and after she put the sleeping baby down in his room, she kissed her ex-husband strongly and he returned her kiss. She told him about Rose's offer of a double wedding. Jeff was elated with the idea and thrilled at the proximity of the date. After ascertaining that her inquiry implied that she was willing to marry him, he urged her to accept Rose's offer.

"I have only one request," he said to her quietly. "I want a separate ceremony. I don't care if it's immediately before or immediately after, but I don't want us to say our I do's at the same time as anyone else."

This time when Jeff kissed her, Marielle returned his kiss with a solid emotional reaction but none of her hoped-for passion.

"I really want to make love to you," he said to her, "but I can tell you're still not a hundred percent convinced about all this."

"I'm ninety percent," she admitted, unable to pretend.

"The last ten's pretty critical," he responded soberly.

"We have a week until the wedding. If I can get one percent a day, we're a go," she promised.

"That's ninety-seven percent," he countered. "I won't ask for more than that."

Rose was aghast. "Of course you'll marry him separately. I didn't mean saying our vows at the same time. Just on the same day. We'll flip a coin. Heads goes first. Done?"

"Done."

Marielle won the toss.

Happy to have the matter decided at last, she threw herself into gear. The next several days became a flurry of preparations. She made phone calls informing her boss and co-workers and various other friends of her plans, invited them to attend, and received their congratulations. She considered, then rejected calling Thomas. No matter how she practiced, "I've decided to get married," it simply refused to come out of her mouth in a neutral tone of voice.

She decided the pale peach dress would serve both occasions, first her wedding then as Rose's bridesmaid. She studied her parents' wedding portrait on her mantel, then searched through her mother's possessions stored in her closet for something "old," the wide-brimmed hat with a white lace veil that her mother had been married in.

She found the hat and took it into the living room to try it on. It had survived remarkably well and was an attractive frame for her face. With a new veil, it would be perfect. She turned the wedding picture toward the mirror and compared herself to her mother.

Under the glass of the old-fashioned frame, the original black-and-white photo had oxidized and her parents' outlines had softened to shades of dark and light umber. Her father, Stephen Jonas, stood stalwart and proud in his stiff army uniform with his arm around her mother; and her mother, wearing a gay polka dot dress, the gold necklace with the cameo reversed and the brave white hat, clutched his arm with a wide, happy smile.

Marielle took from her jewelry box the antique cameo and the small kid-leather bag that held her parents' matching wedding rings. Engraved inside her father's band was "Love always, Téa." As a child, she'd wondered how her mother had managed to have it written inside the ring.

Her mother's matching ring with "Love always, Stephen," was too small for her finger but her father's ring fit perfectly. She fit the heavy gold band onto her left hand. She'd soon be wearing Jeff's ring again and wondered if her parents would approve. She slipped the locket over her head, settled it against her chest, and returned to the mirror. This time she was satisfied.

Shirley was right. There were no guarantees in life. Her mother had married her father with full knowledge that he was going overseas into a dangerous and unpopular war. It was possible that she was pregnant at the time the picture was taken. Certainly, shortly thereafter. Her mother hadn't demanded guarantees, she'd followed her heart.

Times were never going to be simpler. Life was never going to give out guarantees—it was a process of taking risks and managing the potholes as best you could.

The gold necklace had been one of her mother's favorite pieces of jewelry. As a teenager, she'd held the locket while her mother traced an outline of it onto a piece of paper, then cut out the middle and used the pattern to mark and cut a photograph of Marielle to wear inside. She'd copied her mother's actions, placing a picture of her mother in a locket of her own, which, unfortunately, had been lost soon after.

Later, when the soft gold clasp had buckled and the locket became jammed, her mother had always told her that the person she most loved was held inside and she didn't want to get it fixed because she saw no reason to open it.

Marielle tried gently to jimmy the mechanism. The clasp held fast, refusing to cooperate. It was time to put another most loved person inside, she decided. She had a wonderful picture of Jamie that was the perfect size.

The following morning, she and Jeff went to the county clerk's office to apply for their marriage license and from there to the jeweler's shop to pick out wedding rings. Marielle declined a stone and they decided on simple matching gold bands. She asked the jeweler to examine the locket and he indicated that it would be a simple matter to correct. With mixed feelings, she left the cameo with him for repair. Jeff surprised her with a lavish lunch at L'Orangerie and a beautiful gold bracelet as a prewedding gift.

As a final test for herself, she decided to leave Jamie with Jeff on Sunday afternoon and she took herself to a movie. She restricted herself to a minimum of preparation, giving Jeff the details of the baby's usual schedule and the number of the theater. After some initial misgivings, she managed to enjoy the film and when the movie ended, she restrained herself with a great deal of difficulty from calling to make sure everything was all right. When she let herself into the house it was unusually still and an hour past Jamie's normal nap time. She didn't find a note, and the emergency bottle of formula was gone from the refrigerator.

She climbed the stairs to the baby's nursery and when she saw that neither Jeff nor Jamie was in her son's room, she was unable to stifle the initial stirrings of panic. As she passed her own room she saw Jeff lying asleep on her bed, his body curled into a fetal position and snuggled next to him on top of the coverlet was the baby, equally sound asleep.

An instant wave of relief surged through her body

and she tiptoed downstairs to let the two of them sleep. This was a great beginning, she decided; Jeff would make a good father for her child, and if the gods were kind, perhaps a child of their own.

Monday afternoon she picked up the necklace.

"It's all ready for you." The jeweler proudly displayed the locket on a black velvet cloth and pressed the clasp. The cameo lifted open smoothly to reveal a small but surprisingly bright picture of a teen-aged Marielle, ponytailed and smiling. "Looks like you," he said appraisingly.

"It is. My mother put it there. Now I want to put my baby's picture inside."

"If you do that I can't guarantee it won't jam again. This piece wasn't designed to carry photographs," he told her. "There's very little room inside. It was made for a miniature. I wouldn't be surprised to find a painting under this picture."

She nodded permission. He selected a delicate jeweler's tool and with a skilled watchmaker's touch, pried up a corner of the picture of Marielle. As he'd suspected, underneath was an old-fashioned painting of a young man. Marielle caught her breath in surprise.

There was no mistaking the similarity. The color, slightly brighter, and style were identical to the miniature of Lilia. At home that evening Marielle compared the portraits and satisfied herself that they were indeed a pair; she arranged them side by side on her mantel, the golden cameo locket and the small silver frame. She realized the reunited portraits had been created a century ago and were together for the first time in eight decades.

Perhaps it was a cruel destiny, of sorts.

She knew from Jameson's letter to his son that he'd never stopped loving Lilia, and that Lilia had kept Jameson's portrait throughout her marriage to Boyce and had passed it on through her family was surely proof that she had always loved him as well. They'd had a brief time together, had been forced by the circumstance of his marriage and Lilia's pregnancy into separate lives; life had moved on, but their love for each other had endured. ALWAYS had been an apt inscription.

And Marielle knew this knowledge would give her the strength she was seeking in her own choice.

Thomas opened the door to find his home in bedlam. Alissa was raging drunkenly at Thalia. Dana was shrieking in her bassinet, and Thalia was trying to prevent Alissa from entering the nursery.

"You imbecile. You can't expect a blind child to understand anything!" Alissa was in a murderous rage, pounding on the door and shouting over the baby's frightened cries.

When he took hold of Alissa's arm, she whirled to strike him. Thomas pushed his shoulder forward to take the blow and pulled her into the hallway. Thalia immediately shut the nursery door. "What happened? What's wrong?" he demanded.

"What's wrong is that idiot you have taking care of her doesn't know anything," Alissa said furiously. "I think she's probably brain damaged, too."

She walked into the living room and started toward the spiral staircase. "And don't you ever put your hand on me like that again," she warned him as she pulled herself up the stairs by the railing.

Something inside him finally snapped. His life had been twisted sideways and he'd gone along with the program long enough. He'd been hoping for some kind of miracle, but the truth was, the cost would simply have to be borne. He went back to the nursery and tapped on the door. Dana was still wailing, but Thalia opened the door and he took his tiny, sobbing daughter from her arms.

"She got upset because Dana spit up." Thalia was

direct. "I can't deal with this much longer, Thomas," she said to him sadly. "It's terrible for this child and I know you need me to help you here, but Mrs. Saxon is making life impossible for both of us. There's no way I can keep a mother away from her own child and this baby's been in tears all afternoon. That's up to you and God, but I'm telling you right now that I want to leave as soon as you can find someone."

Dana slowly quieted down and took a bottle. Eventually she dropped into an exhausted sleep and Thomas put her down. He and Thalia went looking for Alissa and found her passed out in her exercise room. They moved her inert body into her own bedroom and Thomas called Thalia into the den.

"I'm getting divorced," he told her. "Will you stay until I do?" Thalia gave her agreement and he was grateful. She left to prepare dinner and he picked up the phone and called Barry Cooper.

"I've made a decision," he told his friend, "that you won't like. But I'm through being the nice guy in this mess and I'm going to need someone to cover my ass. Will you to come to my apartment first thing tomorrow morning and bring clean copies of the agreement?"

"What's going on?"

"I'm getting out of this. Whatever it takes, I'm getting out."

Very early Tuesday morning, to beat the rush-hour traffic, Marielle and Jeff, with Jamie strapped in his baby carrier, drove inland up through the Tehachapi Mountains toward Yosemite; they were slowed in their journey by the annual migration of monarch butterflies.

Marielle watched the fragile creatures fluttering through the landscape in their determination to complete their cycle of life against all odds, the survivors circumventing every obstacle that came into their path—natural or a product of the twentieth century—an annual struggle that had been going on for millennia. Their obstacles made hers look like child's play. Life was indeed motion. Anything static died.

With the car moving at a moderate speed, the marvelous orange-and-black creatures could float on the wind up and over the windshield and continue safely on their way north for the winter, so the journey to the park took an hour longer than anticipated. Rose and Cal had driven separately and tomorrow, after the ceremony, they were going on to San Francisco to stay in the honeymoon suite at the Top of the Mark.

The couples arrived in the valley within a half an hour of each other and checked into the gracious Ahwahnee Hotel in the late afternoon. An hour later, Shirley drove in. The fall weather was perfect. Oak and poplar leaves were gloriously multihued, contrasting their beauty against the great gray backdrop of El Capitan, visible from each of their rooms.

Shafts of sunlight splayed like a massive bridal veil through valley clouds. A popsickle orange sun glided onto the tree-covered horizon, creating highlights of mauve and Chinese red.

After dinner, in a last concession to romance, Jeff and Cal decided to batch it together while Marielle and Rose and the baby shared a second suite. It was late and neither could sleep. Marielle showed Rose the portraits of Lilia and Jameson and told her what she knew of their stories.

"I have every intention of lasting that long with Cal," said Rose with confidence. "I made the right decision and I'm going with it. You have too, you just don't know it, yet." She rolled over and was soon asleep.

"Three generations have passed," Marielle considered. "Three generations of unhappiness have come to an end." She looked at the clock. In twelve hours it would be time. She walked out onto the balcony to look up at the granite monument now deepened into solid black against the starlit sky, to soak in its strength and permanence. Above its dome she could see the faint chalk mark of the moon, thin as an eyelash, and was happy there were no longer any questions in her heart.

Wednesday morning, Thomas opened the door to Barry Cooper at nine o'clock. He introduced the attorney first to Thalia Barrett and then to his wife. "I want you to witness the situation," he said formally.

Alissa approached the two men with narrowed eyes. "Hello, lawyer. What's going on?"

Thomas crossed the room and opened his briefcase. Committed, he steeled himself to play hardball, then pulled out a copy of the financial agreement with the crossed-out pages. "Remember this?"

"What is it?"

He saw in her face that she damned well knew what it was. Her chin came up and she was ready and willing to do battle. Great. So be it. "It's an agreement that's no longer worth five million dollars. In fact, it's not worth the paper it's written on," Thomas responded, and continued taking copies out of the briefcase until all four were in his hand. "I've already signed it and I can be held liable for the contents unless I destroy it. Since I intend to do so I've asked Barry to be here so there won't be any misunderstanding later." He had her attention, saw that she had no idea what was coming, and deliberately hit her broadside. "I have proof that your child is not my daughter," he said coldly.

Barry Cooper's head snapped around in surprise. On the other side of the room, Thalia's mouth dropped open in shock. Thomas refused to meet their eyes.

Alissa turned pale but stood her ground. "You're crazy."

"She's not my blood type, therefore not my issue,

right counselor? Ergo, not my problem. You can handle your daughter from now on. I'm out of it."

He was in deadly earnest and felt Alissa's stunned gaze on his face; he met her eyes without expression. She looked from Cooper to Thalia and back again as she tried to decide how to handle the situation. "You're out of your mind if you think you're gonna get away with—"

He cut her off. "I don't think, I know. Further, I'll have no problem proving you got pregnant in order to falsely coerce me into a marriage and I don't think a jury will give you five million dollars for doing it." He shoved the heavy glass-and-metal screen away from the fireplace with his foot and held the papers toward the flames. "In fact, I'm willing to gamble they won't."

"I don't believe you." Alissa found her voice at last. "You won't leave that baby. I know you."

"Now that I know it's not mine, you watch me." He said it coldly and with malice as he pushed the documents into the fire. The signature pages caught fire and he let one agreement slip onto the burning wood in the grate.

"Don't." Suddenly she understood how serious he was. "Don't burn it. Let's talk about this."

"Talk about what? I no longer want the baby. You no longer get the money. I think that's clear enough. What's to talk about?" He let a second copy catch fire and slide out of his hand. "I'm not giving you five million dollars and I'm not supporting a blind child that isn't mine for the rest of its life. End of conversation." A third set of papers went into the flames.

Alissa grabbed his arm and pulled the remaining agreement out of his hand. Several pages of the document were smoking and the pungent smell of scorched paper drifted through the room.

Thalia, stricken at his actions, started toward the kitchen and Thomas was forced to leave the fireplace to stop her. "I know this is unpleasant," he said to her, "but it's important that you witness this, also." Face closed against him, eyes full of pain and disbelief, she returned to a small chair near the doorway, reluctance in every step. When he turned to Alissa, she had rebarricaded the fireplace with the fire screen and was standing guard in front of it.

"I say she's yours and I'm her mother." She was reeling but she wasn't finished.

"Let's not play games, Alissa. It's not mine and you know I can prove it. You want a lecture in Rh factors? I can do that, too."

She went on the attack. "The whole world thinks she's your daughter! You were getting ready to dump me, so you're damned right I made it happen. You try to get rid of me now and I'll drag you through every mud hole in this town and invent some new ones. Tell him whether or not I can do it, lawyer."

Barry Cooper interrupted them. "I wouldn't like this conversation to continue unless she's properly represented," he said firmly. "Do you have an attorney, Alissa?"

"No. I don't need one."

"Yes, you do," said Cooper.

"Well, she better get one, because this ship is sailing," Thomas said ominously.

"Let me call Mason." Cooper picked up a phone. "He'll know someone."

Prominent, well-respected Thornton Sandler, Jon Mason's personal attorney, was in Thomas's penthouse within half an hour. He arrived in tennis gear, thoroughly out of sorts, carrying a briefcase and a gray cellular phone that he deposited on a coffee table with his briefcase. "I'm here as a favor to Jon," he said testily. "Someone want to tell me what this is about?"

"I want a divorce from Thomas Saxon," said Alissa shrilly, "and I want the five million dollars he agreed to give me. We've already signed this agreement and I want you to make sure I'm protected." She shoved the singed papers into the lawyer's hands.

"Thomas hasn't agreed to the changes made after his signature went on it," Cooper pointed out. "The document is void."

"It's signed, that's all that counts," insisted Alissa.

All parties waited while Sandler read the document. "According to this, you two previously agreed to a custody arrangement for your daughter and Alissa crossed out those provisions when she signed it," interpreted Sandler.

"My client has new information and is no longer prepared to sign."

"We've already agreed to it." Alissa's voice was hoarse and strained.

"I signed with the understanding that I would have custody," said Thomas. "If I re-sign it, custody is a part of the deal as originally agreed or see me in court."

"I knew you wanted her," Alissa said triumphantly. "No deal."

"At the time, I accepted her child as mine. Since it's not, and I can prove it, the most I'll do is see that it's provided for." He knew he was being spiteful, but couldn't help loosening the hold on some of his rage. "She's absolutely right. In the public's mind it's my child and it's in my best interest to protect that image. Since I don't trust you to take care of her and I can farm a blind baby out to an institution just as quick as you can, I want total custody as a part of the deal or it's no go." He stared at her, cold and immobile as granite. "It's just business, Alissa."

Sandler raised his voice to intercede. "Wait a minute. The child in question is not your issue?" He reread the paragraph to be sure. "There's nothing in this agreement to that effect."

"No, but I can prove it just the same. She's already admitted she got pregnant in order to marry me."

"Is this true, Alissa?" Tennis gear or no, Thornton Sandler wasn't to be trifled with.

The three men waited out Alissa's stubborn silence.

"I can get a court order to get blood tests if I have to." Thomas held his advantage with a vengeance. "She had surgery when her baby was born—both their blood types are already on record at UCLA."

Finally, Alissa capitulated. "She's not his."

Sandler stepped into the silence that followed her admission. "Well, that does indeed change things, gentlemen. In light of this fact, I can hardly recommend that she give away custody of her child in this or any other agreement.

Thomas shot out of his chair. "I'm not asking you to give that recommendation," he thundered. "It's her decision. Frankly, I don't give a damn what she does, but if she decides to try to force me into paying the bills for a blind, illegitimate kid, I want a jury to know that she's been given adequate counsel."

"Adequate? Adequate!" Angered, Thornton Sandler turned to Alissa. "I can't recommend this agreement, my dear. In hostile hands this could be construed as a sale of your child. Understand if you sign it, you'll be doing so absolutely and directly against my recommendation," he said forcefully.

"What happens if I take him to court?" Jaws set in determination, she watched the lawyer narrowly.

"In my judgment, there's no question that you'd retain custody of your child," he assured her.

"What about the money?"

"If he can prove you married him under false circumstances and indeed it is not his child"—Sandler nodded in Thalia's direction—"which you've just stated in front of a neutral witness, it's entirely possible, in view of his wealth, a jury would still be willing to award a sum of money to be placed in a trust for your daughter.

"Nothing is guaranteed, however, and they could also

refuse to do so," he continued. "If such an award were to be made, I wouldn't be willing to speculate on an amount without a full investigation into all the circumstances, but I should think at least several thousand dollars. Perhaps as much as six figures, but again, there are no guarantees."

Alissa took Sandler's pen from his fingers. "I'll sign it," she said.

The lawyer was thoroughly affronted, unable to remember the last time a client had gone against his advice. "You did understand what I said? It's entirely possible you'd be awarded a large sum of money in trust for the child."

"I got it. I don't sign, I keep the baby. On the money, maybe yes, maybe no, right? I sign, it's five million dollars and he gets the baby."

"That's a crude, but essentially correct, summation," he said stiffly.

"I want to sign. He can have her."

Thomas shrugged and looked away in thinly disguised disgust. Thornton Sandler was nearly irate. Barry Cooper leapt from the couch to dig in his briefcase for the second set of agreements. He handed them to the angry Sandler for his perusal.

After a few minutes, the lawyer nodded that he considered them legally correct and passed them to Alissa for signature. "You do understand that you're giving up custody of your child to Thomas Saxon in anticipation of a dissolution of your marriage, and are agreeing not to challenge him in any way, in court or otherwise, once this agreement is signed?"

"Of course I do. I'm not stupid. I knew what it meant the first time." She calmly signed each copy with deliberation, then handed the pen to Thomas for his countersignature.

Thomas paced the room in agitation for a full two minutes, visibly reluctant to enter into the agreement.

Finally, he signed each document, and both attorneys and Thalia added their signatures as witnesses. Cooper distributed copies to Sandler and Alissa and dropped the rest in his briefcase. Then he took out a set of additional papers. "Here's your copy of the divorce petition," he said to Alissa. "It was filed yesterday morning in the event we were able to come to an agreement. This constitutes official service."

Alissa tossed the papers at Sandler and sat on the couch, her eyes betraying a hard suspicion that she'd been bested at her own game. "Can he do this?"

At Sandler's confirmation, she stood, accepted the consequences of her bargain, and gathered her purse to leave. "The sooner it's final, the sooner I have my money," she snapped to no one in particular. "Yesterday is just one step closer to having it over. I'll send for my things." She slammed the door on her way out.

Thomas stood rigidly at the fireplace, his face fixed in anger. Cooper snapped his briefcase shut. "Well, I guess that handles everything," he said, striving for a cordial tone. "Thanks for accommodating the situation, Thornton," he said to Sandler. "I think we've made the best of a difficult situation."

"No figuring women," answered Sandler. "Thomas, I do hope the next time we see each other it's on the same side of the fence. I assure you I am a great deal better than adequate. No hard feelings?"

"None whatever, Thornton," Thomas replied courteously. "I wanted her to have the best counsel available so nothing went off track."

Cooper walked with a mollified Sandler to the door. When he returned to the living room Thomas was gone and Thalia was nowhere in sight. He found them in the nursery. Thomas had Dana propped against his chest and was patting her back in a gentle rhythm.

Cooper stared from one beaming face to the other,

aware for the first time that he'd been as out of the loop as Alissa.

"I thought I was going to faint dead away when you said you didn't want her," Thalia admonished Thomas. "I'm glad I didn't know what you were doing, I can tell you that."

"If you'd known you wouldn't have been mad at me, and she'd have known something wasn't right."

"Well, I was mad at you all right. I was going to poison your dinner and quit. Well, not poison, but . . ." She laughed again. "I guarantee you'd have been unhappy."

Barry Cooper joined in their laughter. "It was the walk around the room that convinced me," he said with mild approval. "I really thought for a moment that you weren't going to sign it."

"I almost went too far," confessed Thomas. "I just wanted to make sure she bought it."

"If I did, she did," assured the lawyer. "If you ever give up acting, you'd make a hell of an attorney."

32

October 12, 1990

Thomas was in the mood to celebrate. There was no answer at Marielle's, and Jeff's BMW wasn't at the curb in front of her house. It was Joe's day off and the big man was somewhere in Las Vegas trying out a new system of blackjack. Thomas dialed the number for Shirley's office to tell her about the situation with Alissa and Dana.

"She's not here, Mr. Saxon," Louise told him. "She's out of town for a couple of days."

"Let me talk to Jon Mason, then. Tell him it's important."

Mason came on the phone immediately.

"I've got a new public relations situation, Jon. Alissa and I have agreed to get a divorce. I need your office to get into it as soon as possible."

"Wait a minute, what are you talking about?"

"We agreed to a settlement about twenty minutes ago and I'll be flying to Mexico as soon as I can to get a divorce. I'm surprised Alissa hasn't called you already."

"Well, actually, she did, but she was pretty upset and I didn't take her too seriously," Jon Mason admitted. "I was about to call you."

"Where's Shirley?"

"I don't know, she went to some wedding up in northern California. Louise will know. We'll need to get her right on this." He instructed his assistant to have Shirley's secretary pick up the line. "Tell Mr. Saxon where he can reach Shirley."

"Her best friends are getting married and she's driven up to Yosemite for the wedding," said Louise.

"When?"

"She left yesterday."

"No, when's the wedding?"

"It's supposed to be at two."

"Today?" It was nearly noon. "I want to talk to her, where's she staying?"

"The Ahwahnee Hotel." She gave him the number and he hung up.

There was no answer from either Marielle or Shirley at the hotel. He left word, then pounded the receiver into the phone in irritation. Driving was out of the question. The studio's corporate jet was useless.

He called Jon Mason again. "You have any connection with a helicopter service?"

"We've used a couple in the past." Mason was concerned. "Is there something wrong?"

"No, I just forgot the wedding was today and I'm supposed to be there."

"Let me see what I can do. I'll call you back."

Five minutes later Thomas was waiting at the front door of his building for the valet to bring his car around. Across the street he spotted a gypsy cab collecting fares from each of four passengers. He hailed the taxi, ran across the street, and got into the back seat. The driver peered into his rearview mirror in disbelief.

"Tom Saxon? No way Tom Saxon's in my cab."

"I'm in a rush." The name on the certificate read Alberto Pedrosa. "How quick can you get me to the Santa Monica Airport?" He tossed a fifty dollar bill into the front seat. Alberto promptly pulled a U-turn in the middle of Wilshire Boulevard.

"Don't kill anybody doing it," Thomas amended.

"You got in the right cab, Mr. Saxon. I know this town like my mother's face. I was born ten blocks from here."

The taxi charged through a yellow light onto Sepulveda Boulevard and careened through a shopping district to take a hot right turn onto Pico. "Which terminal at Santa Monica?"

"Coast Helicopter Service."

"Where you goin'?" The taxi sped past the row of flame trees in the center divider of the boulevard.

"I'm going to meet a lady," Thomas told him.

"None of my business, but didn't you just get married?"

"No, I just got divorced."

Alberto dodged a slow-moving truck and thought it over. "Aahhh." The cabbie was approving. "You must want to see this lady pretty bad. You in love with her?" Alberto had the accelerator pressed to the floor and Thomas searched for nonexistent seat belts.

"Yes, very much so."

Alberto gave a huge Latin sigh. "I had a lady like that once. She was the love of my life." The car screeched to a halt for a red light. Thomas braced himself against the front seat while Alberto put the gearshift into neutral and raced the engine.

"What happened?"

"She got married to another guy. With a woman like that, you got to take care of business. I didn't take care of business."

The light changed and Thomas was hurled against the back of the cab. He studied the shabby upholstery and wondered at his situation: hurtling through West Los Angeles, about to get into a helicopter that would fly him two hours north to Yosemite. He had absolutely no idea what he could do when he arrived except to try to talk to her before she committed marriage. A little late for "taking care of business."

"You should have talked to her weeks ago," he muttered to himself.

"Sometimes talking don't get it," observed Alberto and wheeled the taxi abruptly through the entrance of the Santa Monica Airport. Seconds later he skidded the car to a stop in front of the Coast Helicopter Service office. "Sometimes you just gotta do something about it. I wish I did, but now it's too late. That's twenty-two dollars."

On the pad a small, speedy Bell helicopter was warming up, rotors spinning. The prop wash sent leaves, styrofoam cups, and other flotsam that accumulates in open spaces in Los Angeles flying against the wire hurricane fence. Thomas felt as out of control as the cup bouncing against the wire. He checked his watch. If the wedding was at two, he'd just make it. He prayed for good weather and climbed aboard the aircraft and introduced himself to the pilot. A few seconds later, the aircraft lifted him over the city and headed north toward the Tehachapi Mountains.

Marielle, dressed in the pale peach gown and no longer nervous, found a heads-up penny on the path and, making a wish, pitched it off the Sentinel Bridge that led to the church; then she walked to the group of people assembling outside the chapel for the small outdoor wedding. Jeff was waiting and took her hand.

"You're sure about this?" he asked one last time. "Last chance to change your mind."

"I'm sure." She kissed him lightly and looked over his shoulder at Shirley carrying her godson against her shoulder, splendid in his little blue "tuxedo" in honor of the occasion.

He'd been good as gold all morning through all the pictures and the attention at lunch from the people who had driven up for the ceremony, and was bug-eyed in four-month-old fascination with his shoulder-high view of the entire proceeding. Shirley took her seat and placed Jamie on his feet in her lap and held him in a standing position so he could see his mother.

A recording of the traditional wedding march sounded, sweet and clear in the still valley sunshine. Marielle's eyes began to mist but she held firm in her decision and smiled at her son, trying to stand in Shirley's lap. She stood tall at Jeff's side in front of the flower-covered bower.

Cal's daughters, in adorable matching peach pink and white dresses and white Mary Janes, came forward in carefully measured steps, tossing rose and daisy petals onto the thin white carpet laid down as an aisle. Their hair in shining ringlets, the little girls carried their white straw baskets filled with petals; Suzie was seriously solemn in her duty while Jennifer smiled and played to the crowd. Reveling in her importance she tossed her petals onto the guests.

They were going to be a handful, but Marielle knew Rose would never regret this day. She turned her attention to the traditional wording of the ceremony and followed the minister's voice carefully.

"If any man shall show just cause as to why this marriage should not take place, let him speak now or forever hold his peace."

Jamie's lusty cry rang out in the silence. The assembled group broke into delighted laughter and, undisturbed at his opinion, Marielle looked at her son with a mother's pride. Shirley responded with a ready bottle and no other voice was raised in objection.

The minister spoke to them in earnest admonishment. "Marriage is a serious and solemn undertaking, and the union of two people is not to be entered into lightly." After a small pause, he continued; his words melted into the serenity of the wooded area surrounding the meadow and quieted the birds to silent attention. "Who gives this woman in marriage?"

"They have a car waiting, sir." The pilot was intent on his craft and checked his instruments repeatedly. The helicopter floated effortlessly, skirting patches of clouds over more old-growth evergreens than Thomas had seen in one place in all his life. Occasionally they passed over huge areas of burned and blackened ground where forest fires had wreaked havoc, then on to more green. The sun had moved to their left as they flew, and he watched the copter's shadow pace their progress on the black-green trees below.

According to the sun, and his watch, it was close to two o'clock.

Passing over a final ridge, the Yosemite Valley was suddenly in view and he caught his breath at its beauty. Thin wisps of waterfalls trailed down the monumental rocks on either side of a wide green expanse with a gargantuan monolith lifting straight up from the center of the valley floor.

The pilot was talking to someone on the ground, his conversation a garble of pilot code and repetition of numbers.

"I told them it was an emergency so they'll let me set down," the pilot told him. "You've just agreed to fund next year's ambulance service for the valley as a penalty for not obtaining prior clearance."

"Good man. I'll be happy to do it."

"Your car's that green station wagon over there on the right. They're going to let me down for twenty minutes, then I have to get this thing out of here. Hang on." More pilot talk and a couple of "yessirs." "They got some kid that's been snakebit. They think he's okay, but they want me to take him over to a hospital in Mariposa to make sure. I can't come back in here after dark, but I can pick you up tomorrow morning, if you want."

"No, I'll figure something out. You take the kid, put it on the bill."

"We'll be on the ground in two minutes." The pilot gave him a friendly glance for the first time during their trip and smiled his approval before returning to the business of landing the aircraft. "You sure you're doing all this just to go to a wedding?"

Marielle questioned her decision one last time. She stood rock still and concentrated carefully on the minister's voice, clutching the spray of flowers in her hand. All the while he was speaking, a part of her wondered if she could abide by such vows, after all? At her side, Rose was holding back tears, so nervous she was trembling.

The minister continued. "Do you take this man to be your lawful wedded husband? To have and to hold, for richer, for poorer, in sickness and in health, for so long as you both shall live?"

After the slightest hesitation, she was able to whisper, "I do."

There was a commotion behind them and a clarion male voice shattered the stillness. "She does not."

Heads turned in unison and mouths popped open in disbelief as Thomas Saxon took giant strides down the path between the assembled guests on their white lawn chairs, toward the couple under the bower.

The minister stepped forward to intercept the intruder in his charge down the aisle, and his face registered astonishment when he recognized the famous actor. "Mr. Saxon, what on earth?"

"I say she doesn't," Thomas insisted. "Not until she talks to me, she doesn't."

The bride whirled on him with fire in her eye.

"Oh, yes, I do!"

The groom revolved slowly to reveal a very puzzled Cal Logan, and Rose Brown pulled at the minister's sleeve. "I said 'I do' and I meant it. I'd like to see who's going to stop me."

The guests sat in shock, too surprised to speak, totally bewildered that Thomas Saxon was in their midst and calling a halt to Rose's wedding.

Thomas, utterly baffled, stared at the indignant bride. "I thought you were . . ." he started. "I'm sorry, I'm clearly in the wrong place." He had no idea what to do now. "Please accept my apology," he said to Cal. "I didn't . . ."

Then he saw Marielle sinking into a seat in the front row next to Shirley, taking her baby into her arms, and staring at him in disbelief. Thomas moved to her side and examined both her hands, checking for a wedding band. It was there, a huge gold one, but it took a full minute for him to realize that it was bent and misshapen, and on the wrong hand. Then he kissed her.

The assembly broke into nervous laughter and conversation; Rose's voice rose above the hubbub and the questions of inquisitive guests. "So, am I Mrs. Cal Logan, or what?"

The minister smiled delightedly and the audience roared its approval.

"I'll say you are," he said, forgetting himself for a moment. "I now pronounce you man and wife. You may now kiss the bride."

"Thank you!" Rose flippantly tossed her bouquet into Thomas's lap and was soundly kissed by her husband while the guests increased their applause. Thomas abandoned Marielle long enough to kiss Rose for luck, then returned to her side.

"What happened?"

"We decided against it yesterday," she said. "I just

couldn't do it. It wasn't fair to Jeff or to the baby. Parents ought to be in love when there's a child to consider."

He took a long look at Boyce Jameson and saw his own dark eyes and miniature eyebrows reflected in the baby's face. "He's mine, isn't he? Don't try to deny it, that kid looks just like me. He couldn't be anyone else's. I'm embarrassed it took me so long to add it up. I plead brain damage. What can I tell you?"

"I didn't get pregnant to—"

"I'm getting divorced." He rode over her explanation. "You want to marry me, or what?"

It took her a fraction of a second to comprehend. "I'll say I do." She laughed, then she kissed him a long, long time.

Jeff walked over and offered his hand. "I want to say this in front of her," he said to Thomas stiffly. "She explained Jamie's your son and I accept that. I just want to tell you that I don't care if you're the King of England, you mess up and I intend to be there."

Thomas shook Jeff's hand and answered gravely, with the understanding that only two men can have with each other. "I don't think I'm going to make any more mistakes, but if I do, I'll deserve to lose her."

Jeff stepped aside to take his place in the receiving line and Marielle joined him. Thomas, holding his son for the first time, felt the joy of fatherhood wash over him yet again. He joined the line of guests.

When he reached Marielle he leaned over and kissed her ear, then whispered, "How about a sister for the placekicker?"

"As many as you want," she answered joyously.

"No, I mean now."

Her eyes widened and she looked at him with sudden tears and understanding. "Dana?"

He turned her around and enfolded her carefully next to the baby in his arms while the wedding guests pretended not stare. "We worked it out this morning. I'll explain later."

She didn't care about explanations or anything else so long as he held her. Always.

Epilogue

The following spring, Marielle Tèa Lilia Jonas McCleary became Marielle Tèa Lilia Jonas McCleary Saxon in a private ceremony at the pine cabin attended by Mr. and Mrs. Thomas Saxon senior, Rose, Jennifer, Suzie, and Cal Logan, Shirley Canfield, nine-month-old Dana and six-month-old Jamie under Thalia Barrett's watchful eyes, Mr. and Mrs. Barry Cooper, and Joe. No press, no helicopters, no "News at Five" despite the fact that *Winter Love* was a major box-office hit in Europe and Thomas had just signed to produce and star in the forthcoming feature, *Hawk Chronicles.*

The bride wore a pale honey gold silk dress, her great grandmother's cameo locket, her mother's hat with a new white veil, and made a beautiful picture next to Thomas Saxon's cream Versace jacket and matching shirt and tie.

It was the beginning of the end of the seven-year California drought and the skies poured rain, but they had anticipated the weather and exchanged their vows beneath a small, flower-bedecked bower in the midst of a huge tent that stood with one end opened to a view of the lake. Suzie and Jennifer Logan served as ring bearers in tulip yellow, and when Thomas repeated, "With this ring, I thee wed," he slipped a simple gold band onto

Marielle's finger next to a massive blue-white, emerald-cut engagement ring he'd given her New Year's Eve.

He was due at the studio the following week to begin preparation for the film, so they spent a honeymoon weekend at the cabin with a pint of crème fraîche and two quarts of strawberries and made love forever. Three weekends later, Marielle, with Dana riding on one hip, and wrapped in her white terry robe, opened the door to Thomas's penthouse to take delivery of a stout wooden crate addressed to Mr. and Mrs. Thomas Saxon.

Joe pried open the crate. A bare-chested Thomas, barefoot and wearing a pair of jeans wet at the top with bathwater, carrying a sleepy Jamie, came in to supervise.

According to the accompanying letter addressed to Marielle, the crate contained a gift from Asantehene Osei III of Kumasi, Ghana, thanking her for her intention of returning the royal treasure and giving his blessing to her marriage. Inside the packing paper, wrapped in silks of splendidly beautiful hues, they found a ram's head mask, a child-size gold scimitar for Jamie, and a fine gold necklace for Dana, as well as a second necklace, and feathered cowrie beads with an exquisite wooden doll attached.

The doll was female and Marielle, strongly suspecting that she was pregnant and saving the news from her family until Dr. Lanier returned from vacation to verify her opinion, had the sudden premonition that her next child would be a girl. Also enclosed was a picture of the new Asantehene surrounded by his staff.

Marielle deposited the impatient Dana among the packing papers to crawl about; the baby's blindness was not yet a handicap and she was an otherwise normally functioning, happy little girl, rapidly exploring the world by sound and taste and feel. Marielle picked up the ram's head and rubbed a small nick in the smooth golden surface with her thumb. "I'd swear this was from the treasure," she said curiously.

The opulence of the gifts was astonishing. Joe disposed of the crate and Thalia came in to collect Dana for her bath; Thomas took the sleeping Jamie into the nursery. When he returned, he found Marielle closely examining the photograph of the Asantehene. Pointing to the picture she began to laugh. "It is the original," she decreed.

Thomas kissed her neck and circled her body in his arms as he peeked over her shoulder at the royal picture.

"Look, he's wearing three of the bracelets I found—the two with sapphires and the one with the diamond designs." She leaned against her husband's body, convulsed with laughter at the royal revelation. "And that thing on the umbrella—that's the finial with the geese. I'd know it anywhere." She examined the nick in the ram's head again. "I caused this. I scratched it on a shelf when I took it out of the bier. I remember being surprised at how soft pure gold is. I felt terrible that I'd damaged it."

Thomas examined the royal photograph more closely. "Are you sure?"

"These are the soul-bearer badges. I know it." She indicated round gold shields worn by several members of the royal entourage, then pointed to a beautifully regal woman with a heart-shaped face and liquid, ebony eyes seated near the king. "That's Meta Kates."

"They stole it?"

"Reclaimed it, I believe, is the proper phrase." Marielle was shaking with laughter as she put it together. "That's why the taxes were paid. What do you want to bet?"

"At this point, I wouldn't rule anything out. What are you going to do about it?"

"Nothing. It's theirs. It was always theirs." She turned in his arms and placed the golden ram's head against his chest, then smiled into his handsome face. "Look what I have—there's not enough gold in this planet to buy what I have." She kissed him fervently. "Promise me one thing, though."

"Anything." Thomas tightened his arms around her.

"Promise you won't tell Jeff. He'd be so upset and . . ."

Thomas's eyes twinkled with wicked intent. He opened her robe and wrapped himself inside, snuggling his body next to hers. "Jeff who?" he asked innocently enough, and began to kiss his wife.

AVAILABLE NOW

DREAM TIME by Parris Afton Bonds

A passionate tale of a determined young woman who, because of a scandal, wound up in the untamed Australia of the early 1800s.

ALWAYS . . . by Jeane Renick

Marielle McCleary wants a baby, but her prospects look slim—until she meets handsome actor Tom Saxon. Too late, however, she finds out that Thomas isn't as perfect as he seems. Will she ever have the life she's always wanted?

THE BRIDEGROOM by Carol Jerina

A compelling historical romance set in Texas. Payne Trefarrow's family abandoned him, and he held his identical twin brother Prescott responsible. To exact revenge, Payne planned to take the things his brother loved most—his money and his fiancée.

THE WOMEN OF LIBERTY CREEK
by Marilyn Cunningham

From the author of *Seasons of the Heart.* A sweeping tale of three women's lives and loves and how they are bound together, over the generations, by a small town in Idaho.

LOST TREASURE by Catriona Flynt

A zany romantic adventure set in Northern California at the turn of the century. When her dramatic production went up in smoke, actress Moll Kennedy was forced to take a job to pay her debts—as a schoolteacher doubling as a spy. Then she fell in love with the ruggedly handsome Winslow Fortune, the very man she was spying on.

SAPPHIRE by Venita Helton

An intriguing historical tale of love divided by loyalty. When her clipper ship sank, New Orleans beauty Arienne Lloyd was rescued by handsome Yankee Joshua Langdon. At the very sight of him she was filled with longing, despite her own allegiances to the South. Would Arienne fight to win the heart of her beloved enemy—even if it meant risking everything in which she believed?

HarperPaperbacks *By Mail*

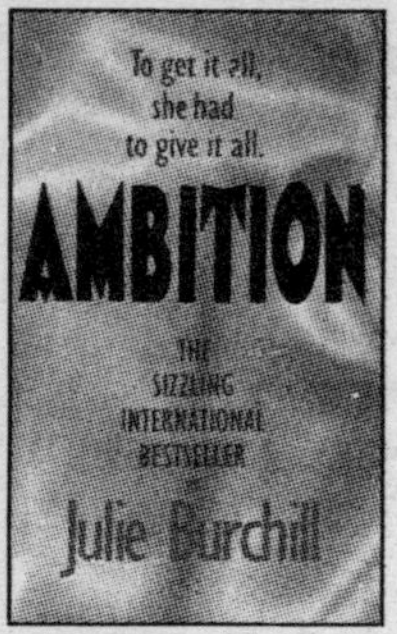

Ambition—
Julie Burchill—
Young, gorgeous, sensuous Susan Street is not satisfied with being deputy editor of the newspaper. She wants it all, and she'll do it all to fight her way to the top and fulfill her lust for success.

The Snow Leopard of Shanghai—*Erin Pizzey—*
From the Russian Revolution to China's Cultural Revolution, from the splendor of the Orient to the sins of a Shanghai brothel, here is the breathtaking story of the extraordinary life of an unforgettable woman.

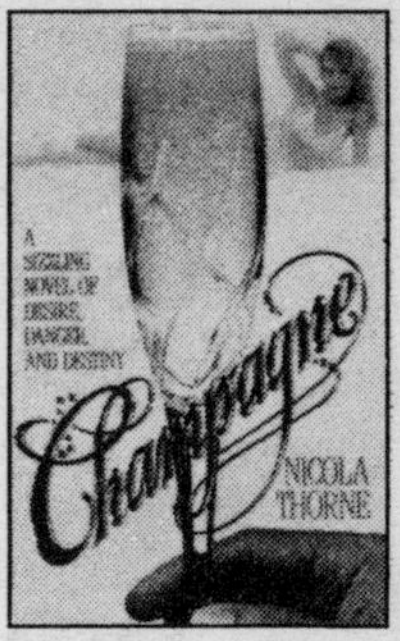

Champagne—
Nicola Thorne—
Ablaze with the glamor and lust of a glittering industry, fired by the passions of the rich and beautiful, this is the sizzling story of one woman's sudden thrust into jet-set power in a vast international empire.

Kiss & Tell—
Trudi Pacter—
Kate Kennedy rises from the ashes of abused passion to become queen of the glittering, ruthless world of celebrity journalism. But should she risk her hard-won career for what might be the love of a lifetime?

Aspen Affair—
Burt Hirschfeld—
Glittering, chilling, erotic, and suspenseful, Aspen Affair carries you up to the rarified world of icy wealth and decadent pleasures—then down to the dark side of the beautiful people who can never get enough.

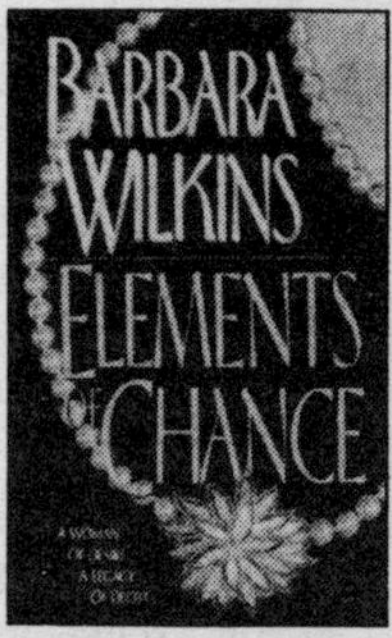

Elements of Chance—
Barbara Wilkins—
When charismatic billionaire Victor Penn apparently dies in a plane crash, his beautiful widow Valarie is suddenly torn from her privileged world. Alone for the first time, she is caught in a web of rivalries, betrayal, and murder.